D0201182

THE ANNIVERSARY

Also by Amy Gutman

Equivocal Death

THE ANNIVERSARY

A Novel

AMY GUTMAN

LITTLE, BROWN AND COMPANY

Boston New York London

Library of Congress Cataloging-in-Publication Data

Gutman, Amy.
    The anniversary : a novel / Amy Gutman. — 1st ed.
        p. cm.
    ISBN 0-316-38120-9
    1. Executions and executioners — Fiction.   2. Women — Crimes against — Fiction.
    3. Serial murderers — Fiction.   4. Psychopaths — Fiction.   5. Maine — Fiction.   I. Title.

PS3557.U885A56 2003
813'.6 — dc21   2002041638

10   9   8   7   6   5   4   3   2   1

Q-FF

Printed in the United States of America

For my family — again

THE
ANNIVERSARY

PROLOGUE

Nashville, Tennessee
Eleven years ago

As soon as the jury came back, she knew.

Faces somber, eyes trained on the floor, they filed back to their seats, these twelve men and women who held his life in their hands. None of them glanced toward the spectators. None of them met his eyes. In her third-row gallery seat, Laura Seton leaned slightly forward. Placing a hand on her throat, she felt a birdlike pulsing flutter. As her fingers traced the delicate bones of her neck, she thought how easy it would be to break them.

Judge Gwen Kirkpatrick looked down on the room from her position high on the bench. She had thick, dark hair streaked with gray and a bright red gash of a mouth. A bronze disk hung on the wall above her, the Great Seal of the State of Tennessee. It floated there like a halo, invoking some higher good. Not that Laura believed in that. She believed in very little these days.

"All right, if the record would reflect that the jury is back in the courtroom after their deliberations." Judge Kirkpatrick took a sip of water, then turned to the jury box. "Mr. Archer, you are still the foreperson of this jury, is that correct?"

"Yes, ma'am." Archer was a stocky man with blue suspenders and a white moustache, recently retired from thirty years in the insurance industry.

"I understand that you've reached a verdict."

"Yes, we have."

Laura glanced at her watch: 10:55 A.M.

For the first time since she'd arrived, she allowed herself to look at him.

A dark-haired man in a navy blazer seated beside his lawyer. His face was beautiful in profile. A high, rounded forehead, straight nose, chiseled chin. He gave the impression of being at once both sensitive and strong. While she couldn't clearly see his expression, she easily pictured it. The vaguely ironic smile. Eyebrows slightly raised. As if he were a little bored but trying to be polite. His deep brown eyes would be shining, like stones from a riverbed.

He leaned toward his lawyer to say something. She willed him to turn around.

Please, Steven, look at me. There's something you need to know.

His back stiffened almost imperceptibly, as if he'd read her thoughts, until a moment later he lapsed into stillness again.

She hadn't planned to be here today, had planned to sleep through it all. She'd gotten as drunk as she could last night before passing out on the floor. But at 4 A.M. she'd snapped awake and stumbled into the bathroom. In the glare of the fluorescent light, she'd looked like she was dying. Haggard face, pallid skin, huge burning eyes. "I'm only twenty-four," she'd whispered. "I'm only twenty-four." For reasons that now eluded her, this had seemed significant.

From the front of the room, the voices pressed on, but Laura barely listened. She forced herself to breathe. She noticed her skirt was too tight. During the past few months she'd gained at least ten pounds, but the effect was oddly soothing. Buried in flesh she felt safer. As if she couldn't be seen.

Memories were flashing through her mind, like a video on fast-forward. Lobsters at Jimmy's Harborside. Camping in the Smoky Mountains. Dancing at 12th & Porter to driving country rock. *I'm in the mood, I'm in the mood, I'm in the . . .*

And then there were the other things. The things she didn't want to remember.

A blood-soaked shirt behind the bed.

Bone fragments in the fireplace.

Knives. A mask. Rubber gloves.

But always an explanation.

Always an explanation. Until one day, there just wasn't.

4

"Mr. Gage, would you please stand and face the jury?" That was the judge again.

Steven Gage got to his feet. He seemed calm and somewhat bemused. Simply going through the motions, as if he were humoring them.

"Mr. Archer, would you read me the verdict as to count one of this indictment."

Archer rubbed a hand over his mouth, then, eyes down, started speaking. "We, the jury, unanimously find that the State has proven the following listed statutory aggravating circumstance or circumstances beyond a reasonable doubt . . ."

The words rolled on, endless and without meaning. A barrage of neat official language to disguise what was happening.

Now, Steven. Look. Now.

But his eyes remained on the jury. He didn't turn around.

The sense of déjà vu grew stronger by the moment. It seemed to Laura that they'd done this all just ten days ago. But after the determination of guilt had come a whole new round of proceedings. They called it the penalty phase. Mitigating factors. Aggravating factors. All of them brought to light. The testimony had lasted for more than two days, but the jury was back in an hour.

Laura's eyes roamed the gallery, the sea of crowded benches. The elderly man beside her smelled like wintergreen. The families were sitting in the front rows, as they had throughout the trial. Dahlia's family to the right of the aisle, Steven's on the left. Dahlia's parents sat ramrod straight, their teenage son between them. The boy, sullen and slightly sprawled, looked utterly out of place. Across the aisle, Steven's mother was flanked by two grown sons. A small, plump woman with bottle-blue hair, she'd shrunk down in her seat. Laura had a sense that if her sons weren't there, she'd slide right onto the floor.

A jagged line of pain shot through Laura's brain. Her mouth was dry as sand. She breathed in hot recycled air, blown from vents in the wall. Dun-colored curtains covered the windows, shutting out the sun. The world had collapsed into this single place. There was nothing outside this room.

Laura felt the words before she heard them, as her heart tore into her chest.

"We, the jury, unanimously find that the punishment for the defendant, Steven Lee Gage, shall be death."

An instant of absolute silence, and then the whispers began.

Laura's stomach heaved, and she pressed her hands together. It had happened, it had actually happened, and she couldn't take it in. She'd tried to imagine how it might feel, but she'd never imagined this. An utter absence of feeling, a blankness akin to sleep. Sentenced to death. *Sentenced to death.* She tried to absorb the meaning. But before the words could fully sink in, something was happening. Up front, a flurry of action. Steven had lunged toward the judge.

"I do not accept this verdict! I do not accept it, do you hear me?" He stood slightly crouched and quivering, glaring at Judge Kirkpatrick. "I am innocent, and *you* are the guilty ones, all of you here today. Those responsible for this will pay. Do you hear me? All of you will pay!"

A muffled roar in the gallery, as Kirkpatrick pounded her gavel. "Mr. Phillips, control your client!"

"Steven. Please. Calm down." George Phillips raised a slender hand, but his client didn't respond. Instead, Gage took another step forward, his eyes burning into the judge.

Two court officers were rushing forward, converging around Gage. The first one, well over six foot five, tackled Gage from behind. He seemed to have gained a hold until Gage bit down on his hand. The injured man stumbled backward, let out an agonized shriek, as his partner, hurling himself toward Gage, wrestled him to the ground. "No! Steven. No! Oh God!" Steven's mother clutched her other sons' arms as her screams gave way to sobs.

Gage fought back from the floor, spitting, writhing, kicking. Everywhere, spectators were jumping up, gawking at the scene. Laura was almost surprised to find she was standing too, craning her neck to watch, to get a better view. Gage's face was a deep bright red. Veins pulsed in his forehead. She didn't want to look, but she couldn't turn away.

This is what they saw, she thought. *This is what they saw.*

He'd managed to get to his feet again when one of the bailiffs grabbed him, jammed a knee in his lower back and hurled him against a table.

"Jesus Christ, get him! Get him!" That was Tucker Schuyler, Dahlia's younger brother. He pounded a fist into his palm, his face as red as his hair.

Another vicious flailing struggle, and Gage broke free again. He flung himself toward the gallery, his eyes bulging grotesquely. A swirl of movement now, as spectators streamed for the door. The jurors, who'd climbed to their feet, seemed astonished, disbelieving. Pretty, blonde juror number four wore an expression of abject terror, one hand clapped over her mouth, her eyes enormous and bright. Jurors number six and seven were edging toward the exit. They'd been told that the system *worked.* They hadn't expected this.

"You motherfuckin' fascists," Gage shrieked. "You don't know what you're doing. Get your fuckin' hands off me!"

He was still cursing and kicking when the handcuffs snapped on his wrists. His body strained frantically, shivered, then went slack. His mouth fell open, and he gazed at the room, drained of energy. For some time the room was quiet, and Steven Gage didn't move. Then, without warning, his body jerked, and his eyes grew wide again. Throwing back his head, he let out an agonized howl.

The cry went on and on, a piercing ululation. The sound of a keening animal caught in the grip of a trap. Laura's skin prickled down the back of her neck, a chill blooming in her heart. This was pure, distilled rage, like nothing she'd ever heard.

Then, suddenly, it was over.

Gage was silent again. His eyes drifted to the gallery. He looked at them. At her.

For a moment their gazes locked. Laura could hardly breathe. It was like a curtain had been ripped away, and she finally saw the truth. The truth that she'd swept aside for so long because she couldn't bear it.

What she saw was an ineffable emptiness, a bleakness beyond

despair. There was something broken and evil in him that could never be repaired. As his eyes bore into hers, a smile flickered on his lips, and in a moment of terrible insight she knew what he was thinking. He wasn't really there, he was floating in fantasy. Imagining how he'd kill her if he only had the chance.

Wednesday, April 5

Sʜᴇ almost didn't see it.

Juggling a pizza box with a load of books, she yanked open the unlocked screen door, her mind on other things. The smell of pepperoni. The sharp spring breeze. Next week's midterm in Abnormal Psych. In retrospect, these thoughts would seem a sort of victory. A sign that, after more than a decade, she'd managed to reclaim her life. But it was days, or maybe weeks, before she realized this, and by then it was too late. She could only look back, helpless, at the world she'd left behind.

By some trick of gravity the envelope stuck, as if tacked against the doorjamb. Later, she'd try to reconstruct this moment, remembering that first impression. An ordinary business envelope. White. Her name — Ms. *Callie Thayer* — in clear black type. Later even that would seem strange, but at the time she'd barely noticed. She'd seen the envelope, grabbed it, stuffed it into her leather bag.

For the next three hours it had been forgotten, a time bomb in her purse.

⁓

"Aɴʏᴏɴᴇ home?"

But of course she knew they were here.

It was Wednesday afternoon, just after five. Anna would be home from school. Rick, who worked an early shift, would have started dinner by now.

Putting down her books, Callie gave herself a quick once-over in the mirror at the end of the hallway. Pale heart-shaped face.

Thick chestnut hair. A vagrant curl had tumbled loose from the clip she'd used to pull it back. Reflexively, she unsnapped the barrette, pushed the tendrils back. Last month, she'd turned thirty-five, and today she looked her age. Faint lines around the large, dark eyes. Two deeper creases in her brow. Not that any of it bothered her, quite the opposite. She watched the shifting landscape of her face with hungry fascination, concrete proof she wasn't the person she'd been ten years ago.

"Hey, babe! In here."

She followed Rick's voice to the kitchen. He was standing at the sink washing vegetables, the Dixie Chicks playing in the background. Wiping his hands on a towel, he stepped toward her for a kiss. Tall and lankily boyish, he wore faded jeans and Birkenstocks with a white short-sleeved T-shirt. He had dark brown hair and a lazy smile. Green eyes flecked with gold. He looked like a carpenter or maybe an artist, someone who worked with his hands. It was still hard for her to believe that she was dating a cop.

As Rick's lips grazed hers, Callie touched his shoulder. He smelled of oregano and mint, a rich, earthy scent. They'd been together for eight months, sleeping together for four, and she was still sometimes caught off guard by the looping surge of attraction. But when Rick's lips moved to her neck, Callie pulled away. Anna was just upstairs. Besides, they had to get dinner ready.

"Here. Take this." Callie held out the pizza box, with its cargo of fat and meat. He set the box on the counter, then turned toward her again. She couldn't read his eyes, but she knew what he was thinking.

"Don't you have things to do?" she murmured with mock severity.

"Like this?"

As he ran a hand down the curve of her back, something inside her sparked. She let her eyes drift shut, her head resting on his shoulder. He pressed against her rhythmically, once, twice, again.

"Not now," she whispered into his chest. "Come on, Rick. Please."

Still, she was almost disappointed when he dropped his arms and stepped away. A last chaste kiss on the cheek, and he was back at the kitchen sink. For a moment, Callie stood where he'd left her, flushed and slightly bereft. Then she went to the refrigerator and grabbed a San Pellegrino. She took a glass from a cabinet, sat down at the table.

"Tough day?" Rick's back was turned to her, and she couldn't see his face.

"Not too bad, really." Callie took a sip of sparkling water, the bubbles sharp in her mouth.

Roseanne Cash was playing now, a song about the wheel going 'round. Outside, the sky was a dappled gray, streaked with red and gold. Callie watched as Rick moved easily through the snug brightness of the kitchen. He pulled three plates from a cupboard, tasted the salad dressing. The flash of arousal she'd felt was gone, replaced with a sense of contentment. A delicious awareness that, just for now, all was as it should be.

"You want me to help?" Callie asked.

"Nope, we're pretty much set."

Again, her eyes moved over the room, a scene of order and comfort. Notched pine floor, granite counters, pots hanging on the wall. Fresh herbs growing on the windowsill: tarragon, basil, thyme. It was the life she'd wanted for herself but most of all for Anna. Callie thought, as she often did, how lucky they were to live here, in this cozy Cape Cod cottage in this picture-perfect town.

Merritt, Massachusetts. Population: 30,000.

White-steepled churches.

Brick storefronts.

Astounding autumn foliage.

A place where kids still went out to play without the bother of play dates.

It was more than six years since she'd moved here, an anxious single mother and student. She'd attended Windham College on an Abbott Scholarship, a special grant for older "nontraditional" students working on their B.A.'s. She'd majored in English and, three years later, graduated with high honors. By then, she'd bought the house and fallen in love with the town.

They'd lived here for going on seven years, and it was lucky she'd bought when she did. She'd been astonished when the house across the street sold last year for more than six hundred grand, purchased by a wealthy family moving from outside Boston. Bernie Creighton had kept his job in the city, commuting two hours each way. It was worth it, he and his wife said, for the quality of life. It seemed a little ridiculous — what was wrong with the suburbs? — but their youngest child, Henry, was Anna's best friend, so Callie was hardly complaining.

She herself had once considered a move to Boston, where job prospects would be better. But after a stressful round of interviews, she'd decided to stay put. She already had the house. And if salaries were low in Merritt, so were her expenses. After finishing her degree, she'd gone to work in Windham's alumni office, a job that gave her flexibility and ample time with Anna. Now that Anna was older, Callie was back in school part-time. She'd switched her focus to psychology and hoped to go on to grad school.

Rick was chopping carrots, intently watching the knife. The steel made a muffled clicking sound on the wooden cutting board. He brought to cooking the same dedication he brought to making love. Callie had teased him about it once, his rapt concentration. "The kitchen," he'd said seriously, "is the most dangerous room in the house." An odd thing to say, she'd thought at the time, though probably accurate.

"So how're things going?" Callie asked. "Did you talk to your dad today?"

"I'm going back down this weekend," Rick said. "I got a cheap flight on Saturday."

Callie looked up, concerned. "But I thought the tests were normal. The electrocardiogram."

Rick put down the knife. Picking up the cutting board, he dumped carrots into the salad. "It wasn't definitive. Now they want to do this thing called a thallium stress test. To find out how much blood is getting to different parts of the heart. Depending on what they find out —"

The phone rang sharply behind her, a shrill bleating sound.

"Go ahead," Rick said, tossing his head back toward it.

Turning in her chair, Callie picked up.

"Hello?" She recognized the voice immediately, soft and hesitant. "Nathan, I'm really sorry, but we're about to sit down to dinner."

"Oh, sure. Sorry."

Callie imagined him flushing crimson on the other end of the phone. She'd never known a boy or man who blushed so easily.

She'd met Nathan Lacoste last fall in Introductory Psych. A Windham junior, twenty years old, he'd somehow latched onto her. Smart, she thought, and not bad looking but painfully self-conscious. She could tell he'd had trouble making friends, and she tried to be kind to him, remembering the pain of feeling lost and alone during her own years in college. Lately, though, she'd come to wish that she'd kept a bit more distance. He'd taken to calling her at home much more than she liked.

"I'll let you go. To eat." But Nathan didn't hang up. For someone almost pathologically shy, he could be very persistent. "I . . . could you just tell me what you're having?"

"Excuse me?" Callie was barely listening. She shouldn't have picked up the phone. As she watched Rick finish the salad, she thought how tired he looked. His parents lived in North Carolina, outside Chapel Hill. This would be his third trip in the past six weeks, and the travels were taking a toll.

"I was wondering what you're having. To eat. I was sort of feeling hungry, but, I don't know, I couldn't think what to make."

He seemed to be angling for an invitation. She had to get off the phone. "Pizza," she said shortly. "Pepperoni pizza. And salad."

"Pepperoni pizza." He slowly repeated the words. "That sounds good. What kind of salad? You know, I never know what to put in the dressing. Sometimes I buy it, but I think that's stupid. It costs —"

"Listen, I really have to go. We'll talk tomorrow, okay?"

"Yeah, okay. Sure." She could tell he was hurt, felt a twinge of guilt, then told herself he wasn't her problem. She could be Nathan's friend to a point, but she wasn't going to adopt him.

"Who was that?" Rick asked when she'd hung up the phone.

"Nathan Lacoste. You know, that kid I told you about."

"The weird one?"

"Well . . ." Callie stopped. It was as good a description as any. "Yeah. That's the one."

"He calls you a lot."

"Not that much." Annoyed as she'd been with Nathan, she could still feel sorry for him. "A couple of times a week, maybe. I'm a mother figure or something."

"Or *something*."

Callie shook her head. "Oh, come on, Rick. He's a kid. He's lonely." She paused, still carefully watching him, ready to drop the subject. "So what about your dad? What were you telling me?"

"I think I pretty much said everything. Hey, could you set the table?"

Callie pulled out three place mats, red-and-white-checked gingham.

"So you're leaving on Saturday?"

"Right."

"I could drive you to Hartford. To the airport."

"I've got an early flight."

From upstairs, the sound of canned laughter exploded from Anna's room.

"How's she doing?" Callie gestured toward the stairs.

"Good. She's fine."

"Really?"

"Sure. She came home. I said, 'How was school?' She said, 'Okay.' Then she grabbed a bag of cookies and went upstairs. No complaints."

"She's supposed to set the table before she goes upstairs."

"I guess she forgot."

Callie sighed. "She didn't forget."

"Well, then, I guess she just didn't want to."

After she'd set out the silverware, Callie plopped back in her chair. "I wish she —"

"Just give her some time, Callie. She's still not used to having someone else around. She's used to having you to herself."

"I know. You're right. I just — I just wish it was easier for her. It's not like we just met. She's had time to get to know you. I don't know what the problem is."

"Let it go, Cal. She'll come around in time. Once she sees that I'm not going anywhere."

Once she sees that I'm not going anywhere. The words were like a gift that she welcomed but didn't quite expect. Her mind held them awkwardly, uncertain where to put them.

"I thought ten was supposed to be easier," she finally said. "I was reading somewhere that nine is a hard age, then things settle down at ten. It's supposed to be one of the ages of equilibrium. I thought there'd be some, you know, *break* before she's a teenager."

"Kids are individuals. They don't grow according to plan."

A pause. Callie stretched her arms overhead, then folded one at the elbow and dropped it behind her back. Using the other hand, she pressed down on the upper arm. A yoga stretch she'd learned years ago, back when she did such things.

"At least she's speaking to you," Callie said. "I guess that's an improvement."

"There you go."

Dropping the other arm, Callie repeated the stretch, this time on the other side.

She was more tired than she'd realized.

She'd love to go to bed early tonight, but she still had reading to do. If she let herself get behind, she'd be screwed by the end of the school year. She was way beyond the age when all-nighters seemed like fun.

"Ready to eat?" Rick was pulling the pizza from the oven, where he'd stuck it to keep warm. The yeasty scent of dough wafted through the room.

Callie looked at him and smiled, the tension subsiding again. She loved their Wednesday pizza nights, haphazard and slightly festive. She got to her feet, stretched again, and headed toward the stairs.

"Just put it on the table. I'll go get Anna," she said.

❦

DO NOT ENTER WITHOUT PERMISSION
THIS MEANS YOU!!!!!
ANYONE WHO COMES IN WITHOUT ASKING
WILL BE IN TROUBLE WITH THE LAW
RICK EVANS YOU CANNOT COME INTO MY ROOM
Signed,
Anna Elizabeth Thayer

The sign on Anna's door was a new addition. With a slight sinking feeling, Callie read the words again. She thought about what Rick had said downstairs, how Anna was simply jealous. The sign on the door was like a cry for help, or at least a cry for attention.

Callie knocked on the door. No answer. From inside, she heard a cartoon character's high-pitched, excited voice. The words were followed by a bonking sound, then a whistling and a crash. Callie knocked again, louder this time, then cracked open the door.

"Hi, bug."

Anna was sprawled on her bed in a sea of stuffed animals. She was wearing gray sweatpants and a Merritt Elementary School T-shirt.

"Hi, Mommy," she said.

"May I come in?"

"Okay." Anna's eyes had moved away from hers, drifting back to the TV screen.

The room was its usual chaos, and Callie had to pick her way through the obstacle course to reach her daughter's bed. A hairbrush, a necklace, a black patent shoe, a Harry Potter book. Callie's old computer, which Anna had begged for, had become an impromptu clothes rack, barely visible beneath a pile of pants, skirts, and sweaters.

Perching on the side of the mattress, Callie leaned down for a kiss. As her lips brushed her daughter's cheek, she smelled something unfamiliar, a cloying chemical sweetness that clung to Anna's hair.

"That smell," she said. "What is it?"

"Remember? We got it in the mail. You said that I could have it."

A shampoo sample, Callie remembered now. One of those minuscule bottles tossed by the millions into consumer mailboxes. A puke-green-colored container with a picture of daisies on the label.

"I like your usual better."

"But Mom, that's *baby* shampoo."

"They just call it that because it doesn't sting your eyes. I use it, and I'm not a baby."

"*Mom.*" Anna rolled her eyes toward the ceiling, as if her mother's views on this subject were too embarrassing to consider.

Callie sighed, and sat back. There'd been more and more of these moments lately, and she had to pick her battles. The mess in Anna's room, for example, was something she didn't push. Maybe once a month or so, she'd insist on a full-scale cleanup. The rest of the time she told herself it was Anna who had to live here. The TV had been another concession that Callie at times regretted. But she limited Anna to an hour a day, and only after homework.

"Homework finished?" she asked now.

"Uh-huh," Anna said.

Cuddled up with her battered stuffed bear, Anna still looked like a child. And yet, Callie was well aware of the crossroads just ahead. There on the wall by Anna's bed was a poster of Britney Spears. Balloonlike breasts. Slick, wet lips. A pale froth of hair. An ominous intimation of the years that lay ahead.

Callie looked at her daughter. "So what's with the sign?" she asked.

"What sign?" Anna said. She kept watching the cartoon. A green squirrel scampered to the edge of a tree limb, not watching his step. The branch ended, but he kept going until he glanced down. Then, in sudden panic, he found he was suspended in space. The knowledge seemed to trigger the force of gravity, hitherto suspended. A whistling, whooshing noise as the squirrel plummeted to earth.

Anna laughed loudly.

Callie, knowing her daughter, could tell the sound was forced. "The sign on your *door*," she said, refusing to be put off.

Still not looking at her mother, Anna shrugged her shoulders.

Callie waited for something more, but Anna didn't go on. After another few seconds of silence, Callie tried again. "What's up with you and Rick? You used to like him fine. Remember how you went sledding last winter, you, Henry, and Rick?"

Still no response.

An explosion on the TV screen sent the green squirrel hurtling through outer space, through the stars, past the moon, past the rings of Saturn.

"Anna, turn off the television."

"But Mom —"

"Turn it off."

With a sigh, Anna clicked the remote, but she still didn't look up.

In the sudden silence, Callie had an impulse just to let it go. But they had to talk about this sometime, and it might as well be now.

"Come on, Anna. Tell me."

Anna shrugged again, more elaborately this time. Her eyes shifted from Callie's face to someplace beyond her shoulder. As if she were seeking an escape route to somewhere her mother was not.

"He's okay," she finally said. "I just don't see why he has to *be* here all the time."

"He's here because he cares. He cares about both of us." Callie studied her daughter. "I think there's something else. Something you're not telling me."

"I don't have to tell you *everything*." Anna stared at her lap, hair shielding her face.

"No. Of course not," Callie said gently. "But you might feel better if you talked about it."

Anna shifted her position, and as her hair fell away, Callie glimpsed her trembling mouth. She looked both defiant and miserable, and Callie yearned to touch her. To do something — anything — to soothe her daughter's pain. But she knew from past experience that this would just make things worse. When Anna was in this sort of mood, she had to wait it out.

"He's not my father."

Anna said the words so softly that Callie almost missed them. She looked at her daughter in astonishment, wondering if she'd heard right.

"He's not!" Anna's voice was stronger now. Her eyes squarely met her mother's.

Callie took a deep breath, trying to compose herself. "No," she said. "You're right."

Her mind was flying now, trying to frame a response, trying to come up with an answer that Anna would find reassuring. At the same time, she was casting around for a clue as to where this had come from. She couldn't remember the last time that Anna had mentioned Kevin.

"You've been thinking about your dad?"

"No!" Anna said. And then, "A little." She'd dropped her head, and once again her face was veiled behind a swath of hair.

"So . . . what do you think about?"

"Just some stuff we did. Like that place where we got pumpkins for Halloween. And at that park, where he pushed me on the swing."

She'd been so young, only three. Callie was amazed she remembered. When she herself thought of Kevin Thayer, almost nothing remained. Just the monotony of trying to pretend that she'd been right to marry him. Even his face was a blur now: plump cheeks beneath the thinning hair, small pug nose. When she tried to picture her ex-husband, she thought of a smooth, round egg. Yet he hadn't been a bad man. Just not the man for her.

"You liked doing those things."

"Yeah."

Callie moved a hand to Anna's back, but Anna wriggled away. After a moment, though, she looked at Callie, her gaze shrewd, assessing. The look of a seasoned gambler weighing the odds of a bet.

"Are you going to marry Rick?"

The question caught Callie off guard. "I . . . I don't know, honey," she hedged. "We haven't talked about it."

"But you *might* marry him."

"Look, sweetie, I'm not going to marry anyone unless . . . unless we both agree. Unless you and I both decide that it would be a good idea."

"Really?" Anna's face lit up. This time when Callie touched her, she didn't squirm away.

Reaching beneath her daughter's shirt, Callie tickled her lightly, trailing her fingers down the narrow back in the way that Anna loved.

"You know, if you want to talk about your dad, you can tell me."

"Okay." Anna's voice was muffled, her face pressed against a pillow.

"Do you . . . miss him?" It was painful to ask the question. Maybe because she wanted so much to believe that she could make Anna happy.

"I'm okay, Mom," Anna said.

Callie didn't say anything. For an instant, she had a strange sensation that Anna was protecting her.

Then, leaning forward, she kissed Anna's flowery hair. "C'mon, honey, let's go downstairs. It's pizza night," she said.

"So you'll be back on Tuesday?"

"That's the plan."

It was a little before eight. They were sitting at the kitchen table. Rick flipped through the *Merritt Gazette*, while Callie scanned the mail — applications for credit cards, catalogues, a sweepstakes entry.

"I'll miss you," Callie said to him. And was surprised to realize it was true.

Rick looked over and smiled at her, faint lines deepening around his eyes. He looked both older and younger, smiling at her like that. In fact, he was thirty-two, three years younger than she was.

They'd met late last summer at a neighborhood barbecue. Rick didn't live in the neighborhood, but his pal Tod Carver did. Tod was Rick's best friend at the Merritt Police Department. He had curly hair, a rueful expression, and Callie was fond of him. He reminded her a bit of a guy she'd dated back in high school.

Like Callie, Rick was a Merritt transplant, having moved up from New York. At the barbecue, they'd traded stories over paper plates of food. "Burnout," he'd said simply, when she asked him why he'd moved. For her part, she'd told him how she'd come here for school, then fallen for the town.

He was so appealing, so easy to talk to, she'd liked him right away. Still, when he'd asked her out for dinner, she'd found herself hesitating. She'd been on her own for so long now. It seemed safer that way. There was no one to tell her what to do, no one to report to. No one to ask her difficult questions, to dredge up the painful past. Her life was simple, streamlined. For the most part, it worked. And yet there was something about Rick that had caused her to reconsider. *I'll go out with him once,* she'd told herself. And that was how it started.

A rustle as Rick turned the page, and a flyer fell to the floor. Pushing aside the mail, Callie reached down to get it. A two-for-one sale on Easter candy, worth remembering. Once again, it was almost time for the neighborhood's Easter egg hunt. When was Easter anyway? Two weeks? Or was it sooner?

She reached into her purse for her Filofax, meaning to check the date. But as she pulled out the date book, she saw that something was caught between its pages. The envelope she'd picked up earlier, the one stuck in the door. She'd totally forgotten about it. Now she pulled it out. Edging a fingernail beneath its flap, she neatly ripped it open. Inside was a single sheet of paper. Two short sentences, typed.

Happy Anniversary, Rosamund. I haven't forgotten you.

The shock was so intense that at first she didn't feel a thing. Like plunging into ice-cold water, unable to catch your breath, hurtling down and down and down, not knowing when you'll stop. She clutched the note tight in her hand. Everything had changed.

"Callie? What is it?"

She started at the sound of Rick's voice, pulled back from the precipice.

"Just a note from Anna's teacher," she lied. "I've got to talk to her."

With thick, unwieldy fingers, she quickly refolded the page. Stuck the note in its envelope back in her Filofax. She was about to close the leather cover when her eyes caught today's date. The large block letters in the small square box said Wednesday, April 5.

She stared at the date, hardly able to believe it.

April 5.

Today was April 5.

How could she have forgotten?

Thursday, April 6

DANCING close.

Her head rests on a man's shoulder, her small hand encased in his larger one. Her dress is long and white, soft against her skin. She's a beautiful girl in a beautiful dress, dancing with her new husband. His leg moves forward as hers slides back. He turns, and she turns with him.

One, two, three. One two three.

A waltz.

Another turn and then another. She's starting to feel dizzy. But when she looks up to tell him, she can't seem to speak. He smiles at her, then, firmly, presses her head back down. As if he can't bear to look at her. She wants to ask him why. But when she tries to move her head, his hand holds it in place.

One, two, three. One two three.

It seems as if the room is growing darker, as if it's going to rain. But then she sees that they're not in a room and everyone else is gone. They're dancing outside, in a parking lot, surrounded by a high fence. In the background, she hears music. I'm in the mood, I'm in the mood, I'm in the mood, I'm in the mood, I'm in the —

One, two, three.

One two three.

She almost starts to giggle as they waltz to country rock.

Again, she tries to look up at him, and this time he doesn't stop her. But his gaze is focused on some distant point, beyond the steel mesh fence.

There are no cars left in the parking lot. It must be very late. His arms grow tighter around her, and he steers her into the fence. He *presses up against her, hard, until the metal cuts into her back. She tries to push him away, but his weight knocks the breath from her. Then his mouth smashes down on hers, and there's nothing but this sensation. Heat shoots up between her legs as she molds her body to his. They kiss for what seems like a very long time, his hand wrapped in her hair.*

I'm in the mood, I'm in the mood, I'm in the mood . . .

His hands slide down her body. She arches up toward him.

Then, stronger than desire, a flame of fear leaps up.

Something's wrong. This isn't real.

She has to get away.

Adrenaline courses through her. She lunges forward, wrenches away, then sets off running. A fog has descended over everything, and she can barely see. Not far behind, she hears his footsteps, rapidly closing in. If she can just keep going, she'll get to the church, and there she'll be safe from him. She skims across the murky landscape, almost as if she's flying. Then a blow to her back. Her feet cut out from beneath her.

She feels the knife before she sees it, pressed against her arm. By now, she's given up. She isn't afraid anymore, doesn't feel much of anything. Just a vague curiosity about what it will be like to die. She watches the blade slice through her flesh, silent and unforgiving. A thin red trail springs up through the paper-white skin of her arm. The color of roses or apples. Of Christmas wrapping paper. So beautiful to look at. Strange that it should hurt.

Again, he lifts and lowers the blade, draws it through her flesh. This time the knife goes deeper, almost to the bone.

No. Please. Stop.

In the distance, she hears the wail of sirens. The knife floats down again. I'm here I'm here I'm here. Whose voice is that, screaming? The sirens are all around her. Why don't they make him stop?

She woke up crying, tears streaming down her cheeks. Which wasn't unusual. It had been this way since childhood, at least once a week. As if some deep enveloping sadness were staking its claim on her. Once her older sister, Sarah, had shaken her awake. "Why are you crying?" Sarah had asked. "I'm not," she'd insisted.

And believed it, until she'd touched her face and felt its salty dampness. The dream, though, where had that come from? She hadn't had it for years.

She pulled on a robe, then went downstairs, found Anna at the kitchen table. Anna was already eating breakfast: leftover chocolate cake. Her hair, jaggedly parted, was yanked in a ponytail, the strands pulled back tightly above the delicate shells of her ears.

Callie almost said something — "Chocolate cake for breakfast?" — then decided that it wasn't such a big deal just this once.

"Did you take your vitamin?" Callie asked.

"Yes."

"Good girl."

Callie got a glass from the cupboard and poured it full of milk. Instead of arguing about the cake, she could simply supplement.

"Here. I want you to drink this up."

"But I don't like milk, Mom."

Callie set the glass by her plate. "Drink it anyway."

Turning back to the counter, Callie started the coffeemaker. She felt fuzzy and disoriented, almost as if she'd been drugged. The nightmare hung in her mind and also something else. *Happy Anniversary, Rosamund. I haven't forgotten you.* For a moment, she wondered if she'd imagined that, if it too might be a dream.

"Mommy, d'you think maybe we could get a puppy? The Johnsons just got the cutest little dog. She's part terrier and part beagle, that's what they think. They got her at the pound, and you don't have to pay any money except for the shots. That's what Sophie said. They named her Florence, and she's so nice with these really big ears. She's sort of —"

"A dog needs lots of attention, Anna. We're not home enough." They'd been through this before. The response was automatic.

Callie took a mug from the cupboard and poured herself some coffee. Brown liquid dripped from the glass carafe and she grabbed a rag to wipe it up. The rag was damp and oily, the splashed coffee hot. It didn't seem like a dream. It all felt very real.

"But why *can't* we? I'll take care of her. I don't see —"

Anna's voice cut into her thoughts; something in Callie snapped. "I said No. N.O. *No*. I don't want to talk about it."

A pink glow spread over Anna's face, almost as if she'd been slapped. She looked at Callie in disbelief. She hadn't done anything wrong!

Callie took a step forward, but Anna was already up. She hopped from her chair, grabbed her backpack and shot past Callie toward the hallway.

The front door slammed behind her.

The sound echoed through the house.

For a time, Callie didn't move, just stood there feeling terrible. She shouldn't have lost her temper, especially after last night. Through the window she saw that the weather had turned. It looked like it might rain. Too late, she realized that she should have told Anna to take her slicker to school.

The coffee in her mug had cooled, but she drank it anyway. Then, leaving the mug in the sink, she went upstairs to get dressed. But when she reached her room, she sank down on her bed and lowered her head to her hands.

When she'd finally finished crying, Callie wiped her eyes. She went to the bathroom and blew her nose, splashed her face with cold water. She glimpsed herself in the bathroom mirror, her skin splotchy red and white. Her expression scared her a little. It was how she'd looked *before*.

Back in her bedroom, she picked up the phone.

"Merritt Police Department." It was Rick's friend, Tod Carver. He had a slow, reassuring voice, like the sheriff on an old TV show.

"Tod? It's Callie." She heard the strain in her own voice but hoped he didn't notice. When she spoke again, she made an extra effort to sound like nothing was wrong. "So how're things going?"

"Good, actually. And you?"

"Okay. Fine. Getting ready for the Easter egg hunt?"

"Yeah, I've got the kids next week for vacation. They can't wait." Tod had moved to Merritt from Virginia last year after a messy divorce. It was hard for him, Callie knew, to be away from his children.

"How're they doing?"

"Great. Lilly's started taking gymnastics. She does this amazing back flip. Scares me to death, but she loves it. Oliver lost his first tooth."

"Wow."

"Yeah."

A pause. She figured she'd made enough small talk. "So is Rick around?"

"Sure. I'll get him. Good talking to you, Callie."

"You too. See you next weekend."

A moment and then Rick was on the line.

"Hey. What's up?" He sounded surprised but pleased. She rarely called him at work.

"Listen, there's this UPS package I was expecting yesterday," she began. "I was wondering if you'd seen it. I called and they said it was dropped off. It's . . . some books for school. I need to get hold of them." With relief, she noticed that she sounded normal, the teariness dissipated. She hated lying to Rick but didn't really have a choice.

"No. Sorry. Didn't see a thing."

"Was . . . did anyone come by before I got home? I mean, did you notice anyone hanging around the house or anything?"

"Uh-uh. No. Why don't you check with UPS again? I bet they made a mistake. Left it at the wrong house maybe."

"Yeah. Okay. I'll do that." It had been a long shot. She'd known in her gut that whoever left the note had been careful to avoid detection. It wasn't so difficult, really. During the day, the neighborhood was quiet, the adults at work or doing errands, the kids all in school. And even if a few people were around, it wouldn't necessarily matter. After all these years, it still amazed her, the things people failed to see.

"Will you be over in time for dinner tonight? I thought I'd roast a chicken." One of Anna's favorites. A small gesture of apology for how she'd acted this morning.

"You know, I think I'm just going to head home after work. I've got to pack, get ready to leave town. I've been a little tired lately."

"Sure. Okay." She was disappointed but tried not to show it. "Tomorrow, then?"

"I'd like to. Really. But my flight's so early."

"So I . . ." Callie let the words trail off.

"What?"

"Nothing." She'd been about to say that they wouldn't see each other again before he left town. But thinking better of it, she'd held back the words, not wanting to add to his burdens. She wasn't close to her parents these days, but both of them were alive, and there was definitely something comforting in simply knowing they were there.

"Okay then," Rick said. "I should probably get back to work."

"Right. Well . . . If we don't talk before you leave, have a good trip."

"I'll call you when I get in."

"Do you . . . d'you think I could get your folks' number? In case. Oh, I don't know." She flushed as she asked the question, feeling as if she were begging. As if she were crowding into some place where she hadn't been invited.

"It'd be better if I called you," he said.

When she hung up the phone, she felt worse.

A single car drove by outside, the sound approaching then fading. Callie hauled herself up from the bed and went over to her closet. She dropped her robe to the floor and pulled off her cotton nightgown. Naked in front of the full-length mirror, she studied her reflection.

Her skin, pale, almost translucent, gleamed back from the glass. Her body was small and slender, with firm up-tilted breasts. As a child she'd taken ballet classes and actually done quite well. In dance, she'd found an arena where she imagined that she'd be *seen*. It was something she'd never talked about, not even to her sister, this sense she sometimes had of being almost invisible. Alone, she'd struggled to find a way out, a way to feel more substantial. And then, when she was nine, she'd had a solo in the spring recital.

Everything was perfect, just as she'd imagined. She'd flown across the stage, the lights beaming down, knowing that out in that velvet darkness all eyes were watching her. But afterwards, when it was over, she'd found that nothing had changed. As her sister and parents hugged her backstage, she'd felt like she was fading. She couldn't believe it was happening. She'd felt stunned, betrayed. She'd been so confident that this one evening would change everything.

After that, with no explanation, she'd quit taking ballet. Her parents, surprised, had questioned her, asked her to reconsider. She'd always loved dancing. Why stop now? But after what had happened, she couldn't see the point. She told them she'd just lost interest. Puzzled, they let it go.

Because she always wore long sleeves, her arms were white as her belly. Now, with a sharp intake of breath, she rolled them slowly forward, examined the tender, pale skin with its orderly tracing of scars. Thin white streaks, from elbow to wrist, more than she could count.

This is real. It happened. It isn't something you dreamed.

The first time she'd slept with Rick, he'd gently touched the markings. He hadn't said anything, just looked at her questioningly. "They're from a bad time," she'd said. "I don't want to talk about it." That was four months ago. He'd never asked again. Now, the past washed over her as she gazed down at her arms. The scars were relics of another lifetime, history carved in flesh.

BACK at work shortly after five, Melanie White struggled to cram an armload of shopping bags into her office coat closet. There were more than half a dozen, and she had to shift things to make them fit. The shiny black bag from Barneys. The blue ones from Bergdorf-Goodman. She'd spent several thousand dollars, but she felt exhilarated. After this morning's victory, she felt as if she deserved it.

Just six hours ago she'd been in federal court, waiting for district judge Randolph Lewis to issue his ruling from the bench. She'd been seated at the counsel table with senior partner Tom Mead. Both of them visibly tense, eyes riveted on Lewis. She knew they'd put on an impressive case, but would that be enough? Judges hated to dismiss on summary judgment, given the risk of reversal. Safer to let the case go to trial and decide it based on the record.

As soon as the judge began to speak, she'd felt a tightness in her chest. It seemed to take him forever to get through the litany of facts — how lives had been ruined, savings lost, sacred trusts violated. No one listening could possibly have doubted his sympathy for the plaintiffs.

Then he'd looked up, paused, and she'd felt a glimmer of hope, a spark that the words he spoke next quickly fanned to light.

"However, reprehensible as the conduct is that resulted in plaintiffs' losses, I find absolutely no legal basis on which to hold United Bank liable. United Bank provided loans to Leverett Enterprises, and this money was allegedly used by Leverett as part of a scheme to defraud the plaintiffs. But even if this allegation is proven true, plaintiffs have failed to show that United Bank had any knowledge of the wrongdoing by Leverett, much less any duty to investigate or to notify the plaintiffs. For the foregoing reasons, all counts against United Bank are dismissed."

Melanie kept her face immobile, but inside she was exultant. *We won. We won. We won.*

Half an hour later, she was packing up amid a swirl of congratulations. As the senior associate on this case, she'd done the bulk of the work, and she could tell by Tom Mead's appreciative glances that this fact wasn't lost on him. She'd be up for partnership in May. Things were looking good.

Then, handing her litigation bag to a junior associate, she caught a glimpse of the Murphys. While the rows around them had emptied out, the couple hadn't budged. Of the $150,000 they'd invested with Leverett, less than $6,000 remained. Penny Murphy had testified that they'd been told the investments were safe. "They knew we were old, that Wilbur was sick, that we couldn't afford any risk." Last year, they'd been forced to sell their house. Penny now worked at McDonald's. Wilbur had had the second heart attack, from which he still hadn't recovered. For a moment, as Melanie looked at the Murphys, the brightness of the moment faded. *What were they going to do?* she wondered. *How would they manage to live?*

Tom Mead's grip was firm and cool as he briefly clasped her hand. "Good job," he whispered to Melanie.

She smiled a tight smile. "Thanks."

Another glance at the Murphys, but this time it wasn't so bad. It was terrible what had happened to them, but it wasn't United Bank's fault. It was like the judge had said. Their client wasn't liable. It was Leverett who'd lied to the plaintiffs, and Leverett should pay the price. The problem, of course, as everyone knew, was that Billy Leverett had vanished. Any assets that might remain couldn't be located. At this point, it would take a miracle for the plaintiffs to get back their money. United Bank had been their last, best hope, and now even that was gone.

Still, Melanie reminded herself, it just wasn't her problem. Her role was to protect her client's interests, and she'd done that admirably. United Bank wasn't an Enron or WorldCom. Its leaders weren't corrupt. At most, she thought, they'd shown poor judgment in getting entangled with Leverett.

From court it was on to Le Bernardin, with a coterie of inhouse lawyers. Melanie ordered tuna carpaccio with a gingerlime mayonnaise. She didn't order an entree. She wasn't all that hungry.

"To Harwich and Young, the best law firm in the city. And especially to Tom and Melanie, who've been on call day and night." Harold Linzer, United's chief in-house lawyer, was raising a champagne flute. He had starched white cuffs and square nails, a gold signet ring.

Melanie toyed with her raw tuna, then took a sip of champagne. As the sparkly radiance flowed through her body, she let her thoughts drift. For the past six weeks, every waking moment had been consumed with this case. It felt like something of a luxury to reclaim her mental space. Briefly, she thought about the Murphys again — *Where were they having lunch?* — then, downing the last of her Veuve Clicquot, she held out her glass for a refill.

The afternoon shopping spree had been her reward, and then she'd planned to head home. But the force of habit was too strong, and she'd ended up back at the office. She needed to check her messages and at least go through her mail. Tom Mead had urged her to take a vacation, but she'd politely demurred. With partnership elections on May 22, she needed to stay on the scene.

"Do a little shopping?" Vivian Culpepper stood in the doorway, delicate eyebrows arched. Her stylish pale peach pantsuit set off her clear brown skin.

Melanie climbed to her feet, smoothing her slim black skirt. She tried to shut the closet door, but something inside it jammed. She reached down to shove back a wayward bag, then managed to force the door shut.

"Congratulations," Vivian said. "I hear you guys were amazing."

The two women embraced, Vivian's exuberant dark brown curls pressed against Melanie's smooth blonde bob.

"I was going to call you," Melanie said. "I just got back to the office." Vivian was a true friend, one of the few she'd ever had. They'd met at Princeton as freshman roommates and become inseparable, the friendship taking root in shared southern origins. Vivian, born and bred in Mississippi, had gone on to Yale Law School, while Melanie, a Nashville native, had opted for UVA. It was funny how they looked alike, despite the difference in race. Both slender, tall, with high cheekbones, large wide-set eyes. As if an artist had painted them as a study in black and white.

"So what'd Paul say?" Vivian asked once they'd settled in, Melanie back behind her desk, Vivian seated across.

"Paul." Melanie looked at Vivian guiltily, Paul's thin, sensitive face floating up through her mind. "I . . . I haven't told him yet."

"You haven't *told* him?" Vivian stared at her. "You win a case on summary judgment for one of our biggest clients and you don't bother to tell your fiancé?"

"It just happened this morning." Even to her, it sounded lame.

Vivian gave her a shrewd look. "Honey, if you've had time to buy out most of Madison Avenue, you've had time to call the guy you're planning to marry."

"I will. Call him."

"You wanna know what I think?"

"Do I have a choice?"

But Vivian had already started. "There's no way you're going to marry this guy. And the sooner you figure that out, the better for both of you. Paul's a nice guy, Mel. Why're you doing this to him? If it's because of Frank —"

"Frank? Are you crazy? *I* left *him*, remember?"

"I remember." Vivian looked at her steadily. As if to say, I remember a lot of things. "So have you called him back?"

Melanie busied herself with the mail. A Legal Aid benefit invitation. CLE schedules. Her corporate AmEx bill. She dumped the CLE stuff in the wastebasket — Harwich & Young had its own continuing-ed classes — and set aside the invitation and bill, starting a pile of things that would need her attention later.

"No. Of course not," she said evenly. "Like I said, I don't want to talk to him."

"I think you should call him."

Melanie stared at her. "Are you serious? You can't stand Frank."

"I'm not saying that you should get back together with him. God, I'd never say that. He's a narcissistic son of a bitch. But I don't think you know that yet. Maybe if you saw him again, if you talked to him face-to-face, you'd get to the point where you could finally see him for what he is. Until that happens, you're still going to be hung up on him. And you'll keep stringing on these perfectly decent guys who you couldn't care less about. Whose main attraction is that they aren't Frank Collier and that you're not in love with them."

"That's ridiculous. Why would I want to marry someone I'm not in love with?"

"Like I said, you don't want to marry Paul."

Melanie rolled her eyes, raised her hands in defeat. She was still too high off today's victory to let Vivian get to her.

"Thank you, Dr. Freud. And now, if you don't mind, I've got to get through a couple of days' worth of mail so I can get home. I've gotten about four hours of sleep in the past two days."

With Vivian out of the office, Melanie got down to work. A Princeton alumni mailing. The City Bar Association newsletter. Draft motions from local counsel in a products liability case. She was almost halfway through when she came to an unstamped white envelope, her name typed on the front. She ripped through the flap with a letter opener, pulled out a single white sheet.

Happy Anniversary, Melanie. I haven't forgotten you.

She stared at the words for several seconds. Even without a signature, she had no doubt whom it came from. But why? That was the question. Why was he doing this? She felt like an insect stuck on a pin, unable to escape. It was bad enough that he'd left that message last week when she'd told him not to call. All she'd asked was that he leave her alone. Was it really so difficult? It certainly hadn't seemed so during the years that they were married. But trust Frank Collier to make an appearance at the worst of all possible times. Like last week, when she'd needed to focus on preparing for today's hearing. And today, when she deserved to be happy, savoring this morning's victory.

Happy Anniversary, Melanie. I haven't forgotten you.

The words seemed to mock her. She hadn't failed at many things, but her marriage had been a disaster. She sometimes felt as if all of her successes were consolation prizes, attempts somehow to compensate for the love she'd never have. Then, sternly, she stopped herself, silenced the creeping self-pity. Her life was not unusual. Marriage, betrayal, divorce. Nothing that hadn't been experienced by thousands of women before her. Hundreds of thousands. Millions. Important to keep perspective. And, she reminded herself, many had it much worse. She was lucky to have a successful career, more money than she could spend. And of course there was Paul Freeman, the man she planned to marry.

Paul.

She really did need to call him. Vivian was right. She also needed to ask him about that cocktail party this week. Was it tomorrow or the day after? She glanced at her flip-page calendar, still turned to Tuesday's date. Today was, what, Thursday? Right. Thursday, April 6.

Thursday, April 6.

It was like she'd been slugged. They'd gotten married on December 17. Frank was more than three months late. Just when she'd thought he couldn't hurt her more, he managed to twist the knife deeper.

Happy Anniversary.

And he couldn't even get the date right.

She welcomed the blast of anger, how it clarified her perceptions. Pressing her lips together, she picked up the sheet of paper. She folded it once, ripped it in half, then tore the pieces in two.

It's over. It's over. It's over.

Frank Collier, you're out of my life.

❧

CURLED in a wooden deck chair, bundled in a heavy parka, Diane Massey stared out over cliffs and dull gray sea. A cold gust whipped her face, and she burrowed deeper into her sweater. One thing she hadn't remembered was how long the Maine winters lasted. But cold as it was out here on the porch, she didn't want to go inside. Back to the cluttered dining room table piled with manuscript pages. Back to the tortured confusion of the story she couldn't tell.

She'd always been a disciplined writer, meeting deadlines with practiced ease. Her true-crime books were read by millions, eagerly anticipated. Eight consecutive *New York Times* bestsellers, and she'd never once been late. But, from the start, this project had been different, plagued by repeated setbacks.

For months, she'd struggled in her New York apartment, trying to find a rhythm. But the more she worked, the more confused she got. Something wasn't working. For the first time in her writing career, she'd begun to avoid her desk. Started to accept the dinner invitations she'd never had time for before. Even took to answering the phone during the time she'd blocked out for writing.

Her subject was Winnie Dandridge, the Houston socialite killer, a charming woman who paid her mobster lover to knock off her wealthy husband. The pair's ties to organized crime had caused Diane some concern. Especially after two anonymous letters warned her off writing the book. And it wasn't just the issue of safety, though that preyed on her mind. There were problems with the story itself, in how she wanted to tell it.

Then, suddenly, March was almost over, her June 1 deadline looming. It was then that she'd thought of Maine, of her parents' house on Blue Peek Island. The island would be all but deserted, the perfect place to work. Just a handful of year-round residents, mainly fishermen. Three days later, she was packed and gone. Only two people knew where she was, her editor and her agent.

She'd arrived in Maine about a week ago, determined to get down to work. But much to her chagrin she'd found that the change of scene wasn't helping. She took long walks, stared at the sea, and worried about her deadline. Every afternoon at five, she ran a three-mile loop, the daily ritual reminding her how little she'd accomplished. She'd mastered the art of excuses, blaming circumstances. Light had become an obsession, its absence or profusion. During the day, she blamed the bright sunlight; at night, she blamed the darkness.

Of course, she knew deep down that this was all in her mind. If she'd really wanted to work, nothing would have stopped her. She'd worked under far worse conditions for many, many years. Once she'd written all night in a motel room while a couple made love next door, their cries and moans mingling in her mind with those of the story's victims. Death and sex. Sex and death. How often they came together, the explosion of hate following love in some sort of cosmic dance. She'd written in a sort of trance, forgetting where she was. Then there were the years of reporting, when she'd written in a noise-filled newsroom, colleagues on the telephone, editors screaming for copy. No, if she were ready to work, the words would be right there.

In the distance she saw the ferry chugging back to the mainland. She might as well pick up the mail now, get that out of the way.

The post office was just down the street, a demure white clapboard structure with a sprightly American flag. Nothing had changed since childhood, when she'd spent her summers here. She remembered waiting at the counter for stamps, unable to see the top.

A bell tinkled as she opened the door.

"I'm still sorting, Diane. It'll be at least ten minutes." Jenny Ward, a sturdy island native, was a few years younger than Diane. She'd taken over as postmistress when her mother retired.

"That's okay. I'll wait." The room was bright and warm, smelling of coffee and glue. Rows of small brass-fitted boxes lined the long front wall. Diane sat on a wooden stool tucked beneath a window.

"So how's the book going?" Behind the counter Jenny was working, her hands flying through the mail.

"Oh . . . it's okay." Diane's lips curved in the same false smile she smiled at her friends in New York.

"Well, I hope you finish it fast 'cause I can't wait to read it. I don't know how you write all those words, I really don't."

Neither do I, Diane thought. *Believe me. Neither do I.*

Jenny kept up a stream of chatter, a running commentary on island life. Lobster season. A new baby. Last year's property tax increase. She seemed so utterly at ease with her life. Diane envied that. Though at this moment she might have envied anyone who didn't have to write a book.

"Here you go."

Jenny handed her FedEx packets from her editor and her agent.

Diane turned to her editor's packet first, quickly ripping it open. Inside were three smaller envelopes in a range of soft pastels. Pale pink. Pale blue. White. They reminded her of Easter eggs. A note was clipped to the stack in Marianne's familiar scrawl: "Looks like fan mail," she wrote. "Thought you could use a boost." Diane smiled, though a bit uneasily, reminding herself that Marianne couldn't know how far behind she really was.

Diane opened the pink envelope, skimmed the spidery cursive. "My daughter gave me *Dreams of Dying* and since then I've read every one of your books. Are you ever afraid that some of the people you write about might come after you?"

The next envelope she opened was white. She unfolded the single thin white sheet and read the short typed message.

Happy Anniversary, Diane. I haven't forgotten you.

Happy Anniversary?

Puzzled, she turned the paper over, looking for an explanation. There was her AA anniversary, of course, but that was months away. Again, she looked at the envelope. No postmark or return address. Maybe she should call Marianne, find out where it came from. For now she stuck the mail in her purse. She'd open the rest at home.

She said good-bye to Jenny and headed up the road. Between buildings she glimpsed the flat sea against the backdrop of sky. Mild cramps pinched her stomach. She'd been drinking too much bad coffee. While she'd brought out a stash of French Roast, it didn't taste the same. The old aluminum percolator worked a curious alchemy, transforming the beans' dark richness to something sharp and bitter.

Longingly she thought of her home in New York, the lights, the traffic, the noise. She lived in a loft in Tribeca, a sun-drenched open space. On an ordinary day, she'd have breakfasted at Le Pain Quotidien. She could almost taste the flaky croissant, the bowl of caffe latte. After a few hours at her desk, she'd have headed off to the gym. Worked out with Bob, her personal trainer, maybe had a massage. Back home, the mail would have arrived, with its cache of invitations. Book signings and film openings. Requests to come and speak. She had a life in New York, friends and dinners and parties. All those distractions she'd come to escape seemed endlessly alluring.

Back at the house, she went straight to her desk and forced herself to sit down. *Keep your butt in the chair. No more procrastinating.* She worked for a couple of hours, then made a tuna fish sandwich — a far cry from the take-out sushi she'd have picked up back home. Sandwich in hand she returned to her desk and continued to work as she ate.

By three o'clock, she was amazed to find that she'd written more than two thousand words. She stuck another log in the woodstove, then printed out the new pages. At her desk, she reread what she'd written that day, making penciled notations in the margins. It was good, much better than she'd thought.

When she next looked up it was almost five. A solid day's work. The best she'd done in months. Standing up, Diane stretched her legs, then headed upstairs to change. She tied back her hair, pulled on a hat, dropped her necklace under her shirt. On impulse, she picked up the phone and dialed a New York number.

Her editor's assistant picked up.

"Hi, Kaylie? It's Diane. Is Marianne around?"

"Sorry, Diane. She's in a meeting. Anything I can do?"

"No. Well. Actually, I was wondering . . . I just got the mail you forwarded, and there was a letter, something without a return address. It must have been dropped off. Anyway, I was trying to figure out who it was from."

A pause. "Oh. Yeah. Someone dropped it off in reception. I don't have a name, though. If you want, I can check to see if they have a record down there."

"Great. That would be great." Diane heard phones ringing in the background, someone calling down a hallway. "One more thing. Do you know when it came in?"

"Sure, let's see." A flipping of pages. "We got it yesterday."

After she hung up, Diane grabbed a Polartec jacket and headed outside for her daily run. Every day her route was the same. Up Harbor Road, the main island thoroughfare, then off toward Carson's Cove. Down a spruce-shaded dirt path, past Fischer's abandoned boatyard, then onto the rocky promontory that ran along the water.

She always felt better once she started to run, and today was no exception. The wind rustled in the tall old trees; empty sky arced above. It was easy to lose perspective, to forget how lucky she was. She found herself thinking about Nashville, the place where it all began. Remembering the chance meeting from which everything had followed. From the vantage point of where she sat, it could seem inevitable. But when she was honest, she had to admit how much she owed to luck.

Her first job was at Nashville's morning paper, general assignment reporting. Weather stories and car crashes. Filling in at school board meetings. Tedious in retrospect but exciting at the time. Of course, she hadn't stood a chance of covering the Gage trial. That plum had gone to Bryce Watkins, the paper's veteran court reporter. But like readers everywhere, she'd been riveted by the story, mesmerized by the drama unfolding in the Davidson County Courthouse. She read every word she could get her hands on, pumped Watkins for information. A couple of times, she played hooky from work to watch parts of the trial.

Still, she would have stayed on the sidelines if it hadn't been for Laura Seton. They met at an AA meeting at a church in downtown Nashville. Because she was seated at the side of the room, she saw Laura walk in, watched her slip quietly into a seat in the very last row of chairs. Despite the dark glasses and hat, Diane recognized her. She lost all track of what was being said as she concentrated on Laura, wondering how she might approach without scaring her off. She had a brief tussle in her mind about the ethics of this maneuver, knowing that she'd be taking advantage of Laura's vulnerability. But even as she argued with herself, she knew what she had to do. Gage's former girlfriend was the prosecution's star witness. An exclusive interview with Laura Seton would be the story of a lifetime.

At the end of the meeting, she rushed forward, caught Laura on the steps of the church. "You looked upset," she babbled. "I wanted to give you my number. If you ever want to talk, call me anytime." She handed Laura a piece of paper with her home number scribbled on it.

Laura was looking down. "Thanks," she muttered softly. She stuffed the paper into a pocket and quickly turned away. After that, weeks passed, but Laura didn't return. Not that Diane was really surprised; it happened all the time. A newcomer checked out a meeting or two, then went back to drinking.

Steven Gage's trial continued.

The night after he was sentenced, Diane awoke to a ringing phone sometime after 2 A.M.

"I need to talk," Laura said, sobbing, the words barely audible. "I'm sorry, but I had your number. I didn't . . . know who to call."

Diane rushed over to Laura's apartment, where she dumped out half-empty bottles of vodka, then listened as Laura talked. For hours, the words poured out in a self-lacerating stream. Laura seemed to assume that Diane knew who she was. Either that or, because of the booze, she wasn't thinking clearly.

"I loved him so much," Laura said, weeping. "And even with . . . everything that's happened, I still do. Love him. I can't believe I've done this. I've killed the man I love."

"You didn't kill him, Laura. You had to tell the truth." She said the words mechanically, patting Laura's shoulder. One part of her present, comforting, another part taking notes. Her mind was already on overdrive, thinking about the book.

More than ten years later, she was slightly appalled by the ambitious young woman she'd been. Appalled but also grateful. While all her later books had been bestsellers, her first had been a smash. Eight years after its initial publication, *The Vanishing Man* was still in print, having sold millions of copies in twenty-three languages.

Diane had emerged from the woods and was back on Harbor Road. She ran past a timeworn wooden barn caving in on itself. She was thinking about what to make for dinner; she didn't have much at the house. Maybe pasta with red sauce, something simple and quick. Then she'd go back to work until it was time for bed. If she could keep up today's momentum, she might even meet her deadline. Today was, what? April 6. She had almost two months left. If she could just —

Happy Anniversary, Diane. I haven't forgotten you.

A thought ricocheted through Diane's mind, the present and past colliding. She glanced at the date on her Cartier watch. Today was April 6. If the letter came yesterday, as Kaylie said, that meant it had arrived on April 5. It was a date that stuck in her mind, a date she'd never forget. Odd how she'd been thinking of him just before she made the connection. As if her subconscious, leaping ahead, had already found the link.

April 5, five years ago.

The date of Steven Gage's execution.

THAT night, Callie was relieved to find that Anna was in good spirits. Between two helpings of roast chicken, she chattered about Harry Potter, seeming to have entirely forgotten their breakfast confrontation.

"Mommy, don't you think Henry looks sort of like Harry Potter?"

"Yeah, I think he does."

"Except he's not a wizard."

"You never know, Anna."

"Mommy, if you went to Hogwarts, what house would you want to be in? If you couldn't be in Gryffindor?"

"But I want to be in Gryffindor," Callie said playfully. That was Harry's house.

"But . . . you can't. So which one?"

"Well . . ." Callie made a show of serious consideration. "I wouldn't want to be in Slytherin, of course."

Anna looked approving.

"Maybe Ravenclaw. Isn't that Cho's house?"

"Uh-huh."

"I could be friends with her."

It was one of the nicest evenings they'd had in quite a while.

Not until she'd tucked Anna into bed did Callie realize how tired she was. Lately, she'd had to put in overtime at the Windham alumni office. The Fifth Reunion directory was overdue at the printer's, and with Debbie Slater on maternity leave, it was just her and Martha. The student intern they'd managed to snag wasn't helping matters. Her name was Posy — Posy Kisch — but they called her Kabuki Girl. She wore white pancake makeup and red lipstick. This week her hair was green. On a good day she called when she planned to skip work. Most days she didn't bother.

Regardless of how tired she felt, she had to get some reading done. Leaving the dishes in the sink to soak, Callie went straight to her desk. After months of trial and error, she'd found this was the only way. She turned on her halogen desk lamp and pulled out a syllabus. *Now You See It, Now You Don't: Unconscious Transference and Mistaken Identity*. Riffling through a stack of articles, she found the one she needed.

As Callie's eyes moved across the page, the world seemed to fade away. They were studying memory, and the material intrigued her. Eyewitness testimony, the author wrote, was heavily relied on by juries. A single credible eyewitness could put a defendant behind bars. And yet time and again, sworn witness accounts had proven false. "In some instances victims lie, but many more are simply mistaken. Far too little attention is paid to the vagaries of memory."

A tapping somewhere at the back of her mind, the past paying a visit.

Things she remembered or thought she did.

Things she'd prefer to forget.

She finished the introductory section and moved on to the rest, the case studies the author used to demonstrate his thesis. In the first, a ticket agent pointed to a sailor as the man who'd robbed him at gunpoint. But the totally innocent sailor had an alibi. It was later discovered that the sailor had bought tickets in the past. It was simply because he looked familiar that he'd been picked from the lineup. In a second example, a psychologist stood accused of rape, again having been selected by the victim from a lineup. But at the very moment the rape was occurring, the psychologist was live on TV. The explanation? The victim had been watching the program when she was assaulted, and the memory of what she'd seen on screen had apparently merged with the rape. Another classic case of unconscious transference, a glitch in memory.

Unconscious transference.

Callie wrote down the words. She stared at the phrase for another few moments, thinking through what she'd read.

Far too little attention is paid to the vagaries of memory . . .

Far too little attention. Maybe.

But sometimes far too much.

She'd like to know more about these witnesses, so confident and unyielding. Was there a personality type especially prone to making such mistakes? Or how about another type, who constantly doubts herself? Who knows exactly what she's seen yet refuses to acknowledge it? She herself would fall in this second group, of that she was sure. Asked to identify someone, she would be plagued with doubts. However confident she might feel, a small part of her would wonder. She thought of a girl named Laura Seton, recalled her haunted eyes, pictured her on the stand at trial, pointing at Steven Gage. She thought of Sharon Adams, Dahlia Schuyler's friend. Even at the time, she'd reflexively wondered how you knew for sure. Wasn't there always that shade of doubt that whispered you might be wrong?

Over the years, she'd taught herself to push certain facts aside. It was a skill she'd carefully cultivated, a tool she'd used to survive. First she'd done it for her daughter; later, for herself. For years, the habit had served her well, and she'd never questioned it. Only now did it occur to her that the strategy had its drawbacks. The note she'd found in the door last night, she'd pushed it from her mind. Now she forced herself to take it out of the desk drawer where she'd stowed it.

Happy Anniversary, Rosamund. I haven't forgotten you.

Callie picked up a spiral notebook and turned to an empty page. Licking her lips, she stared at its blankness, thinking where to begin.

Who could have left the note?

That was the obvious question.

It had to be someone who knew where she was, someone determined to find her.

Through the window over her desk, Callie stared into the night at the delicate black-lace tree limbs arced against the sky. Across the street, a single light burned in a second-floor window, while Bernie Creighton's black Mercedes loomed in the shadowed driveway. She'd already checked the doors and windows. Set the household alarm. And yet, when the wind rustled through the leaves, she imagined she saw someone.

Impulsively, Callie got up and reached toward the window to yank down the bamboo shade. It fell with an explosive clatter, blocking out the night. She took a deep breath and sat back down, willing herself to calm. Again, she turned to the blank white page with its pale blue lines. It wasn't just a question of who, it was also a question of why. Why would someone have done this, left this note in her door? What would be the purpose? What would they hope to gain?

Money, maybe. Blackmail.

Or possibly revenge.

For an instant, the thought danced through her mind, sharp and bright with danger. Then, firmly, she told herself that it wasn't, couldn't be, true. Steven Gage was dead.

Unless . . .

A new thought pushed through her brain, horrifying in its logic. *He could have planned it before. He could have set it up.*

The idea was like an electric charge, surging through her body. The moment it occurred to her, she knew that it was true. At first, she felt as if she'd lost her breath. Her thoughts flew in all directions. Then, slowly her mind began to clear, leaving her with questions.

Who would he have recruited?

Who would have agreed?

The response was almost immediate: She thought of Lester Crain.

What had happened with Steven Gage and Lester Crain had been the ultimate outrage, a final insult to the grieving families left behind by both of their victims. Crain, a rapist and murderer, was a scrawny, tough-talking punk. He was just seventeen when he committed the murder for which he was sentenced to die, the gruesome torture-killing of a runaway teenage girl. After repeatedly raping his victim, Crain strung her from the ceiling, tore off her nipples with a pair of pliers, and injected her vagina with bleach. By the time he finished with her, what was left was barely human. But the source of Crain's notoriety wasn't just his crime. It stemmed from the cassette tape he'd kept of his victim's agonized screams.

Gage and Crain met on Tennessee's death row and quickly forged an alliance. Gage was already a living legend; Crain became his disciple. The incredible course of events that followed began in the prison library, where Gage had honed his legal skills as a practicing jailhouse lawyer. With Gage's help Crain won a new trial, convincing a judge that the torture tape heard by the jury had been obtained in an unconstitutional search. Later, at a press conference, Crain gleefully announced that he owed this second chance to Steven Gage. He'd do his best, he promised, to repay the favor someday.

That part was bad enough, but it wasn't close to the end.

While awaiting his second trial, Lester Crain escaped from prison. The uproar provoked by Crain's flight didn't let up for months. In addition to the Tennessee murder, he was a suspect in other crimes. Two brutal Texas rape-murders. Another in south Florida. Fueling the fear were experts' predictions that Crain would kill again. Sexual psychopaths like Crain, they said, didn't simply stop.

For months, then years, the nation waited for Crain to pop up somewhere. But as time passed, it seemed more and more likely that one of three things must have happened. Lester Crain could have died or become incapacitated. The third possibility was that he'd managed to flee the country. Crain had spent several dissolute years prowling the Texas border, living with his alcoholic father outside El Paso. The hardest part would have been making it from Tennessee to Texas. But if Crain had somehow reached the border, he could easily have slipped across.

All of this was far in the past, seven, eight years ago. But if Crain was alive, he had to be somewhere. Could he be here, in Merritt?

Abruptly, Callie stood up, adrenaline flooding her body. She had an overpowering urge to speak to another person. Rick was probably asleep by now, but she couldn't stop herself. Her hand curled around the phone as she punched in his number. After four rings, the machine picked up, and she heard his recorded voice. She almost left a message, then changed her mind and hung up.

The box was high on a closet shelf, behind a row of shoes.

She climbed onto a step stool and reached up to take it down.

Sitting on the bedroom floor, she placed the box between her legs. It looked like one of the dozens of boxes she kept in her Windham office, a simple white container for the storage of file folders. For a moment she stared at the cardboard lid, covered with a layer of dust. She thought fleetingly of Pandora and that other mythical box. But keeping the lid on her own box wouldn't keep her safe. The thing she feared was out there somewhere. It couldn't be contained.

The contents of the box were tightly packed: File folders. Notebooks. Snapshots. She carefully pulled out items and placed them on the floor. A file of yellowed newspaper clippings. A small blue spiral notebook. Her stomach clenched at the sight of letters in a strong sloping hand. She sat for a moment staring, almost afraid to touch them.

The box was almost empty when she found what she was looking for. As she pulled out the book, she averted her eyes from the picture on the cover. She didn't want to see his face. Not now. At least not yet. She saw that the binding was coming loose, shrinking away from the pages. Careful not to loosen them, she flipped to the title page.

The Vanishing Man: The Secret Life of Serial Sex Killer Steven Gage
By Diane Massey

Slowly, she turned to the first chapter, the familiar opening lines.

In the months before his arrest in Nashville, Tennessee, Steven Gage roamed the country. There was something frenzied in his travels, which often took place at a moment's notice for no apparent reason. From Boston to San Francisco to Miami, then back to Boston again. From Nashville to Phoenix to Burlington. From Charlotte to Indianapolis. When the evidence was pieced together — the gasoline receipts purchased with stolen credit cards, the plane tickets bought under assumed names — it would turn out that he covered more than 30,000 miles in those final desperate six months. And everywhere he went, women died . . .

Minutes passed. Callie read on, her eyes skating over the pages. Each line, each word, each image, cast her into the past.

Looking back, it would seem astonishing that he could have escaped detection. He drove his own car, often used his own name, moved easily in the daylight. Later, some would speculate that he'd actually wished to be caught. And yet, for at least a decade, Gage killed with impunity. Even witnesses he'd spoken to were hard-pressed to describe him. All agreed that he was tall, handsome, but no one could say much more. Good-looking yet eminently forgettable, the perfect disguise for a killer. He didn't need to wear a mask. His own face served that function. He glided into his victims' worlds, taking them with him when he left. Even when the bodies were found, he left no trace of himself. No hair. No fibers. No fingerprints. They called him the Vanishing Man.

It all washed over her, again, the horror of what he'd done. And it wasn't just the victims but those they'd left behind. Now, with a child of her own, she found the pain past imagining. She thought of Dahlia Schuyler's family, the families of all the others, dozens, hundreds, of broken lives, never to be the same. She thought of Dahlia's younger brother, who blamed himself for her death, believing that if he hadn't been late to meet her, Dahlia could have been saved. And all the other lives snuffed out, the endless list of names. Fanny Light. Clara Flanders. Dana Koppleman. Dozens of young, beautiful women, with long, straight blonde hair.

It happened slowly, not all at once, but something inside her was changing. Beneath the turmoil of her racing thoughts, something was growing clear. A belief that she could do what it took to protect the life she'd built.

Slowly, she closed the book and stared at the face on the cover. She forced herself to study it, refused to look away. Bulging eyes, distended veins, teeth bared in rage. She wasn't frightened anymore, just filled with a sense of purpose. Gazing at the book, she whispered, "This time, you're not going to win."

Monday, April 10

THE Prada suit fit perfectly.

As one of Mr. Lin's best clients, Melanie had convinced him to complete the alterations on Saturday. Now, heading down the hall toward her office, she sensed the admiring glances. The long black skirt hugged her hips, flaring out slightly at the bottom. The black jacket clung to her body, nipping in at the waist. She felt both armored and seductive, a heady combination. A woman who could afford this suit wasn't someone you'd want to mess with. She smiled to herself as she walked down the hall.

Look, just don't touch.

"Wow. You look great!"

"Thanks, Tina." Melanie smiled at her secretary, turning as she reached her office door. "Listen, I've got to take care of something. Will you hold my calls for a while?"

Closing the door behind her, the smile faded from Melanie's face. There was a reason she'd worn this suit today. She wanted to feel in control. Outside, twenty-two floors below, traffic streamed down Park Avenue. She watched the scene for a bit, then turned to the phone. It was just after eight-thirty, but Frank got to work early. One of the things they'd had in common. One of the few in the end.

"Frank Collier, please. This is Melanie White."

"Yes, Ms. White. I'll get him." The secretary's voice was unfamiliar, but she obviously knew who Melanie was. Waiting for Frank to come on the line, Melanie wondered what she'd been told. *Can you believe that she left him? She sounds like a total bitch.*

"Hi there, Melanie. Thanks for gettin' back to me." The familiar drawl gave her a queasy feeling. Even hundreds of miles away, Frank Collier filled up a room. She pictured him in his spacious office, with its views of the U.S. Capitol. An imposing six feet four inches, with steel-gray hair, eyes a guileless blue. He'd be leaning back in his leather chair, an easy smile on his face, as if he had absolutely no doubt that he'd end up getting his way.

"Sorry it took me a while. I had a summary judgment hearing." She sounded polite but distant, just as she'd hoped to sound. She had no intention of letting on how much she'd dreaded this call.

"So how'd it go?"

"Good. We won, actually. The judge ruled from the bench." The pride in her voice annoyed her. As if she were a cat, dropping a bird at his feet. Seeking a laying-on of hands from Frank Collier, megalawyer. Maybe it wouldn't have bugged her so much if it hadn't been true for so long.

"I'm not surprised, Melanie. You're a wonderful lawyer." She heard condescension in his words, but maybe she imagined it. Anyway, it hardly mattered. Time to cut to the chase.

"Listen, Frank. You've got to stop contacting me. I mean the calls, that note. Enough."

"The *calls?*" He seemed bemused. "Melanie, I only called you once. When I left a message last week. As for a note, I have no idea what you're talking about."

"But I . . ." Melanie stopped, confused. This was one response she hadn't anticipated. Who else could the note be from? And yet, why would he want to lie? If he'd sent the note, she couldn't think why he wouldn't admit it.

And then he was speaking again. "Melanie, please, believe me. We're in total accord on that point. I actually called you for a reason."

A long, pregnant pause, the trademark Collier staging. "I thought that I should tell you. I'm getting married again."

At first she almost laughed, thinking it was a joke, but the silence that followed his words told her she was wrong.

For an instant, the world around her froze. Time seemed to stand still. Then everything started moving double-time, and she was too angry to speak. *You bastard. You fucking bastard.* She was tempted to announce her own engagement, to throw *that* back at him. But even as she felt the urge, she knew that she'd waited too long. Coming on the heels of Frank's proclamation, hers would smack of defeat. A pathetic attempt to convince him that she was still desirable. If only she'd told him *before*, but that was wishful thinking. The best that she could do right now was pretend she didn't care.

"Congratulations," she said coolly. "I hope you'll be very happy."

❧

DIANE Massey was in a foul mood.

She typed another few words on her laptop, then stared off into space. It had all started this morning, when she went down to pick up the mail. Jenny had mentioned that a man had come by asking if she was around. He hadn't wanted to give his name, claimed to be another writer. He too, he'd said, was seeking seclusion but good to know she was here. No need to mention him, he'd said. He wouldn't want to intrude.

Diane hadn't bought it.

Right away, she'd thought of Warner.

They'd broken up more than three months ago, but he hadn't given up. Back in New York he still called her several times a week, begging for another chance, insisting they needed to talk. These messages, which she never returned, always left her feeling tense. The contrast between who he was and the man she'd thought she'd seen. Jenny's description had calmed her somewhat — Warner didn't have a beard — still, just the thought he might have tracked her down had made her distinctly uneasy.

She worked fretfully another few hours, but her concentration was gone. She was relieved when five o'clock came. Time for her afternoon run. She grabbed her Walkman on her way out the door, along with a Garbage cassette. Usually, the silence soothed her, but today she wanted noise. Something raucous and angry to block out the anxious thoughts.

Another monochromatic day. A study in shades of gray. Slate-gray water. Bleached gray sky. Tall charcoal trees. Almost impossible to believe that spring would come, let alone the brightness of summer. She watched a car approach but barely heard its roar, the blaring music on her headphones erasing all other sound.

As she turned down the dirt road that led to Carson's Cove, the woods closed in on her. Spindly fir trees, impossibly tall, layer upon layer of them. On most days, running raised her spirits, but today it didn't happen. The thing that bugged her most was the imminent sense of intrusion. It was probably a little irrational. She didn't own the island. But she couldn't escape the prickly feeling of being imposed upon. It was exactly the sort of thing she'd argued about with Warner. He'd never been able to understand her need to be alone. But she wouldn't think about that. There didn't seem to be an answer. In the end, the choice was always the same: work or love. Not both.

For a time, she'd thought that Warner was different. The exception that proved the rule. He worked so much himself, she'd thought they might reach an understanding. But finally even he'd grown angry, wanting more from her. In the end, like all the others, he'd wanted to be taken care of.

There was always that stark moment when she saw that it wouldn't work. It always came in a sudden flash that caught her by surprise. She imagined it would be a gradual thing emerging over time, a slow accretion of evidence, like building a case at trial. But as far as she could remember, it never happened like that. Instead, there was that single moment when everything crystallized.

In every relationship, she could pinpoint precisely when it happened. With Don Bishop, the cardiologist, it had come after dinner one night. He'd looked around, bemused, at her library, and said, "Think you've got enough books?" With Phil Brooks, the turning point had been when he'd left the message, "It's me." It wasn't the words so much as the tone, the fatuous self-absorption. Right then she'd stopped returning his calls, and finally, he'd given up.

With Warner the moment had come the first time he'd raised

his voice. Her mind slipped back to that final night, the last time they'd seen each other. They'd had dinner at Raoul's, around the corner from her loft. Even then she'd sensed something dark, a current beneath the surface. Between bites of steak au poivre she'd thought about saying something. Then, back at her apartment, they'd had that terrible fight.

Now she was on the narrow path leading to the water. But just as she caught the first glimpse of sea, a blow struck her from behind. Breath flew out of her lungs. Her only thought was, *Whaaa?* As she watched her body fly through the air, her reaction was pure surprise. It might be good or bad. She really wasn't sure. She tried to break the fall with her hands, but she wasn't fast enough. Her face smashed into the earth, and her mind seemed to implode. There was a moment before the pain hit, when everything went still. Then, as if someone had hit a switch, sensation flooded her body. Tendrils of pain rushed through her. Everything seemed to blur. Her mind, her body, the sky, the earth — none of it made sense.

Somewhere dimly above her, she heard the sound of breathing.

Her nails dug into the hard dirt path as she struggled to climb to her knees. But just as she raised herself onto an elbow, a foot pressed into her back. A foot and behind it a body's weight. She heard the cracking of bone. She flung out an arm in mute appeal, grasped at empty space. She tried to scream, but she had no breath, and her cry was a soft yelp. Then, the weight bore down on her, knees clamped around her sides. She saw a pair of heavy muscled thighs encased in black denim. She felt something around her neck, twisting slowly tighter. Fear spilled into the pain, and she couldn't think anymore. She wanted to live, *to live.* Her lungs fought for air.

Hands rolled her roughly onto her back. She was choking and crying at once. Her eyes traveled up past the black shirtsleeves until she saw his face. He didn't say anything, just looked at her without blinking. Even with the beard, she recognized him. She never forgot a face.

You, she thought. *Why you?*

She really wanted to know.

Then the thing around her neck grew tighter, and she couldn't breathe again. Above her the wind rustled through the trees, and she was floating toward them. An explosion of colors behind her eyes, and she thought of Dahlia Schuyler. The last thing she thought before the sky went black was, *So this is how she felt.*

HE stared at her sprawled on the ground, his heart still heaving from the struggle. He was filled with a sense of exhilaration that he'd never known before.

Of all that is written I love only that which is written in blood . . .

The words of the great German philosopher bloomed red in his mind.

After another second or two, he reluctantly glanced at his watch. The large hand pointed to the number two, the smaller down by six. It took another moment for him to realize that it was just 6:10. Could it really have happened so quickly? It seemed impossible. With a start he wondered if his watch had stopped. What time was it really?

It was then that he noticed the gold watchband circling her pale wrist. With a gloved hand he turned over her arm to see the face of the watch. He caught the name *Cartier* on the watch's face. Even he knew that name. It must have cost thousands — five or ten grand — to the $29.95 he'd paid for his. But the time on both of their watches was the same. He found this satisfying. Timex. Cartier. It didn't matter. Time was one of the few things in life that was absolutely fair.

Life isn't fair. He'd grown up hearing that. As if it were something you had to accept. As if you were powerless. Well, by God, he wasn't accepting it. He was a man of action. Maybe you couldn't change the past, but at least you could avenge it. Over the years, he'd come to conclude that people were essentially weak. They'd prefer to whine about what had happened instead of doing what had to be done. They didn't seek out opportunities, they sought out excuses. How many of them would have had the guts to do what he'd just done?

Can you be judge of yourself and avenger of your law?

Yes and yes and yes again. And finally, he'd proved it.

Again, his eyes drifted to the splayed body, tossed across the path. He'd have liked to stay there for quite some time, letting the image sink in. But even though the island was all but deserted, he couldn't dispense with caution. He had to finish up with the body, then head back to the boat. He'd brought it in under cover of night, he'd leave the same way. He needed to stick to his schedule, to take care of things and get out.

Formula of my happiness: a Yes, a No, a straight line, a goal.

The familiar words echoed in his brain, reminding him of his purpose. He had to wind up his work here, to get back to Merritt in time.

Tuesday, April 11

CALLIE sat on the side of her bed, picking fuzz balls off her sweater. There was something calming about the task, its total mindlessness. She'd finally cleared the right side and turned now to the left, plucking off the furry bits of wool and flicking them into the trash. When at last she looked up, she felt vaguely dazed. Twenty minutes had passed.

She'd been this way for almost a week now. Preoccupied. Distracted. The world around her had come to seem more and more unreal. It was at night, as she lay unconscious, that she sensed reality. The old nightmare returned now almost every night. Steven Gage in the parking lot, his hands exploring her body. The heat of desire, the fear of death, intertwined in sleep. Even worse, the dream was mutating, as if it were a living thing. Sometimes Steven was Lester Crain. Once he'd had Rick's face. This last shift had appalled her. It had felt like a betrayal. Moments after she'd snapped awake, she'd gone to the toilet and thrown up.

She was no closer to deciding what to do than she'd been last week. She'd spent hours on the Internet, seeking news of Lester Crain. But just as she'd thought, there was very little that she didn't already know. She told herself this was reassuring; he might be dead, after all. All the experts agreed that a killer like Crain wouldn't have simply stopped. Yet during the years since his escape, no crimes had been linked to him.

If only she had someone to talk to, but there was no one now. She thought of her parents back in Indiana, how much older they'd seemed last Christmas, her father's skin pouched around his eyes, her mother somehow fragile. After everything she'd put them through, she couldn't dump this on them. Besides, even if she talked to them, what could they possibly do? They'd only worry as they had before, as they had for so many years. And once again they'd be helpless to protect the daughter they loved. Imagining how she'd feel in their place, she was filled with guilt. She couldn't think of anything worse than fearing your child was in danger.

Her older sister, Sarah, had always been her closest confidante. But calm, perfect Sarah now had problems of her own. Sarah and her husband had been sharply hit in the nineties tech-stock crash. Gary had been laid off, and Sarah, a doctor, had gone back to work full-time. She had two young children, one of them autistic, and wanted to be home with them. Instead, the kids were in day care, while Gary looked for work.

The only other possibility was her ex-husband, Kevin Thayer. At least he knew the history. She wouldn't have to explain. Kevin with his round pink face, his smell of Ivory soap. Strange, that of all the options, he was the most appealing. She and Kevin had barely spoken for years. Their divorce had not been smooth. She doubted if he'd forgiven her for walking out on him. Still, at this point, even he had to see that the marriage couldn't have lasted. And now that he had a new life, he had to be less angry. Last she'd heard, he had a son and a baby on the way. He worked for a Chicago accounting firm. His wife was a stay-at-home mom.

There was another reason to call Kevin, of course. Callie thought of Anna. Even if she hadn't received the note, there was still that conversation. Anna missed her father. That was the simple truth. She owed it to Anna to talk to Kevin, to try to repair the damage. Remorse washed over her as she thought how blind she'd been, how she'd had absolutely no idea what Anna was going through. The fact that she simply hadn't known didn't seem like an excuse. She should have suspected something. She should have thought to ask.

Kevin's number wasn't in her Filofax. She had it somewhere locked in a file drawer along with her divorce decree. Squatting by the drawer, she flipped through folders, then finally pulled one out.

The notepad page where she'd scribbled his number was yellowed and dry with age. How long ago had she written it down? Was it even good anymore? She stared at the digits, uncertain, pondering what to do.

It would be so easy to pick up the phone, simply to place the call. But once she'd taken that step, there was no going back. Maybe she should at least put it off until Anna wasn't home. What if Anna overheard? Or happened to pick up the phone? Rick, too, that was another thing. He'd be getting back tonight. He'd be over in just a couple of hours, and she needed to shower and dress.

Not a sound from Anna's room. Callie wondered what she was doing. Restless, she finally stood up and went into the hallway.

As she knocked on Anna's door, Callie noticed that the sign was gone.

A rustle from inside. "Come in," Anna called.

Automatically, Callie's eyes moved to the bed, but Anna wasn't there. Instead, she was at her computer, her eyes glued to the screen. The clothes that had covered the monitor were now piled high on a chair. Anna was staring at the screen, her hand glued to the mouse.

Callie stepped up behind her.

"Wait, okay?" said Anna. She was staring at a square filled with brightly colored boxes that were rapidly disappearing. A click of the mouse and a box was gone. Finally, none was left.

A celebratory burst of canned music.

"There," Anna said.

"Whatcha doing?" Callie asked.

"Just this game Henry showed me."

"Something on the Internet?"

"No, it's on a disk."

Good, Callie thought. But didn't say anything. She'd limited Anna's AOL access to the kids-only areas. Still, she worried about who might be lurking in those so-called kids' chat rooms. She'd stressed to Anna the importance of abiding by strict ground rules. *Never give out your real name. Never say where you live. Tell me right away if anyone wants to meet you.* She'd have liked to bar Anna from the Internet, but the kids all had AOL.

"Homework done?"

"*Mah-um.*" It was the two-syllable version.

"Well?"

"Yeah. You want to see it?" Chin thrust out, defiant.

"That's okay. I trust you."

"No you don't," said Anna. "If you trusted me, you wouldn't ask. It's like you have to be with me every second. I mean, all weekend, I had to do stuff with you. The *whole* weekend."

It was true, Callie thought. She'd been more protective than usual, wanting Anna close by at all times. But something pushed her to deny it, an impulse of normality.

"That's not true," she said. "What about Sunday? You spent the afternoon at the Creightons'."

"You still came over *twice.*"

"I needed to talk to Henry's mother."

"Why? You don't even like her."

Callie looked at Anna, surprised. What had she ever done or said that Anna guessed her feelings? And it wasn't that she didn't *like* Mimi Creighton, just that they had nothing in common. Mimi, with her Harvard M.B.A., ran her family like a corporation. Before she and Bernie had children, she'd worked for a consulting firm. Now she focused her energies on raising perfect children. Mimi talked about her kids as if they were investments. Benjamin's stellar S.A.T.'s, Emma's soccer trophies. And Henry, well, he was the smartest one. Practically a genius.

"Rick's coming over later," Callie said, quickly changing the subject.

"Oh," Anna said. "I thought he was away."

"He was, but now he's back."

Anna didn't answer.

Callie wanted to say something — *I understand. I just want you to be happy* — but the words stuck in her throat. Instead, she reached down mutely and stroked her daughter's hair.

I'd do anything for you, she thought.

Then Anna squirmed away.

Back in her bedroom again, Callie picked up the phone. She'd left the number on the table beside it. Now she punched it in. If he wasn't in, she told herself, she wouldn't leave a message. If he wasn't in, it would be a sign. If he wasn't —

"Hello?"

A soft, almost childlike voice. The second Mrs. Thayer.

"Donna? This is Callie."

A pause, and then, "Oh!" It had taken her a moment to place the name. "I . . . Kevin isn't in." There was a guardedness to her voice that hadn't been there before. "I'm afraid he's out of town. Business."

In the background Callie heard the TV, the sound of kids arguing.

"Is this an emergency?"

"No," said Callie. "But I do need to talk to him. It's about . . . well, could you just ask him to call me, please? Not at home, though. Here, let me give you my cell phone number."

"I'll be talking to him later tonight. If I had a number for him, I could give it to you, but he's . . . well, they're sort of moving around."

"No problem," said Callie.

"He should call before too long, though. I'll be sure to give him the message."

Callie thanked her profusely and hung up.

As she put down the phone, she realized that she could have asked Donna for Kevin's cell phone number. She considered calling back, then changed her mind. She might catch Kevin at an awkward moment, and she didn't want to annoy him. Better to wait for him to call. She'd hear from him soon enough.

❧

ANNA waited until she heard her mother's door close. Then, with a click of the computer mouse, she signed on to AOL. She checked her Buddy List and saw that TheMagician93 was still online. She clicked to send him an instant message. The box popped up on the screen.

Bttrfly146   *Sometimes I really hate my mother.*

But as soon as the words appeared, she felt bad seeing them. She didn't hate her mother. It just seemed that way sometimes.

A chiming sound and more words flashed up. He was answering her.

TheMagician93   *I told you, you don't have to stay there. She can't make you stay.*

Anna chewed on a piece of hair. Was that really what she wanted? Could she run away? She looked around her room — the blue-and-white bedspread she'd picked out last year, the mounds of stuffed animals. Her favorite books and posters. She really liked her room. But sometimes her mother made her so mad, she could hardly stand it anymore. If she ran away, her mother would be sorry. Maybe things would change. Besides, she wouldn't have to stay gone all that long. Just enough to scare her.

Bttrfly146   *Where would we go?*
TheMagician93   *Wherever we want . . .*

THE doorbell rang, and Callie raced down the stairs. She fumbled with the lock, threw open the door. Suddenly, there he was. His face was dimly illuminated by the pale yellow porch light. He didn't smile at first, just gazed at her solemnly. He was wearing khakis and loafers with an old brown leather jacket. She thought of all the times she'd seen that jacket over the past eight months. Once at the movies, when she was cold, Rick had draped it across her shoulders. At that moment, she'd felt closer to him than she'd ever felt before.

He was back, he was really back.

It hadn't seemed real until now.

She hurled herself into Rick's arms. His mouth smashed down on hers.

They stood there silent, kissing, for what seemed like a very long time. She looped a hand behind his neck. He stroked the back of her head. Rick's skin was cold, or maybe hers was hot.

"How's your father?" she whispered.

"Better. A lot better."

As Callie locked the front door, Rick wrapped her in his arms. Gently, he turned her toward him, until her eyes met his. Something happened then, some bright internal spark. The blood turned silvery in her veins, as their bodies flew together. Their mouths were welded tight as he pressed her against the wall. She hooked a leg around one of his, pulling him closer still. She felt the butterfly bones of her pelvis, sharp against his thigh. She'd never felt this way, so weak with love and longing. Grabbing his hand, she quickly led him up the carpeted stairs.

Anna's door was closed. She'd be asleep by now. They slipped into Callie's room, locked the door, then collapsed on the bed. They lay on top of the bedspread and his mouth was everywhere. As she sank into sensation, images flashed through her brain. Rick's leather jacket. Steven's eyes. *Happy Anniversary* . . .

Rick roughly pulled up her shirt, pushed aside her bra. As his tongue circled a nipple, Callie closed her eyes. Their bodies moved together, the rhythm already begun. The emptiness was coming faster now and she gave herself up to it. She twisted a hand in his hair, hard. His lips touched her other breast. She took hold of one of his hands and rubbed it between her legs. Pushed herself against his palm, wanting wanting wanting.

It was going on too long. She wanted him inside her.

"Now," she whispered. "Now."

She heard the rip of a condom packet.

Then, after seconds or forever, finally he was back. As she raised her hips, he began to move, slowly and then faster. Callie's hand touched his lower back, the concave dampness of it. As they thrust against each other, her blood seemed to dance. There was nothing beyond this pleasure, nothing beyond this place.

They rolled over, still in one piece, until Rick lay beneath her. Callie sat astride him, her arms braced against his shoulders. For a moment, they stayed there still, eyes locked together. Then everything was moving, a rapid-fire surge of feeling. Callie threw her head back, as she rode him into the night, harder and faster and harder and faster, until the flame ignited.

Yes, yes, yes.

She heard him cry out below.

Afterwards they lay there, quiet, the stillness of the house around them. Rick's eyes were closed. His chest rose and fell. Callie kissed his shoulder. Spooning her body into his, she wondered if he were sleeping.

Safe, that's how she felt. *Safe*. Still a novelty.

During the early months with Rick, she'd bounced back and forth between fear that he'd stay and fear that he'd leave. She was determined not to lose the independent life she'd struggled so hard to build. At the same time, as their bond grew stronger, an older fear crept in. The fear that one day he'd find her wanting, that one day he'd be gone.

She was like a child, a two-year-old, who wanted contradictory things. Once when Anna was about that age she'd thrown a tantrum halfway up the stairs. As Callie knelt beside her, she'd choked out an explanation. She wanted to be both upstairs with her toys and downstairs with her mother.

With Kevin she'd managed to avoid this conflict by just not caring that much. They'd met one Sunday at her parents' church, at the weekly social hour. She'd watched his round face brighten as they sipped tea from china cups. He gave an impression of earnestness, pleasant but not exciting. He'd talked a lot about his sister's kids. She could tell that he loved children. The blandness of her response to him had struck her as reassuring.

They'd married in a small church ceremony, attended by just their families. Callie had carried a mixed bouquet. No roses, though. No roses. They'd bought a small house with a bright green lawn in an Indianapolis suburb. For years, she'd simply drifted, numb and rudderless. She watched TV, talked on the phone, took care of her infant daughter. In the two-plus years they'd lived in that house, she hadn't made one friend. It was almost as if she'd known that she'd be leaving and didn't want to waste time. And yet, thinking back, she hadn't been unhappy. Happiness, as she now knew, was entirely relative.

It was after Anna's second birthday that the doubts really set in. She looked at herself through the eyes of her child and didn't like what she saw. She relied on Kevin for everything, had no goals of her own. What kind of a role model would she be as Anna began to grow up? Kevin watched her warily, urged Prozac and counseling. But the clearer she got, the more she saw that the marriage had been a mistake.

Rick murmured something she couldn't hear, pulling her back to the present. Her body was smooth and amphibious against the rise and fall of his chest. Even more than when they were making love, he felt like a part of her. Her leg began to cramp, but she didn't want to move it, didn't want to do anything that would break this fragile peace. Gently, she folded her hand into his. Her eyes dropped to her arm. To the thin white rows of scars that bound her to the past.

When she looked up, she saw that Rick was awake. His eyes gleamed in the dark. He didn't say anything, just studied her intently. She had an urge to turn away but made herself keep looking. One more small victory in the battle to connect.

"I think we should get married." He spoke the words so softly that she wasn't sure she'd heard right.

"Callie, will you marry me?"

She lay there still, barely breathing, then rolled her head away. She felt something but she didn't know what, couldn't name the feeling.

"Callie? Cal?" Rick rubbed her shoulder. "Sweetheart, what's wrong?"

"I . . ." Her face pressed into the sheet. Her cheeks were hot and dry.

"What is it?" Rick said again. His breath smelled of mint.

Still, she didn't answer. What was there to say?

Finally, she rolled her head toward him. "It's Anna," she said. "We can work it out."

"I . . ." She had a sensation of unraveling, her life coming undone.

"I love you, Callie," Rick said.

Tears filled her eyes. She'd turned her head toward the ceiling again so he couldn't see her face. If only everything were as simple as he seemed to think it was.

"How do you know?" she asked him.

"Know? Know what?" Rick had propped himself up on an elbow to get a view of her face. She turned her head farther, let hair fall over her eyes.

"How do you know . . . that you . . . love me?" The words came out haltingly. "Because, the thing is, once someone told me that, and I . . . I believed him. I believed everything he told me, but all of it was lies. And so . . . if I believe you now, what would it really mean? Because I've been so wrong before, and I'm still the same person I was. Different in some ways but still the same. Maybe I don't understand what love is. Between a man and a woman. When I think about it, my mind goes blank. I can't seem to —"

"I'm not your ex-husband, Callie."

Startled, she turned her head toward him, the tears having stopped.

"I'm not Kevin. I'm not going to leave you. You know me better than that."

"Oh . . ."

He must have sensed her unease. "You're talking about Kevin, right?"

"No," she said. "It was someone else. Kevin was . . . afterwards."

It struck her again how little he knew of the basic facts of her life. Was he aware of the gaping holes? The pieces that didn't fit? So many lies, large and small, piled on top of each other. Even if she told him the truth, would he ever be able to trust her?

"I wonder," she said, "if you can know someone. Really know who they are. I used to think you could. I used to think I did."

Then something was shifting in her chest, shifting and growing larger. Without warning it exploded. She began to cry. But this time she didn't turn away. This time she let him see.

"I love you, too," she whispered. And held tight to his hand.

It was like the words had been torn from her heart, leaving a gaping wound. But with the pain came a strange lightness, as if something had begun.

Rick rocked her in his arms, whispering into her hair. He softly stroked her back while she cried, sobbing into his shoulder. He showed no sign of annoyance, no sign of discomposure. He seemed to accept without question the chaos of her emotions. She could almost believe that he would understand, almost believe she could tell him.

Almost believe, almost believe . . .

Almost, but not quite.

After she didn't know how long, the tears finally stopped. Exhausted, she lay against Rick, matching her breath to his. It was like she'd been swept up onto this bed from some wild storm-tossed sea. But one of her arms lay across Rick's chest, and again she glimpsed the scars. *You belong to us*, they seemed to say. *This is who you are.*

Wednesday–Saturday, April 12–15

CALLIE sat at the kitchen table, reading, drinking coffee. Memories of the night before tumbled through her mind. Sun poured in through the windows, warming up the room. She'd been there for a couple of hours, unable to concentrate. Twice she'd reread the same page, but nothing registered.

Her cell phone rang, breaking her loose. She grabbed it from her purse. Kevin. It was Kevin. She instantly felt queasy.

He barely bothered to say hello. "Is something wrong?" he asked.

His voice was just as she remembered, a nasal monotone. At the same time, his voice was a stranger's voice. He was someone she didn't know. She'd thought that she might talk to him, tell him about the note. Now that she had him on the phone, she saw how mistaken she'd been.

"No," she said firmly. "No. Nothing's wrong."

"Well, you called me," he said curtly. "I suppose you had some reason."

"Right," she said. "There was."

Despite the hundreds of miles between them, she felt his irritation. She'd been wrong in thinking that time would have softened his feelings for her. Kevin might be slow to anger, but he knew how to hold a grudge. If it hadn't been for Anna, she'd have hung up right away. But now that she had him on the phone, she forced herself to speak.

"I wanted to talk to you about Anna."

"What? What about her?" He bit off the words like he didn't care, but she could tell that he was listening. She so much didn't want to have this talk, but she didn't have a choice.

"Anna misses you," she said. "Would you consider seeing her?"

A long pause on the other end. "Why now?" he finally said. She could hear the bitterness.

"She's been asking about you recently." It took some effort to say that.

He snorted. "Well, that's a surprise. How does she even know I exist? I thought you took care of that."

"You thought *I* took care of it? Me? How do you figure that?" It had taken less than five minutes to trigger their old patterns, Kevin coldly blaming, she emotional.

"You made the decision." His voice had no inflection.

"It was both of us," Callie said. "You didn't object."

"Would it have done any good?"

An answer leapt to the tip of her tongue, but she managed to hold it back. "Let's just focus on the present, okay? Let's just think about Anna. She wants to see you now. How do you feel about that?"

"I don't know," he finally said. "I really don't know. I'll have to talk to Donna. My wife. I'll have to think about it."

"Fine. You talk to her and think about it, and then you can let me know. Don't call me at home though. Use my cell phone number, the one you just called. I don't want Anna to answer. Or you could try to get me at work. Here, I'll give you the number."

She heard him writing it down. She took this as a good sign.

"Thank you," she said.

"For what? I haven't said I'll do it. And even if I do, it won't be for you."

Again, she was struck by the bitterness. Time hadn't changed a thing. Then she told herself to let it go. She was doing this for Anna.

The conversation left her off balance, but the feeling eased with time. It was the usual busy Wednesday, and the hours flew past. It wasn't until dinner that night that she thought of Kevin again, really considered for the first time the forces she'd set in motion. What if Kevin tried to turn Anna against her? What would happen then? What if Anna decided to live with him?

How would she survive? Never mind that Kevin hadn't even said he wanted to see Anna. Her mind relentlessly spun out the worst possible outcomes.

"Want another piece?" Rick asked her, gesturing to the pizza.

"Sure," Callie said.

She pulled away a yeasty slice and took a large bite.

Anna was eating industriously, leaving the crusts behind. Judging by the pile of half-moon scraps, she was working on her third piece. Gradually, Callie's anxiety calmed. Why go looking for trouble? From the sound of Kevin's voice, she doubted that he'd even want to see her.

Now that Rick was back, she found it was easier to stay grounded. The shapeless fears that had tormented her seemed to have far less power. For example, her thoughts about Lester Crain — what evidence did she have? After all, if someone wanted to hurt her, why bother leaving a note?

Whoever it is knows where I live. Someone came to our house.

But she wouldn't think about that part. At least, not right now.

On Thursday night, Rick worked late. She and Anna dyed eggs. On Friday, Rick took her out for dinner while Anna stayed with the Creightons.

Saturday was cool and luminous with the promise of early spring. Rick came over for pancakes and bacon, and then they went for a hike. Mt. Holyoke was a deep blue peak ten miles out of town. A wide, gently sloping path wound up toward a breathtaking lookout. While Anna and Henry ran ahead, Callie and Rick lingered. They strolled slowly, hand in hand, neither of them talking. It meant something, Callie thought, when you didn't have to speak. Everyone talked about communication, the importance of sharing words. But so often the need to fill a silence reflected the absence of something.

They reached the mountain's peak, capped by the Summit House. Once a fashionable hotel, it now served as a museum. The windswept expanse of its balcony offered spectacular views: the tiny, perfect town of Merritt, patchwork farms and fields, the blue Connecticut River cutting through it all.

Callie leaned against the railing, the sun warm on her face. Down below, she could hear Anna and Henry calling out to each other. Rick came up from behind and slid his arms around her. For a moment they stood there, resting, taking in the view. Then Rick pulled her gently closer, whispered into her hair. "So have you been thinking about it? Getting married, I mean." The world seemed to darken slightly. "I have to think," she said.

That night, after Henry went home, they watched a video. Over Chinese food, Callie filled baskets for tomorrow's Easter egg hunt. Anna kept sneaking chocolate eggs until Callie made her stop.

"He ate more." Anna pointed at Rick, who looked a little chagrined.

"Well, I'm sure if his mother were here right now, she'd tell him he'd had enough."

Anna had already gone to bed when Rick got up to leave. "Are you sure I can't help?" he asked her, pointing to the baskets.

"No. It's fine. Really. I do it every year."

They kissed good night on the front porch. Callie went back for the baskets.

The sky was a tumbled bowl of stars as she stepped down into the grass. She paused a moment in the silence and breathed in the crisp night. Her eyes sought out the Big Dipper, the white crust of moon. Down the street, she saw another flashlight bobbing in the bushes. Naomi or Morton Steinmetz. Or maybe David Enderly. Callie waved toward the bouncing light, then settled down to work.

Kneeling down beside the porch, she shoved a basket under the stairs. Anna had been attending the Easter egg hunt since she was four years old. Callie had piles of snapshots, stuffed into boxes and albums. Anna at five, looking horrified as she stared at a bright blue egg. A smug eight-year-old Anna, surrounded by rows of baskets. This hunt, however, would be Anna's last. Ten was the cutoff age.

As she stood up, Callie was hit by a sense of time's rapid flight. Each moment, so substantial and real, was gone before you knew it, consigned to an uncertain fate in the outposts of memory. This evening, the warmth and laughter they'd shared, how long would it be remembered?

For the next half hour, she moved around the yard, distributing the baskets. Anna always complained that she made things too easy, so this year Callie had come up with several new hiding places. One basket went into a recycling bin, beneath a pile of plastic bottles. The next she hid in the mailbox. Okay, so it was obvious, but she'd never used it before. She was especially pleased with the niche she'd found for the final tiny basket. Squeezed behind a bush, next to the house, she edged it into the drainpipe. The basket fell out a couple of times, but she finally wedged it tight.

She'd just emerged from the bushes, when she startled at a noise. It seemed to have come from across the street, somewhere in the Creightons' yard. The crackling sound of branches breaking, then a muffled thud. Frightened, Callie stood there, waiting for what came next. But now there was nothing. Nothing unusual. Just the faint, dim hum of distant traffic, wind moving through the trees.

Happy Anniversary, Rosamund.

The words rose up in her mind.

She glanced down the street, but the flashlight was gone. She was all alone now. Walking quickly across the lawn, she headed for the house.

Back inside, she locked the door, checked the burglar alarm. Tried to forget the feeling she'd had that someone was watching her. What she'd heard was maybe an animal or a branch falling to the ground. No reason to get excited. Nothing to worry about.

⟐

AFTER she vanished into the house, he waited for the light to snap on upstairs. In a moment, he saw the golden glow seeping out from behind her blinds. He was tempted to wait another few minutes, to see if she might raise them. Sometimes, he knew she did that, right before she went to bed, stood there staring into the night, her expression cloudy and lost. A look she never wore during the day at times she might be seen. It was a private expression confined to times she believed herself alone.

For years, she'd assumed so much, with no justification. Assumed that no one was watching her. Assumed no one could find her. And, really, it had been quite simple. Just some basic computer searches. Her identity had stayed secret only because no one had really looked. It had been the same with Diane Massey, that false sense of control. All he'd had to do was chat up her doorman, claim to be an old friend. The doorman didn't have the details, but he thought she'd gone to Maine. She'd talked about Blue Peek Island in interviews. And sure enough, there she was.

He stared hard at the closed blinds as if he might see through them. Then, regretfully, he turned away. It wasn't safe to linger.

He crawled across the tree house floor until he came to the opening around the trunk. Carefully, he lowered one leg until his foot touched a wooden step.

Almost to the ground, he let himself drop into a thick bed of leaves. A rich, moist odor floated up, moldering leaves and dirt. The smell caught him by surprise. It was almost exactly the same. Deeply inhaling the cool night air, he thought of Diane Massey.

Timex. Cartier. It doesn't matter. Only time is fair.

Still crouching, he scanned the Creightons' yard, making sure no one had heard him. Another few seconds, then he started to move around. Twigs and stones dug into his palms as he palpated the ground, searching for the binoculars that had fallen from his hands. He couldn't believe that he'd let that happen, especially with her right there. She'd actually heard the sound. Startled, she'd wheeled around. Luckily he'd already ducked down behind the tree house wall.

When he finally found the binoculars, he hung them around his neck. Through a gate, he could see the Creightons' backyard sheltered by a tall white fence. The back door opened onto a deck with a gas grill and picnic table. All the accoutrements of family life, sturdy and ordinary. Yet the sense of safety, the perfect calm, could be shattered in a flash. Dahlia had grown up in a house like this, pretty and safe and secure. But none of that had protected her on the night she met Steven Gage.

He crept through a dense wall of trees until he reached the

curb. Briefly he hesitated, then stepped into open space. Beneath the glow of a single lamp, he quickly crossed the street. His footsteps slapped against concrete, and then he was in her yard.

His destination was the shrubbery along the front of the house. When he'd seen her disappear back there, he'd figured this was the place. There was an opening between two bushes, and now he slipped between them. Squatting beside wooden shingles, he peered into the shadows. He ruffled the branches of a gnarled shrub, then ran his fingers across the earth. She'd come back here with just one small basket, and when she'd come out it was gone.

It had to be somewhere, he told himself. But where, damn it, where? Then, at that instant, he caught sight of it, the pale scrap of ribbon. Gingerly, he reached up the drainpipe spout until he grasped the basket. It was wedged tightly in the narrow pipe, and it took a while to dislodge. Impatiently, he pushed against the straw until it fell away.

As the basket slid out of the chute, candy tumbled out. He picked up a foil-covered chocolate egg, unwrapped it, and popped it in his mouth. Sweetness melted across his tongue, as he reached down into a pocket. From inside, he pulled out another egg, this one made of hollow pink plastic. When he turned the ends, the egg fell in two, and he looked at the object he'd placed inside. He wondered how long it would take her to realize its significance. She was smart, he had to give her that. He doubted that it would take long.

I am not a man, I am dynamite.

He smiled at the philosopher's words.

After snapping the plastic egg back together, he placed it in the tiny basket. The egg looked so innocent resting there. Who could guess what it held? He took a moment to straighten the bow before restoring the basket.

Once he was sure it was securely stowed, he climbed back to his feet. Everything was in order now. Everything was ready. Now it was time for him to go home, to get a good night's sleep. The only thing he had left to do was make sure that Anna found it.

Sunday, April 16

A N N A ' S gotten so tall! How old is she now?"

"Ten," Callie said. Across the street, she watched as Anna beat through the Creightons' shrubs, joining the horde of neighborhood kids in their search for eggs and baskets.

"So this will be her last one?"

"Mmm." Callie felt a pang.

Naomi Steinmetz shook her head, short gray hair bobbing. The thick lenses of her oversized glasses seemed to magnify her eyes. A Latin professor at Windham, she'd recently retired. She'd always reminded Callie of a large yet friendly insect.

It was one of those magical early spring days when time seemed to stand still. The sky was a bright primary blue dotted with puffy white clouds. All around kids laughed and shrieked as they scrambled for hidden bounty. There had to be more than twenty of them; the event had grown each year. Parents mingled in the background, irrelevant and ignored, their smiles nostalgic and a bit wistful as they watched the frenzied search.

"Mommy, I found *another*! Here." Anna thrust a basket into Callie's hands, then dashed away again.

Naomi laughed. "A lot of energy, that one."

"Yes," Callie said. On days like this, when Anna seemed so happy, she could almost forget the rest, almost convince herself that Anna's moods were simple growing pains.

As Naomi stepped away to find her husband, Callie walked to the porch. She added Anna's basket to the growing pile and checked her watch again. After eleven-thirty. Rick was running late.

From the porch, Callie watched the Henning twins toddle toward a cache of eggs. One two-year-old twin stared straight at them, then promptly turned away. The other ran a few short steps, teetered, and fell down, at which point he lost all interest in everything but his left shoe. He studied the sole with intensity, then stuffed it in his mouth.

"Just wait 'til next year," Callie called to their mother. "You won't be able to stop them."

Across the street, Anna and Henry romped with a neighbor's dog. The puppy grabbed hold of an Easter basket, and galloped across the yard. *Camera,* Callie thought. And went into the house to find it.

As she came back out, she was putting in film, fiddling with the roll. She closed the compartment and listened for the buzz that would tell her the film was loading. As she held the camera to her ear, she heard a noise behind her. But before she had time to turn around, hands came down on her shoulders. In that instant, her blood seemed to freeze. She shrieked and wheeled around.

But it was only Tod Carver standing there, wearing a sheepish expression.

"Geez, Callie," he said, abashed. "I didn't mean to scare you."

She'd dropped the camera. He picked it up. "Hope this isn't broken."

"It fell on the grass. I'm sure it's fine." She smiled at him, embarrassed. "Sorry that I screamed. You just caught me by surprise."

Of course, that wasn't the only reason, but how was he to know?

"Kids here?"

Tod gave her his rueful smile. "Nope. I left Oliver and Lilly at home and came to the Easter egg hunt on my own. Thought I'd use my superior size and strength to beat out the other children."

"And if that doesn't work, you can always flash your badge."

"Now you're talking." Tod grinned.

Callie grinned back, calmed by the familiar banter.

"They're over there," Tod said, pointing toward the Steinmetz yard. Callie caught a glimpse of Lilly, with her long hair and pipestem legs. Tod just adored his daughter, who was two years younger than Anna.

Like Rick, Tod was an unlikely cop, low-key and warm. He was boyishly good-looking, with an open face and hair the color of copper. Looking at him, she couldn't imagine why he didn't have a girlfriend. But Rick said the divorce had hit Tod hard. He still wasn't ready.

"Where's Rick?" asked Tod, as if on cue.

"He should be here by now." Again, Callie looked around.

"Hey, Tod, Callie!" Mimi Creighton swooped down on them, a smile planted on her face. Gucci loafers, streaked blonde hair, a Louis Vuitton handbag. Mimi might have left the city but she'd kept all the trappings.

"Isn't it a *beautiful day?*" Mimi looked excited, almost giddy, her small eyes shining. Taken separately, Mimi's features weren't pretty, but together, they somehow worked. She had a slight overbite, a bumpy nose, and small gray-green eyes. But she conveyed an impression of energy that substituted for beauty.

"Sure is," said Tod, smiling and laconic.

Mimi barely seemed to hear him. Her eyes had lighted on her son. "I just can't believe this is Henry's last year."

"Anna's too," said Callie.

"Oh, well," said Mimi brightly. "I guess they have to grow up."

She didn't seem too bothered. Already, Callie sensed that she was charting Henry's future, mapping his path from Merritt Elementary to the nation's halls of power. Her other two kids were already in college, one at Yale, one at Brown. Henry's birth, Callie suspected, hadn't exactly been planned.

Callie glanced toward the Driscolls' yard, where Anna was sprawled with Henry. Their heads were close together as they talked over who-knew-what. Henry was sort of cute, Callie thought, in a gawky boy-genius way, a look that gained a sort of cachet with the Harry Potter craze. He was small and slender with quick bright eyes behind thick horn-rimmed glasses. Like Anna, he sometimes seemed older than his age and at other times far younger. It struck Callie as a little odd that Anna's best friend was a boy, but things had changed since she was a kid and boys were the source of cooties.

"Greetings, neighbors." Bernie Creighton appeared, tossing a casual arm around his wife.

Bernie exuded an air of enormous self-satisfaction. *Well upholstered* was the term that came to mind when Callie looked at him. He was short — a bit shorter than his wife — maybe five foot six or seven, barrel-chested with a neat moustache, and slightly overweight. But somehow the extra pounds only added to the effect. He gave the impression of being well fed rather than out of shape.

"I *made* Bernie come today," Mimi said. She sounded pleased with herself. "We saw this video last week, where the father didn't know the daughter's middle name. He didn't even know she *had* a middle name."

"*The Royal Tenenbaums*," said Callie. "We saw it too."

"Yeah, that's what it was. Anyway, I told Bernie that he's going to forget his kids' *first* names if he doesn't see more of them."

Callie and Tod laughed politely. It didn't seem so funny.

Bernie shrugged. "We've got a trial coming up. That's just how it is."

"He's even taken an apartment in Boston," Mimi said.

"Just until after the trial."

The conversation went on in this vein with Callie zoning out. She heard Tod making the appropriate sounds. *Yes. No. Really?* With the Creightons, you never had to worry about a topic of conversation. Mimi and Bernie were more than happy to talk about themselves.

Scanning the street for Rick again, Callie started at an unexpected sight: her classmate Nathan Lacoste on a bike slowly pedaling toward them. She hadn't talked to him since that night he'd tried to cadge an invitation for pizza. *The weird one*, Rick had called him. What was he doing here? Quickly, Callie turned away, hoping he wouldn't see her. Maybe he was heading for the Windham campus, just a few blocks away. But he lived on the other side of town. She was hardly on his route.

When she looked back up, she saw with relief that he didn't seem to be stopping. He rode his bike straight through the throng, stopped at the corner, then turned.

"Hey there, buddy!" she heard Tod call.

She looked back, and there was Rick.

"Sorry, babe. I overslept. Forgot to set the alarm."

The day got subtly brighter, as Rick leaned down to kiss her. Callie took his large, warm hand and folded hers into it.

The festivities were winding down now, and Callie snapped a last few pictures. Clusters of kids lay sprawled about, baskets piled around them, happily gorging themselves on sugar in all of its various forms. Chocolate rabbits and malted eggs. Marshmallow chickens and jelly beans. Not one of the children that Callie could see was eating a hard-boiled egg.

Bernie and Mimi, arm in arm, headed back toward home. When Tod's kids straggled back, the three of them left as well.

"You look tired," Callie said to Rick. They were still holding hands.

Rick shrugged. "I'm okay. Just haven't been sleeping well."

"Hungry?" Callie asked.

"Now that you mention it."

Anna bounced into view. She was wearing jeans and a yellow shirt that picked up the gold in her hair.

"I like the light blue eggs best," said Anna. "They're like robins' eggs but bigger."

Callie and Rick headed inside, Anna trailing behind them.

In the kitchen, Callie pulled out bread, mustard, leftover chicken, and lettuce.

"So how's your boyfriend?" Rick teased, as he took plates from the cupboard.

Callie rolled her eyes. "C'mon Rick. That was twenty years ago." Rick always ribbed her about Tod's resemblance to her high school beau, Larry Peters. Thinking of Tod she was reminded of how happy he'd seemed today.

"It must be hard on him, having his kids so far away."

"It is," Rick said. He didn't elaborate.

Callie spread mustard on a slice of bread. "Why'd he move way up here when they're down in Virginia?"

"I think he wanted to start over. He lived in the area when he was a kid."

"I could see how he'd want to come back. Still, he must be lonely." Callie gave Rick a covert glance. "I've been thinking about fixing up Martha and Tod."

"Martha?"

"You know, I work with her. She got divorced a while back."

"The one with the fuzzy hair?"

"It's not *fuzzy*, it's curly. Women pay lots of money for hair like that."

"Well, I'm glad you're not one of them."

"Is that the problem? You don't think she's pretty enough?"

"Honey, that's not it."

"So what's the problem, then?"

Rick shrugged. "If you want to, give it a shot. I just don't think he'll go for it."

"Well, there's no harm in asking. We could have them over for dinner or something. It wouldn't have to be a real date."

From the living room, she heard Anna. "Wow!"

"What is it?" Callie called.

A beaming Anna appeared in the doorway, something clutched in her hand.

"This watch is so cool!"

A watch? Callie walked toward her. "Let me see," she said.

Looking at her mother warily, Anna opened her hand.

The watch had an intricate golden bracelet. On its face was the word *Cartier*.

Callie took the watch from Anna and balanced it in her hand. She had little experience with fine jewelry, but this seemed like the real thing. She'd once owned a knock-off watch, a two-tone fake Rolex. Its flimsy metal components had felt nothing like this.

"Where did you find this?" Callie asked.

Anna gave her a baffled look. "It was in the plastic egg, in the Easter basket. The one you put in the drainpipe."

"Where's the basket?" Callie's voice was level, but she felt a stir of alarm. She wasn't sure what was going on, but she knew that she didn't like it.

Anna shrugged. "I don't know. In the living room, I guess."

"What's up?" Rick turned toward them.

There was no point in trying to hide the facts. "A watch," Callie said. "Anna found a watch in an Easter basket."

Rick had drifted over to the counter, where he surveyed the abandoned makings of their meal. "What do you say I finish up the sandwiches?"

"That would be great. Thanks."

She was already on her way to the living room, where she found the basket with its yellow ribbon. Plastic green grass was scattered around, like so much exploded stuffing. On the floor lay the pieces of a hollow pink egg. Callie picked them up, looked at them, snapped the halves together. She remembered eggs like this from when she was a kid, but she hadn't seen one in years.

She took the plastic egg back to the kitchen, where Anna was slumped in a chair. "The watch, it was in here?"

Silently, Anna nodded. "Mom, just give it back to me. I'm the one who found it."

"Honey, it's a mistake. I didn't put it there."

"Well, it's still *mine*," Anna said. There was an edge of defiance to her voice now. "Someone left it in a basket, and I'm the one who found it."

Callie shook her head. "It may belong to someone. We have to find out who."

"But Mom, it's not *fair*. I found it."

Anna looked like she might cry. "Okay. *Fine*." She shoved back the chair so hard it almost fell and ran out of the room.

Callie stared at the watch.

Upstairs, she heard Anna's door slam shut. So much for the perfect day.

"Let me see," said Rick.

Wordlessly, Callie showed him the watch. Rick looked at it.

"You really think this is the real thing?" he asked.

"Why? You don't?"

Rick shrugged. "It just doesn't seem very likely. Why would someone hide a Cartier watch? It's probably just a fake someone found when they were cleaning out their house or something."

Callie had to stop herself from launching into explanations. How she was the one who'd filled this basket, and she hadn't put a watch inside. But before she spoke, she realized that this would only make things worse. It would only lead to further questions, and then what would she say? If she convinced Rick that the watch was authentic, he'd want to take it to the station. And she — she wanted to keep hold of it. For what she couldn't say.

She reached out and took the watch from Rick. The time was 12:10. She dropped it into a pocket.

"You're probably right," she said.

⊸⊷

IT was a little before nine on May 7 when 20-year-old Dahlia Schuyler jumped into her white Saab, a birthday present from her parents, and made the short trip to Donovan's Bar & Grill, where she'd planned to meet friends for a quick drink. The pretty blonde Vanderbilt junior had originally begged off, saying that she had to study for an organic chemistry exam, but finally let herself be persuaded. "We told her that you're only young once," recalled sorority sister Cindy Meyers. "She would rather have stayed home, but she didn't want to disappoint us. That was what Dahlia was like. She always put her friends before herself. I know this sounds like a cliché, but everyone just loved Dahlia."

Those words are echoed again and again by Dahlia Schuyler's friends and family. By all accounts, the vivacious pre-med had lived a charmed life. The daughter of a wealthy Nashville real estate developer and his socially active wife, she had enjoyed a privileged childhood. She attended Harpeth Hall, a private girls' school, and was always near the top of her class. Her classmates recall her as a popular girl, always at the center of a circle of friends, and her academic success was balanced with a healthy *range of interests. For many years, her first love was horseback riding, and she rode whenever she could — on weekends, after school, and during the summers — taking ribbons in many competitions. As a young girl, Dahlia hoped to become a veterinarian. She also loved children, and by the time she arrived at Vanderbilt, she'd decided to become a pediatrician, a dream that would stay with her for the rest of her short life.*

By that spring, Dahlia was deservedly pleased with her life. With a 3.8 G.P.A. and stellar faculty recommendations, Dahlia knew she had a good shot at being accepted at virtually any of the nation's top medical schools. And if the spring had been a little rocky — just six weeks earlier, she'd broken up with her boyfriend of two years — she had the loving support of family and friends and a bright and promising future. "We all knew that Dahlia had been a little down," said sorority sister Meyers. "But she never wanted to talk about herself. Dahlia's reaction to feeling blue was to focus on other people. You'd start out asking how she was and then end up talking about yourself. She was a very strong person, very mature. With a lot of people, it's like they expect to be happy all the time, but Dahlia accepted the bad with the good and just tried to focus on the positive."

In light of these words, it's perhaps not surprising that the last thing Dahlia did before heading off to join her friends was place a call to her younger brother. The siblings were just two years apart, and they had always been close. But while Dahlia had sailed through life, 18-year-old Tucker had always struggled. Since graduating from high school the previous year, he'd been floundering, picking up a series of low-paying jobs in Nashville restaurants and spending, Dahlia thought, far too much time alone. "She sort of felt guilty about Tucker," said Meyers. "Like it made it harder for him that she was doing so good. Like she was this perfect creature and he was this total failure." On this particular night, Tucker had sounded especially troubled, and Dahlia invited him to join her and her friends.

Donovan's is a dark, old-fashioned sort of place, popular with newspaper reporters and local politicians as well as college students. That night, it was doing a brisk business. Dahlia quickly found her friends. Cindy Meyers and Sharon Adams had arrived an hour or so earlier and were now on their second round of frozen margaritas. After sitting down with the two young women, Dahlia tried to flag down a waiter but failed to get his at-

tention. She decided to go to the bar for her Diet Coke. She was feeling tired, she told her friends, but wanted to wait for Tucker.

It was almost twenty minutes later when Cindy and Sharon, immersed in conversation about an end-of-year dance, realized that Dahlia hadn't come back. "When I looked over at the bar, I saw she was talking to this guy," Cindy Meyers said. "It looked like they'd been talking for a while. I remember feeling glad because she hadn't been too interested in anyone since she broke up with Jim. I was thinking this might be a good sign. Dahlia was sitting on a bar stool and the guy was leaning toward her. I almost went over to say something, but I didn't want to interrupt. I guess Sharon and I went back to talking and then we'd finished our drinks and Dahlia was still talking to the same guy. Anyway, we were fixing to leave, so I finally just walked over, but as I got closer, he whispered something to her and kind of slipped away. I told her we were going home, but she said she was going to stay. Tucker still hadn't got there, and she was waiting for him. That was what she said. But also, I could tell she wanted to keep talking to the guy she'd been talking to. She said his name was Steven."

It was just after ten when Cindy and Sharon headed back to the Vanderbilt campus.

By eleven o'clock, when her brother showed up, Dahlia Schuyler was gone . . .

Callie put down the book and leaned back against her bedroom wall, legs loosely extended before her, bare feet splayed. She picked up the watch from the floor beside her and closely examined it. For a fleeting moment, she wondered if maybe she was going crazy. Could she have put the watch in Anna's basket and then somehow forgotten? She'd actually have preferred that scenario to the one now facing her. The noise she'd heard in the yard last night. Someone *had* been watching. The watch and the anniversary note. There had to be some connection.

It was almost one in the morning.

The book lay open in front of her. Now, closing the cover, she absently turned it over, stared at the glamorous photograph on the back of the dust jacket. Diane Massey's hair was swept to one side, and she gazed out from under it. Perhaps because she wasn't smiling, she appeared slightly disdainful. Her arms were folded across her chest. On her left wrist, she wore a watch.

Dumbly, Callie stared at the picture, told herself it couldn't be true.

This couldn't be the same watch that Anna had found. It couldn't. It just couldn't. Because if it was, if it was . . .

Her mind wouldn't process the thought.

Callie picked up the watch and looked at the photo again. The image was so tiny. She needed a magnifying glass. They had one somewhere in a kitchen drawer that Anna used for science class.

Downstairs at the table where they ate their meals, she studied the photo again. She raised, then lowered the glass, until the watch came clear.

The same gold bracelet.

The same white face.

While she couldn't make out the inscription, she had no doubt what it said.

Monday, April 17

"WHERE were you supposed to meet her exactly?" The woman on the phone was skeptical, polite, but just barely. Her name was Marianne North, and she was Diane Massey's editor.

"At my apartment. For lunch. She was supposed to come over yesterday, but she . . ." Callie hesitated. "She never made it."

"At your apartment *in New York?*"

"Ummm . . . Yes. That's right." Callie twirled a piece of hair in her fingers, thankful for caller-ID block. She wished that she'd spent a little more time thinking through her cover story. For all she knew, Diane was in L.A., out of the country even.

She decided to cut her losses and just plunge ahead. "Look, you can believe me or not. But what's the harm in checking?"

Seconds later, when she hung up the phone, Callie felt defeated.

It was shortly after one o'clock, a cool, overcast day. She'd planned to work this morning, to catch up on reading for school. Instead, she'd spent most of the morning trying to reach Diane. Not surprisingly, Diane had an unlisted number, so she'd called Diane's publisher. At Carillon Books, she'd been transferred, put on hold, disconnected. She'd left numerous messages, none of them returned. She'd been about to give up and try the New York police when Marianne North had called back.

From her perch on the side of her bed, Callie's eyes moved to the watch. It was sitting on her nightstand. Now she picked it up. On the back of the face were numbers and letters: 1120, followed by 157480CD. A serial number, she supposed, proof of ownership. She reminded herself that she couldn't be sure that this watch belonged to Diane. But even as she tried to reassure herself, her anxiety was growing.

She hadn't eaten since breakfast. Maybe food would help.

As she walked downstairs, she was conscious of an overpowering silence, broken only by the muffled sound of her footsteps on the carpet. Faces in the photographs lining the wall watched her slow descent. She and Anna on a Nantucket beach. Anna at Disney World. A formal portrait of Anna at six. Anna on a sled. She found herself wondering about these pictures, why she had so many. It was almost like she was building a case that she really had a life. *See, we were here. And here and here and here.* For a moment, it struck her as slightly bizarre, almost embarrassing.

In the kitchen, she opened the refrigerator and stared blankly at its contents. If she'd had the time she might have cooked something, a childhood comfort food. Meat loaf and mashed potatoes. Macaroni and cheese. Instead, she settled on a peanut butter sandwich along with a glass of milk.

She put the sandwich on a plate and sat down at the table. As she ate, she looked around the kitchen, but something didn't feel right. The pleasure she normally took in this room was sharply diminished today. Everywhere she looked, she confronted hidden dangers. The knife block on the kitchen counter. A long three-pronged fork. The gas jets on the kitchen stove, odorless yet lethal. For the first time, she fully grasped the truth of Rick's observation. She could see how the kitchen was, in fact, the most dangerous room in the house.

Tuesday, April 18

DEPUTY Tim O'Hara drove his Jeep Cherokee off the ferry onto Blue Peek Island. He wished that he'd had time to change before coming out today. In a Shetland sweater and freshly pressed khakis, he was feeling a little self-conscious. He looked like the clueless college kid he'd struggled to prove he wasn't.

O'Hara pulled out of the parking lot and turned onto Main Street. He hadn't been on the island since summer and was struck by the bleakness of it. During July and August, the island's population grew to over a thousand, but during the long dark winters, it shrank to a couple hundred. By June, the summer people would start trickling in and Main Street would burst to life. Today, though, it was hard to believe that this change would ever take place. Everywhere he looked was gray. The place felt like a ghost town.

Last summer, he'd been the deputy assigned to island duty, a standard first-year rotation in the Hanson County sheriff's office. Blue Peek Island was forty-five minutes offshore but technically part of the county. Four days a week, for three long months, with almost nothing to do. He'd taken to driving around the island, patrolling its quiet streets. He'd given several speeding tickets, arrested a mailbox vandal. As he saw it, he was just doing his job, something to earn his paycheck. But the islanders had rolled their eyes. They'd called him Mr. Columbo. He'd gritted his teeth and pretended to laugh, but he hadn't thought it was funny. So he was only twenty-three. He still deserved respect.

Today would be different, though. At least that's what he hoped. Maybe, just maybe, he'd finally catch his first real case. A major step toward his long-term goal of joining the Maine State Police.

He'd been on his way to pick up his fiancée when the sergeant's call came in. They'd planned to have dinner with Molly's folks after a trip to the mall.

"I need you to check out a call on Blue Peek Island. Missing person report. I'd send Barrett out," the sergeant said, "but he doesn't know the island."

"No problem," O'Hara responded. "I'll take the next boat out."

A missing person report. This could be interesting.

He'd pulled out a long thin notebook and flipped open the cover. At the bottom of the first page, he scrawled a *1*. If the notepad was ever introduced in court, that could be important. Consecutive numbering could help to prove that the evidence hadn't been altered.

"Name's Diane Massey."

O'Hara's pen, poised to write, stayed in midair. "You kidding me?" he said.

"You know her?"

"Well, sure, I mean she's . . ." O'Hara stopped. No point in making the sergeant feel like a total idiot. "She's a writer. She wrote this book about Steven Gage. You know, the serial killer."

"I know who Steven Gage is." The sergeant sounded aggrieved. "So you know this Massey woman?"

"Not know her exactly. I mean, I saw her around last summer when she visited her parents. They've got this gigantic house right on the tip of North Point."

"Yeah, that's what I hear," the sergeant said. "Anyway, here's the deal. I got a call from this woman in New York. Her name's — let me see — Marianne North. Says she's Massey's editor and she can't get in touch with her. Probably nothing, you know, but this woman was real insistent."

Probably nothing.

But maybe not . . .

O'Hara parked in an empty space. Today he had his pick. The Massey house was just up the road, overlooking the Narrows. The house was visible from where he stood, fog-shrouded and imposing. It had been built by one Thomas Massey, more than a hundred years ago.

Last summer, he'd spent a couple of hours at the Blue Peek Island History Museum, learned about the wealthy Boston families who'd built the first summer homes. They'd called themselves rusticators and relished simple pleasures. Their summers were filled with a festive round of sailing, parties, and picnics. These days, descendants of those first settlers returned with their own children. But the summer people wouldn't start to arrive for another month at least. The island was all but deserted now. Why was Diane Massey here?

A set of granite steps led up to the house, which was shielded by a stand of pine trees. From where he stood, he could just make out a corner of the shingled roof. As a breeze came up, he heard a rustle of trees tossing in the wind. He flipped the latch on a low gate and headed up the stairs.

O'Hara rapped on the back door, three sharp knocks. He waited a bit, then tried again. Still no response. The porch where he stood wrapped around the house. Now he walked toward the front, his footsteps sounding hollowly on the worn wooden planks. Below him, a vast expanse of lawn ended in granite cliffs. By summer, the grass would be emerald green, a smooth velvet carpet. Today, it was still scruffy and brown with weeds poking through it.

By the front door, he saw a wooden folding chair with a blue canvas seat. Beside the chair, on a rickety table, was an ashtray filled with cigarette butts. A few more knocks. Still no answer. He tried the door. It opened.

"Ms. Massey? Are you here?"

He was standing in a two-story foyer with a broad staircase to his left. At the end of the central hallway, he saw a closed door.

"Hello?" O'Hara called.

It was darker in the house than it was outside. O'Hara flipped a light switch. A heavy wrought-iron chandelier sent out a dusty glow.

Then, as he inhaled, he smelled something, a faint scent of rot. He walked down the hall. The smell grew stronger. His hand moved to his gun. For an instant he considered calling Dispatch, then decided against it. If it turned out to be a false alarm, he'd be asking for it. He'd already taken enough ribbing for that Mr. Columbo bit. Better to handle this on his own. Not get too excited.

When he reached the door, he pushed it open and found himself in the kitchen. The room was empty, no one here, but the smell almost made him retch. He found a light switch on the wall, clicked it, and scanned the room. There was an ancient woodstove and, next to it, a modern gas-fueled one. A dining table with four cane chairs. Dishes set out to dry. Everything appeared to be clean, in order. Where was that smell coming from?

Over beside the woodstove, he noticed a narrow door.

He approached and flung it open, peered into its depths. Brooms and mops. Cleaning products. Just a utility closet.

From where he stood, the stench was fainter. It was stronger nearer the hallway. Testing, he moved in that direction. Yes, he was getting closer. Beneath the sink was a cabinet. He knelt down and opened it. Breathing in, he almost gagged, enveloped in rotting foulness.

Jesus.

Breathing through his mouth, he gingerly fished out the plastic wastebasket. Tuna fish cans, molding rice and beans, a gelatinous stinking mess. Who would have thought that ordinary food could give off such a stench? Stomach heaving, he closed the cabinet. His mind continued to work. During the summers, the island dump was open on Tuesdays and Saturdays. But even if the schedule were less frequent off season, she'd have put her trash outside. Could she have gone off island, forgetting to take it out? That was possible, of course, but it didn't seem so likely.

His skin felt prickly, like when he was a kid and his dad would take him hunting and he knew that something was about to happen but wasn't sure what or when. Leaving the kitchen, he went down the hall, heading for the stairway.

He walked past the shrouded living room, furniture covered in sheets. For the first time, he noticed another door on the other side of the room. Crossing the floor, he opened it and found himself in a study.

Unlike the other rooms, this one showed signs of use. On the massive desk was a Sony laptop attached to a portable printer. There were stacks of papers on the desk and floor, a space heater in the corner. Newspaper clippings were everywhere, spilling out of folders. Glancing at one of the headlines, he saw the name Winnie Dandridge. Everything suddenly fell into place. Diane Massey had come here to write.

O'Hara walked back through the living room and into the entrance foyer. From there, he proceeded up the stairs, into another hallway. Off the hall were half a dozen doors, all but one of them closed. He went toward the door that was slightly ajar.

"Ms. Massey? Are you there?"

His heart was beating faster now, and he kept a hand on his gun. But when he looked inside the room, he saw that it, too, was empty. White curtains. Water views. Two single beds. One of the beds was rumpled, the other piled with clothing. At least half a dozen pairs of shoes were lined up beneath it. Running shoes. Hiking boots. A pair of sandals with heels so high that he couldn't see how she'd walk. The only time he'd seen shoes like that was on that TV show Molly made him watch, the one with the four cute New York girls who had sex with everyone.

He checked the closets, under the beds, then moved to the other rooms. Then, back downstairs, he did a sweep of the areas he hadn't covered. Now that he was sure that the house was empty, he considered his next move. Who would Diane have been most likely to see? He thought of Jenny Ward. Someone as famous as Diane Massey had to be getting mail. The post office closed in the afternoons. Jenny was probably home now. O'Hara turned on his cell phone and got the number from information.

"Yeah?" It was a man's voice, Jenny's husband, Phil.

"Is Jenny there?"

"Who's calling?"

"It's Tim O'Hara. From the sheriff's office."

Something that sounded like a snort from the other end of the phone. *And what can I do for you, Mr. Columbo?* O'Hara felt himself flush. While he hadn't been to the island for months, his reputation survived him.

"She there?"

Silence and then Jenny was on the line.

"Hello?" Jenny said. As if she were asking a question. He remembered her, pleasant and matter-of-fact. She'd always been nice to him.

"I'm trying to find Diane Massey. I understand she's been on the island."

"Yes, she's been out here writing. I told her I think she's crazy staying up there on the water. The house isn't winterized, you know. Even with space heaters, she's still got to be freezing. And then there's the danger of fire. I really think —"

O'Hara broke in. "I was wondering if you'd seen her in the past few days."

A pause.

"No," Jenny said finally. "Not for a week or so. Why?" In the background, a baby had started to cry.

O'Hara hesitated. This wasn't a conversation he wanted to have on an easily monitored cell phone. "Listen, would you mind if I stopped by? Just for a couple of minutes."

"Uh, just a sec." Muffled sounds in the background, then Jenny was back. "We're about to go out."

Her voice sounded artificially bright, and he could tell that she was lying. "It won't take long," O'Hara said.

"Well . . ." She sounded helpless.

"I'll see you in about five minutes."

Before she could answer, he hung up.

THE Wards lived in a snug white house halfway across the island. This neighborhood was a world apart from the grand homes lining the shore. These houses were stolid, compact dwellings built for year-round living. The lobster traps piled in yards attested to hard daily work. Parked in the driveways were pickup trucks, older Fords and Chevys.

Jenny greeted him at the door, a baby slung over her shoulder. "So what's this about?" she asked him, once they'd both sat down.

"It's probably nothing," O'Hara said, echoing the sergeant.

Jenny bounced her enormous baby. *Man, that kid was ugly.* Smiling at the pie-faced child, O'Hara pulled out his notebook.

"I've just been trying to catch up with Ms. Massey. She isn't at the house. You have any idea where she might have gone?"

As he spoke, he quickly numbered the pages: 6, 7, 8 . . .

Phil Ward lumbered into the living room, a dark, hulking man. "We gotta go to my mother's now. We're already late," he said.

Jenny looked up. "I thought she said five."

Her husband scowled at her.

"The sooner we get through these questions, the sooner I'll be gone." O'Hara kept his tone polite, though it really took some effort.

"Whatever you say, *Mr. Columbo.*" Phil Ward shambled out. O'Hara heard him in the kitchen, popping open a can.

Jenny's brows were knit together. She looked distracted now. Still bouncing her huge kid, she glanced toward the other room.

"About Ms. Massey?" O'Hara prompted. "Can you think where she might be?"

Jenny shook her head. "She pretty much stays at home. She doesn't even hardly go to the market. She brought food from the mainland."

"She have any visitors?"

"No. At least, I don't think so. She came out here to finish this book. Have you read any of the ones she's written? They're all really great. The first one is still my favorite though, the one about Steven Gage. I can't remember what it's called. Something about disappearing."

"The Vanishing Man."

Jenny looked at him, pleased. "Yeah. That's right. You read it?"

"Yup." He quickly moved ahead. "When was the last time you saw her?"

"I'm not exactly sure. Not this week. Maybe early last week? The last time she was in, she picked up some FedEx packages. We'd have a record of that. I could —" Jenny broke off. "I just thought of something. Diane went running every day, out by Carson's Cove. She said it helped her think. Gosh, I hope she's okay."

The baby let out a fretful wail. Jenny patted its back.

"She's probably fine," O'Hara said. "Made a trip to the mainland or something."

"Maybe." Jenny didn't sound convinced. "We've had some trouble with a few boys shooting off guns in the woods. I should have reminded her to wear bright colors. She's from the city, you know? She might not have remembered."

THE rutted dirt road that led to Carson's Cove was lined with towering trees. As O'Hara drove down the curving path, the shadowy air grew cooler. The road ended in a small clearing, and O'Hara parked his Jeep. He jumped out and headed for the break in the woods that led to a narrow footpath.

It hadn't rained for a couple of weeks, and the path was covered with dry brown leaves. Even if Diane had been through here, she wouldn't have left footprints. It occurred to him that he hadn't seen a car when he'd stopped by the Massey house. He should have thought to ask Jenny if Diane had brought one over.

He'd just caught the first glimpse of slate-blue sea when he noticed a change in terrain. A few yards back, the leaves and pine needles had formed a smoothly packed bed. Here they were looser in places, as if they'd been disturbed. He got down on his hands and knees to study the ground more closely. Twigs and pine cones gouged his palms as he slowly edged forward. But there still weren't any footprints that he could see, no sign of human presence. The most likely explanation, he decided, was some sort of animal.

O'Hara climbed to his feet. A bird cried shrilly. Leaves and dirt clung to his pants. He brushed at them with his hands. The woods seemed to close around him, silent and oppressive. Continuing down the path toward the water, he walked just a little bit faster.

Twenty feet farther, to the side of the path, he saw an abandoned shed. Its weathered boards had shrunk apart and the roof was caving through. In front, there was a gaping hole where a door must once have been.

Making his way through the undergrowth, O'Hara peered inside. He aimed a flashlight into the shed, exploring its dark corners. The cavernous space was overflowing with what looked like the refuse of a lifetime. A rusting boat trailer. Woodworking tools. Ancient lobster traps and buoys. Slowly, O'Hara moved the light from one object to another. No sign that anyone had been through here anytime recently. When he was through, he clicked off the flashlight and went back outside.

Later, he couldn't say exactly what drew his attention to the side of the shed, to the thick tangle of fallen branches piled against a wall. But as he moved in for a closer look, he glimpsed something there behind it. There was a sparking sensation in his mind and heart. For an instant, he couldn't think.

She was curled up on her right side, her body stripped of clothing. O'Hara crashed through the underbrush and knelt down beside her. Flat brown eyes stared blankly at the tops of his leather boots. A stream of dried blood ran from her mouth, the color of molten rust. Her face was bloated and deeply bruised, but he had no doubt who she was.

The smell floated up around him, like fish or shrimp gone bad. There was something wrapped around her neck, a tight black ligature. He checked the ordinary human impulse to reach down and loosen it. His job was to protect the crime scene, leave everything as it was. The body had to stay as he'd found it until the state police arrived.

Then he noticed something else, and his body seemed to clench. Her arm, it was something on her arm, a series of deep gashes. All in a row. Orderly. Someone had taken their time. The image was something that he'd seen before but only in a book, in a homicide manual showing examples of serial killers' work.

A shiver passed through O'Hara's body, and he felt a little lost.

For the first time, it occurred to him that he'd never seen a corpse before.

Then he was back on his feet, pulling out his cell phone.

Cutting his eyes away from the body, he placed the call to Dispatch.

Thursday, April 20

After an exhilarating post-graduation trip to Europe, I settled into the training program at Lowell, Cafferty, a brokerage firm in Boston. It was there that I met Joe Flick. Right away, we knew we were soul mates. Both of us were marathon runners, and could think of no better way to spend a Saturday night than to search out great live music. Perhaps most importantly, though, we discovered a shared obsession with Fresh Samantha's Vanilla Almond Soy Shake! Last Christmas, we announced our engagement. If all goes as scheduled, we'll be married by the time you read this and settling into our new apartment in Boston's Back Bay.

Callie looked up from the Fifth Reunion report she'd been editing for the past two hours. She was awash in stories of promising lives, a sea of self-congratulation. A bit cynically she wondered how the reality measured up. These seamless records of accomplishment, what did they leave out? She thought, too, of the graduates who hadn't sent in the survey, of those who'd provided just name and address or hadn't responded at all. Maybe they'd tried to answer the questions, then finally given up, overcome with a sense that at age twenty-six they'd already lost the race.

Callie rubbed her eyes. Time for a break, she thought.

Crossing through the reception area, she dropped a stack of edited pages on Posy Kisch's desk. As usual, Posy was on the phone. She didn't look up. Her hair, a purplish red today, almost matched her lipstick. "So I was, like, no way. And he told me to, like, shut up . . ."

Martha was at her desk, typing away on something. She looked up, slightly distracted, as Callie came through the door.

"What are we going to *do* about Kabuki Girl?" Callie asked, once she'd shut the door.

Martha gave a helpless shrug. "What *can* we do?" she asked. "Anyway, it's just for another month. Next year, maybe we'll do better."

Callie plunked herself in a chair. "Windham College. Where the student rules. That should be the motto. Next year, we should definitely insist that we at least get to interview."

"Yeah. I guess you're right." Martha took a sip of coffee from a blue ceramic mug. "At least she's here," she said mildly.

Callie rolled her eyes. "For once."

In recent weeks, Posy's sporadic attendance had become even more erratic. An overdue paper. A sick ferret. A malfunctioning alarm. At this point, Callie didn't even bother asking why she hadn't shown up. "Just call us if you're not coming in," she'd said tiredly. Sullenly, Posy had said she would. Then she'd skipped three days.

"How's she going to hold a job once she gets out of school?"

"Thankfully, that's not our problem," said Martha.

"I guess you're right," said Callie.

A swirl of dark hair fell over Martha's forehead, and she shoved it back absently. She had square capable artist's hands, the nails clipped short. Along with her job at Windham, she worked as a ceramic artist. She'd married young, divorced, and now had two teenage kids. Martha seemed to take life as it came, and Callie admired that.

"So how've *you* been?" Martha asked after another sip of coffee. "I've hardly seen you this week. How was that Easter thing?"

Callie felt a dip in her stomach. "Fine," she said. "Fun."

"Anna doing okay?"

"She seems to be. No recent explosions."

"And Rick?"

"He . . . he's *good*." Callie struggled to convey a confidence she was far from feeling. In fact, things with Rick were compli-cated. She wasn't sure where they stood. His proposal still hung over them, a floating question mark.

"He's a great guy," said Martha.

"Yes," said Callie. "He is."

As she met Martha's serene blue eyes, Callie felt a twinge of guilt. Why should she have Rick while Martha had no one? Cal-lie knew Martha was okay with it, that she didn't need a man. At the same time, she knew that her friend would be happier if she had a partner. She'd answered the occasional personal ad, been fixed up by friends, but except for a few amusing stories had little to show for her efforts.

Impulsively, Callie leaned toward her. "There's someone I want you to meet."

Martha raised her eyebrows, as if to say, "Shoot."

"He's a cop, a friend of Rick's. He lives in my neighborhood."

Briefly she described Tod Carver. Martha seemed interested. "Rick thinks he's still not over his ex-wife. But you have to start somewhere. He has two kids, both pretty young. Is that a prob-lem?"

"Nope."

Callie smiled. "Okay then. I'll talk to him this week. I could have you both to dinner."

A knock on Martha's closed door, then Posy poked her head in. There was something eerie about the makeup covering the fresh young face. Not for the first time, Callie wondered why she did this to herself. A desperate bid for attention, or did she just like how it looked?

"A guy named Nathan's here to see you," Posy said to Callie.

Nathan. Callie groaned to herself. She'd half forgotten their plans. Nathan had called early this morning to ask if she'd have lunch. She'd begged off, saying that she was too busy but finally agreed to coffee.

"He says you're expecting him," Posy said.

"Thanks. I'll be right out."

Posy closed, almost slammed, the door. The office reverberated.

"You could always say no," Martha mouthed, as Callie stood to leave.

"Why didn't I think of that?" Callie whispered. "Next time, definitely. Hey, are you through with the *Globe?*"

"Take it," Martha said.

Callie grabbed the paper from a bookcase and went out to meet Nathan.

He was standing next to Posy's desk, all gangly arms and legs. He shifted from one foot to the other, his eyes trained to the floor. As Callie approached, his head jerked up, and color flooded his face.

"Hi, Callie." He seemed on edge, more so than usual.

Callie made a quick decision.

"Nathan, I'm really swamped today. I don't have time to go out. If you want, we can have a cup of coffee here. Then I've got to get back to work."

At first she thought he was going to object, but he seemed to think better of it.

"Okay," he said, with an awkward shrug. "Let's just stay here then."

As she handed Nathan a mug of coffee, Callie noticed Posy watching. In the place of her usual bored detachment was an almost avid interest. For an instant, Callie wondered what Posy was thinking. Then Nathan started to talk.

They carried their coffee into Callie's office. She didn't close the door. Directing Nathan to the visitor's chair, she sat behind her desk.

"Did you miss me?" Nathan asked, once they'd settled in. He was looking at her intensely, an odd smile on his face.

"Miss you?" Callie said lightly. "I didn't know you were gone."

His smile turned petulant. "I was sick. I had the flu. Didn't you see that I wasn't in class? I usually sit with you."

"I'm glad you're better," Callie said.

Nathan didn't answer. Now he was looking around the room,

as if preoccupied. "I saw this great video the other night, this Nazi propaganda film. Incredible pictures of Nazis kissing babies. Lots of stuff like that."

Callie stared at him. Had he always been this creepy? When they first met, she'd thought he was strange but sweet. Now he just seemed strange.

"That doesn't sound like it's up my alley," Callie finally said.

Ten minutes later, when they said good-bye, Callie felt a vast relief. She stood in the doorway of the office suite until he turned the corner.

As Callie headed back to her office, Posy asked, "Who was that guy?"

"He's a junior," Callie said. "His name's Nathan Lacoste."

"How do you know him?"

"He's in one of my classes. What's with all the questions?"

Posy was blushing now. "Nothing," she mumbled, ducking her head. "I was just wondering." Beneath the thick layer of white pancake, her face was a mottled pink.

Posy was interested in Nathan! Callie almost laughed. Nathan and Kabuki Girl. What a perfect pair. At least it was something to keep in mind if Nathan showed up again. Who knew? Maybe it would even work. Maybe they'd be good for each other.

Back at her desk, Callie launched into the next stack of questionnaires.

After graduation, I moved to New York, where I worked as a paralegal at Cravath, Swaine & Moore . . .

God, it was all too tedious. She grabbed the newspaper she'd snagged from Martha and skimmed the front-page headlines. She wouldn't mind seeing a movie this weekend, though not the one Nathan had mentioned. She flipped through the newspaper's sections, searching for the listings.

Diane Massey

The name jumped from the page. For an instant, she thought she'd imagined it, but another part of her knew. Blood rushed to

Callie's head. Her heart began to race. Deep inside her, a voice was saying, *This is what you've been waiting for.*

For a moment, the name seemed to float, unattached to anything else. Then, slowly, her focus widened, and she could read the surrounding words. MYSTERY DEEPENS IN CRIME WRITER'S DEATH. And beneath the boldface headline, in smaller type: DIANE MASSEY LED QUIET LIFE IN FINAL DAYS ON ISLAND.

She read through the article quickly once, then again more slowly.

It obviously wasn't the first report, maybe not even the second. It wasn't until the end that the facts of the crime were recapped. Diane had gone to the island for quiet, to finish work on a book. It appeared that she'd been ambushed during her daily afternoon run. As of yet, no suspects had been publicly identified. The cause of death was blunt force trauma, and Diane had also been strangled. When her body was discovered, a black nylon stocking was twisted around her throat.

Callie's eyes froze on the printed words.

A black nylon stocking.

In a haze, she lurched up from her chair and into Martha's office. She wasn't feeling well, she said. Maybe a touch of the flu. Martha's expressions of concern seemed to come from far away. At the same time, sensations in her own body seemed strangely magnified. She could feel the blood flowing through her veins, the skin clinging to bone. Every cell of her being seemed to vibrate at lightning speed.

Callie walked the seven blocks home barely paying attention. A Volkswagen bug screeched to a halt as she crossed against the light. Through the windshield, she glimpsed the shaken driver, her eyes two small moons. Vaguely, Callie realized that she could have been hit, but this fact barely registered. *What am I going to do?* she thought. *What am I going to do?* She couldn't handle this alone anymore, that much was clear. But where could she turn for help? Whom could she talk to? It had to be someone who knew her history. Someone she could trust.

Then, as Callie unlocked the front door, a face flashed from the past. She ran quickly through her mental checklist. A match on every score. Smart and incisive, knew the past, and one added draw: For professional reasons she'd be bound to keep any secrets she was told.

For the first time since she'd seen the paper, Callie's mind cleared a bit. Inside, she bounded up the stairs and went straight to her room. She still had her old address books, stuffed in a jumbled desk drawer. She dug out the black one with the vinyl cover and flipped to the W's.

"Ms. White is no longer employed with the firm."

Callie's heart sank. "Do you know where I could reach her?"

A pause. "I'll transfer you."

It took some time, but she finally got a forwarding phone number. As soon as she hung up the phone, she picked up and dialed again.

"Harwich and Young," a voice said.

Callie's heart was pounding. "I'm calling for Melanie White," she said.

A click and then a ringing.

"Melanie White's office." An impersonal female voice.

Callie clutched the phone. The moment seemed unreal. "I . . . I need to . . . ," she began. "May I speak with Melanie?"

Callie was sitting on the side of her bed, leaning slightly forward. She'd twisted one leg around the other, and they both felt slightly numb.

"I'm sorry, but Ms. White is in a meeting now. Would you like to leave a message?"

"Just . . . just that Callie Thayer called. It's important that I speak with her."

Half an hour later, Callie tried again.

"Please," she said. "This is urgent."

"If I could tell Ms. White what this is about —"

Callie sensed an edge of annoyance.

"No," she said. "I'm sorry. It's . . . it's personal."

After she'd hung up again, Callie slumped back on her pillows. She lay there for another twenty minutes, barely moving at all.

She felt totally exhausted, as if she'd been up for days. She had an urge to pull back the covers, to climb under them and sleep. But another part of her was wide awake and knew what she had to do.

Still lying flat on her back, she picked up the phone. She didn't have to look at the number. She had it memorized.

"Ms. White's office." The same cool voice.

In an instant, the past flashed through Callie's mind, the path that had brought her here. It was like she was standing at the edge of a cliff, poised, about to leap. She didn't want to take that step, but she didn't have a choice. She took a deep breath, closed her eyes.

"Please tell her this is Laura Seton."

❧

"Laura Seton?"

Melanie White looked up from the floor where, crouched amid a sea of boxes and papers, she was spot-checking the production work of a team of junior associates. Outside the sky was a brilliant blue, but Melanie hardly noticed. The documents still had to be photocopied and shipped out by midnight.

"It's the same woman, I'm sure. The one who's been calling all morning." Tina Dryer was small, just five foot one, and very, very pregnant. Her pursed lips signaled disapproval of this waste of Melanie's time.

"I . . ." Melanie stared at Tina, caught totally off guard. The facts of the Connor Pharmaceuticals case collided with the past, thoughts of market share and dominance giving way to a sharp nostalgia.

Far below, horns blared and tires screeched, but Melanie didn't hear them. She was back in Nashville in a rented Ford Escort, driving out I-40 toward the prison. The Riverbend Maximum Security Institution. Tennessee's death row. A huge red sun was beating down as she frantically talked on her cell phone. *How much more time? Have you heard anything? Isn't there one more, one more, one more . . .*

Then she was in a smoke-filled hotel room with Mark Kelly

and Fred Irving. It was in watching the senior partners' haggard faces that she'd realized it was over. They were still drinking coffee, smoking cigarettes, talking strategy. But in the hard, clear eyes of the older lawyers she'd recognized the truth.

"I tried to get her to tell me what's so important, but . . ." Tina made a helpless motion with her hands, then dropped them to her tight round belly.

"Laura Seton," Melanie said, lingering on the words. As if by simply repeating the name, she could find an explanation.

Decisively, she got to her feet. "Okay, Tina, I'll take it."

A slight lift of plucked eyebrows, but Tina didn't say anything. She simply turned and left the room, closing the door behind her.

Melanie picked up on the phone's first ring. "Melanie White," she said, sitting down behind her desk.

"Melanie? It's . . . it's Laura Seton. I know it's been a long time."

The voice caught Melanie by surprise. Husky and stronger than expected. Not at all the voice that she recalled. Or imagined that she recalled. Not a voice that she'd ever have connected with the Laura Seton she'd known.

In her mind's eye, Laura was a hazy image, fading out at the edges. And it wasn't just the passage of time; it had been that way even then. Laura had always given the impression of being slightly out of focus. As if she were being observed through a camera in need of adjustment. Perhaps it was the waves of fawn-colored hair that tumbled over her face, the vague ineffectual gesture she'd make to push it back. Even now Melanie remembered how the gesture had come to annoy her. She'd had to suppress an impulse to grab hold of Laura's hand.

"You remember me?" the Laura, not-Laura, voice said. The words framed a question but it sounded more like a statement. An awareness that the passage of time could never erase what they'd shared.

"Yes," said Melanie. "Of course."

Another wave of memories flooded over her. The heady excitement of her early days as a lawyer at Watkins & Graham. She'd just moved to Washington, D.C., after taking the bar exam. She had a tiny apartment in Dupont Circle, just two Metro stops from the firm. The day she was called to Mark Kelly's office began like any other. She was working on a lengthy memorandum dealing with choice of law. Kelly, harried and intense, eyed her appraisingly. "I've got a pro bono assignment for you. We'll be handling the appeal in Steven Gage's case."

At the time it had seemed like an incredible coup, but of course, she'd been naive. Only years later did she understand the reason she'd been picked. Like Dahlia, she'd been raised in Nashville. Their families were even neighbors. It was almost as if Dahlia herself had been fighting for his life. None of this mattered legally; it was a question of atmospherics. But faced with an uphill battle on appeal, they'd decided it couldn't hurt.

In the end, though, none of it had made a difference. They'd killed him anyway. And there she'd been, a fifth-year associate, all but useless to the law firm. An expensive item on a balance sheet, hard to justify. She'd made countless courtroom appearances, many more than other lawyers her year. But death penalty expertise was not a transferable skill, would be of scant use in the commercial cases that she'd now be expected to manage.

In retrospect, she could see that she'd been partly to blame. She at least could have made an effort to stay on a dual track, to take some lucrative corporate cases along with her pro bono work. But at the time, the bread-and-butter cases had seemed so trivial, hardly weighing in the balance against her fight to save a man's life. That this man had perhaps killed a hundred-plus women was something she didn't dwell on. She'd tried to push those thoughts aside, to focus on the principle. The death penalty was barbaric. Regardless of what he'd done.

Still. More than a hundred women. The number weighed on her. By most accounts, Steven Gage was the nation's most prolific serial killer. Ted Bundy, for all his notoriety, lagged far behind. He was thought to have killed just thirty-some women before his apprehension. Such statistics, of course, were debatable. No one knew for sure. But whatever way you looked at it, Gage's crimes were stunning.

She reminded herself that Steven Gage was far from the world record holder. There was British physician Harold Shipman, with more than two hundred victims. And Pedro "Monster of the Andes" Lopez, linked to more than three hundred deaths. But the specter of such atrocities hardly minimized Steven's. *More than a hundred women.* She'd struggled to comprehend it.

But all that was in the future. At the start, she'd just been thrilled. One of the first things she'd done after getting the assignment was to read Laura's trial testimony. Laura, Steven's longtime girlfriend, had been a devastating witness. For months she'd tracked his movements, copied phone and credit-card bills. It was credit-card records that had linked Steven to the last place Dahlia was seen. He'd been at Donovan's on May 7, the day she disappeared.

Melanie had pored over Laura's words, preparing to interview her. The goal was to find a discrepancy, something that didn't add up. She'd met with Laura a number of times, but they'd never really connected. While they'd been the same age, twenty-five when they met, they'd had little else in common.

Now, breaking out of her reverie, she realized that Laura was waiting. "How are you?" she quickly asked.

"Fine. I . . . things are very different now."

Melanie said simply, "I'm glad." Because it was hard to imagine any changes that wouldn't have been for the better.

"I hope you don't mind me calling." On its face, the question was deferential, but the tone belied the words. "I needed to talk to someone. Someone who . . . knows about my past."

There was a pause, as if Laura were thinking. Then she spoke again.

"I go by a different name now. It's Callie, Callie Thayer. Thayer is my ex-husband's last name, and I just kept using it. I live in — well, it doesn't really matter where, but no one knows who I am. At least, that's what I thought. I work at a small liberal arts college, in alumni affairs. My life has been very quiet. I went back to school and I . . . But I don't need to tell you all that. The reason I'm calling is this letter I got. It started with a letter. Someone left it in my door, and I realized . . . I realized they knew. At first, I was really upset, but then I sort of calmed down. I figured that at worst it was blackmail, and it might even be a prank. You know, some kid on the Internet who managed to track me down.

"Then last Sunday we had this Easter egg hunt. It's an annual neighborhood thing. I'd hidden one of the baskets in this drain-pipe by our house. But by the time my daughter found it, someone had switched the contents. I'd filled the basket with chocolate eggs, those little ones wrapped in foil. But when my daughter found it, they'd been replaced with this pink plastic egg. When you opened the egg, twisted it open, inside there was a watch.

"Right away I knew something was wrong. I just didn't know what. Then later, I was looking at *The Vanishing Man* — Diane Massey's book — and in the picture on the back she's wearing it — the watch my daughter found. I called her publisher's office last week and told them they needed to find her. Then, yesterday I read the paper . . ."

The flow of words trailed off.

"Yes?" Melanie prodded. She felt both confused and wary. A letter. A watch. A plastic egg. It sounded totally crazy.

"Well, Diane was killed, you know. Last week. Up on an island in Maine."

"Diane Massey was murdered?" Melanie sat up straighter. Suddenly, the profusion of words came sharply into focus. Briefly, she wondered if it were true. Wouldn't she have heard? But then she'd been working around the clock. She'd barely scanned the papers.

Melanie signed on to the Internet and pulled up the *New York Times* website. She typed in a search for Diane Massey's name. Two articles popped up.

"She was strangled," Callie said. A pause. "The killer used a black stocking."

For a moment, Melanie's pulse beat faster. "Have you called the police?" she asked.

"No," said Callie. "No, I can't." She sounded almost frightened.

"Why not?" It was the obvious question.

"My daughter," Callie said. "I . . . I don't want her to know about this. If I went to the police, the publicity . . . I've kept my past a secret here. I need to keep it that way."

"How old is your daughter?" Melanie asked.

"Ten," Callie answered.

It didn't make sense, Melanie thought, *not to go to the police*. She was about to argue with Laura, but then she stopped herself. Before embarking on this line of discussion, she wanted more information.

"What makes you think that the watch was Diane's?" As she spoke, Melanie realized that this was far from the only thing in doubt. The only facts she knew for sure were those she'd read on the *Times* website. Laura had been telling the truth when she said Diane was murdered. As for the Easter basket story, the verdict was still out.

"It's exactly the same as in the picture. But it's not just the watch. It's everything. The timing. The letter I got."

"And this letter, what did it say?"

"Didn't I tell you that?" Callie sounded dazed.

"No, you just told me that you got a letter. That someone left it at your door."

"It said 'Happy Anniversary, Rosamund. I haven't forgotten you.' Rosamund — that's what Steven used to call me. This stupid joke we had. Because I loved red roses. He used to buy them for me."

Melanie had reached for her calendar to check tomorrow's schedule. Now her hand dropped to the desk. "Happy Anniversary?"

"Right. That was the message. It was dated April fifth."

"April fifth," Melanie repeated. The room felt suddenly cold.

"The date of the execution." Callie's voice was flat.

In a flash, it all came clear. She thought of Frank's bemused denials when she blamed him for the letter. Her ex-husband had been telling the truth. He hadn't sent the note.

Melanie's head was spinning now. She had to get off the phone.

"I'm terribly sorry, but I have a meeting. Could I get back to you this afternoon?"

"When?" Callie asked.

"Later. Before the end of the day."

"I . . . well, okay." Callie was reluctant to let things drop, but she didn't have an option.

Melanie had almost put down the phone when she thought of one last question.

"Laura?"

"Yes."

She was still there.

"Why did you call *me*?"

Callie hesitated. "Well . . . I knew that I could trust your judgment. And then, there was the privilege."

"The privilege?" Melanie didn't follow.

"I knew that whatever I told you, you had to keep it confidential."

Melanie's body tensed. The attorney-client privilege, that's what Laura meant. The sacred rule prohibiting disclosure of a client's secrets. But Laura wasn't her client, was she? She'd called up out of the blue. With a sinking feeling, Melanie saw she was in much deeper than she'd realized.

THE Harwich & Young library was on the sixty-third floor. It was the realm of junior associates, and Melanie had rarely been there. When she arrived at the firm four-plus years ago, she'd already been fairly senior, handing out research assignments herself rather than slogging through them. It was a little after seven by the time she got there, and darkness had already fallen. Far below, the teeming city was a sparkling sea of lights, visual compensation for the tedium of the junior associate's life.

"Need some help?" A night-shift librarian looked up from her terminal.

Melanie smiled at the owl-like woman. "No, thanks," she said.

The reading room was a hushed enclave of polished mahogany. Desk lamps burned in the private carrels, where several young lawyers worked. A fresh-faced blonde in a gray pantsuit had kicked off a Gucci pump. She was avidly reading and taking notes, jouncing a manicured foot. Melanie had a disconcerting sense of looking at her younger self. She had a sudden impulse to warn her, to say, *It's not too late*. The thought took her by surprise, and she wondered where it had come from. After all, she loved her job. Her job wasn't the problem.

Cutting her eyes away, Melanie entered the stacks. As she roamed the aisles, scanning the shelves, she felt conspicuous. She sensed the younger lawyers looking at her, wondering why she was here. She could have done the research on her office PC, paid for the Westlaw research. But then there would have been a record, something she didn't want.

She finally located the CPLR, a compilation of New York laws. She found the volume she needed and took it to a carrel. She read through the statute once quickly, then turned to the commentary: "The attorney-client privilege is perhaps the oldest of the common law evidentiary privileges, and New York courts continue to draw heavily upon common law developments . . ."

She scanned a list of case summaries, looking for relevant law. What professional obligation did she have to Laura? That was the basic question. At this point, Laura wasn't a client, but she didn't think that mattered. Prospective clients, as best she recalled, fell within the scope of privilege. But was Laura even a prospective client? Had she called seeking legal advice? Maybe this was more a situation of a friend calling on a friend.

But even as she tested the analogy, she knew it didn't ring true. When they'd talked on the phone this morning, Laura had been quite clear: Her call had been premised on the belief that what she'd said would be kept confidential. A rule popped into Melanie's mind from some long-ago ethics class. *If someone reasonably thinks they're a client, the attorney-client privilege attaches.* She didn't remember the name of the case, but the rule was clear in her mind. The point was, you had to be careful. And always, until now, she had been. At parties, on plane trips, talking to friends, she'd been meticulous. *Of course, I can't give you legal advice. I'm not speaking as your attorney . . .*

Melanie scribbled down a few citations, then got up to find the books. Back at her carrel, she started to read, fast, without taking notes. She was doing what she did best: examining a legal issue. Taking stock of its strengths and weaknesses, finding the chink in the wall. Beneath the surface calm, though, she was frustrated, almost angry. Not with Laura. No. She was angry with herself. She, who was always so careful, had let Laura catch her off guard. It would have been so easy to say, "I can't give you legal advice."

At best, her situation was murky, which left her with just two options: She could talk to Laura and try to explain that there'd been a misunderstanding. The second option, even less appealing, was to go to the partnership. She could present the matter to the Ethics Committee, seek guidance on how to proceed. But the thought of going to those three men was difficult to stomach. She could already see their bland faces, the subtle calculation. The very fact that she was there before them would be proof that she'd screwed up. Partnership elections were just weeks away. Was it really worth the risk? At this point, she should be bringing in paying clients, not creating trouble.

By the time Melanie finished reading, almost an hour had passed. She was supposed to meet Paul at nine at a restaurant down the street. But picturing him, the evening ahead, she felt her resistance growing.

She pulled her cell phone from her purse and went out into the hallway.

"Hi, honey," she said when Paul came on the line. "Listen, I'm really sorry, but I have to work late tonight. The client . . . well, you know how it is. They want a draft of the brief tomorrow. I thought we'd have another day."

Muffled voices on the other end, Paul sounding authoritative. "Right, put them in the blue folders. We decided that last night." Then he was back on the phone. "Sorry. What were you saying?"

She repeated the story one more time, her voice artificially bright. She waited for him to notice, but he seemed preoccupied.

"Don't worry about it," he said. "We're pretty busy here too."

More muffled voices from the other end of the line. "No, I think Joe has them," she heard Paul say. And then, annoyed, "Well, *ask* him."

In her mind's eye she pictured her fiancé's office, just five blocks away. Books stacked neatly on his desk. To-do lists beside the phone. The millefleurs paperweight she gave him for Christmas holding papers in place. Funny how, when she thought of Paul, it was always his office she saw.

This time, when he came back on the line, he didn't apologize. "Shall I stop by later, then? What time do you think you'll get home?"

"You know, I've had this headache. I should probably just go to sleep."

"Sure? I could give you a back rub."

"Oh, that's sweet, but . . . How about tomorrow? I'm sure I'll feel better by then."

As she ended the call, Melanie realized that she actually did have a headache, a sharp, pulsing pain coiled at the base of her skull. The only thing she'd eaten all day was some low-fat coffee yogurt. She wandered down the hall to a kitchenette with coffee and vending machines.

She bought a Snickers bar, wolfed it down, then felt a wave of disgust. A particle of chocolate stuck to her hand, and she flicked at it with a finger. But instead of removing the sticky fragment, she'd rubbed it into her skin. Repelled, she stared at the dark brown smudge, its warm waxiness.

She threw the candy wrapper into the trash and washed her hands at the sink, dried them roughly on paper towels, then crossed the hall to the rest room. Luckily no one else was there. She entered a stall and threw up. Except for the candy she'd just eaten, her stomach had been almost empty. She flushed away the evidence and leaned against the door. Her forehead was damp with perspiration. She wiped it away with a hand.

When she finally emerged, she went to a sink, one of three in a row. In her purse, she kept a travel toothbrush in a blue plastic case. As she brushed her teeth, she concentrated on the texture of the bristles. She counted the strokes off one by one, an effort to keep from thinking. When she'd finished, she combed her hair and painted her lips pale pink. She looked at the mirror but avoided her eyes, not wanting to see the shame. It had been so long since she'd succumbed to the urge, but the feeling was just the same.

She'd always associated eating disorders with adolescent angst. She herself had passed through the teenage years utterly unscathed. At a time when her peers had grown plump and splotchy, she'd stayed clear-skinned and lean. She'd never thought about her weight, not that she recalled. She'd looked in the mirror and liked what she saw. She was beautiful and strong. It hadn't hurt that she'd been popular. The phone rang off the hook. When she agreed to go out with boys on dates, they'd always seemed so grateful. During those years, she'd never had any doubt that she was the one in control.

What a shock, then, to find herself at thirty, heaving over a toilet. The first time it happened was after she found Frank in bed with Mary Beth. She still didn't know what had prompted it, where the idea had come from. But afterwards she'd felt a sweeping relief, and that had been the beginning. She'd known it wasn't a long-term answer, but this knowledge had stayed abstract, somehow remote from her daily life, while the solace was very real.

She'd been relieved when, after she moved to New York, the urge had sharply abated, assuming that by this time the behavior had served its use. But then, shortly after Paul had proposed, the cycle had started again. During the past few months she'd been better, hadn't purged at all. She'd kept track of the time on her calendar: 108 days. Again, she'd almost convinced herself that the problem had disappeared.

There was a full-length mirror by the rest room door, and she gave herself a quick once-over. She was reassured to see that from the outside she looked just fine. And who was to say that it wasn't real, this image in the mirror? As long as she could still look like this, everything would be okay.

On her way back to the library, she ducked back into the kitchenette, filled a paper cup with water and swallowed two Advil. She was glad that Paul had been distracted, that he hadn't known something was wrong. But beneath the relief was a vague unease that she couldn't quite explain. It wasn't that she'd wanted him to read her mind, just maybe to notice *something.* Frank would have noticed immediately, asked what was bothering her. Before she could push the thought away, she felt it pierce her heart. She put her books on a reshelving cart and decided to call it a night.

Twenty minutes later, she walked into the lobby of her Central Park South apartment. "Good evening, Ms. White," the doorman said. She couldn't remember his name. He was new, had been there less than a month, part of a rotating cast. The building had several hundred units, a staff of more than a dozen. Each year she wrote out more than a thousand dollars in Christmas checks for the staff.

Her apartment was on the fortieth floor, with magnificent views of the park. Two bedrooms, a large living room, a galley kitchen, and bath. While she'd lived here now for more than four years, the rooms were sparsely furnished. A white sofa and armchair. A few good antiques and rugs. She'd come here straight from her marriage, still numb and despairing. She'd wanted someplace impersonal, a temporary refuge. The apartment had been a place she could hide, a place to lick her wounds. While she couldn't seem to forget the past, at least she could shut it out.

Tonight, she went straight for the refrigerator and pulled out a bottle of wine. She uncorked the chilled Chardonnay and poured herself a glass. All it took was one long sip, and she felt an instant buzz.

Already feeling calmer, she drifted into the living room. On an end table next to the couch, her phone message light blinked red. Wine in hand, she sat down and punched the replay button. One call from her father. Another from Vivian.

She found herself recalling Vivian's words about Paul. *You're not in love with Paul.* The words still stung. She knew that tone of voice, the self-confidence behind it. Still, Melanie told herself, even Vivian could be wrong. She didn't love Paul the same way she'd loved Frank, but that didn't mean she didn't love him. If anything, the opposite was true. Her love for Frank hadn't been healthy. With Frank, she'd lost all sense of who she was, a moth drawn to a flame. With Paul, she felt exactly the same as she had before they met.

The wine was making her pleasantly dizzy. She kicked off her shoes and lay down. Her mind floated back to Laura Seton, to the news about Diane. She remembered Diane as she'd last seen her, a beautiful, vibrant woman. It was hard to believe that she was dead, that she didn't exist anymore. But then, death was always hard to comprehend. She thought of Steven Gage. Even though she'd expected his death, it had still seemed unreal.

After a while, she got to her feet and went over to a built-in bookshelf. Beneath the shelves was a row of cabinets. She knelt down and opened one. The book was right where she'd thought. She pulled it out, turned it over. Her eyes went straight to the watch. A classic Cartier Panther. She herself wore a Cartier watch, though a less expensive model. She'd bought the Tank watch with the crocodile strap with part of last year's bonus. The watch had cost about eight thousand dollars; the Panther ran around twelve.

Turning the book back over, she stared at Steven Gage, stared at the handsome, rage-filled face of the man whose life she'd tried to save. Veins pulsed grotesquely in his forehead, his eyes bulged wide. His teeth were bared in a wild grimace more animal than human. You had a sense of some terrible pressure building inside his brain, growing stronger and stronger until the skull couldn't hold it.

She folded open the cover and turned to the title page.

The Vanishing Man: The Secret Life of Serial Sex Killer Steven Gage
By Diane Massey

She flipped ahead. The section she was looking for was somewhere toward the end. It took just a few minutes to find. Standing up, she began to read.

It was a week or so before Dahlia Schuyler's death when Laura noticed the missing pair of panty hose, one of three she'd bought at a drugstore several days before. Two of the pairs were skin-toned. The other pair was black. Laura was sure she'd stashed all three in a drawer in her bedroom bureau. But searching the drawer as she dressed for work, she couldn't find the black pair. All that was left was an empty box. No sign of the stockings. Laura knew that she hadn't opened the box, of that she was positive. She was equally sure that Steven had been the only other person who could have. No one else had visited her apartment since she'd made the trip to the drugstore, which was why she asked him, when he arrived that night, if he'd taken the stockings for some reason.

He'd looked at her without answering, then gone to the kitchen for a drink. Vodka, she thought, with orange juice. That's what he was drinking in those days. She'd followed Steven to the kitchen, asking him again. She'd actually been a little annoyed, which was rare in her dealings with him. She hadn't had another pair of black panty hose and she'd had to change her outfit. Because of that, she'd been late to work. Laura hated being late.

Still, he hadn't answered. He'd downed the drink in a single gulp, then filled the glass again. This time the drink was all alcohol. He didn't add any juice. The whole time, he was watching her, his gaze strangely blank. As he drained the second drink, she'd stepped forward, suddenly worried that he might be ill. After that, she'd forgotten all about the stockings until much, much later. Until after Dahlia Schuyler's death, when, finally, the facts slammed home. At night, she'd lie awake for hours, searching for an explanation. Not just for the stockings, but for all the things she'd struggled so hard to ignore.

The time she'd found a blood-soaked shirt stuffed behind his bed.

The time she'd swept out her fireplace and found pieces of bone.

The time she'd found a bag in his car holding knives, a ski mask, gloves.

The incidents scrambled in her head until she could barely think. Alone at night, she could convince herself that they added up to something. But then day would come, she'd see him, and her doubts would fade again. This was the man whom Laura loved, the man she hoped to marry. Finally, after many false starts, her life was coming together. Steven was working as a paralegal, and soon he'd go to law school. She'd support him while he studied, and then they'd have a family. She imagined their future, a home of their own, beautiful, perfect children. This dream had to be preserved at all costs. Truth was the casualty.

Over the years, she'd struggled valiantly to accept her lover's stories, done her best to accept his incredible tales at face value. The bloody shirt? Steven could explain. He'd used it as a bandage, wrapped it around an injured driver at the scene of a car accident. Never mind that he'd never mentioned this before, was vague about time and location. Laura swallowed the story whole. Or told herself she did. He needed the mask and gloves, he'd claimed, because of his allergies. He'd planned to take the knives to be sharpened. The bones were from fried chicken.

Melanie realized she was shaking her head, slowly, back and forth. It was Laura's failure to come forward that had left Gage free to kill. How many lives might have been saved if Laura had acknowledged the truth. Certainly Dahlia Schuyler's. And maybe many more. *How could you not know?* That had always been her question. Because of this, she'd never fully trusted anything Laura said. In her meetings with Laura, she'd done her best to hide this skepticism. But despite her best efforts, she'd always suspected that Laura sensed her feelings.

Still holding the book, Melanie went to the couch. As she settled into its cushioned depths, she stared out into the night. *Hindsight is always twenty-twenty,* her father used to say. For the first time, she tried to look at events as Laura might have seen them. Laura had needed love. Steven had offered it. *Just like you needed Frank. It's really just the same.* Like Laura, she'd seen what she'd chosen to see, pushed the rest aside.

She thought of how easily she'd accepted Frank's self-serving explanations. So he'd been married twice before. He just hadn't found the right woman. His first wife hadn't had a sense of self. She'd looked to him for that. He'd loved her, he said, he really had, but you couldn't live that way. Next he'd swung to the other extreme, married a hard-core careerist. She hadn't been capable of intimacy. He'd been unbearably lonely. After these seductive confessions, he'd gaze into Melanie's eyes. With her, he'd say, he'd finally found the love he'd always longed for.

In fairness, she'd only been twenty-six, still a work in progress. Frank had been fifty-two, powerful, well connected. He'd gone all out to dazzle her and, predictably, she'd been dazzled. For the first year or so of the marriage, everything had been fine. Immersed in her work on the Gage appeal, she'd barely noticed the shift, that Frank was coming home later and later, making more out-of-town trips. In the ensuing months, he'd left countless clues, but she'd refused to see them. Only when she'd found him with another woman did she finally face the truth.

She closed Diane's book and put it on the coffee table. She still hadn't figured out what to do about Laura's phone call.

Happy Anniversary, Melanie. The words rose up in her mind. Were the notes connected to Diane's murder? Was Laura right about that? If only she hadn't destroyed hers. She'd have liked to study it now. Again, she reminded herself that Laura might be lying. Laura herself could have sent the letter, dropped it off at the firm. As for the watch, if it even existed, Laura could have planted it. She'd certainly offered no proof on the phone that the watch had belonged to Diane.

But why would Laura go to such trouble? Melanie had to think. Was it possible Laura had come to crave her former notoriety? Could she have written the note in an effort to capture attention, viewing Diane's murder as a chance to regain the media spotlight? During the trial, Laura had briefly been a reluctant celebrity, her trial testimony raptly followed by people all over the world. The public's hunger for information had seemed insatiable. What was it like to share your life with a psychopathic killer? Through it all, Laura had refused to give a single interview, insisting that she wanted nothing to do with the media feeding frenzy.

But if Laura had really felt so strongly, why had she talked to Diane? Why had she given the interviews that appeared in *The Vanishing Man*?

Mulling this over, Melanie stood and headed for the kitchen. She shouldn't be drinking on an empty stomach, but she still didn't feel like eating. She poured herself another glass from the cold, beaded bottle, admiring the golden glow as it cascaded into the crystal. Paul, something of a connoisseur, disparaged her fondness for white wine. The reds, he said, were more complex. Melanie didn't care. She had no interest in complexity, in her life or in her wine.

On the way back to the living room, Melanie tripped on a rug. She held the glass aloft, managing not to spill. Funny, she didn't feel the least bit drunk, but at this point, she must be. Still, her mind seemed clear as glass, her thoughts unencumbered. If anything, the alcohol was helping her, clarifying her logic.

That's what alcoholics think. You really need to be careful.

But that was one problem she didn't have. She rarely drank at all. She didn't like the out-of-control sensation that alcohol usually gave her. Laura had been an alcoholic, though she'd stopped drinking by the time they met. Perhaps that was part of the reason she'd always seemed so raw. As if her skin were literally thinner than that of a normal person.

Melanie took a long sip of wine. Something was bothering her. The scenario she'd come up with. What was wrong with it? As she sank down on the couch again, she realized what it was. The time frame, that was the problem. The chronology didn't work.

According to the *Times*, Diane's body hadn't been found until Tuesday. It would have taken another day at least for the news to hit the papers. Yet the letter had arrived at her office almost two weeks before then. It was dated April 5, and she'd received it the following day. Again, that was almost two weeks before Laura could have known.

Unless, that is, Laura herself had been involved in the murder.

Laura Seton a murderess? Now that was really a stretch. Laura had been unstable, but she'd never shown signs of violence.

Laura was the classic female depressive, all anger turned fiercely inward. At least, that's how she'd been before, at the time Melanie had known her. In the intervening years, could she have changed so much? Then Melanie thought of the voice on the phone, so surprisingly strong. If Laura's voice could change so dramatically, might her temperament have changed as well? There was still the question of motive, though. That took another few seconds.

She thinks that Diane's book ruined her life. She did it for revenge.

Disconcerted by the thought, Melanie put down her wine glass. Laura had been angry about the book, Melanie remembered that now. She seemed to think that Diane had broken some sort of unspoken agreement. The reaction was hardly surprising in light of how she'd come off. But if Laura had killed Diane for revenge, then why call Melanie? Why take a step that could only increase the risk that she'd be caught?

Even that, though, Melanie decided, could be explained in terms of psychology. Killers often volunteered to help solve their victims' murders. Often, they stayed bizarrely close to the scene of the crimes they'd committed. That was the reason that investigators photographed crowds at crime scenes. Amazingly often the killer was there, lurking on the sidelines. Perhaps Laura's call was something like that, a variation on a theme.

Laura. Laura's call. With a start, Melanie realized that she'd accepted this too without question. But how could she know that the woman who'd called was really Laura Seton? Laura's voice had been breathy, her sentences full of false starts. Again, she thought of the caller's voice, the core of confidence. She'd noted the difference right away but hadn't made the logical leap. Perhaps the caller hadn't sounded like Laura because she was someone else.

Tucking her legs beneath her, Melanie finished her wine. But the warm glow she'd felt earlier continued to dissipate. The phone rang. Melanie's body tightened. She let the machine pick up.

"Hi, sweetie. You there? Hello?" Paul's disembodied voice echoed through the room. "Guess you must have gone to bed early. Talk tomorrow. Love you."

Love you.

The words drifted in the empty air. Briefly here, then gone.

But do I love you? Do I love you?

The words danced in her mind.

When she'd heard the phone, she'd instantly assumed that it must be Laura. Laura or whoever the woman was who'd called her at work today. Her number was listed, after all, easily available. The fact that the caller hadn't tried her at home was slightly reassuring. Or maybe she just had the sense to know that Melanie wouldn't pick up.

Melanie lay back on the cushions, staring up at the ceiling. The fog from the wine had come over her slowly but now it was thickening. She felt as if she'd been here for hours, but she'd yet to find her answer. She kept coming back to the fact that she needed more information. She'd thought about going to the police herself, reporting the note she'd gotten. But like Laura — or the woman who claimed to be Laura — she too wanted this kept quiet.

She had no intention of becoming fuel for some lurid tabloid story, especially not with partnership elections coming up next month. Harwich & Young was an old-school firm, circumspect in the extreme. A whiff of scandal might tip the balance. She wouldn't let that happen. Her career had already been derailed once because of Steven Gage. She'd been lucky to get a second chance. She couldn't screw it up.

You need to talk to her again. You need to see her in person.

At first the thought surprised her, but it made a sort of sense. By insisting on a face-to-face meeting, she'd force her caller's hand. If it turned out that the caller wasn't Laura, she might simply disappear. And if the woman *was* Laura? What would happen then? Melanie tried to think it through, to weigh the pros and cons. Would a face-to-face meeting further complicate an already messy situation? Of course it was a possibility, but she didn't have much choice. At least this time she'd be prepared. She'd have to take the risk.

Sunday, April 23

IT was a three-hour drive from Merritt to Manhattan, less if you drove fast. Callie had planned to leave earlier, but she'd lingered over breakfast with Anna. They'd made blueberry pancakes and fresh-squeezed orange juice. By the time she dropped off Anna at the Creightons', it was after nine o'clock.

Driving down I-91, she thought over what she planned to say. She'd been surprised by Melanie's proposal that they meet face-to-face. On the phone, she'd been pretty sure that Melanie didn't quite trust her. She had to remember that the last time they'd met she'd been a total mess. Melanie had no way of knowing how much she'd changed since then. Today, she'd stick to the facts. That was the best approach. She'd brought the note and watch, as Melanie asked. Concrete evidence.

As she approached Manhattan, traffic became a tangled, frantic snarl. Cars and trucks dodged in and out of lanes, barely avoiding collisions. A yellow cab cut in front of her, almost clipping her fender. The driver gave her a murderous look. She clutched the steering wheel. Ahead, the city skyline loomed, jagged and imposing.

They'd arranged to meet at the Lowell Hotel, Melanie's suggestion. By the time Callie had parked her car, she was almost half an hour late. If she'd had Melanie's cell phone number, she could have tried to call her. Instead, she took off down the street, hoping Melanie had waited. She made her way across Park Avenue, with its rows of blank-face buildings, past the Met Life tower, past a red-brick church.

When she reached the hotel, she rushed past the doorman, down a short flight of stairs. Breathless, she almost collided with a thin, tall blonde.

For a moment, the two of them stared at each other.

The woman was Melanie.

A strange look played on Melanie's face — surprise, regret, confusion. Then she quickly regained her composure and held out a manicured hand. "Hello, Laura," she said.

Callie's body tightened. It was one thing to hear the name on the phone, another to hear it in person. Laura Seton was a figment. She lived only in memory.

Callie forced a smile. "Please call me Callie," she said. "I'm so sorry to be late. Thanks so much for waiting."

"I figured you must have gotten lost. I hope you could follow my directions."

"The directions were perfect," Callie said. She was feeling a little dizzy.

A brief uncertain pause. Then Melanie was briskly steering her toward an elevator. "We'll have tea upstairs in the Pembroke Room," she said. "Or lunch. Whatever you want."

They stepped out on the second floor.

Classical music played in the background as they took seats at a small round table. The room was an elegant oasis; the city seemed miles away. There were lace curtains, swooping draperies, soft carpets muffling footsteps. The china was white with blue-and-gold trim. There was a candle on the table.

"It's been a long time," said Melanie, as she picked up her napkin and placed it on her lap. "You look wonderful."

"Thank you," said Callie. Then, falsely, "You too."

In fact, Melanie did not look good. For one thing, she was far too thin. Her black knit sweater clung to her ribs as if it were a second skin. The impression was one of angles and edges, something tightly wound. But most of all, it was Melanie's eyes where Callie saw the change. Still the same remarkable blue, they seemed somehow colder. *Extinguished* was the word that came to mind, as if a light had gone out. The gleaming hair that once fell to her shoulders now skimmed her jaw. It, too, seemed subtly cooler. Moonlight rather than sun.

Behind their table, Callie glimpsed an enormous display of lilies. Their scent floated through the room, gently perfuming the air. But despite the tranquil atmosphere, Callie was on edge. There were a dozen or so tables, two others occupied. In one corner sat a sedate threesome, consuming tea and scones. A larger table was occupied by a laughing group of young women. More people than Callie had expected, certainly more than she'd have liked. She found herself questioning Melanie's judgment, wondering why they had come here. This was hardly the setting she'd have picked for a private conversation.

Callie opened her menu.

Melanie did the same.

"It's on me," Melanie said quickly, as Callie scanned the prices.

When the waiter arrived, Melanie ordered the full afternoon tea. Uncertain and not terribly hungry, Callie followed suit.

The waiter left and Callie saw that Melanie was watching her.

"I don't mean to stare," said Melanie, when Callie's eyes caught hers. "It's just that you seem so . . . different."

Callie gave a faint smile. "I am different," she said. "I'm a totally different person."

"So you're living in Massachusetts?"

"Merritt. The western part of the state."

"The Berkshires?"

"Not too far from there. Closer to Amherst and Northampton."

"There's a college there, isn't there?"

"Windham," Callie said. "I finished my degree there — my bachelor's. Now I work in the alumni office and take a few classes on the side."

"I was up that way a few years ago. Lovely part of New England."

Pleasant but utterly impersonal, the conversation drifted on. Callie had the sense that they were marking time. Was Melanie waiting for something?

The waiter arrived with plates holding rows of triangular tea sandwiches. Beside these edible pyramids lay a single flower.

As she waited for her tea to cool, Callie ate a sandwich. Her appetite suddenly returned, and she found she was ravenous. She finished a salmon sandwich and picked up a cucumber one.

"So you moved to New York from Washington?" Callie said between bites.

"That's right," Melanie said. "I've been here going on five years. I love living in the city."

"And your husband?" Callie asked. "How does he like it here?"

Melanie's features seemed to freeze. "I'm not married," she said.

"I'm sorry," Callie said. "I thought —"

"I was married, but I'm not anymore."

Something in Melanie's tone warned Callie to back off. "These sandwiches are delicious," she said, returning to neutral terrain.

Melanie was on her second cup of tea, but she hadn't eaten a thing. Now she pushed her plate away, with a look of vague distaste.

"I had a late breakfast," she said. "I'm really not very hungry."

Callie had finished her own sandwiches and looked at Melanie's. "Do you mind if I —"

Melanie waved a hand. "Please. Be my guest."

The waiter brought strawberries. Callie continued to eat. Over Melanie's shoulder, she watched the festive group of young women. Peals of laughter floated over from their large round table. A bridal shower maybe. Or a sorority reunion. Whatever their reason for being here, it was nothing like her own.

Callie spooned up clotted cream and dropped it on her berries. She looked expectantly at Melanie, wondering what came next.

As if reading her mind, Melanie leaned forward.

"I wasn't sure that it would be you." She spoke very softly.

For the first time, Callie noticed the traces of a southern accent. She looked at Melanie, baffled. "What?"

"When you called me, you sounded so different. I thought it might not be you, that it might be some sort of trick. That's why

I wanted to meet like this. I thought maybe you wouldn't show up. Or if you did, you'd be someone else."

"Well . . ." Callie had no idea what to say. The admission astonished her. She'd certainly sensed Melanie's wariness but never grasped its extent. If Melanie had questioned her identity, what other doubts might she have?

"What about the letter, the watch? Do you believe what I told you?"

Melanie bit her lip. She seemed to be thinking something through, then came to a fast decision. "We should talk about this privately," she said. "My apartment is just a few blocks away. We'd be more comfortable there."

Callie quickly agreed. Melanie tossed out a platinum credit card. Soon they were on the street. Neither of them spoke during the short cab ride to the building where Melanie lived.

The elevator glided the forty floors up to Melanie's apartment.

"This is beautiful," Callie said. She'd just stepped through Melanie's door and caught sight of the sweeping views. "You can see the whole city from here."

"The East Side. The park." Melanie flipped on a light. "Here. Have a seat."

Callie sank into the couch and looked around curiously. White walls, white sofa, white armchair. *Melanie White, in her home of white*. It was like a fairy tale. Was it intentional? An affectation? Or did she just like white?

Except for a few framed photographs, the room seemed impersonal. As reluctant as Melanie herself to disclose any information.

"May I get you anything? Coffee? Seltzer?"

"No," said Callie. "I'm fine."

Melanie sat down across from Callie in the overstuffed white chair. The chair's massive size underscored her fragility. For the first time, it occurred to Callie that Melanie might be sick. She wondered about Melanie's marriage, when it had broken up.

"Before we start talking," said Melanie, "I have to clarify something. I can't give you legal advice. I can't act as your lawyer. I'm meeting with you now as . . . as a friend, I guess. I want to be clear on that from the start. I need to be sure you understand that."

Melanie seemed suddenly uncomfortable, but Callie wasn't sure why. "That's right," she said. "That's what I assumed. I mean, I'm not paying you."

Melanie visibly relaxed at the words, which made Callie uneasy. She had a sense of missing something and wanted to ask what it was. But before she could frame a question, Melanie was speaking.

"Did you bring the watch?"

"Yes. The watch and the letter both."

"Could I take a look at them?"

"Sure." Callie reached into her purse.

The watch was in a small cardboard box. Melanie took off the lid. "I probably shouldn't touch it," she said. "Even though it's been handled since your daughter found it, there still might be latent prints."

Fingerprints. Callie started. Why hadn't she thought of that? But as soon as the question flashed through her mind, she instantly knew why. Steven had never left fingerprints. Never. Not one time.

Melanie examined the watch, then replaced the lid. She carefully set the little box on a table beside her chair. "The letter?" she said, looking up at Callie.

Callie held it out.

Melanie hesitated. "Wait a minute," she said. She got up and went to a hallway closet, returning with a pair of black leather gloves.

"Not exactly standard issue, but I guess they're better than nothing."

After pulling on the gloves, she took hold of the envelope and removed the letter. Black pants, black sweater, and now black gloves. All that white around her, and everything she wore was black.

Even with the gloves on, Melanie held the paper gingerly, taking hold of it at the edge between a thumb and forefinger. Her head was bowed as she examined it, and Callie couldn't see her face.

When she finally looked up, her expression was troubled. "Do you have any idea who might have written this?"

Callie dropped her eyes. "Not really. I mean, I don't have any evidence."

"But you have some idea?"

"It's probably stupid, but right away I thought of Lester Crain."

"Lester Crain?" Melanie stared.

"The day Steven was sentenced, he said that all of us were going to pay. He looked around the room at us, and you could just feel the hatred. Everyone just wrote it off as some sort of crazed reaction. But I . . . I knew him very well. He meant what he was saying. And then, well, he couldn't get revenge himself. He'd have to have arranged it with someone, someone who owed him a favor. Steven helped Crain to get a new trial. Crain said he'd find a way to thank him."

Melanie put a hand to her forehead. "I . . . this is hard to believe."

"I'm not saying it's true," said Callie. "It's just what I've been thinking."

"I think you should go to the police."

Already, Callie was shaking her head. "No," she said. "I can't."

"Why not?" Melanie asked.

There was something in her tone, a deference, that put Callie on the defensive. She had an impression that Melanie was trying to manipulate her.

"You have to do something," Melanie continued, when Callie didn't answer. "You can't just ignore what's happened. The police need to investigate, to get to the bottom of this. If there's a link between Diane's death and these items, they'll be able to figure it out. And if not, if it's something else, they can look into that too."

Callie nodded slowly but didn't say anything.

"It might not be Diane's watch." Melanie's voice was soothing. "It's just an ordinary Cartier watch, the same brand that I have."

She extended her wrist so Callie could see the gold Tank with its black strap. But all Callie could think was, *They're not at all the same*.

"They're totally different watches," she said, stating the obvious point.

"But the same brand," Melanie said. "The same manufacturer."

"So what?" Callie said. She felt a little dazed. "The watch Anna found is exactly the same. Like the one in Diane's picture."

Leaning forward in her chair, Melanie clasped her hands. "Look, you asked me if I believed you. I'm not sure why, but I do. But you've put me in a difficult position. When you called me, you caught me by surprise. It wasn't until you'd finished talking that you mentioned the attorney-client privilege. It hadn't occurred to me. The thing is, something like this — I can't just keep it to myself. It would be unethical. There's an ongoing murder investigation. What you told me could be relevant. You could be in danger yourself. You have no idea who's behind this. You don't know what they'll do next."

"I know that," Callie said sharply. "You think I haven't thought of that?"

A long, tense silence.

Thoughts swirled through Callie's mind. She now understood why Melanie had been so careful to establish the context of their conversation. Not lawyer-client. *Friends*. Of course there'd been a reason. It had to do with the privilege. There must be limits on it. If Melanie wasn't officially her lawyer, perhaps the privilege didn't apply. That possibility seemed so obvious now, though it hadn't occurred to her before. But she'd trusted Melanie to keep this confidential. Didn't that mean a thing?

"I'm sorry," Callie said. "I didn't mean to get upset."

"It's an upsetting situation."

"Yes," said Callie. "It is." She fought to keep her voice steady. "But what I do about it — if anything — that should be my decision. That's why I called you instead of someone else. I thought that because you were a lawyer, you'd have to respect my confidences."

"I understand that," Melanie said. "But even where the privilege applies, it isn't absolute. For example, if you told me you were going to commit a crime —"

Callie jumped to her feet. "But it isn't like that," she said. "It's not the same thing at all."

"No," said Melanie. "You're right. Still, it's not the sort of thing I can ethically keep to myself. At the very least, I need to talk to one of my law firm's partners. I work for them. They need to know about this. The conversation we've had today — there isn't a privilege issue. Before we started talking, we both agreed that I'm not acting as your lawyer. When we talked on the phone before — to be honest, that's a bit unclear. But even if a conversation is privileged, I could still talk to lawyers I work with. Any privilege that exists would extend to members of the firm."

"Oh," said Callie. She bit her lip. She hadn't realized that. "Would they tell anyone? The police, I mean?"

"That would depend," Melanie said. "I couldn't say for sure."

"You haven't told anyone yet?"

A pause.

"No," said Melanie. "I haven't."

A brief moment of relief. At least she still had a chance. But the situation was spiraling out of control, and Callie was at a loss. All she knew was that she had to do something to stop Melanie from talking.

"I called you because I trusted you." Before she thought it through, the words were out. While she wasn't even sure they were true, they had the desired effect. Melanie seemed to hesitate, and Callie pressed her advantage.

"If you don't want to get involved, fine. I can understand that. But I don't want anyone else to know. This is my problem. I can handle it."

"Actually," Melanie said, "I'm not sure that you can. It's not just about you, you know. Other people could be in danger."

Startled, Callie stared at her. "What do you mean?" she asked.

"Just that . . . Diane's killer is still out there." Melanie didn't meet Callie's eyes. She seemed suddenly uncomfortable.

"There's something else," Callie said. "Something you're not telling me."

A shadow passed over Melanie's face, and Callie knew she was right. But just a fraction of a second later, her features settled back in place. When Melanie spoke, she seemed remote, her face a smooth mask.

"What more would there have to be? Diane was murdered shortly after you received a threatening letter. The letter was sent on the anniversary of Steven Gage's execution. Diane wrote about Steven. A few days after the murder, someone sent you her watch. It doesn't take much to connect the dots. This isn't good, Laur — Callie."

"It said 'Happy Anniversary.' That's not exactly a threat."

Melanie looked at her, shaking her head. She didn't argue the point.

Callie tried again. "And like you said, it might not be her watch. Maybe I'm totally wrong."

"You might be," Melanie said. "Then again, you might be right."

Abruptly, Callie stood up. She walked over to the wall of windows and looked out on the city. She was surprised to find it was still light outside. It seemed like she'd been here days. Her eyes drifted over to the photographs on the bookshelf to her right. Melanie in cap and gown, standing with an older man. A pretty African-American girl in front of the Eiffel Tower. Several rows of smiling men and women gathered on a college campus. Looking at the small collection, Callie thought about what was missing. No sign of the former husband. No sign of Steven Gage. This is how you created a past, plucking out bits and pieces. You put on display the parts you chose, banished all the rest. And then if you were very, very lucky, you managed to forget.

From behind her, Callie heard Melanie's voice. "I have an idea," she said.

"Okay," Callie said cautiously. She folded her arms and waited.

"Do you remember Mike Jamison?"

"The name sounds familiar."

"He was with the FBI. The Investigative Support Unit."

"The profiler." She remembered now. "He did all those interviews with Steven. Right before —"

"Yes."

All these years later, they both still avoided the words. *Right before the execution.* Right before his death. Right before the state of Tennessee stuck a needle in him.

"So what about him?" Callie asked.

"It's just an idea," said Melanie. "I haven't spoken to him for years. The last I heard he'd retired from the Bureau and joined a corporate security firm. He's a good person. I got to know him pretty well during the appeal, and I . . . I always liked him."

Melanie seemed oddly self-conscious, a flush rising in her cheeks. The sudden shot of color threw her pallor into relief.

Quickly, she went on.

"I was thinking that I could give him a call. He's very well connected in the law-enforcement world. He'd have access to a lot more information than either of us has. He could have the watch and letter checked for fingerprints. He could also probably find out if the watch really belonged to Diane."

Callie sensed her heart beating faster. "And if it did belong to her?"

"If it did . . . I don't know. But let's not jump ahead."

"And you wouldn't tell him who I am, where you got the watch?"

Melanie hesitated. "I wouldn't have to at first," she said. "Not unless the watch could be traced to Diane, and then . . . I'd have to talk to someone at that point. I don't see any way around it. Even now, it seems problematic to be keeping this to myself."

Putting herself in Melanie's place, Callie understood. But if Melanie wasn't barred from talking, why was she cooperating?

"So why are you?" Callie said, suspicion creeping into her voice.

Melanie flushed again, this time more deeply. "When we first spoke, you believed you were speaking to me in confidence. I'd like to respect that if I can."

"I see." Once again, Callie had the sense that Melanie was hiding something, that she had some secret agenda she hadn't yet revealed. She'd have liked to know what this agenda was before reaching a decision. But she could tell from Melanie's closed expression that she wasn't going to discuss it.

"And if I don't agree?" asked Callie. "Then what will you do?"

Melanie's response was immediate, her voice clipped and assured. "Then I'll speak to some partners at my firm. We have an Ethics Committee."

The sun had slowly started to shift, dappling the room with shadows. Callie looked at her own Swatch watch. The time was 3:35. She needed to be on the road within the next hour or so. Rick was out of town again, visiting his parents. When she'd dropped Anna off at the Creightons', she'd promised to pick her up before dinner.

Callie turned and faced Melanie, squarely meeting her eyes.

"So I don't really have a choice," she said.

"I'm afraid that's pretty much right."

⤜⤚

THE paintings were god-awful. Sickly pastels on cheap cardboard, the worst sort of tourist crap. Sunsets over the Hudson River. The Empire State Building. Two fat children with lurid smiles skating in Central Park. As luck would have it, he'd positioned himself in front of one of the worst. But this was where he needed to stand to get a clear view of her door.

"You like that one? I can make you a deal." The painter — you couldn't call him an artist — was fat with a bright red face. He had dirty fingernails and bloodshot eyes. He smelled of gin and tobacco.

"I'll have to think about it." He flashed a smile at the painter, then quickly turned away. Careful as he'd been with his disguise, there was no need to tempt fate. He was pretty sure the painter was alcoholic, hardly a credible witness. Still, it was always possible that the man would remember him. Regretfully, he decided not to return to this spot. He'd have to find another place from which to observe her building. Luckily it was cold today, hovering around forty. No one would think it strange that he wore a heavy coat, gloves, and hat.

He decided to cross the street, move in for a closer view.

But just as he stepped down off the curb, he saw her coming toward him. For an instant he froze, unable to move, an animal caught in headlights. His brain seemed to float. He couldn't breathe. *How could she be here?*

A wild confusion rolled over him as he dove back into the crowd. It was like some strange, impossible dream with everything out of place. This was Melanie's apartment building. Manhattan. Central Park South. For a brief hopeful moment, he thought he must be mistaken. He'd seen someone who resembled Laura, not Laura herself. The optimism lasted another few seconds, until he looked again.

As she stood on the corner hailing a cab, there was no mistaking her. She wore that same look of lost confusion he'd seen when she was alone. Of course, she wasn't alone right now; crowds surged around her. But despite the throngs of passersby, he felt her isolation. The marked unhappiness on her face provoked a stab of joy. She *should* be unhappy. She *should* be alone. This is what she deserved. Still, his pleasure in her suffering was dampened by a growing fear. What was she doing at Melanie's? How had she come to be here?

A yellow cab screeched to a stop. Laura climbed inside. An instant later the cab wheeled right, and then she was out of sight. He stared after her for another few moments, then walked up Fifth Avenue. His legs wobbled beneath him. His heart rolled in his chest. Around him, everything was swirling. His mind was a sea of questions.

Turning into Central Park, he walked aimlessly. He ambled past a set of swings, a zoo, a shallow pool. Everywhere, people smiled. He wished that they were dead. A woman with a small white dog gave him a pleasant nod. The smile faded from her red lips as he stared at her stonily. Over and over the same question screamed in his brain. *How had Laura come to be in Melanie's apartment?*

He walked and walked, thinking hard, trying to sort it out. Trying to adjust his plans in light of this development. So Laura and Melanie had found each other. That much was obvious. He was pretty sure that Laura's visit was linked to the letters and watch. But how much did they know? What had they figured out?

For a moment, he had the disturbing thought that he'd underestimated them. He'd known both women were smart, of course, but he'd never expected this. The thought of them together, talking, filled him with a burning rage. They had no business meeting. This wasn't what he'd planned. Well, at least he knew what was going on. For that much, he was grateful. At least he'd discovered the connection. An amazing stroke of luck. He savored this last thought for a time, relishing their ignorance. Gradually, like a shift in the wind, his confidence flowed back.

He made his way down a sheltered path beneath a canopy of leaves. As he breathed in the scent of fresh, damp earth, his thoughts moved to Diane. Ironic how this springtime smell would always make him think of death, would always remind him of how he'd left her, sprawled and still and white.

Again he thought of Melanie and Laura, their private assignation. Perhaps his presence here today wasn't a coincidence. *Write with blood: and you will discover that blood is spirit.* What he'd seen today, he told himself, was a timely call to action.

⁓

It was almost eight o'clock, and the dining room was abuzz. Clarence was the hot new downtown restaurant. You came to see and be seen. This is what Melanie told herself as she dutifully scanned the menu. Still, with each passing minute, her irritation mounted. The list of entrées was ridiculous, each dish more preposterous than the last. Beef cheeks glacé? *You've got to be kidding.* Salmon profiteroles?

Across the blue-lacquered table, Paul put on reading glasses.

Brow furrowed, he studied the menu as if it were a client's prospectus. He looked so humorless sitting there, she had to needle him.

"Think they'd make me a burger?"

Paul looked at her, annoyed.

"Geez. I'm just joking." Then she felt a little bad. Paul had been excited about tonight. He loved checking out new restaurants.

A waiter banged into the back of her chair. Melanie gritted her teeth. With resolve, she turned to the menu again, but nothing appealed to her. She found herself thinking of the pork barbecue she'd loved as a kid in Nashville. Not the fern-bar version but real soul food. It was a taste she'd shared with her father, much to her mother's chagrin. Their maid, Ruby, used to sneak in cartons from a place near her home in North Nashville.

Again, she read through the offerings. Duck confit? Baby lamb chops?

She closed the menu and pushed it aside. "You pick for me," she said.

Paul looked up, clearly pleased. "Are you sure?" he asked.

"Of course. Why not?" she said.

And after all, it was true.

For the past two weeks, she'd barely eaten, just yogurt, carrots, and juice. She'd tried to force down some oatmeal this morning but choked after two mouthfuls.

Paul was talking to the waiter now, ordering food and wine. His light brown hair was thinning. In five or ten years he'd be bald.

"You're sure that's okay?" he asked her.

"Absolutely," she said.

A waiter walked by carrying plates stacked high with elaborate turrets of food. She caught a whiff of exotic scents, anise and maybe mint. Paul picked up a crisp bread stick and swiped it through a bowl of dip. There was something subtly annoying in the sound he made as he chewed.

He patted his mouth with a napkin. "So how was your day?" he asked.

Melanie sipped her water. "Fine," she said. "Yours?"

That was all it took. He launched into a report. How he'd spent an hour on the StairMaster before going in to work. How pleased Jason Fisk — a powerful partner — had been with the brief he'd drafted. She grimly wondered how long it would be before he noticed her silence. Then, abashed, she told herself that she wasn't being fair. If she wouldn't talk, she couldn't blame Paul for taking up the slack.

Still, the more he went on, the more he wore on her nerves.

Food arrived at the table. Paul continued to talk. She found herself thinking of Mike Jamison, wondering how he'd changed. She hadn't seen him in almost five years, since Gage's execution. Where Paul's smile was quicksilver bright, Jamison's had an edge. She remembered the first time she'd seen that smile, how something in her had responded. It seemed to have layers of meaning: amusement, irony, sadness.

She'd called Jamison earlier tonight, left a message on his office voice mail. Luckily she had the name of the firm where he'd gone to work. She'd received the announcement when he left the FBI and had taken down the information. When she flipped through her office Rolodex, there was his name and address.

"So how is it?" Paul's voice pulled her back to the present, to the table filled with food.

"Fabulous," she said. "It's great."

"You've hardly eaten a thing."

Melanie looked down at her plate. There were layers of yellow, green, and orange over something white. What was it that Paul had ordered for her? It looked like some sort of fish. She saw that she'd been cutting off pieces, arranging them in rows.

She forced herself to take a bite, then pushed her plate toward Paul. "I guess I'm just not hungry," she said. "Why don't you have mine?"

"Fine," Paul said shortly. She could tell that he was angry.

They didn't say much for the rest of the meal. They didn't order dessert. It was a relief when Paul put down his espresso and asked to be brought the check.

Outside the restaurant, the night was brisk. It took some time to get a cab. They waited silently, hands raised, as if they were almost strangers. Paul gave her a cool kiss as he put her into the taxi. He didn't ask to come home with her, one thing she was grateful for.

The first thing she saw when she got home was the flashing red light on her phone. Without waiting to remove her coat, she quickly crossed the floor.

She'd forgotten how deep his voice was, strong and self-assured. Just the sound of the recorded words swept her back in time, back to those desperate weeks in Tennessee before the execution. He'd been so absorbed in his work, that's what she remembered most. It was hard to imagine him in private business, retired from the FBI.

"Melanie. God, it's good to hear from you." He sounded as if he meant it. "Listen, if you get in tonight, give me a call at home. Don't worry about the time. I'm up late." He left a 703 number. *Virginia*, she thought.

It was a little before nine. Slowly, Melanie walked to a closet and hung up her coat. She hadn't expected him to call so soon. For reasons she didn't quite understand, the message unsettled her. There'd been a bond, an understanding, between them, at least that's how she had felt. At some level hard to articulate, Mike Jamison had been important. He'd liked her. He'd believed in her. Perhaps it was that simple. If she talked to him, she risked finding out that what they'd shared was gone. Perhaps because she'd lost so much, she clung to what was left.

Jamison had arrived in Nashville just weeks before the execution. At the time, he was a star profiler in the FBI's Investigative Support Unit, lead author of a landmark study on sexual predators. It was Gage who'd requested Jamison's presence after reading some of his work. He'd written Jamison a flattering letter, asking to meet with him. The tone of the letter had been collegial, one expert speaking to another. Gage had dangled the tempting possibility that he might finally open up, disclose the locations of dozens of victims whose remains had never been found. By this point, Gage had been grasping at straws, aware time was running out. The offer had been an obvious ploy to defer his execution.

Gage's courting of Jamison had horrified his lawyers. She recalled the disbelief on Fred Irving's face when Gage announced his plans. Jamison, of course, hadn't cared what Gage's motives were. The chance of interviewing Steven Gage was something he couldn't pass up. Once it was clear that they couldn't stop Gage, his lawyers had gone along. Irving had tapped Melanie to talk to the profiler. At the time, she'd taken this assignment as proof of the partners' trust. Only later did she realize that they'd simply given up.

In retrospect, it was hard to see how the interviews made any difference. Melanie even thought that Steven had shown a level of shrewdness. As the nation's most prolific serial killer, Gage had had a certain power. He'd known how tantalized Jamison would be by the prospect of meeting with him. It hadn't been illogical for Gage to seek Jamison's help, to think that the profiler might do what he could to preserve his specimen.

Her first talk with Jamison took place over coffee at a Waffle House near the prison. It was late at night, and, except for them, the restaurant was nearly empty. For obvious reasons, there'd been strict limits on what she was able to say. As Gage's lawyer she couldn't discuss the obvious facts of his guilt. At the same time, nothing had prevented her from listening to Jamison. They'd sat there for several hours in the stiffness of the booth, drinking cups of oil-black coffee under harsh fluorescent light. She'd made her case for sparing Gage's life, then listened as Jamison talked.

Jamison had the easygoing manner of an aging college athlete. There was something about him that inspired trust. You wanted to confide in him. Was it something he'd learned, she'd wondered, or something he'd always had? But the thing that had impressed her most was his passion for his work. She'd certainly known driven men and women before. Her husband. Her classmates and colleagues. But in Jamison she'd sensed a purity entirely new to her. He wasn't driven by money or power but by the need to know.

They'd talked about the insanity defense and whether Steven might have used it. By this time, of course, the point was moot, even if he'd reconsidered. Jamison had said Gage wasn't insane, at least not legally. But she'd heard the irony in his voice and pounced on the distinction.

"You don't think he's really sane," she'd charged.

Jamison had shrugged. "He knew what he was doing, and he knew that it was wrong. That's your basic legal definition. No question he's well within it. But sane in any meaningful way? Not to my mind, no. A lot's been made of the fact that Gage was able to control his impulses. When he was in danger of being caught, he kept a low profile. After Dahlia Schuyler was killed, there were no more Tennessee murders. He managed to restrain himself until leaving the jurisdiction."

"So what then? What are you saying?"

"What I'm saying is, so what? C'mon, Ms. White. You're a smart woman. What's wrong with this picture?"

"I'm his lawyer, Mr. Jamison. I can't answer that." Even to herself, she sounded priggish, but it was something that had to be said.

"Okay, then. So let's speak *hypothetically*." Again, the ironic tone. "A guy manages to restrain himself from this — if not un-controllable, let's say *compelling* — need to murder women, to have sex with their corpses and then dismember them. You hear about a guy like this. Based on your personal definition, would you consider him sane?"

"No."

"What I'm saying is that the legal definition isn't all that use-ful. At least not from a psychological perspective, which is where my interests lie. When we ask if someone is able to *control* an im-pulse to kill other human beings, to my mind we've skipped right over the most interesting questions. For normal people, these urges don't exist. We don't have to control them. You and me — most people — we have no idea what it's like to have this drive to kill. This sort of killer is profoundly different from the rest of us. To say that he could have *controlled* the impulse — it's sort of ludicrous. A way to reassure ourselves that the world is comprehensible. We say, 'He's not insane, he's evil. He chose to do what he did.' But the sort of choice we're talking about isn't the kind we make. It's the choice to resist an impulse that no normal person feels. Ultimately, I think we'll find the explanation in some sort of neural wiring. There's all sorts of research going on pointing in that direction."

Melanie still remembered that talk as if it were yesterday. It had been the first of several they'd had during that strange and terrible time, as the weeks and days ticked away toward the execution date.

Then, suddenly, it was over, and Steven Gage was dead. She woke up to find the cause that had obsessed her had vanished into thin air. While she'd known it would happen, tried to prepare, she couldn't take it in. The first day, she felt utterly numb, bereft of all emotion. She packed up the files, her clothing, as if she were a machine. Not until she talked to Jamison did she finally burst into tears. It was Jamison who'd spent that night with her, talking and drinking whiskey.

The next day, she'd flown back to D.C. and found Frank with Mary Beth.

If not for the collapse of her marriage, she'd have kept in touch with Jamison. But at the time, she'd needed all her energies simply to survive. Until then, her life had gone according to plan. She'd had a sense of control. Then, in quick succession, came three devastating blows. Gage's execution. Her husband's betrayal. The derailment of her career.

"I hope you understand," Fred Irving had said, his bald head shining in the light. Behind his massive desk, he'd actually seemed a little nervous. "It's nothing personal. You did a splendid job on the Gage case, but your skills are limited."

She'd wanted to scream, "And whose fault is that?" Instead, she'd sat there, nodding. Already, she was thinking ahead. She'd need his recommendation.

Then came the divorce, the move to New York, the years at Harwich & Young, where, thanks to her friendship with Vivian, she'd managed to find a job. While she'd never forgotten Mike Jamison, they'd long ago lost touch.

Melanie picked up the phone and dialed. He answered on the second ring.

He didn't say hello, just repeated her name. Something in his tone, a depth of feeling, filled her with a sudden warmth.

"How *are* you?" he asked.

"I'm . . . *fine*," she said. And then, "Not really. Actually, I have a problem."

"I figured as much," he said. "What can I do to help?"

He was acting as if no time at all had passed, which was strange but comforting.

"I . . . I need to talk to you. In confidence."

"Of course." He didn't hesitate.

It was easy, far easier than she'd expected. She told him everything. Without identifying Laura — Callie — she ticked off the relevant facts. How this woman she knew had received a letter on the anniversary of Gage's death. How weeks later, a Cartier watch had been found by the woman's daughter, left in a plastic Easter egg at a neighborhood Easter egg hunt. He already knew about Diane Massey's death, had followed it in the papers. So when she told him that the watch resembled Diane's, she didn't have to explain.

"You think it's the same watch," he said. A statement, not a question.

She tried to hedge a bit. "Of course, I really don't know. But the whole thing is troubling. It's a lot to ask, but I was hoping . . . hoping that you could help. That maybe you'd have some way of finding out if Diane's watch was missing after her death."

"I have some connections in the Maine state police. I could certainly talk to them. The thing is, if it's true, they'll be all over me. They'll want to know the source of my information. They'll want all the facts."

"Right," said Melanie. "I know that. But I was thinking —

what if you don't mention a watch, just act like you're curious. Like it's some sort of personal interest linked to your crime scene research. And then, if the watch was missing, well, then we go from there. I'll go back to . . . this woman, and tell her she needs to come forward. I think if she really knows for sure, then she'd be willing to do that. She just doesn't want to go through the ordeal if it doesn't lead anywhere."

"I don't think I could do that, Melanie." His voice was regretful but firm. "I couldn't lie to these guys. If I approach them, I've got to be honest. Now, I could tell them I'm withholding certain information, but if there's anything to all this, it's not going to end there. They'll want to talk to you. They'll want to talk to this woman. If you don't come forward voluntarily, there's the possibility of a subpoena."

Melanie let what he'd said sink in.

"The woman who told you all this. Do you think she could have staged this? That she might be using Diane's death to get attention for herself?"

"That occurred to me too," Melanie confessed. "But after talking to her, I really don't think so." There was also the issue of chronology, her own note arriving before Diane was killed. But she wasn't prepared to discuss that. At least not yet.

"Does she have any theories? Of who might be behind it?"

Melanie took a deep breath. "Do you remember Lester Crain?"

"Lester Crain? God, yes. But why . . ." His voice trailed off, and she could almost hear his mind spin. "Because of that thing with Gage, right?"

"Exactly. She has this idea that Crain might be trying to avenge Gage's death."

"So this woman, did she know Gage herself?"

"I . . . I can't get into that."

On the other end of the phone line, she heard a sharp intake of breath. "My God, Melanie, is it you?"

"Me?" She gave a short, dry laugh. "No. No, of course not. If it was me, I'd tell you."

"I hope so," he said seriously. "Because the thing is . . . if this all is for real, if it's not a ploy, then it could be very, very serious. This woman, whoever she is, could be in danger herself. Does she realize this? Is she taking precautions?"

"I'm not sure what she's doing. I'll talk to her, though. Warn her."

"Please do that." The heavy seriousness of his voice left Melanie slightly dizzy. It was the first time she'd fully grasped the potential risks she herself faced. Perhaps she'd focused on Callie's dilemma to avoid facing up to her own.

"Do you have any particular suggestions? For what she should do, I mean?"

"She should go to the police," he said promptly. "That's what she should do."

"I know, but it's complicated. There are reasons she doesn't want to do that."

"Then she should be very careful. If she has the money, hire private security. If not, do whatever she can to make sure her house is protected. Get a good alarm system. Does she live alone?"

Melanie hesitated. While that was the impression she'd had, she realized she didn't know. "Except for her child, I think so."

"Well, let's just hope this whole thing is a false alarm. Maybe it's a practical joke."

"Right," said Melanie. A joke. At the thought, her spirits briefly lifted.

"So what do you think?" Jamison asked. "What do you want to do?"

"Well . . . what if you go to the Maine police and tell them that you have some potentially significant information. That you've talked with someone in possession of a watch that might have belonged to Diane. I have the watch right here. I could give you the serial number. If it belongs to her, she probably has the documentation somewhere. You usually need to take it in when you get a watch like this serviced."

"And if it turns out to have belonged to Diane? They'll want to talk to this woman."

"I could go back to her then. Explain that she has to talk to the police. That she really doesn't have a choice."

"They could do their best to protect her. Keep her identity confidential."

"I'll tell her that," said Melanie, though she doubted that Callie would be reassured. Callie, she had a strong feeling, wasn't used to trusting people.

"Okay, then. I'll make the calls first thing tomorrow morning. You want to give me the watch information?"

"It's a Cartier Panther. Panther's the model. Let's see, there are two numbers on the back — eleven-twenty and then, below that, one-five-seven-four-eight-zero-CD."

In the background, she heard the scratch of pen on paper.

"I was thinking about fingerprints," she said. "Do you think it's worth trying to lift them?"

"Let's wait on that. Let me talk to the guys in Maine first."

"Sure. Okay."

There was a break in the conversation, as if each of them was waiting for the other to speak.

"So, how *are* you?" he asked again. "God, it's been a long time."

"Yes," she said. "It really has. It seems like another lifetime."

"Still practicing law?"

"I'm at a firm in New York now. Harwich and Young."

"Sure. I've heard of it."

"I'm actually up for partner soon. Things are looking pretty good."

"Congratulations."

"Well, we'll see. And you? How've you been?"

"Let's see. I guess it's been about three years since I left the Bureau. I took a year off after that. I needed to spend some time with my kids. Get my life together. I started this new gig last year. Corporate security. Employee background checks. Psychological assessments. After September eleventh, the industry exploded. It's . . . different from what I did at the Bureau, but I'm not sure that's a bad thing."

"And your wife? How's she doing?"

"She's . . . well, she's fine, but we're not together anymore. We split up about four years ago. Mainly my fault, I think."

"I'm so sorry," said Melanie.

"It was for the best," he said. "It was hard for the kids at first, but I think they're doing okay now. Both of them were already in college. That made it easier."

"I got divorced too," Melanie said. "At just about the same time." She didn't mention her engagement. She didn't mention Paul.

"Ah, Melanie. That's tough."

"No kids, though," she said. "And we weren't together so long."

"Still. It's never easy."

"No," she said. "It's not."

A pause.

"You know," he said. "I'm in New York a fair bit. It would be great to get together."

As he spoke, she realized that she'd been waiting. "I'd like that," she said.

Tuesday, April 25

THE Windham College cafeteria had embarked on a somewhat unsettling series of meals with themes. Some of them were
pleasant enough, mildly appealing diversions: Cajun Day. Chocolate Madness. Veg-Stravaganza. But on other days, Callie had to
wonder what drugs they had in the kitchen. Today, for example,
had a carnival theme, complete with carousel music. The sound
screeched out tunelessly from somebody's old boom box.

Callie slid her tray past the steam tray, Martha trailing behind
her. Foot-long hot dogs and hot pretzels. A lurid vat of yellow
popcorn.

Callie turned to Martha. "Salad bar?" she asked.

Martha wrinkled her nose. "Absolutely," she said.

They found two chairs at the end of a table in the crowded dining room. As she speared a leaf of lettuce, Callie thought about
Thursday's party. She'd broached the subject with Tod last week,
and he'd happily accepted. She hadn't described it as a fix-up,
just an informal dinner. Along with Martha and Tod, she'd decided to invite the Creightons. Anna spent so much time at their
house, she really owed Mimi and Bernie. Besides, this way Anna
could stay with Henry Creighton and his sitter.

Callie looked at her watch. "I've got to shop for the party this
afternoon. The rest of this week is crazy."

"Are you sure I can't bring anything?"

"Nope. I've got everything in hand."

"What are you going to wear?" asked Martha.

"Oh, it's totally casual. I may wear a skirt but just because I'll
be more comfortable."

Looking at Martha, her pretty, worn face, Callie felt a need to caution her. "Look, I really don't know what the deal is with Tod. Rick thinks he's still hung up on his ex-wife, so I'm not sure he's available. But he's a really nice guy. I thought it was worth a shot."

Martha pushed back a wave of hair. It was wavy, *not* fuzzy, whatever Rick might say. "Believe me," Martha said, "I'm not expecting a thing."

"It'll be fun," Callie said. "And anyway, who knows?"

Martha had started to smile at something over Callie's shoulder. "Don't look now, but right behind you, Kabuki Girl and Nathan are having lunch. From the looks of it, she's talking his ear off. But he doesn't seem to mind."

"You know, I thought something might be going on. When he stopped by the office the other day, she really seemed interested."

Callie tried to steal a covert glance, but she wasn't fast enough. At the exact moment she turned her head, Nathan looked up. Even at the distance, she saw him flush, then he was on his feet, picking up his tray of food, moving toward their table.

Watching Nathan's retreating back, Posy glared at Callie.

"Damn," Callie muttered. "Why did I have to look?"

Then Nathan was in front of them. "Okay if I join you?" Beneath the pink flush of his face, the skin was dry and flaking. The plate on his cafeteria tray held two foot-long hot dogs.

Martha looked helplessly at Callie.

Callie balled up her napkin and tossed it onto her tray. "Actually, we're finishing up. We were just about to leave."

If Nathan hadn't shown up, she might have stuck around for coffee. As it was, Callie decided she might as well get moving. Tomorrow would be hectic. She had a lot to do. Rick had some sort of training that would take him to Springfield for the night. The trip would keep him from helping out with their usual Wednesday pizza.

She decided to drive out to Atkins Farms to pick up food for the party. The upscale indoor farmers' market would have everything she needed.

*   *   *

As she turned off Route 9 onto 47, the mountains rose up around her, cradling her in the restfulness of their ancient rocky hold. The landscape never failed to calm her. It was what had brought her here. Before then, she'd been so completely lost, living with Kevin outside Indianapolis. It was during that time, after Anna was born, that she'd started to think about finishing school. She'd discovered Windham's Abbott Scholars program at a local college placement office. But academics weren't the main attraction, at least not initially. What had captivated her at the start was a campus photograph. The brochure showed Windham's red-brick buildings nestled against the mountains. Instantly she'd been transfixed, had thought, *I could be happy there.*

The Atkins Farms parking lot, jammed on weekends, was half empty today. Callie quickly found a parking space and headed for the long, low building. Inside, she took a sensual delight in the jewel-like mounds of produce. Red tomatoes. Purple eggplants. Dark, leafy greens. She grabbed a shopping cart and reached for her list. First stop, the meat counter. She'd decided to cook a pork roast, easy and always good. The menu was wintry for this time of year, but nights were still quite cold. She'd serve the roast with spinach, spiced onions, and red potatoes.

In less than an hour, she was finished.

She put her bags in the back of her Subaru and headed back to Merritt, munching on a cider donut as she listened to NPR. Traffic was picking up now, as the early shift headed home. By the time she pulled into the driveway, it was almost three o'clock.

She saw it on the porch, a white florist's box. Instantly, she thought of Rick with an upwelling of warmth. He knew that she'd been stressed lately, and there'd been some tension between them. Her hesitation over his proposal. Anxiety over Anna. But as usual, Rick was reaching out, trying to bridge the gap. Looping the grocery bags over one arm, she reached down and picked up the box.

Sun poured through the windows as she stepped into the kitchen. She put down the bags on the counter, then turned to open the box. Carefully, she peeled off the gold seals that held the top in place. She took off the cover, looked at the flowers, and instantly went numb.

Roses. Red roses.

She felt a mounting panic.

The scent floated up in a cloying cloud, everywhere at once. She was hot, cold, dizzy. Her heart raced in her chest. As if from a distance, she watched herself slowly back away. When she reached the other side of the room, she stood there, silent, help-less. And still she could smell the flowers, their violent, deep per-fume. She wanted to scream, to break something, but she couldn't seem to move. All she could do was stare, aghast, at the box of long-stemmed flowers. He knew how much she hated roses. What had he been thinking?

What had he been thinking?

And then, skin prickling, she realized.

The roses weren't from Rick.

Wednesday, April 26

IT was almost eleven o'clock, and the law firm had fallen silent. It was Melanie's favorite time to work, the time she got the most done. During the day there were endless phone calls and meetings, crises demanding attention. Late at night, she could finally concentrate, work without interruption.

For the past two hours, she'd been at her computer, skimming case citations. She'd been drafting a response in the Leverett appeal when she'd decided to check the case law, to be sure that none of the cited cases had been overturned since the hearing. At first, she'd planned to check just one or two, the key opinions relied upon. But one thing led to another, and now, here she was. Of course, she could have assigned the task to some junior associate. But while the task was largely mechanical, it was vitally important.

For some reason, she was feeling sad tonight, and at first she didn't know why. Then she saw them in her mind's eye, those two scared faces: Penny and Wilbur Murphy. The couple who'd lost their savings. It wasn't her fault. *It wasn't.* Still, the guilt was there. She'd gone to law school with the notion of making the world a better place. *I used to be a nicer person,* she thought. The sadness weighed on her.

The phone rang on her desk, a shrill insistent sound. She picked it up right away, grateful for the distraction.

"Melanie White," she said.

"Melanie. It's Mike."

At the sound of his voice, an electric current seemed to run through her body.

"Is it okay to talk?" he asked tersely. "I've got some things to tell you."

Before he said anything further, she knew why he was calling. "The watch," she said. "It belonged to Diane."

"I just got the call," he said.

Melanie rolled her chair from the desk, turned away from her computer. She stared out the window blankly, holding the phone in her hand. "So what's next? What happens?"

"They want to get hold of the watch. And whoever this woman is who had it, they want to talk to her."

"I'll call her." Melanie was thinking out loud. "Explain the situation."

"Tell her they'll try to work with her. To protect her privacy."

Melanie's heart was pounding. *Happy Anniversary, Melanie.* The words flashed through her mind. She didn't want to think about what they meant, those letters sent to her and Callie.

"So what's the status of the investigation?" she asked. "Are there any significant leads?"

"None that's gone anywhere, at least so far as they'll tell me. They've talked to the guy Diane Massey was dating, but he's pretty much been cleared. They were also looking into possible links to the book she was working on. When she was killed, she was finishing up a book about Winnie Dandridge."

"That Texas black widow?" Melanie asked.

"Right. That's the one. Diane had been threatened by a pal of Dandridge's, but nothing's panned out so far. This guy, he's still the strongest lead, but he's got pretty good alibis. The thing is, no one's had any reason to think that her murder could be linked to the Gage case."

"What about Lester Crain? Did you look into that at all?"

"The watch will be checked for fingerprints, but Crain didn't kill Diane Massey."

"Why? How can you know?"

"The crime scene. It's not Crain's. The signature of a sexual sadist always stays the same. There may be some variation, but the core — it's always there."

"The signature?" Melanie recalled the term, but wasn't clear on its meaning.

"Think of it as a calling card. A sort of identifier. Crain always tortured his victims before killing them. His gratification didn't come from killing. It came from causing pain. Now the ways that he tortured his victims varied. That led to some confusion. It took some time for the different jurisdictions to see that the murders were linked. They were focusing on the techniques instead of the act of torture itself. In fact, the shifts in techniques were just efforts at improvement. Crain changed his M.O. — his specific techniques — as he found more effective ones."

Melanie's mouth felt dry. "And Diane. You're saying she wasn't tortured? So Crain couldn't be the killer?"

"That's right."

"But I don't understand. People change."

"I've never seen a signature change, not the essential parts." There was something in his voice, a certainty, that stopped Melanie from pressing. It sounded a bit far-fetched. *Never?* But Jamison was the expert.

Another thought occurred to her. "What about Gage's signature? Are there . . . similarities?"

"No. Totally different. Gage was a necrophile. He killed women to control their bodies. He killed them and then he raped them."

"Right." Melanie's stomach churned. It was something she'd always tried not to think about, that particular fact. He'd killed them, *then* had sex. The women had been just bodies to him. He'd referred to them as *subjects*.

Jamison was going on. "According to the M.E.'s report, there's no sign that Diane was molested. The victimology is different, too. Crain targeted runaways and prostitutes. Women living on the edge. Heavy makeup. Big hair. That was his physical type."

"And the victimology — that stays the same too?"

"Not always," Jamison admitted. "Especially when the killer's under stress, he may jump victim pools. Take Ted Bundy, for example. He had a type. Pretty, young women with long, dark hair parted down the middle. Then when he started to decompensate, he killed that child in Florida. But that was the beginning of the end for him. A sign he was falling apart. Under normal conditions, these guys stick with a type."

"Like Steven killed slender blondes."

"Right."

Women who looked like me. She thought but didn't say that before quickly moving on.

"What about forensic evidence — fibers, fingerprints, anything like that?"

"I don't know," Jamison said. "It's an ongoing investigation. They wouldn't tell me much. There's something else I meant to ask you. That anonymous note you mentioned. What did it say again?"

"Just 'Happy Anniversary. I haven't forgotten you.' And then her . . . this nickname she used to have." At this point it seemed slightly absurd to be concealing her identity. But she felt some sort of obligation to keep the secret while she could. She could still let Callie come forward herself, allow her that measure of control.

"What sort of paper?"

"White, eight-and-a-half-by-eleven. Some sort of lightweight bond, I guess."

"Handwritten?"

"No, it was typed. Or maybe printed from a computer." The line of questioning was filling her with a vague sense of foreboding. "Where are you going with this?" she asked.

"The detective in charge of the investigation had been going through Diane's correspondence. When I mentioned the note to him, he had a lot of questions. I'm thinking that there's a pretty good chance Diane got a similar note."

As she walked through the door that night, Melanie realized with surprise she was hungry. When was the last time she'd felt that way? She really couldn't remember. The craving for barbecue she'd had the other night returned with renewed force. She could almost smell the smoky meat, taste the bite of pickle. She thought of Virgil's near Times Square, Brother's somewhere downtown. But chances were slim to none they were open, and even less they'd deliver.

Flipping through the Yellow Pages, she had a sudden thought. The pork buns you got at Chinese restaurants, maybe they'd do the trick. Not that the taste would be the same, but the texture was pretty close. The spongy bread, the tender meat. At least it was worth a try. Chinese restaurants were everywhere, open day and night. She found an ad for one nearby, called, and placed an order.

Hanging up, she almost started to laugh, imagining her father's reaction. He'd be amused at her ingenuity but still horrified. They'd both been purists about barbecue, refusing to compromise. "Daddy," she whispered softly. Tears pricked her eyelids. She yearned for the closeness she'd had with her father until Steven Gage.

As a baby, it had been assumed that Melanie would be her mother's child. After four sons, Patricia White had been thrilled with her infant daughter. She'd named her after Melanie Wilkes, the perfect lady in *Gone with the Wind,* an exemplar of the traditional virtues of southern womanhood. As a child, Melanie had found herself dressed in pale pink dresses with starchy lace. White ruffly anklets. Shiny patent shoes. She slept on an enormous canopy bed with piles of silky pillows, took ballet lessons twice a week, had dozens of flaxen-haired dolls.

But the older she got, the more Melanie chafed at her mother's instructions. She'd excelled at sports, running track and developing a mean backhand. When she was eight, her mother had told her, "Never beat a boy at tennis." By then, she'd already known that her mother was the enemy. She'd respectfully listened to this new injunction, nodded and said, "Yes, ma'am." But she'd sat there silently thinking, *That's the stupidest thing I ever heard.*

Richard White was an eminent labor lawyer with a national reputation. It had always been assumed that at least one of his sons would follow him to law school. Maybe not all of them, but at least one or two. Over the years, though, all four had taken different paths, so when Melanie opted for a legal career, her father had been thrilled. Like her father, Melanie had gone to Princeton, then law school at UVA. In the back of her mind, she'd thought someday she might join her father's practice. Even after she married Frank, the fantasy stayed alive. He'd retire long before she did. By then, they'd have kids. Nashville was a great place to raise children. She'd move down with her family.

If it hadn't been for Steven Gage, might she have gone home? At times, she thought it was likely. Other times, she didn't know. The only thing she could say for sure was the case had changed everything. "You cannot represent Steven Gage." That's what her father had said. At first his reaction had surprised her. She saw now she'd been naive. It wasn't that his values didn't have substance, just that they weren't absolute. After all, her parents and Dahlia Schuyler's parents moved in the same social set. The families lived just blocks apart in the wealthy enclave of Belle Meade. While her father had never much liked the Schuylers, that didn't seem to matter. Their differences were more akin to family squabbles than the battles of warring clans.

Melanie had argued with her father for hours, called him a hypocrite. He'd taught her that everyone deserved representation, regardless of what they'd done. But this argument hadn't swayed him. He'd thundered back at her, "I'm not saying he shouldn't have appellate counsel. But it doesn't have to be you!" For the first time in her life, she'd openly opposed him. For a year, they hadn't spoken. He'd never forgiven her. Was he more upset that she'd represented Gage or that she'd disobeyed him? All these years later, she still wasn't sure.

Glancing down at the phone, she saw the flashing message light. She listened to the recording and found a message from Paul. Listening to her fiancé's voice, she felt not the slightest emotion. He mentioned plans for next weekend, a play they had tickets for. They'd barely spoken since Sunday night, that disastrous dinner at Clarence. There was something in his tone that told her he expected an apology.

Quickly she erased the message. She didn't call him back. Instead, she found her thoughts returning to her talk with Jamison. She tried to think about the implications, for herself as well as for Callie. But while her rational mind told her that she could be in danger, somehow she couldn't feel it. The burst of adrenaline, the beating heart — all of that was missing. It was like she was two different people, one of them observing.

She reminded herself that as of yet Jamison's theory was speculation. He didn't know for sure that Diane had received a note. But the watch — the watch had belonged to Diane. Callie had gotten a note. The three of them had all known Gage. There had to be a connection. The safest thing would be to go to the police, to follow the advice she'd given Callie. But at this point, she simply couldn't predict what consequences would follow. On the eve of partnership elections, she'd be embroiled in a murder case. She thought of the risk of scandal, always the kiss of death. It wasn't fair, of course. None of this was her fault. But by now she'd learned her lesson: Fairness didn't matter.

It would be one thing if the information she had was of great significance. But, assuming that Callie stepped forward, how much would it really add? Callie's story would establish the link between Diane's murder and Steven Gage. That would be sufficient to alter the frame of reference. Besides, while she could always step forward, she couldn't take anything back. It made sense to think this through carefully before saying anything.

As for personal safety, she just wasn't worried. Maybe she was in denial, but it didn't feel that way. The thing was, her life was so circumscribed, it was hard to imagine how she'd be at risk. She lived in a high-security building, protected by a team of doormen. Before admitting any visitor, the doorman on duty called up. At work, the Harwich & Young reception desk was manned by security guards. Visitors had to wait downstairs for a firm-employee escort. You couldn't enter the building without showing your pass card.

A buzzing on the intercom phone by her door. She hoisted herself off the couch.

"You've got a delivery," the doorman said.

"Thanks. Send him up."

As she hung up the phone, her stomach growled in pleasant anticipation. She stood by the door with her wallet until she heard a knock.

She unlocked the door, opened it, then stood there in confusion. Instead of an Asian deliveryman, she was facing a bearded white guy holding a long white box. His baseball cap was pulled down low. She couldn't see his face. Flowers, that's what it looked like. Maybe they were from Paul? But even as the thought occurred to her, she knew it wasn't right. Paul wasn't in any mood to make this sort of gesture.

The man at the door took a step forward. "Can I get your signature?"

"Uh. Sure." But he wasn't holding a pen or clipboard. What did he want her to sign?

She had a fleeting sense that something was wrong, and then he was up against her. His breath smelled of garlic and coffee. He seemed to radiate heat.

Before she could step away, he gave her a powerful shove. Then she was tumbling backward, falling into space. Colors exploded behind her eyes. She tried to catch her breath. A jolt of fear. *What was happening?*

She heard the door click shut.

Thursday, April 27

A RICH perfume filled the house, the smell of roasting meat and spices. Callie had spent most of the day preparing for the dinner party. Since the roses had arrived two days ago, they'd never been far from her mind, a fierce, nagging anxiety verging on obsession. It seemed surreal that her life could be proceeding on this dual track: cooking a casual dinner for friends, fearing for her life.

It was almost six o'clock now. Her guests would be here soon. Tired and distracted as she'd been all day, she needed to concentrate. She'd already set the dining room table with the good china and silver. Put out glass bowls of olives and nuts, a plate of cheese and crackers. She had vodka, rum, bourbon, and wine, purchased for the occasion.

As she pulled a tray of mushroom puffs out of the oven, Callie heard the doorbell ring.

"Hi, honey." It was Martha. She entered on a wave of cold night air, pink-cheeked and animated. Her hair, an electric dark brown cloud, danced around her face.

She peeled off her gray wool cape and handed it to Callie.

"What's that fabulous smell?" she asked, gesturing toward the kitchen.

"Peasant food. Nothing fancy. Roast pork, potatoes, spinach, and onions. I made a pear tart for dessert."

Callie hung up Martha's cape, then led her back to the kitchen.

"Wine?" Callie asked.

"Sure."

"Red or white?"

"Red."

On the counter were an open bottle and a cluster of large wine glasses. Callie poured wine into one and handed it to Martha.

"Where's Anna?" Martha asked, after taking a sip.

"She's across the street with her friend Henry. His parents will be here tonight. Mimi and Bernie Creighton. He's a big-shot lawyer in Boston, and she's this yuppie mom. To be honest, I'm not crazy about them, but Anna spends so much time over there, I owe them an invitation. Oh, and Bernie's bringing some guy he works with. Another partner at his law firm. So if things don't work out with Tod, who knows? Maybe this guy will be an option."

The doorbell rang again.

Callie looked up from the mushroom puffs. "Would you mind finishing up with these? Just arrange them on this plate."

She quickly wiped her hands on a towel and went to answer the door.

When she caught sight of Rick through the peephole, Callie felt a catch in her throat. He was smiling that slightly bemused smile and holding a bunch of tulips. For a moment, she wished with all her heart that it was just the two of them.

As she opened the door, Callie saw that Rick wasn't alone. Tod was standing next to him, holding a bottle of wine.

"Hi, sweetheart." Rick handed her the tulips and leaned down for a kiss. She briefly lingered in his arms before turning to Tod.

"Welcome," she said, extending a hand. "I'm so glad you could make it."

Tod looked wholesome and a little bit shy in khakis and a hunter-green jacket. He handed Callie the bottle of wine, a tentative smile on his face.

Another ring of the bell. The Creightons with their guest.

A profusion of greetings and air kisses, a potent blend of smells, the sharp floral of Mimi's perfume, Bernie's aftershave. Bernie's colleague was dark and heavy with an inward, brooding look.

"Callie, I'd like you to meet John Casey. Like I told you, he's one of my partners. We're working together on a case."

"So nice of you to have me."

As he spoke, Callie was startled to hear the traces of a southern accent. For a moment, she stood there, staring at him, her mouth suddenly dry. The memories were so close these days. Anything could trigger them. A certain kind of light. A melody. The sound of a southern voice.

Quickly she pulled herself together, managed to force a smile.

"Not at all," she said. "The more the merrier."

A round of greetings and shedding of coats as Martha emerged from the kitchen. With a sudden surge of protectiveness, Callie wrapped an arm around Martha's waist.

"You remember Rick," she said.

"Of course." Martha smiled.

More introductions followed, with Tod coming last. As Callie presented Martha to him, she sensed Rick's watchful eye. It wasn't a coincidence, she thought, that Rick and Tod had come together. Rick would be protective of Tod, just as she was of Martha.

"Nice to meet you, Martha," said Tod.

The two of them shook hands.

"I've got to put these in water," said Callie, holding up the tulips. "Why don't you all go into the living room? Rick can get you drinks."

"Need any help?" asked Martha.

"Maybe if you could get the hors d'oeuvres — put them on the coffee table."

"I'll help," Tod said promptly.

Not bad, Callie thought.

In the kitchen, Tod picked up the mushroom puffs. Martha took a tray with pâté. "Pretty cute," she whispered to Callie, as she slid past her toward the doorway.

Callie picked out a vase of deep blue glass for the tulips that Rick had brought. As she fanned out the bright orange and yellow flowers, her mind flashed back to the roses. How time had seemed to stop as she stared at their crimson mass. As soon as the shock had dissipated, she'd thrown them into the trash. Then, not content to have them merely out of sight, she'd taken the garbage out.

That night, she'd mentioned the roses to Rick, hoping that she'd been wrong. But Rick didn't know anything; he'd told her to call the florist. "They must have made a mistake," he said. "They went to the wrong address." In fact, she'd already made that call, already knew the answer. The florist didn't have a single order that day for a dozen long-stemmed roses. The box must have been salvaged from some past delivery.

From the other room, Callie heard muffled talk, then a sudden burst of laughter. Strange how totally alone she felt with friends just steps away. Her eyes settled on a bottle of wine, now half empty. The crimson liquid that it held was the same color as the roses. The room seemed to dissolve behind it, throwing the bottle into sharp relief. She was suddenly hit with an astonishing urge to raise it to her mouth.

She hadn't touched a drop of alcohol since the night of the sentencing, but all these years later, she remembered everything. The way the world seemed to dissolve and soften, filled with secret meaning. In AA they'd told her that alcoholism was an incurable disease. She'd never argued with the diagnosis, though she hadn't exactly agreed. The way she saw it, drinking resembled some wildly destructive talent. Others less gifted genetically sought refuge in work or shopping. For her, though, alcohol had always offered the fast road out of herself.

Now, staring at the bottle, she felt almost afraid. It was the first time in many years that she'd really wanted to drink. She picked up the cork from the kitchen counter and jammed it into the neck. Once all the guests left, she'd pour it down the drain. *There isn't any problem that drinking won't make worse.* That was one thing she'd heard in AA that she'd never doubted was true.

"Callie?"

She turned around quickly, guiltily, as if she'd done something wrong. Rick was standing in the doorway holding the wine Tod had brought.

"Got a corkscrew?" He looked at her, took a few steps forward. "Hey, are you okay?"

"I . . . sure. I'm fine." But she didn't sound that way.

Rick put down the wine. She walked straight into his arms. Closing her eyes, she relaxed against him, breathing in his soapy scent. As her body shaped itself to his, she felt a creeping warmth. She'd have liked to stay with this sensation, fan it, let it build. The touch of bare skin. Darkness. The obliteration of sex.

Rick put his hands on her shoulders and gently pushed her back. "You look really tired."

"I didn't sleep well last night."

"We'll make this an early evening. It's a weeknight anyway."

Callie opened a drawer and rummaged around for the corkscrew. "You go back to the party. I'll be out in a few minutes."

Rick pressed his lips to her forehead. Then, turning, he was gone.

Alone again, Callie checked on the roast, a luscious, fragrant brown. The onions and potatoes were warming in the oven; the spinach would take just minutes. She decided to have a drink with her guests before the final preparations. Not that she felt like socializing, but after all, she was the hostess. She mixed herself a seltzer with cranberry juice, then headed for the living room.

She was pleased to find that Martha and Tod had taken adjoining chairs. Tod seemed to be listening intently to whatever Martha was saying. Martha looked pretty tonight. Lively, almost carefree. The deep blue of her scoop-necked blouse brought out the blue of her eyes.

Across the room, Bernie and his colleague were absorbed in conversation. Callie had the distinct sense they'd just as soon not have come. Mimi sat on the sofa with Rick, expensive blonde hair gleaming, toying with the strap of an elegant small purse. She seemed tense tonight, more so than usual, her face somehow taut. Her eyes darted back and forth between Rick and her husband.

Callie walked over to Martha and perched on the arm of her chair.

"What's up?" she asked.

Tod turned toward Callie. "Martha was telling me about this dance thing she does. It sounds like a lot of fun."

Callie laughed. "Contra dancing. She's been pushing me to try it for years now."

Tod looked back toward Martha. "So it's sort of like square dancing?"

Martha made a haphazard gesture pushing back her hair. Her hand disappeared in the dark brown mass floating around her head. "Some of the steps are the same, but it's done in long lines."

"Do you have to take lessons?" Tod asked.

"Absolutely not," said Martha. "It's informal. Really friendly. Sometimes they give a lesson before the dance, but basically you learn as you go."

"So where do you do it?"

"It's every weekend in Greenfield. People come from miles around, even out of state."

Tod grinned. "You know, I haven't danced for years, but I'd like to try it sometime." He looked at Callie. "Maybe the four of us could go. You and Rick and Martha and me."

Callie struggled to hide her delight. "Sure," she said. "Why not?"

Relieved that things were going well with Martha, Callie got up to circulate. She approached Bernie and his law partner — John Casey, that was his name. "You both doing okay?" she asked.

"We're fine." Casey gave her a fleeting smile. Swirling his amber drink, he asked, "So where you from, Callie?"

"You mean, where did I grow up?"

"Your accent." The drawl was stronger now. "I guess we're both from the South."

Callie looked at him, unnerved. "I didn't know I had an accent. I . . . I lived in the South for a few years, but that's not where I grew up."

"Whereabouts?" Casey asked. "No, wait. Don't tell me, lemme guess. Alabama? Or maybe Tennessee?"

Callie felt the blood rush to her face as she stared down at Casey. For a moment, she couldn't seem to move, but she had to get away. She looked at her watch, put her hand to her mouth, then looked up, as if distracted. "I had no idea it was so late. I've got to get on with dinner."

By the time the dinner guests filed out, it was almost ten o'clock. Anna, who'd been across the street with Henry, had come home an hour ago. As Callie closed and locked the door, fatigue settled over her. She let the muscles of her face relax, the fixed smile fall away. Silently, Rick reached for her, gathered her in his arms. She rested there a few long moments, then stepped back to look at him.

"So how d'you think it went?" she asked.

"Everything was perfect."

"It was a little disjointed, I thought. Bernie and that guy he brought sort of kept to themselves."

Rick smiled. "As did Tod and Martha."

Callie mustered a smile in response, though even that took some effort. Behind her forehead, beneath her skull, she felt a sort of pulsing. Not a headache exactly, but something that might become one. "I was wondering if you'd noticed. Surprised?"

Rick shrugged. "I still don't think it will go anywhere."

"He wants us all to go contra dancing."

Now he *was* surprised.

"Dancing? Tod?" Rick started to laugh.

"No, really. That's what he said."

Rick shook his head. "I'll believe it when I see it. Hey, want some help cleaning up?"

The living room was littered with crumpled napkins and the pale ends of melting drinks. They piled up the sticky glasses and plates and carried them to the kitchen. As she dumped dregs of wine down the drain, Callie caught an astringent whiff. Quickly, she squeezed out a glob of detergent and rinsed off the glass.

They cleared the dining room table, then loaded the dishwasher, Rick rinsing the glasses and plates while Callie arranged them inside. Something seemed to be bothering her, tugging at her mind. She realized it was Bernie's colleague, John Casey, that offhand comment he'd made.

"Do you think I have an accent?" Callie asked.

"What?" Rick handed her a plate.

Callie put it in the dishwasher. "A southern accent. Do you think I have one? Is it something you've ever noticed?"

Rick shook his head. "No. I don't think so. At least not that I remember."

"Not that you remember? What does that mean?"

"Maybe when I met you, I might have noticed that you didn't sound like you're from around here. But I don't know if that was your voice or just . . . how you are."

"Oh." It wasn't a very satisfying answer, but she didn't know what else to say.

"Cal, why are you so upset? I mean, who cares? So he guessed that you lived in Tennessee. Why's that a big deal?"

"I'm not upset," Callie said. "I just don't see how he knew."

"Well, he's from down there himself. Maybe he's more sensitive to it."

"Yeah. I guess. Maybe." Callie slammed the dishwasher shut and started the wash cycle. As much as she'd wanted to be alone with Rick, she now wanted him to leave.

The telephone rang.

Welcoming the interruption, Callie crossed the room.

"May I speak to Callie Thayer?" The voice was male and unfamiliar.

"Speaking."

"This is Mike Jamison calling."

Mike Jamison. It took just a second or two for Callie to make the connection. The former FBI profiler whom Melanie had planned to call. Anger rushed up in Callie, a sort of emotional flash flood. Was it really too much to ask for Melanie to have warned her?

Conscious of Rick's eyes on her, Callie tried to keep her voice even. "I'm afraid this isn't a good time. Could I call you back tomorrow?"

"I'm afraid not, Ms. Thayer. I'm calling to tell you that Melanie White was attacked in her apartment last night. She's in the hospital now."

The breath rushed out of her body, and for a moment she couldn't think. In her mind's eye, she saw Melanie's face, the clear ice-blue eyes. "But I just saw her," Callie whispered.

"On Sunday," he said.

"Yes. That's right."

"You're a . . . a friend of hers?"

There was just a shadow of a pause.

"That's right," Callie said again.

Rick was at her side, touching her arm, concerned. She knew that he could tell from her voice that the call had brought bad news. With effort, she collected her thoughts, tried to decide what to do.

"I need a few minutes," she finally said. "I'll call you right back, okay?"

She scribbled down a number. When she hung up the phone, she turned to Rick. "I have to be alone now."

He looked at her intently. "Who was that on the phone?"

Callie stared at the ground. The churning noise of the dishwasher seemed to fill the room. Somewhere in the distance, she heard Rick let out a sigh.

"Callie, what's going on? For weeks now you've been . . . I don't know. Something strange has been happening."

"You're right," she said, still looking down. "But I . . . it's complicated."

"Is it something about me?" he asked. "Something about us, I mean?"

Callie gave a short, quick laugh, then pressed a hand to her face. Her skin felt dry and very hot, as if she had a fever. "Oh, God," she said. "No. No, it's nothing like that."

He took a step closer, then hesitated, as if afraid to approach her. "So what is it then? What aren't you telling me?"

It was like she was trapped inside a bubble, and he was on the outside. She could hear what he was saying, but he didn't have the power to touch her. In her hand, she clutched the piece of paper with Jamison's phone number.

"I'm sorry, but you have to go now."

Rick stared at her another few moments, then silently turned away.

She heard him get his coat from the closet, the rustle as he pulled it on. Without saying another word, he shut the door behind him.

His footsteps echoed on the pavement.

She heard his car door slam.

A roar of the engine, a squeal of tires, as he pulled away from the curb. *He must be very angry,* she thought. But right now that didn't matter.

Back in the kitchen, she picked up the phone, paused, then put it down. She needed to clear her mind a bit before calling Jamison back. *It could just be a coincidence.* The thought brought a ray of hope. Maybe the attack was a random thing. Or maybe it was personal. A violent boyfriend. An angry client. Nothing to do with Steven.

What did Jamison know? That was another question. What did he know about the watch and note? Did he know who she really was?

The watch. The note.

Callie froze. She'd left them with Melanie. She wondered where they were right now. Had Melanie's attacker found them?

She punched in Jamison's number. He answered on the first ring.

Their greetings were brief, perfunctory, then Jamison ran through the facts. How Melanie's attacker had come disguised as a florist's deliveryman. How the law firm had sent someone looking for her when she didn't show up at work.

"It happened around one this morning, but they didn't find her until nine or so. She didn't show up at an early meeting. They couldn't reach her on the phone. So the law firm sent a paralegal over to look for her. In one way she was lucky. Right after the attacker went up, she got a delivery of Chinese food. When the delivery guy knocked on the door, he must have scared the attacker. It looks like the attacker fled when the Chinese food guy went back downstairs."

"How is she?" Callie asked. "What did he do to her?"

"She was hit with some sort of blunt object, a glancing blow to the side of the head. When they found her, she was unconscious, and they rushed her into surgery. She had what they call a sub-dural hematoma — that's a bleeding in the brain. The bleed was pushing against the brain, compressing the brain tissue."

"Surgery," Callie said faintly. "Is she . . . will she be okay?"

"At this point, we don't know. She's still in intensive care. She was conscious for a few hours after the operation. That's when she told me to call you. Then, well, she had a relapse. She's in a coma now."

"My God," said Callie. "I'm so, so sorry." She realized that she was crying. A tear rolled silently down one cheek. She wiped it away with a hand.

"The flowers that the guy who attacked her brought, do you know what kind they were?"

"I don't know," said Jamison. "Any special reason you're ask-ing?"

"No, I just . . . I don't know." Callie realized that she was shak-ing. Thoughts whirled through her mind. "What did Melanie tell you about me? Why did she ask you to call me?"

"She kept repeating several names. Yours was one of them. Your number was in her book. The rest I figured out myself."

"The rest?"

"She told me about the watch and letter, that a woman she knew had received them. She didn't give me a name. But you're that woman, right?"

Callie swallowed hard. "Where are they?" she asked. "Did he find them? That watch and the letter, I mean."

"Luckily, no. They're in the hands of authorities now. The Maine state police will want to talk to you about them. And about the Massey case."

"The watch —"

"It belonged to Diane. We've already checked that out. Melanie was going to tell you. Apparently, she didn't have a chance."

Too late Callie thought that she shouldn't have been so open, shouldn't have been so quick to admit her connection to the letter and watch. Until then, Jamison was going on suspicion. Now he knew for sure. At the same time, she had a helpless feeling. What did it really matter? Even if she'd kept her mouth shut, it was only a matter of time.

"Both Diane and Melanie had ties to Steven Gage. Is that also true for you?"

She could tell that he was feeling his way, like a blind man in a strange room. His instincts were good. He was sensitive. But he didn't have the facts.

"I don't mean to be rude," said Callie. "But I'm not going to answer that."

"Fair enough," he said. "You don't have to tell me. But you do need to tell the police, Ms. Thayer. There's a killer out there."

"But how do you know that I can help? How do you know it's connected?"

A pause.

"I don't know," Jamison said finally. "But I intend to find out. And I hope you'll do whatever you can to help with this investigation."

"I . . . of course, I will. But I'm not sure —"

Before she could discover what she'd meant to say, Jamison cut in.

"Melanie told me that you have a child, that you're worried about privacy. I have children too. I understand your concerns. But even if you're willing to risk your own life, other people are involved. If you'd gone to the police in the first place, this thing might not have happened."

"We can't know that," Callie said. But the words had hit their target. She'd put Melanie in harm's way, and then she'd tied her hands. She was the one responsible. Just like before.

Just like before.

Remorse washed over her.

"I'll talk to the police," said Callie. "I'll do whatever I can. Will they . . . do you think they can keep it confidential, the fact that I'm involved?"

"I'm sure they'll do whatever they can to work with you on that."

"Do you have a phone number?"

"In Maine, you need to talk with Jack Pulaski. He's with the state police." Callie took down the name and number as Jamison read them off.

"The police in New York and Maine — are they working together on this?"

"Not yet," Jamison said. "It takes a while for multijurisdictional investigations to get up and running. The links have to be established, and this thing with Melanie just happened. But soon, I hope, they'll be collaborating. You can help with that. You provide a link between Diane and Melanie."

Upstairs, Callie heard the toilet flush. Anna was awake.

"I'll call first thing tomorrow," she promised.

"Good," Jamison said. "In the meantime, I hope you won't mind if I pass on your name and number." She heard the words as a warning. If she didn't step forward herself, they'd come after her.

Anna appeared in the doorway, her face crumpled and pink, mouth turned down at the edges in an expression of accusation.

"You woke me up," she said.

Callie raised a hand to signal she'd be just a moment. "I guess that's it," she said.

"For now. And Ms. Thayer — please be careful."

After she'd hung up the phone, Callie pulled Anna into her arms, rubbed her nose against the silky hair. "Sorry, sweetie," she said.

"What's wrong? Is something wrong?" Anna was waking up now.

Callie forced a smile. "Not a thing. Let's get you back to bed."

She walked Anna upstairs, then tucked her under her blankets. Anna sighed contentedly, then rolled over on her side. In the shadowed dimness of her daughter's room, time seemed so precious. She'd always planned to tell Anna the truth at that distant point called *someday*, but the luxury of this delay was one she no longer had. Tonight — right now — her secret was safe, but tomorrow that might change. Gazing at the face of her sleeping daughter, she wondered what to say.

Friday, April 28

*S*HADOWS. *Shapes. Voices.*

Her eyelids were so heavy. She had to get to work. A meeting on the Leverett case. But something was holding her down, keeping her from moving. Who was in the room with her? Where was she, anyway?

Another voice. A man's: "How's she doing? Is she waking up?"

A mumbled response in the background that she couldn't quite make out.

Lying there, she realized they must be talking about her. "I'm fine! I hear you!" she wanted to say. "Just help me to get up."

Then, confused, she knew that she couldn't be fine, after all. If she was fine, she wouldn't need their help. If she was fine, she'd just sit up.

What had happened? What was wrong? She strained for the memories.

She was eating dinner with Paul. He was mad at her.

Alone in her Harwich & Young office, she stared at her computer.

The images flickered through her mind, like frames in some home movie. But nothing she saw could explain to her what was going on.

She sensed a darkening overhead, someone leaning forward. Panic. A jolt of fear. Steven Gage had found her. Somewhere, deep inside, she'd known it would happen. It didn't matter that she'd tried to help him, that she'd tried to save his life. She'd always sensed that when he looked at her, he wanted to see her dead. She'd tried to tell herself it wasn't so, but, always, she'd known the truth. Steven was a predator. That was just his nature.

Then the fear seemed to break, give way to a certain acceptance. She was floating on a bank of clouds, could see things in perspective. Maybe she deserved what was happening. Maybe it made sense. She'd always been one of the lucky ones, but luck could always change. Why should she be alive to protect him, while so many women were dead?

Slowly, the shadow receded. Whoever had been there was gone. And it couldn't have been Steven, anyway. Steven Gage was dead.

Steven Gage was dead. So what was she afraid of?

At that moment, it all came back to her: Happy Anniversary.

MIKE Jamison gazed at the thin form beneath the starched white hospital sheet. He still wasn't exactly sure what he was doing here.

He'd learned of the attack yesterday when he'd called Melanie's office. She wasn't there, and when he inquired, her secretary told him why. Even before he hung up the phone, he'd started making plans. He had his assistant reschedule meetings and rushed home to pack. Three hours later he was on a plane, heading for New York.

Now he studied Melanie, the bruised motionless face. She'd been in a coma since last night, a postsurgery relapse. As he sat by her side, there'd been a constant stream of doctors, nurses, technicians, but their faces faded to a blur as he focused on Melanie. The white gauze wrapped around her head resembled a snowy turban. An intravenous tube ran from her arm through a metal pole. Wires attached to her chest connected to the EKG monitor, while some sort of strange metallic device measured her brain pressure. The high-tech equipment should have reassured him, but it just made him more anxious.

A nurse came into the room and adjusted Melanie's bed. She had rosy cheeks, curly hair, and a calm, efficient manner. She examined Melanie's eyes with a flashlight, pushing back the lids. Then she checked the fluid level in the intravenous feeding bag. "Do you see any changes?" Jamison asked. He couldn't help himself. "Don't worry," she said soothingly. "There's still plenty of time." But the edge of pity in her voice gave him a hopeless feeling.

When the nurse left, he pulled his chair closer. Visitors in intensive care were normally limited to family, but with the help of a pal in the NYPD he'd managed to talk his way in. Which still begged the question: What was he doing here? He had an arrangement with Leeds Associates to consult on outside cases. It was one of the terms he'd negotiated when he'd joined the private firm. Until now, he'd scheduled these consultations around his paying clients. This time, though, he'd dropped everything, without a second thought.

As an FBI profiler, he'd spent more than a decade studying sociopaths, delving into the darkest parts of their deeply troubled minds. He'd met Melanie shortly before Gage's execution, still immersed in the death-row interviews that became his best-known work. They'd known each other so briefly, and yet he'd remembered her. They came from totally different worlds, but he'd sensed a kindred spirit.

If they'd met in other circumstances, would the feelings have been the same? Impossible to answer that. The facts were what they were. He thought about their first meeting back in Tennessee, both of them running on adrenaline and coffee as the hours ticked down. They'd shared the same obsession, and that had created a bond. Melanie hadn't said a lot — as Gage's attorney, she couldn't — but he could tell that she was drinking in every word he said. And it certainly hadn't hurt that she was so damn pretty. Tall and blonde with that deep blue gaze, at once skeptical and earnest.

Of course, he hadn't said any of this. He couldn't at the time. He was with the FBI. She was one of Gage's lawyers. Besides, even more to the point, both of them were married. The night after Gage's execution, he'd sat up with her all night. Later, he wondered what might have happened if both of them had been free. After his divorce, he'd briefly thought about getting in touch with her. But he'd assumed she was still married. And what would have been the point?

He glanced at his watch. Fifteen more minutes. He wondered where the hell her family was, hoped someone would be here soon.

He leaned forward a little more, bracing his hands on his knees.

"Melanie. Can you hear me?"

No response. Nothing.

That brief window of consciousness seemed like a mirage. Just yesterday she'd talked to him, begged him to call Callie Thayer. She'd been groggy, her voice weak, but she'd gotten her point across.

The NYPD had released Melanie's apartment late yesterday afternoon. Under cover of getting her some personal items, Jamison had slipped in. Even though he'd known what to expect, the sight had been a shock. All that white upholstery. All that dried red blood. On an arm of the couch was a trail of handprints, as if she'd tried to stand up. The image had seared itself into his mind. He wished he hadn't seen it.

The slope-bellied super watched him closely as he opened closets and drawers. Picked out a nightgown, some bedroom slippers, a pink quilted robe. He'd had no idea where to look, but he'd acted like he did. Relieved, he'd found the watch and note still safe in a dresser drawer.

A slight ripple, a movement, beneath the crisp sheet. At first he thought he'd imagined it, and then he heard a sound.

"Noooooo . . ." The word was uttered softly, a barely audible moan.

In an instant, Jamison was on his feet, rushing to the hall.

"She said something," he called to a nurse. "I think she's waking up."

Back at Melanie's bedside, Jamison held her hand. The nurse walked briskly into the room with the neurosurgery resident. The young doctor, dark-eyed and intense, stood across from Jamison. "Ms. White, can you hear me?" he asked. "Can you open your eyes?"

Jamison's eyes were on Melanie's lips, waiting for her to speak. For several minutes, nothing happened, then it came again.

"No-no-no!" she mumbled. Her voice was louder now. She seemed almost agitated, as if she were afraid.

"It's okay," Jamison told her. "You're safe here. No one will hurt you. The person who hurt you is gone now. Everything's okay."

"Noooooooooo," Melanie said. Her eyes fluttered open. For an instant, she seemed to look straight at him, then her eyelids shuttered down. But after a moment, her lips trembled.

"Not," she said.

Not what? Jamison wondered. And then his body tensed. She hadn't been saying no at all; she'd been saying something else. Something that confirmed what at some level he'd suspected all along.

He leaned so close to Melanie's face that his cheek brushed her hair.

"*Note.* Is that what you're saying? Did you get a note like Callie's?"

For a moment, nothing happened.

Then she squeezed his hand.

Monday, May 1

CALLIE sheered off I-91 onto Route 2A, heading east toward Boston. In something under three hours she was crossing into Maine. She passed through the shipbuilding town of Bath, through picturesque Wiscasset. Shortly after noon, she stopped for lunch, at a place called Moody's Diner.

Inside, she sat in a green vinyl booth and waited for a menu. Even months before tourist season, the room was bustling. Single diners, mainly men, ate at the yellow counter. At a neighboring booth two gray-haired women worked on pieces of pie. "Chowdah?" Callie heard a waitress ask a couple seated nearby. She'd forgotten how Mainers dropped their *r*'s, how distinctive the accent was.

Her lobster roll came toasted, with sides of coleslaw and shoestring fries. She ate quickly, eager to get back on the road. When she'd placed the call to the Maine state police, she'd been afraid they'd want to come to Merritt. She'd been relieved to find that they were more than willing to let her come to them. Merritt was such a small town. People noticed things. As it was, she'd still had to explain this unexpected trip. She'd told Rick she needed a night alone, time to rest and think. She and Martha had just finished up the Fifth Reunion report, so under the circumstances the story almost made sense. With profuse thanks to Mimi, she'd packed Anna off to the Creightons'.

She almost missed the state police barracks. It looked like a small white house. She pulled into a circular driveway and parked right in front. After giving her name to a receptionist, she took a seat on a turquoise couch. But before she had time to settle in, a man was coming toward her.

"Jack Pulaski." He held out a hand. His grip was firm and warm. He was of middling height, with a low-key demeanor, dressed in a light gray suit. Brown hair, brown eyes, a pleasant face, nothing the least bit striking. But for some reason, as she looked at him, Callie felt somehow safer.

Pulaski's office was small and neat, looking out on a patch of grass. He had the requisite office fittings — file cabinet, guest chairs, desk. There were two picture frames on his desk, though Callie couldn't see the pictures. A wife, she assumed. A couple of kids. That's what she'd expect. On the edge of the desk sat a brass nameplate: Jackson D. Pulaski, Detective.

He asked if she wanted something to drink.

"Water would be great."

When he came back, glass in hand, another man was with him.

"This is Stu Farkess," Pulaski said. "He'll be here with us today." Farkess was taller than Pulaski, thin, with red hair and a spray of freckles.

For a time, the three of them made small talk. The weather — warm for this time of year; her drive — the directions were perfect. Callie knew that they were trying to put her at ease, and, to an extent, it worked. She felt the muscles in her back unclench, her grip loosen on her chair. By the time they touched on the reason for her visit, Callie's hands lay in her lap.

"Now, Callie," Pulaski said — they'd quickly moved on to first names — "when we talked on the phone, you expressed concern about keeping this confidential. We want to respect your wishes on that. Like I said before, we'll do everything we can. Now, if this comes to trial, well at that point, you might have to testify. We can't do anything about that. But as for the investigation itself, there's no reason that what you tell us today can't stay between us and other investigators working on the case."

"And the media?" Callie asked. "What about reporters?"

"You don't need to worry about that. We tell them very little in any ongoing investigation. They won't even know about you."

"Thank you." He seemed so earnest, so genuine, Callie liked him more and more. A part of her knew that it was tactical, that she was just succumbing to technique. But another part of her didn't care. She liked him all the same.

"So why don't we start with the watch you found," Pulaski said. "If you can tell us how you came to have it."

She'd already rehearsed this part in her mind, and now she went over it. How she'd hidden the Easter basket in the drain-pipe, filled it with chocolate eggs. How, by the next morning, when Anna found it, the contents had been replaced.

As the two men listened to her, Callie felt the strength of their attention. Their expressions stayed calm and easy, but she sensed they were missing nothing.

"Now, this Easter egg hunt," Pulaski said. "It's for the whole neighborhood?"

"That's right," Callie said.

"So the kids look for eggs and baskets all over the place, not just in their own yards."

"Yes."

"So that particular basket, there was no way of ensuring that your daughter would be the one to find it?"

"I guess not," Callie said reluctantly. *Unless, unless* . . . A thought surfaced, then disappeared before she could quite grasp it.

"Still, you have some reason to think that the basket was meant for your daughter. You think that the person who hid the watch intended for her to find it."

"Yes."

"Could you tell us why you think that?"

She felt it rushing toward her, the moment of no return. For the first time in almost ten years she would tell her secret to someone new. The fear that she'd anticipated was strangely ab-sent, though. Instead, she had a feeling of almost reckless exhila-ration.

Callie took a deep breath.

"I'm sure you both know about Steven Gage."

"Sure," said Pulaski. "The serial killer. Diane Massey wrote a book about him."

Callie nodded. "I . . . I was one of the main sources for that book. For several years, I was Steven Gage's girlfriend. During that time, I was known as Laura Seton."

The room was absolutely silent. The air seemed electric.

"There's more too," Callie said. "On the fifth of April — about ten days before my daughter found the watch — I received a note. No postmark. It was stuck in my front door. A single sheet of white paper, typed, not signed. It said 'Happy Anniversary. I haven't forgotten you.'"

The detectives traded glances, a quick shift of the eyes.

"What?" Callie said.

"We have the note," Farkess said. "Jamison sent up a copy along with Diane's watch. He thought we might want to look at it."

A sudden spark of insight. "Diane. Did she get a note too?"

Neither of the detectives answered. Instantly, Callie knew she was right.

"I'm afraid we can't discuss that," Pulaski finally said. "Like what you're telling us today. The details of the investigation have to be kept confidential."

"I see," Callie said. It didn't exactly seem fair, but she didn't have much leverage. "Melanie White — the woman who was attacked in New York — she was one of Steven's lawyers. She helped represent him on appeal. Right until the very end."

Again, the two detectives nodded, but they didn't seem surprised.

"So that makes three of us," Callie said. Now she was thinking out loud. "Three women, all of us connected to Steven. Someone killed Diane. Someone tried to kill Melanie."

Pulaski squarely met her eyes. "I suppose I don't have to tell you that you need to take precautions."

Callie bit her lip and nodded.

"Let's think about motive," said Pulaski. "Do you have any idea why someone might be doing this? Any idea at all of who might be responsible?"

"Well, I guess it's pretty clear that what's happening is somehow linked to Steven. All three of us are women. All three of us knew him. The other thing that we have in common is that all of us betrayed him. At least, that's how he would have seen it. That's how he *did* see it. I testified against him at trial, star witness for the prosecution. And Melanie, while she tried to help him, she didn't manage to save him. Diane's book, well, you must have read it. Steven comes off badly. He wanted to be seen as this brilliant guy. Diane didn't buy it. She was the first — the only — writer to question his intelligence. She dug up Steven's grades and test scores, showed how they were only average. I'm sure that infuriated him. He despised mediocrity."

Pulaski thought a moment, stroking his chin with a hand. On the fourth finger of his left hand, Callie saw a thick gold ring. "So you think it's about revenge?"

"Yes," Callie said. "I do."

"Any idea who would have done these things?"

"Well . . . I keep thinking of Lester Crain. You know who he is?"

Pulaski and Farkess nodded. Again, Callie saw that her speculations weren't any surprise. Melanie must have told Jamison, who'd passed them on to these guys.

"Any other thoughts?" Pulaski asked. "Aside from Crain, I mean?"

Callie studied Pulaski. "You don't think it's him," she said.

"Without getting too far into the details, I'd say it's pretty unlikely. Sexual psychopaths follow certain patterns. Ms. Massey's murder, the attack on Ms. White — they don't conform to Crain's."

As Pulaski spoke, it hit Callie that this wasn't what she'd wanted to hear. At least with Crain she'd had something concrete, an anchor for her fear. Now, set free of its object, the fear was everywhere. *If not Crain, then who?*

"There's Steven's family," she said slowly. "They stuck with him 'til the end. He had two brothers, both younger. Drake and Lou were their names. Last I knew, both of them were still living in Nashville. Drake was in construction. Lou did something with computers."

"Their last name was Gage as well?" That was Farkess talking. For a time, he'd been a silent presence, quietly jotting notes.

"They're half brothers," Callie said. "Their last name was Hollworthy. Steven's father left when he was small, then his mother remarried."

"Anyone else?" Pulaski asked.

"Well, there's his mother, Brenda. She was high-strung. Unstable. Totally relied on her husband and sons, could hardly function on her own. When Steven was a kid she tried to kill herself. I don't think he ever forgave her. He found her in the bathroom, barely breathing, blood everywhere. I can't imagine her planning this, though, let alone doing it. Although . . . I guess people do change. And he was her son, after all."

"She also lived in Nashville?"

"Last I knew. But that was years ago." Callie gave a humorless laugh. "I certainly haven't kept in touch."

A rustling sound as Farkess turned a page in his small spiral notebook.

Callie realized her mouth was dry. She sipped from her glass of water.

"Who else?" Pulaski asked. "Any other names come to mind?"

"I don't know. I guess all the groupies — there were a lot of them. They wrote him letters, came to the trial. I don't know where you'd get the names. Maybe someone saved the mail. It was bizarre, you know? During the trial, these women threw themselves at him. They proposed to him, sent him presents. One woman, I don't remember her name, knitted him a sweater. I always wondered if they thought he wasn't guilty, or if they just didn't care."

"What about friends?" Pulaski asked.

Callie gave a crooked smile. "Steven didn't really have friends. Except for me, that is. He said that he was too busy. Which, in light of everything that came out later, I guess was probably true. It's funny, I always thought it was strange that he wasn't more successful at work. I mean, here was this smart, intense guy who couldn't seem to get things done. He had this paralegal job, and he always seemed to be behind. I told him he had to stop being such a perfectionist. I figured that was the problem. But that wasn't it at all. The whole time he had another job that to him was far more important. It must have taken incredible focus to murder all those women. To kill them and get away with it for all the years that he did."

By four-thirty, Callie was on the road again, heading back toward Merritt. She felt utterly depleted, hardly able to drive. Briefly, she considered finding a motel and going right to sleep. But she still had a couple of hours of daylight. She flipped on cruise control.

She'd been driving for half an hour or so before she realized that the streets seemed unfamiliar. She saw a shopping center. A hospital. Had she passed by these before? It was possible, of course. She'd been preoccupied. But it was equally likely that she'd made a wrong turn back when she'd left the barracks. She caught the names of cities on signs, but they didn't mean anything. Augusta. Bangor. Lewiston. She didn't know their locations. As she looked for a spot to turn off the road, her skin began to prickle. BLUE PEEK ISLAND / CARTWRIGHT ISLAND FERRY. The arrow pointed straight ahead.

Callie's heart was pounding. Her foot moved to the brake. Until now Blue Peek Island had seemed unreal, a fantasy more than a place. But now, here she was — practically, almost, there. At first, the sign's appearance struck her as amazing. One of those impossible accidents that almost have to mean something. But a moment later, she realized that it wasn't so strange after all. It made sense that the investigators would be somewhere near the island.

She was driving close to the water now, through a vaguely industrial landscape. She saw a smokestack in the distance, corrugated metal buildings. The sky was gray and sultry, with seagulls swooping down. Then, on the right-hand side of the road, she saw the ferry landing. A low white building steps from the harbor, the huge docking structure.

She didn't feel as if she had a choice. She turned into the parking lot.

Down here, close to the water, the air whipped against her face. She heard boat riggings snap in the breeze, a mournful distant clanging, the raucous cry of seagulls circling overhead. The water spread out in front of her, green-black rather than blue. On the building, a streaming electronic display announced arrivals and departures.

CARTWRIGHT ISLAND 8:15 . . . 11:15 AM . . . 2:15 . . . 5:15 PM

BLUE PEEK ISLAND 8 . . . 10 AM . . . 2 . . . 4 PM

Callie looked at her watch: 4:20 P.M. Even if she'd wanted to go, she'd missed the last boat out. Not that she would have made the trip, she hastily told herself. She'd done what she came to Maine to do. Now she had to get home.

She stood there another few aimless moments, then walked back to the car, climbed in, and pulled out her road atlas to figure out where she was. It took just a couple of minutes to see that she needed to turn around. She flipped the key in the ignition and drove back toward the road. Before pulling out into traffic, she looked from side to side. It was then that she saw the Old Granite Inn, just across the street. At first she thought it was a large stone house; then she saw the sign.

There was a break in the flow of traffic, but Callie didn't pull out. She hesitated in the parking lot, uncertain what to do.

Maybe they won't have vacancies.

It wouldn't hurt to check.

You have to stay someplace.

Why not just ask?

A tall man with glasses answered the door, a black cat in his arms. Another cat rubbed against his leg, peering up from below.

"Do you have any rooms tonight?" Callie asked.

"As a matter of fact we do."

Tuesday, May 2

8 A.M. A huge swooshing of water as the ferry pulled away. Callie leaned against the railing on the top deck, wind whipping through her hair. For the first time since arriving in Maine, she smelled the acrid sea.

They passed a long granite breakwater with a lighthouse at its tip. Callie's thoughts flashed to Diane, trying to picture her here. The Diane she saw in her mind's eye was the young woman she'd known. She tried to imagine what the years had done to that fiercely intelligent face. Diane would have aged well. She had no doubt about that. The high cheekbones, the fine, straight nose — these would have stayed the same.

When Callie thought of Diane now, it was hard to know what she felt. Beyond the horror of what had happened, her feelings were more complex. Sadness, pity, resentment. Anger and gratitude. She barely remembered their first meeting, at that Nashville AA group. She'd been so distraught — and so hungover — everything was a blur. Diane had followed her out of the meeting, pressed a phone number on her.

She'd needed someone to talk to. That had been part of it. Diane had been an excellent listener, patient and sympathetic. She'd known when to talk and when to keep quiet, when to give advice. From the start, Diane had been honest about her job, but she'd promised to keep their friendship secret from even her editors. Now, more clear-sighted, Callie saw she'd had a plan. It had been self-interest, not loyalty, that had kept their meetings secret. Diane had had no intention of letting her paper get wind of this story.

Diane had kept her word, though. She'd obtained Callie's —
Laura's — approval before selling her book proposal. At first,
she'd resisted Diane's cajoling, but later she came around. In the
end, it had all boiled down to money, and they'd finally struck a
deal: Fifty thousand dollars up front and 10 percent of Diane's
royalties. At that point, Callie had had no idea of how much that
might be. By now, she'd received several hundred thousand dollars, and checks still trickled in. It was money she'd received from
The Vanishing Man that had paid for the house in Merritt. It had
paid her Windham College tuition, established a trust for Anna.

If she had it to do over again, she had no doubt that she would.
Still, she'd never entirely recovered from reading Diane's book.
At first she'd been wildly angry, consumed with a sense of betrayal. She'd trusted Diane totally. Was this how Diane repaid
her? She'd had thoughts of filing a lawsuit, even sat down with
pen and paper. But when she reread the book, her reaction
started to shift. Hard as she searched she couldn't find a single in-
accuracy. Every word Diane had attributed to her — she'd really
said those things. The only difference between the book and life
was the things that had been left out. The days when nothing bad
had happened. The days when Steven was kind.

Still, when you took out these interludes, this is what was left:
an endless series of bright red flags she'd done her best to ignore.
The blood-soaked shirt. The mask and gloves. The unexplained
absences. The blue Honda Civic that someone saw before Lisa
Blake was killed. The Atlanta woman who'd had a frightening
encounter with a man whose name was Steven. She'd met him at
a bar, and he'd bought her a drink. It tasted strange, she said. He
told her he'd get her another one, but when she looked up, he
was gone. A grad student in biology, she'd taken the drink to be
tested. And found that it was laced with GHB, the well-known
date-rape drug.

But everything had been so confused back then, an alcohol-
soaked blur. Callie remembered nights on the couch, with her
second bottle of wine. In her mind, she'd match up his absences
with the dates women disappeared, feel herself teeter dangerously

at the edge of a precipice. Then, sharply, she'd pull herself back, tell herself it was crazy. Would he use his own name if he were a killer? Park his car in plain view? Would he leave evidence for her to find, the shirt, the knives, the bones? Later, she'd tried to tell herself that he'd wanted to be caught, but the experts traced his seeming carelessness to grandiosity.

She still remembered the first time she'd felt that lurching sense of doubt. A Friday night. She'd been watching TV after Steven cancelled a date. She'd been drinking wine, feeling sorry for herself, when a news report came on, a recent murder attributed to the infamous Vanishing Man. Her name was Lisa Blake; she was a Memphis college student. Her picture showed a brilliant smile, smooth, straight blonde hair.

It was like the twist of a kaleidoscope, as pieces fell into place. She'd staggered up to find her date book. To find out where he'd been. Lisa Blake had disappeared on a Saturday night just two weeks before. Steven had cancelled that night, too. He'd said he had to work. In later weeks, she'd checked the dates of half a dozen murders. On none of these days did her calendar show that she'd been with Steven. She didn't always make note of their dates, especially casual ones — a cheeseburger at Rotier's, drinks at 12th & Porter. Still, the suspicion had taken root. She couldn't let it go.

On some days, she was filled with doubt, filled with remorse and guilt. How could she have such terrible thoughts about the man she loved? No wonder Steven was losing interest. He knew who she really was. A desperate, jealous, angry girl, out to get her boyfriend. *No wonder he's not around,* she thought. *You're out to destroy him.*

When they moved to Nashville, Steven's childhood home, the plan was that they'd live together. Steven went down to find a place, while she stayed back in Cambridge. But after finding an apartment, Steven decided to live alone. He was planning to apply to law school, that was his excuse. He'd need to study for the LSAT. He needed solitude.

For once, she stood up for herself, demanded an explanation. If he didn't even want to live with her, why should she move to Nashville? To her astonishment, he started to cry, begging her to stay. "I need you," he told her — the first and only time. "Please, please don't leave me." The tears had reassured her in a way his words could not. Finally, after so much time, she'd finally believed he loved her.

Once she arrived in Nashville, though, things went from bad to worse. And the more elusive Steven grew, the more frantic she became. She devoured dozens of self-help books, tried to improve herself. The problem was they all offered conflicting advice and information. They urged her to be understanding, to listen to his pain. Then they told her that she was making herself too easily available. She tried not calling him on the phone, not answering when he called her. He mentioned it a couple of times, but mostly he didn't notice.

Foggy as this time was, it was clearer than what came later. After his arrest, her life unfolded in an endless haze. Through days in the airless courtroom, she felt like a sleepwalker. And then one night, watching TV news, she suddenly snapped awake. She could still feel the chill that had passed through her as she listened to an interview with Dahlia's brother. "He ruined my life. He ruined my family," Tucker Schuyler said. "Death is too good for him. Anyone who causes this sort of pain, they should be forced to suffer."

The words cut clear through her. She felt their searing truth. With a prescient chill, she knew then that this boy would never recover. He'd been late to meet his sister, and when he showed up she was gone. He'd live with that for the rest of his life, the burden of his guilt. Until then, there'd been something abstract about Dahlia Schuyler's death. In that instant, though, she clearly saw the truth of what Steven had done. He had destroyed this family. And she'd played a role in that. For the first time, it hit home, the degree of her complicity.

The ferry pitched high to one side as the wind cut across the boat. They were passing a rocky island now, lined with jagged trees. In the distance, rolling blue-gray hills rose against the sky. The effect was one of layers upon layers, different shades of blue.

The air was growing colder. Callie went downstairs.

She slid into a seat in the almost empty cabin. The air, heavy and damp around her, smelled like salt and oranges. Behind her a heavy gray-haired woman was finishing off a snack. As she peered through a foggy window, Callie glimpsed land. At first there was just the rocky coast, then the occasional house. The woman behind her gathered up bags. A sleeping man woke up. They must be getting close now. Callie's stomach dipped.

Ten minutes later, the ferry heaved left, and a village came into view. A cluster of shingled buildings, a long wooden pier. They were moving between two islands now through smooth, glassy water. The village grew larger and clearer as the ferry pulled closer in. She caught the words on several buildings. Gray's Yacht and Boat Builder. The Lobster Pound Restaurant. Then she felt a solid bump as the ferry touched the pier.

She waited in her car until the ferry official signaled for her to pull out. Then, following a flatbed truck, she drove down the metal ramp. She couldn't believe she was here. *She couldn't believe she was here.* It was almost as if some outside force had taken control of her body.

She turned left out of the parking lot. No choice, it was a one-way street. Slowly, she drove down a winding road past a library and post office. She saw an art gallery closed for the season, an American Legion post. Another curve in the sloping road, and then there it was: the shingled house where Diane Massey had spent her final days.

Because she'd seen its picture in the paper, she knew that this was the place. Quickly, she glanced in her rearview mirror. No cars or people in sight. She pulled into the gravel driveway and followed it up a hill. The driveway circled behind the house, shielding her car from view.

The soles of her boots scrunched on the gravel as Callie walked toward the back porch. Using her hands to cut the glare, she peered through a back window. What she saw was a rustic old-fashioned kitchen. Nothing unusual. Stove. Refrigerator. Table and chairs. Just what you'd expect. The porch wrapped around the house, and Callie continued on. There were three windows on the side of the house, two of them in the kitchen. Through the last window in the row, she saw a living room. Again, nothing striking. No sign of what had occurred.

It was actually a bit unnerving how untouched everything seemed. Callie realized that, at some unconscious level, she'd expected to find a crime scene. Yellow tape across the door, everything cordoned off. But Diane hadn't been killed at home. She'd been attacked some ways off. Besides, it had been days — weeks — since the body was found.

When she reached the front door, Callie paused, reluctant to continue. Even with the wall of trees by the porch, somebody might see her. She reached for the knob and gave it a twist, sure that she'd find it locked. But to her surprise, the handle turned. The door creaked open.

She gazed into a shadowy hall, its upper reaches veiled in darkness. She felt poised for something, though she didn't know what it was. She had no business being here, but something pulled her on. There wasn't any logic to it, yet she couldn't seem to stop.

Just five more minutes, she thought. *Then I'm out of here.*

She walked down the hallway toward a closed door that she assumed must lead to the kitchen. But just as she reached out to push it open, she heard an explosive crash. The house went black. She couldn't see. Everything started to spin. Some animal instinct seemed to kick in, and she crouched close to the ground.

Time passed, seconds, then minutes. She wasn't sure how long. In the black silence of the looming house, she could almost hear her heart. Then, as her eyes grew accustomed to the dark, she glanced quickly around. No sign of another person. The hall was perfectly still. After another moment, she stood and walked to the front door. She opened it and looked outside. Nothing but sky and trees.

She could see now what had happened: a breeze. The door had slammed shut.

Still shaky, she walked out onto the porch, closing the door behind her.

It was reassuring to hear the familiar sound of her sturdy Subaru's engine. She drove slowly down the driveway and turned back onto the road. For a while, she drove aimlessly, hardly paying attention, letting herself recover from the shock she'd had in the house. She passed a Chevy Blazer and a Ford Escort, turned right on an unmarked road, drove past an overgrown field full of boats, a cemetery, a farm.

After a time, she saw water again, narrow glimpses through trees. The dirt roads that led off into the woods didn't seem to have street signs. Briefly she wondered about that, then figured that they weren't needed. Anyone likely to be out here would know their way around. But just as this thought went through her mind, she *did* see a sign. Black block letters on unfinished wood. CARSON'S COVE, it said.

Callie stepped on the brake.

This was where it happened.

She pulled her car to the side of the road and checked for traffic behind her. No cars, no people, nothing, just a long, flat stretch of pavement. She backed up to the entrance and turned left at the sign.

Bumping down the deeply rutted dirt road, she was glad for her all-wheel drive. She splashed through a muddy pothole, crunched over stray tree limbs. To either side were towering trees as far as she could see, the soft white of birch bark contrasting with the evergreens.

She'd driven about a mile when the road ended in a clearing. It seemed she'd gone as far as she could. Now she'd have to walk. A slender break in the wall of trees led to a narrow footpath. Callie parked, got out of the car, and headed for the opening.

Beneath the deep green canopy, she carefully picked her way. She didn't know what she was looking for, but she felt like she was looking for something. The path was littered with small pinecones, twigs, rocks, and leaves. The air seemed colder than it had before, the sky a deeper gray. She passed a dilapidated shed. Somewhere, birds were chirping. She heard the tapping of a woodpecker, impossibly sharp and fast. But by far the loudest sound of all was the wind rushing through the trees.

Again and again, she asked herself, *What are you doing here?* The words became a sort of refrain as she moved down the path. The impulse that had drawn her here wasn't a simple thing. And it wasn't just about Diane, although she played a role. It struck Callie that perhaps this trip was a pilgrimage of sorts. She'd come to do penance, that was part of it, to bear witness to the past. To pay tribute in some visceral way to all the women who'd died. For so long she'd tried not to think about them, not as individuals. Even at Dahlia Schuyler's trial, she'd tried to block things out.

Without realizing it, Callie's steps had slowed until she was standing still. Lost in thought, she startled at the sound of footsteps behind her. The sound was soft but growing louder, approaching not retreating. For the second time in less than an hour, adrenaline washed through her. Frozen, she stood there listening for another long moment. Then she started to walk again, but this time more quickly. Up ahead a few dozen yards, she saw a patch of sun. Her rapid walk became a run as she sprang toward the light.

She heard the sound again. Someone, or something, behind her. Still running, she reached into her purse and grappled for her cell phone. The footsteps behind her seemed to speed up, keeping time with her own. With a burst of energy, she broke through the trees, emerged on a windswept beach. Black water lapped against the shore, an expanse of rocks and seaweed. She'd hoped to see houses or even people, but the area was deserted. To her left the island curved inward, and she couldn't see around the bend. Not sure what else to do, she jogged in that direction.

She had to be careful not to trip as she fumbled with the cell phone buttons. The bright beep as she turned on her phone filled her with sudden joy. Then, glancing behind her, she saw a man step out of the woods. Wearing dark clothing and a baseball cap, he impatiently scanned the landscape. Even as she started to run more quickly, she realized that she was trapped. Her only possible hiding place was a pile of boulders down the beach. But long before she reached it, he'd be on top of her.

"Hey!" he called. "Wait up. I wanna talk to you."

She'd already dialed 911 and was waiting for the call to go through. Holding the phone to her ear, she kept her eyes on him. The glassy water broke against the shore, bursting into foam.

The phone still wasn't ringing.

She looked at the screen: NO SIGNAL.

She stared at the words, incredulous. This had never happened before. Just last night she'd called Anna from her room at the Old Granite Inn. A wave of fear engulfed her. What was she going to do?

She felt clumsy and weighted down in her parka and heavy boots. When she next looked back, she saw the man was fast gaining on her. She reached down, grabbed a rock, and started to run again. Her heels sank into the stones on the beach and she ran awkwardly. Her purse, clutched close to her side, banged against a hip.

"Hey! Hey!" She heard his voice from behind.

Finally reaching the pile of boulders, she scrambled up one side. On top, she hopped from one rock to the next, struggling to keep her balance.

Then, almost to the other side, she suddenly lost her footing. With a sickening lurch, her ankle twisted, and her foot slid out from beneath her. She grasped at air, then fell, hard, landing on her hip. Her fingers scrabbled at moss-covered stone as she tried to stand up again. But when she managed to reach her feet, pain shot through her ankle.

With a huge effort, she reached the next boulder, dragging her injured leg. From behind, she could hear the pounding approach of footsteps, growing louder. Somewhere along the way she'd dropped the rock. She had no way to protect herself. Then in a flash it occurred to her that he didn't know about the phone.

She wheeled around to face him. He was nearer than she'd

thought. He'd reached the base of the boulders and was looking up at her. Up close, she could see that he wasn't large, not much taller than she was. He had sharp features, pitted skin, and narrow, slouching shoulders. For an instant, she wondered if she could take him on but quickly dismissed the idea. Even apart from her injured ankle, there was something that warned her off. She sensed a sort of wiry strength at odds with the slender frame.

Now he smiled up at her, showing small yellow teeth. He reminded her of the evil foxes in fairy tales she'd read to Anna.

"You gotta be careful up there," he said. "Them rocks is slippery."

Callie met his eyes. "Stay away from me," she said. "I've already called for help."

The smile flickered, then faded. "What're you talkin' about?"

"I've got a cell phone with me," Callie said. "I've already called the police. They know I'm out here, that you're following me. They'll be here any minute."

Shaking his head, he raised his hands and slowly backed away. "Ma'am, you got the wrong idea," he said. "I ain't gonna hurt you. I was just comin' to tell you that you shouldn't be out this way alone. A woman was killed 'round these parts not too long ago."

Callie's ankle had begun to throb. She looked at him, uncertain. Could he be telling the truth? She had no way of knowing.

"Look," she said. "I'm just a little nervous. I didn't mean to attack you. It's just that when I heard you behind me, well, I guess I sort of panicked."

"You knew about the murder?" he said.

"Yes," said Callie. "I knew."

He peered at her more sharply, with something like suspicion. "Who are you, anyway? You some sort of reporter? Someone from the papers?"

"No. I'm . . . I used to know the woman who was killed. I was sort of a friend of hers."

"Huh." He nodded slowly a few times, then looked at her again. "You need some help gettin' down from there? You hurt yourself when you fell?"

"No," said Callie. "Really. I'm fine."

"Okay, then." He cocked his head. "Well, I'd better get going. You be careful now, hear?"

As he sauntered back down the beach toward the woods, Callie watched his figure get smaller. Once he'd disappeared in the trees, she began to climb down off the rocks.

Now that there was no need to move quickly, she stayed on her hands and knees. Painfully, she crawled down off the boulders, then made an effort to stand. Her injured ankle was pounding, the pain growing worse by the minute. She limped forward, step by step, toward the path back to her car.

When she reached the edge of the woods, she tried her phone again, but there was still no signal. For all her network's vaunted claims of coverage, they must not have service here.

It was almost one o'clock. The next ferry was at three. She needed to get back on the road and find her way to the landing.

As she stepped back onto the gloomy path, her throat seemed to close up. Again, fear washed over her. What if he'd been lying? She told herself that he'd had his chance. If he'd wanted to attack her, he would have. Chances were he was just who he'd claimed to be, a concerned passerby. Besides, she couldn't just stand here all day. She had to get back to her car.

Pale sun flickered across the ground as Callie struggled forward. It was her left ankle that she'd hurt, and she tried to favor it, but even minor pressure sent pain surging through her. When she finally glimpsed her parked car, she almost started to cry. She realized that a part of her had been afraid that it wouldn't be there. Amazingly, she'd managed to keep hold of her purse. She reached into it for her keys.

Inside, the car had its familiar smell of fresh plastic and coffee. On the seat beside her lay the road atlas, still opened to Maine. In the backseat, she saw her overnight bag, exactly where she'd left it. These simple objects seemed miraculous; she had to reach out and touch them. As she turned the key in the ignition, she felt a burst of gratitude. How lucky she was to be here! How lucky to be alive! She backed up and turned around, heading back to town. To the ferry that would carry her toward home, to the place and people she loved.

~

HIDDEN inside the abandoned shed, Lester Crain watched her go.

She was limping — he'd known that she was hurt — as she staggered into her car. The dependable motor of the Subaru quickly sprang to life. Rigid, he stood there watching as the blue car pulled away. The roar of the motor blended with the drumbeat in his brain. He knew what it meant, tried to stop it, tried to think it through. But the drumbeat just grew louder. There was nothing he could do.

A tiny voice in the back of his head was telling him he'd screwed up. He shouldn't have come to the island. He shouldn't have stayed this long. It was getting harder and harder to keep himself under control. At night, when he slept, he could hear the screams, almost smell the blood. He saw their faces, crimson-lipped with bright, desperate eyes.

Things were getting all mixed up, the past confused with the present. Sometimes he'd forget why he was here, forget Steven Gage was dead. When he'd seen *her* coming down the trail, he'd wondered if he'd gone crazy. But he wasn't seeing things after all. She was real. Here.

He wondered if she had any idea how close she'd come to dying. It had taken an incredible effort to keep his hands off her. Even though she wasn't his type, he'd almost given in. But once she let loose about the phone, he'd managed to pull back. The bitch was probably lying, but he didn't know for sure. And he wasn't so far gone yet that he planned to take the risk.

Still, hard as he tried, he couldn't get her off his mind. He looked at a beam high overhead and imagined her dangling there. Mouth gagged, eyes bulging, terrified of what came next. The drumbeat in his head was faster now, pulsing through his body. Quickly, he unzipped his pants and jammed a hand inside.

When he was finished, he leaned against the wall, waiting for his head to clear. The relief was only partial, though, and he needed something more. He couldn't get over the feeling that he'd let a chance go by. Of course, that's what he'd learned to do. Gage had taught him that. Strategy. Discipline. Self-control. He'd learned these lessons well. He'd learned to assess opportunities. He'd learned to hide the bodies.

But the pounding in his head wouldn't stop. The rules were falling away. Ever since Diane Massey, things hadn't been the same.

As the car disappeared down the tree-lined road, a plan was taking shape. Again, he repeated the letter and numbers until he knew them cold.

23LG00.

Her Massachusetts license plate.

Thursday, May 4

THE dining room at Rebecca's was bathed in a peachy glow. Self-conscious on crutches, Callie followed the hostess back. When the young woman stopped at a table for two, Callie hesitated. She'd be sitting with her back to the door, and the prospect made her anxious.

"I . . . could we have one of the banquettes? What about over there?"

The hostess smiled, amenable. She didn't seem to care. Her heavy topknot gave her head the look of a nodding flower.

Rick held her crutches, as Callie slid onto the cushioned bench. She'd told Rick that she'd twisted her ankle stepping out of her car. The hostess offered to take the crutches. Callie said no.

"I'll just put them against the wall. They'll be out of the way."

For the first time, the hostess seemed slightly put out, but she didn't say anything. Instead, after Rick had taken his seat, she said, "Enjoy your meal."

As she folded open the menu, Callie glanced toward the entrance. She hadn't wanted to come out tonight, but for once, Rick had insisted. They needed to talk, he'd said to her. The words seemed ominous. A week had passed since the dinner party, and they'd barely spoken since. Yesterday, Rick had even cancelled pizza night.

"You know what you want?" Rick's voice was polite but coolly impersonal. They might have been a couple on a bad first date, the kind you just wanted to end.

"The duck, I think," said Callie.

Across the table in his navy blazer, Rick was a handsome stranger. He seemed as remote and alien as a model in a magazine. Callie hadn't bothered to get dressed up, just couldn't make the effort. As a last-minute concession, she'd put on dangly lapis lazuli earrings.

A waitress came by to take their orders, and then they were alone again.

"So I —"

"I was —"

Both of them spoke at once then stopped, elaborately courteous. Out of the corner of her eye, Callie watched a couple enter the restaurant. As the man took the woman's coat, he said something and she laughed.

Rick began again. "Callie, we need to talk."

"Yes," she said. "I know."

This was the moment she'd been dreading, and yet she felt oddly detached. As if this wasn't happening to her. As if she were someone else. There was something restful, almost comforting, about this state of mind. She didn't have to fight anymore. She could just let things go. She was so tired of trying to manage her life, of trying to control things. It reminded her of that AA phrase, she could just *turn it over.*

Calmly, she took a roll from the basket and started to butter it. When she'd finished, she took a bite. It was sourdough, very good.

She knew that Rick was watching her, sensed his rising annoyance. But, again, it had nothing to do with her. All she could do was wait.

Rick leaned forward, hands clasped, elbows on the table. "I want you to tell me what's going on. Something is happening with you. I want to know what it is. The way things have been with us — it can't go on. I feel like you don't trust me. I haven't asked any questions. I haven't wanted to press you. I've kept hoping that you'd — we'd — get to the point where you'd want to let me in. Where you'd want to tell me your secrets. Want to tell me about *this.*"

Before she knew what was happening, he grabbed hold of her arm. He flipped it over, pushed up the sleeve, and touched the tracing of scars.

And then it was like she'd gone away. Her mind was set adrift. Instead of listening to Rick, she was thinking of Melanie. She needed to call the hospital, to find out her condition. She wondered if they'd tell her how Melanie was if she called and asked. She should have protected Melanie. She should have protected the others. Once again, she'd second-guessed herself. She hadn't trusted her instincts.

"Callie? Are you listening to me?" Rick's voice jarred her back to the present.

"I'm sorry," she said. "I sort of spaced out."

"Have you heard a thing I've been saying?"

"I — I heard the first part."

He looked at her, jaw set.

The waitress arrived with their meals.

The crisp, brown duck smelled delicious, but Callie wasn't hungry. Unwilling to meet Rick's eyes, she picked up her fork and knife. She cut off a tiny sliver of duck and moved it around on her plate. It was then that she noticed the single rose in the flower display on their table. The rose was the palest yellow, not red. Still, her body clenched.

"I want to get a gun," she said abruptly.

Rick looked at her, dumbfounded. "Is there any particular *reason?*" he asked.

She didn't like his tone.

"I'm a citizen," she said stiffly. "I have a right to protect myself."

"Callie, this is Merritt. Protect yourself from *what?*"

Suddenly, she felt angry. She shouldn't have to explain. The gun was her decision. It had nothing to do with Rick.

"You know," she said, squarely meeting his eyes. "There are things you don't know about me. Some of them are . . . important."

He leaned closer, across the table. "What the hell is going on?"

She had a sense that if he could have, he'd have reached across the table to shake her. Then something in him seemed to collapse, and he sank back into his chair. When he looked back up, he seemed defeated, and she felt a pang of guilt. Suddenly, she thought of Rick's father, his ongoing heart problems. How long had it been since she'd even asked Rick how his father was doing?

"I'm sorry," she said softly. "I'm sorry for everything."

Rick just looked at her, shook his head. His face was expressionless.

"Something's got to change," he said. "We can't go on this way."

Saturday, May 6

H E shouldn't be here, he shouldn't.

And yet, here he was.

Lester Crain drove slowly past the house on Abingdon Circle. Right away, he knew he'd found the place. Her car was parked out front. The blue Subaru with the license plate 23LG00. Then the front door was opening. He pulled to the side of the road. He watched as she stepped down off the porch with two men and another woman.

The four of them walked to the curb where a battered Jetta was parked. They opened the doors and climbed inside, and then they were off.

Without taking time to think, he fell in behind them.

The drumbeat was growing louder now.

He knew what he had to do.

⌘

"WHAT'S a grange anyway?" asked Callie.

They were zipping up I-91 in Martha's Volkswagen Jetta, Tod and Martha in the front seat, Callie and Rick in the back, heading for the weekly contra dance at the Guiding Star Grange in Greenfield.

"They were started by farmers after the Civil War," said Martha. "Community organizations to promote the well-being of farm families. They fought the railroad monopolies but also did a lot of social activities. Square dances, suppers, sing-alongs, that sort of thing."

As it turned out, Callie was just as happy to be in a group

tonight. There was no denying the tension that now suffused her dealings with Rick. They hadn't talked since Thursday night, when he'd left her abruptly at the front door. She'd even thought that he might cancel tonight, say he just didn't want to see her. But, perhaps in deference to his friendship with Tod, he hadn't opted out.

"Actually," said Martha, "this particular grange almost closed in the early nineties. There was a lawsuit over handicap access and not enough members left to pay for renovations. We — I mean the dancers — we'd been renting the hall, and when we found out what was happening, we asked the farmers how we could help. The solution we figured out was for the dancers to join the grange."

"That's interesting," said Tod.

"Yes," Callie chimed in.

Rick's face was dim in the shadows. He didn't seem to hear. Callie wondered what he'd say if he knew where she'd spent her day: in Springfield, at the Smith & Wesson Academy, taking a gun safety course. Today she'd stood on a shooting range, firing at paper targets. She'd learned to squeeze the trigger slowly, waiting for the recoil. The revolver was heavier than she'd expected. She felt subtly changed. Now, with her safety certificate in hand, she was free to apply for a license.

They swung off 91 onto 2A and headed down Greenfield's Main Street. Callie had a moment of déjà vu; she'd taken this route to Maine. They passed through town, then swung a left down a side street of clapboard houses.

The Guiding Star Grange was a large white building that might have been a country church. It was only seven-thirty, but the lot was filling, and it took some time to park. Inside, the hall was huge, with wood floors and tall windows. A table by the door held an open fiddle case piled with dollar bills. A sign on the case said $7.00, the price of admission. "I'll pay for you," Callie said to Rick and counted out fourteen dollars. "Thanks," Rick responded. He barely glanced at her.

Callie's spirits lifted slightly as they moved inside, and she heard the lively music, a haunting, energizing blend of Celtic and American. Onstage, someone played the accordion, and a few other musicians played strings. Out front, a few eager couples danced, mirroring each other's movements, swirling in circles, suddenly stopping, then doing a sort of scuff kick.

The growing crowd ran the gamut from aging hippies to tattooed kids. There were even a few svelte couples in black who looked like they hailed from Manhattan. Callie was smiling at the random mix when she caught sight of Nathan and Posy.

Callie ducked behind Martha. "Kabuki Girl's here. With Nathan."

Martha looked at her, stricken. "I should have told you she comes sometimes. I'd totally forgotten."

"It's not a big deal," said Callie. But a part of her wished she'd known. The thought of dealing with Nathan tonight was more than she could take. People were still pouring through the door, filling up the hall. Perhaps the crowd would be large enough that he wouldn't notice her.

Someone on the stage was talking.

"That's the caller. We're about to start." Martha looked at Callie and Rick. "Maybe the two of you should split up, at least for the first few dances. It's easier to pick up the steps with someone who knows what they're doing."

"Okay," said Rick, with an alacrity that Callie found disconcerting. He headed off into the crowd, leaving Callie with Martha and Tod.

"I don't want to strain my ankle," said Callie. "I just got off those crutches."

"See how it feels," Martha said. "You can always sit down if you want to."

Martha was looking over Callie's shoulder. "Al!" she called. "Come dance with my friend. It's her first time here."

Callie's partner was a balding man with a small potbelly and an impish smile. Below khaki shorts, his legs were white. He wore tube socks and sneakers.

The crowd had divided itself into three long lines of couples.

From the stage, the caller gave instructions. Callie did her best to follow.

Do-si-do. Star Left. Swing your partner. Circle right.

Some moves were familiar from childhood square dances; others were totally new. The most complicated step, called a *hey*, involved four dancers weaving in and out. Callie couldn't seem to get it straight. She kept bumping shoulders and knees.

"Don't worry about it," Al said reassuringly. "Just have a good time."

The music started up, spirited and infectious.

Before she knew what was happening, Callie found herself dancing. Someone grabbed her hand. She turned around. Then Al clasped her from behind. He spun her around, first slowly, then faster and faster.

"Meet my eyes," she heard him say, as the room began to blur. "It'll keep you from getting dizzy."

She raised her head, reeling, smiling. Then someone else grasped her hand.

There was a pattern to the dance, Callie saw, though it took a while to catch on. She and Al had started near the top of their line and were moving toward the bottom, dancing with the couple just behind them, then moving on to the next, repeating the same pattern of steps with each successive couple.

Once she got the hang of it, she fell into the rhythm. Before long, she was extending a hand, not waiting to be grabbed. Now when Al spun her around, she leaned farther back, letting the weight of her body add to the momentum. It was like being a child again, twirling as fast as she could, getting a kick out of trying to make herself dizzy enough to fall down.

Glancing around, Callie thought how *wholesome* the whole thing seemed. As if they'd all been transported back to some simpler time and place. A community barn raising, a church potluck supper. It really was a lot of fun, festive and exhilarating. So different from the type of dancing she'd done when she was younger. The dark rooms, the beer and sweat, the loud pounding music. *I'm in the mood, I'm in the mood, I'm in the . . .*

With a start, she pulled her thoughts back to the safe, well-lighted present.

When the music ended, everyone clapped. Al thanked her and moved on. But before she could look around for Rick, someone else had asked her to dance. She danced with him and then another man, a professor at UMass. By the end of the third dance, her ankle throbbed. She had to take a break.

Chairs lined the sides of the hall, and she headed for an empty one. She was just about to take a seat, when someone called her name.

"Hi, Callie. Will you dance with me?" Nathan's face was pink and shiny. His white T-shirt clung damply to the bones of his narrow rib cage.

Callie shook her head. "Sorry, Nathan, but I'm beat. I've got to take a break."

"Maybe I'll take a break with you. I'm pretty wiped out too."

The music had started again. But instead of the rousing contra music, the musicians were playing a waltz. Couples slowly dipped and turned to the *one*-two-three, *one*-two-three beat. Across the room, Callie saw Martha, taking the floor with Al. She wondered what he'd been thinking when he put on those thick white socks.

"Where's Posy?" Callie asked Nathan.

He shrugged. "Don't know," he said.

Then, with relief, Callie saw Tod, coming toward her through the crowd.

"Hey," he said. "I was looking for you. Want to give it a whirl?"

"Sure!" said Callie. She looked at Nathan. "Sorry. I promised him." She glimpsed Nathan's disappointed face as Tod took her hand. He stood there, slack-faced, staring, as she moved to the floor with Tod.

"What was that about?" asked Tod, taking Callie in his arms. He felt different from Rick, shorter and more compact. She had an impression of solidity. He smelled of wool and lime.

"It's not worth going into," said Callie. "Someone I know from school."

They danced for a while in silence, Tod's arm firm around her waist. Callie hadn't waltzed since the ballroom dancing classes she'd taken as a kid, but to her surprise, she found that she could easily follow Tod.

"You're good at this." She grinned up at him.

"You sound surprised," he said.

"No. Oh, maybe. I guess I just don't think of people waltzing anymore. It seems so old-fashioned. Like something our parents did."

"My wife — ex-wife — liked to dance," said Tod. "She made me learn."

There was a neutral quality to his voice. Callie couldn't see his face. She debated whether to follow up or let the subject drop.

"So do you still miss her?" Callie finally asked.

Tod circled her to the right.

"I don't even know anymore. Lately I've been thinking that maybe it's just a habit. Something I've got used to saying without really thinking. The thing is, we didn't really get along. We're very different people. But for some reason both of us kept thinking we could change the other person. Stupid, huh? I mean everyone knows you can't change someone. So why do we keep thinking we can?"

"That's a good question," said Callie.

"Martha's a really great person," he said, after another pause. "Thanks for introducing us."

Callie felt a glow of warmth for him. "Sure," she said. "No problem."

When the dance was over, everyone clapped. Callie saw Tod watching her.

"You okay?" he asked, after the applause died down. "You look a little tired. Want something to drink? I think they have stuff downstairs."

As a crowd of dancers surged toward the door, Callie and Tod moved with them. Downstairs the throng converged on a table filled with refreshments. Callie and Tod bought lemonade, then headed for an empty table, one of several shoved against the walls of the busy room. As she sipped her drink, Callie saw Martha and called out to her.

"Hey, you guys," said Martha. Her face was bright and flushed. She pushed a swath of hair up on her head and fanned the back of her neck.

Tod scooted over another few inches so Martha could sit down. She touched his shoulder briefly. "Thanks. But let me get lemonade."

Upstairs, the music was starting again.

"Have you seen Rick?" Callie asked her.

Martha scanned the room. "I danced with him a while ago, but I haven't seen him since."

As Martha made her way to the refreshment table, Tod turned to Callie. "How's Rick been doing?" he asked her. "He seems sort of quiet tonight."

Callie wasn't sure what to say. "Yeah," she finally said. "I know."

"How's his dad doing?" Tod asked.

"Better, I think," she said. "At least, the last he told me. He doesn't really tell me much."

"I know what you mean," said Tod.

These last few words made Callie feel better. At least it wasn't just her. But the sense of relief didn't last long. Rick's father was the least of their problems.

Martha rejoined them, paper cup in hand, and hopped up onto the table. Then, from across the room, Callie saw Nathan coming toward them.

"I'm looking for Posy," he said to Callie once he reached their table.

Relieved that he wasn't asking her to dance, Callie managed a smile. "Haven't seen her," she said. "It's quite a crowd tonight."

Nathan looked at her suspiciously, as if he didn't believe her.

"Well, if you see her, tell her I looked for her. I'm tired. I'm going home now."

As Nathan walked away, Martha turned toward Tod. "How about it?" she said. "You up for another one?"

"Sure," he said. Then turning, "You coming up, Callie?"

Callie took one more look around the rapidly clearing room. Most of the dancers had gone back upstairs. Still no sign of Rick.

"My ankle's hurting a little bit. I think I'll sit this one out. But I'll come back upstairs with you. I think I'll just watch."

In their absence, the dance hall's temperature seemed to have shot up. The crowd had grown as the evening passed, and the room was now jam-packed.

At the next break in the music, Martha and Tod stepped onto the floor, joining one of the long lines that ran the length of the hall. As the music started up again, Callie started to walk, slowly edging her way around the room's chair-lined periphery. A sharp cool breeze blew in through a window, and she paused there gratefully. A boy with a pierced eyebrow asked her to dance. Callie politely said no. Continuing around the room, Callie watched the dancers. Again and again, she scanned the crowd, but she didn't see Rick anywhere.

GODDAMN *it*.

She wasn't going to cry. She wasn't.

Crying was totally lame. And besides, it would wreck her makeup.

Posy Kisch pressed two fingers against the skin beneath her eyes, carefully blocking the tears that threatened to erupt. Her lower eyelashes left traces of black on the tips of her black-nailed fingers. She wiped them off on her short black skirt, bought specially for tonight. She wished she had a mirror to check the rest of her face. The dark red lipstick. The white foundation. The spots of pink on her cheeks.

But then, why did she give a fuck?

What was the point, anyway?

She was such a stupid girl. *Stupid, stupid girl.*

When Nathan agreed to come with her tonight, she'd thought that it meant something. She'd thought that it would be almost a date. The two of them together. There were always tons of people at a contra dance, but Nathan wouldn't know them. And since he was incredibly shy, she'd expected he'd stick with her.

When that bitch Callie Thayer had walked in the room, she could hardly believe her eyes. Of course, Martha was a regular, but she'd never before brought Callie. It had taken Nathan about five seconds to figure out she was here. She was old enough to be his mom. The whole thing was totally stupid. Besides, Callie *had* a boyfriend. It fucking wasn't fair.

She was standing outside in the parking lot crowded with dark cars. From back inside, she could hear the music, the sound of people dancing. Looking up at the silvery stars, she wondered what the point was. She'd hated high school. She hated college. Maybe she hated life. She had never fit in anywhere. Maybe she never would.

Again, she felt the tears rush up. Again, she pushed them back. *Don't cry. Don't cry.*

Don't be a stupid girl.

She'd thought she was all alone out here, but someone was calling her. "Hey. Over here." The voice was urgent, low.

Confused, she turned toward the sound. It seemed to be coming from someplace close, but she didn't see anyone. Maybe back behind the building. She couldn't see back there. Most of the parking lot was well lit, but that area was darker.

"Nathan?" she said hesitantly.

"Yeah. Over here."

"Why are you talking like that?" she said. "Where are you, anyway?"

Then there was a light in her face, and she couldn't see anything. "Nath — " she said. But before she finished, hands closed around her neck.

Monday, May 8

In the silence of the Windham library basement, Callie found her carrel, the place where she always sought refuge when she had to get some work done. The carrel wasn't really hers — it was assigned to an honors senior — but the only sign of its rightful occupant were some books about ancient France.

As she started to unload her backpack, she gave herself a pep talk. It was understandable, she told herself, that she hadn't kept up in school. Diane's murder. Melanie's attack. The overnight trip to Maine. It was hard to believe that all these things had happened in a few short weeks. At least Melanie was doing better, and that was a huge relief. When Callie called the hospital several days ago, she'd learned that Melanie had been released. She'd sent her a card and a spring bouquet but hadn't telephoned yet, unsure if Melanie would welcome the call, under the circumstances.

But she had to put these thoughts aside, at least for a couple of hours. She was here to focus on the term paper due in just two weeks. Today she'd look over the assigned readings and settle on a topic. She wanted to write about memory but needed to find a thesis. From a loose-leaf notebook, she pulled out a copy of an excerpt from a Harvard psychologist's book. It discussed what the author called memory's "sins." There were seven of them.

Most intriguing, Callie thought, were the so-called sins of commission — cases where a memory was inaccurate or unwanted. Of the four sins in this category, the first was misattribution — for example, believing that a friend had told you something you'd read in the paper. The concept seemed familiar, and Callie wondered why. Then she realized that it reminded her of the reading on unconscious transference.

Farther down, she discovered that there was, in fact, a link. This excerpt, too, recounted the story of the innocent sailor accused of robbery because in the past he'd bought tickets from the victim of the crime. Again she read about the psychologist wrongly accused of rape due to the fact that, during the rape, the victim had watched him on TV.

Such mistakes, the author wrote, may be traced to "binding failure," the failure to connect a memory to its proper time and place. Now here was a topic she could write about, one that would hold her attention. That someone could be sure they knew something and yet be totally wrong.

She was thinking that she should go find the book when a shiver passed through her body. Suddenly, it struck her how alone she was down here. She'd turned on the light above her carrel, but the book-lined stacks were dark. Behind her a row of empty carrels faded into the shadows. She looked up sharply, quickly, as if expecting to see something, a flicker of light, a movement, as someone tried to hide. There was something suspect about the stillness; it felt like a sort of trick. Again she peered up, around, craning her neck to see. She had an impulse to speak out loud, to test the strength of her voice. Would anyone hear her if she called out? Could someone have followed her?

Right then, she wanted to grab her things and head for the elevator, for the populous realm of the reading room, the busy reference desk. But another part of her sternly exhorted herself to stay put. The killer had taken a lot from her, but she wouldn't give him this. She'd come here to get some work done. She'd stay until she finished.

She sat there another few seconds, heart pounding in her chest. Then, her stomach growled, a homely sound, and she hit on a compromise. On the other side of the basement was a lounge with vending machines. She'd take a break, have a quick snack, then get back to her reading.

Her footsteps sounded unnaturally loud on the gray cement

floor. Towering shelves of dusty books floated in the vaultlike gloom. In a movie, this would be the scene where the heroine was attacked. A sense of foreboding washed over her, and she walked a bit faster.

She stepped into the bleak, windowless room as if into a bath. Even the harsh fluorescent lights seemed cheerful and welcoming. Two young women sat at a table, heads bowed over books. One of them tapped a foot against her chair in a steady, rhythmic beat. Another time the sound might have been annoying, but right now it calmed her.

From the vending machines that lined the wall, Callie bought Raisinettes and cheese crackers. She ate the candy standing up, scanning a bulletin board. Yoga classes. A desk for sale. Someone seeking a roommate. After she finished the Raisinettes, she decided to get some coffee. She deposited her thirty-five cents. The machine spit out a cup.

Back at one of the tables, she sipped the tepid brew. The uneasiness she'd felt just minutes ago had totally disappeared. Her heart was back to its normal rate; she could hardly feel its beating. Once again, her mind was clear. She could think about her paper.

Misattribution.

Unconscious transference.

She asked herself why these theories had such a hold on her. Mistakes — sins — of memory. Is that what she'd once hoped for? That the women who thought they'd seen him had somehow all been wrong? For a moment, she had the crazy thought that maybe they *had* been wrong. That whoever had killed Diane in Maine had also killed the others. If that were true, *if that were true,* Steven had been innocent. But, of course, it was just a fantasy, and a far-fetched one at that. She had no doubt of Steven's guilt. She had no doubt of her own.

So who had killed Diane? Who'd brought her the watch and letter? With the force of an unpleasant habit, her mind moved to Lester Crain.

She had the impression that the Maine state police had written him off as a suspect. But despite their confidence, she wasn't convinced, at least not all the way. It just made so much sense that Crain would be the one. He'd admired Steven, owed him his life. No one knew where Crain was. This notion that the signature didn't change seemed somewhat dubious. Psychological theories were, by definition, always works in progress. Theories were true until proven wrong. That's the way it worked. The fact was, when she thought of Diane's killer, she pictured Lester Crain. Or not pictured, exactly, since she couldn't recall what he looked like. She must have seen pictures when he escaped, but she couldn't remember them.

"Hey, Callie. What's going on?"

She raised her head with a jolt to find Nathan there beside her. Right away, Callie stood up.

"I was just getting back to work," she said. "How're you doing, Nathan?"

"How come we never hang out anymore?" His voice had a plaintive tone.

She turned and faced him squarely. Okay, the moment of truth.

"Nathan, you need to find friends your own age. I'm sorry, but I'm just too busy. I have a job. I have a daughter. I have other friends."

There. She'd finally said it. But instead of feeling relieved, now she just felt bad. Nathan's face seemed to crumple up, and she thought that he might cry.

"C'mon, Nathan," she said with a laugh, trying to lighten the mood. "You've got other friends too. I think Posy really likes you."

Nathan shook his head. "No chance. She ditched me at that stupid dance in Greenfield."

"Ditched you. You mean broke up with you?"

"No. Just left without me. I saw her talking to this other guy. I think she went with him. I've tried to call her a bunch of times, but she doesn't answer her phone. She's probably screening her calls. She doesn't want to talk to me."

Callie wasn't sure what to say. "Maybe it will all work out," she said, not feeling terribly hopeful. If Posy had really left him at the dance — well, it didn't sound promising. But this just wasn't her problem. *It really wasn't her problem.*

A cluster of students walked into the lounge, all of them squealing with laughter. One of the women had a glossy braid that almost reached her waist. Callie balled up her crackers wrapper and tossed it into the trash.

"Give Posy another call," she said. "It could be a misunderstanding."

As she turned to leave, she tried to avoid the pain on Nathan's face.

Saturday, May 13

Ring Bell for Firearm Permits

ALL OTHERS SEE DESK OFFICER AT WINDOW
BEHIND YOU

The bell was on the counter beneath the sign. Callie tapped it with her palm. A short, bright ring, and then a female voice. "Be right there. Just a sec."

Nervously, Callie glanced around once more at the small police department lobby. While she knew Rick was visiting his parents again, she half expected to see him.

"What can I do for you?" The woman behind the window had short brown hair and a soap model's flawless skin. Callie was relieved to find that she didn't look familiar.

"I'm here for a license to carry," said Callie.

"You've filled out the application?"

"Yes." Callie pulled it out. She handed it over along with the safety certificate from her Smith & Wesson class.

The clerk opened a door and gestured Callie back. "That'll be thirty-five dollars."

After taking Callie's money, she turned back to the forms. Covertly, Callie watched, trying to read her expression. There were several places on the four-page application where she hadn't been sure what to write.

Are you or have you ever been under treatment for or confinement for drug addiction or habitual drunkenness?

She'd never been to rehab — though perhaps she should have gone — so she figured the answer was no. AA wasn't a treatment program, more a form of self-help.

Have you ever used or been known by another name?
If yes, provide name and explain.

Her first thought had been to stop right there, to forget all about the license. In bold-faced letters, the application warned against providing false information, listing penalties ranging from a five-hundred-dollar fine to a two-year prison sentence. Maybe the warning was exaggerated, but she didn't feel like testing it. The only other option was to put down her maiden name.

Laura Seton

Laura Caroline Seton

Laura C. Seton

She'd written down the various versions, trying to see them with fresh eyes. Even if the name seemed vaguely familiar, would it prompt more than a fleeting thought? There were millions of people in the world. Many had the same names. In the end, she'd settled on the full name: Laura Caroline Seton. It was both the most accurate and, she thought, the least likely to be recognized.

The clerk looked up at her.

"Where it says reason for request, you put down personal protection."

"Yes."

"You'll need to speak with Lieutenant Lambert."

"Is . . . is that standard? Talking to him, I mean?"

"If you want a gun for personal protection. Not if it's for target practice."

Damn.

Briefly, Callie considered changing the reason she'd put down. But to do so now, she decided, would be a transparent ploy. Better to stick with what she'd written, as if she had nothing to hide. At least this Lambert wasn't someone she knew, someone Rick talked about.

She was photographed and fingerprinted. One by one, Callie watched as the lacy black prints appeared, the second time in the past two weeks she'd been through this process. In Maine, they'd needed her prints for elimination purposes, to compare with anything they managed to lift from the note or the watch.

They started with the right hand, moved to the left, then did a second set. Finally, the clerk took a single print of Callie's right index finger.

"This one will be for your license," she said.

"Why? Why just that one?"

"For most people it's the trigger finger."

"Oh," Callie said.

In less than twenty minutes, it was over.

Callie was on her way out the door when a question crossed her mind. "The application says it could take more than a month — to get a license, I mean. Is there any way to speed that up? Any way to expedite?"

"You'd need to ask Lieutenant Lambert about that too. I really couldn't say."

Lambert. Callie had forgotten that part.

"Actually, I think he may be in. Want me to see if he's free?"

The young woman picked up the phone and talked briefly to someone. When she hung up, she looked at Callie. "He can see you now. I'll take you back."

"Lieutenant Mark Lambert. Nice to meet you, Ms. Thayer." He was Asian, something she hadn't expected, not given the name. Tall and slender with high cheekbones, he had short jet-black hair. Instead of a uniform, he wore a crewneck sweater and neatly pressed khakis.

There was a table with two chairs in the small white room. He gestured for her to sit. Taking a seat across from her, he briefly studied her face.

"So, Ms. Thayer, you want a gun for self-protection. Can you tell me a little about that?"

His eyes, almost black, fixed on her face. She had a brief unsettling feeling that he could read her mind.

"There's not really much to tell." Callie laughed self-consciously. "I'm a single mother with a ten-year-old daughter. It just seemed like a good idea. My father had a gun while we were growing up, and it always made me feel safer." This last part was a total fabrication, but who was going to check?

"I see," Lambert said. His tone didn't change. "Are you concerned about something in particular?"

"No," Callie said, perhaps a bit too quickly. "No, it's nothing like that."

"Where do you live, Ms. Thayer?"

"On Abingdon Circle," Callie said. "Walking distance from downtown."

"That's right near the college?"

"Yes."

"Almost no crime in that area. Just a break-in now and then when folks go out of town and forget to stop the mail. Last one must have been a couple years back."

"The Reillys," said Callie. "Two Christmases ago."

"That sounds about right."

A knot was building in Callie's chest. She hadn't expected to be grilled.

"It's not like I plan to *use* the gun. I just want to have it."

"I'm sure you know about the dangers of having a gun in the house. As careful as you are, there's always a chance that your daughter or a friend could get hold of it."

"So . . . I don't understand," said Callie. "Do I have to convince you of something? I've taken the required safety course. I've never been convicted of a crime. I've never done any of those things on the list that keep you from getting a license."

For a long moment, Lambert looked at her. "I have some discretion," he said.

There was something in his gaze that Callie found unnerving. It was like he suspected a subterfuge. Or knew more than he was saying.

Now he was sitting back in his chair, his eyes still on her.

"Officer Evans came by to talk to me. He's a little worried about you."

Callie looked at him in astonishment. "What did he say?" she asked.

"He's concerned about your having a gun in the house. He

seems to think you've been a little . . . tense, maybe not seeing things clearly."

Tense. He'd picked the word carefully. What he meant was *unstable.* Damn Rick for interfering. This wasn't his concern. Before she could think better of it, hot words tumbled out.

"This is ridiculous. If *Officer Evans*" — she bit off the words — "had something to say, he should have talked to me about it."

Lambert looked at her warily. "I was under the impression he had."

"He doesn't think I need a gun. I'm aware of that. But I'm not a child. He isn't my father. This is my decision, not his. I'm a citizen of this community, just like anyone else. It's not up to the man I've been *dating* to make the decision for me."

"Whoa," said Lambert, raising his hands. "Look, Ms. Thayer. I think we're going off in the wrong direction. Officer Evans is just concerned about your safety. It's not about someone controlling you, telling you what to do."

"I think I'm the best judge of that," Callie snapped. "And from where I'm sitting right now, that's exactly how it feels."

A long pause. Callie's face was hot, and her heart thudded in her chest. A tiny voice in her head was saying, *This isn't helping any.*

She pressed her lips together, let out a long breath.

"I'm sorry to get so upset," she said. "But this really isn't Rick's business. Unless he told you anything specific that makes you think I'd pose a danger. If he did, I'd like a chance to respond. I think I'm entitled to that much."

Lambert studied her another few moments. Finally, he spoke again. "I'll let the application go through," he said. "But I'd advise you to think about this when you're feeling a little calmer. Think about whether it really makes sense to keep a gun at home."

She couldn't get out of there fast enough, away from Lambert's questions.

As Callie emerged onto the street, she took deep, full breaths. She stood there squinting in the morning light as her eyes adjusted to the sun.

It was one of the first warm spring days, the air both soft and bracing. The sky was the same flawless blue it had been on Easter morning. The police department shared the street with a picturesque row of shops. People milled about window-shopping, but Callie barely noticed.

Still standing in the shadow of the police station, Callie pulled out her cell phone. She didn't even have his parents' number. She'd have to leave a message. Rick had a cell phone, but he rarely used it, and she didn't have that number either.

When she turned on the phone, it let out a beep, telling her to check voice mail. She'd listen to the message later. Once she'd talked to Rick. She called his home phone and left a message asking him to call her. On the short walk home, she left the phone on, which she didn't usually do.

She walked through town along Main Street, past boutiques and coffee shops. Merritt had awakened today and tumbled onto the streets. There were mothers with babies and skateboarders, musicians, and college students. A tiny woman in an orange caftan fed ice cream to her dachshund.

When Callie reached home, she stalked up the steps and jammed her key in the lock. She was glad that Mimi had taken Anna and Henry to Six Flags today. Inside, she headed straight for the phone. A single message was waiting.

At first she thought it was a wrong number, maybe someone drunk. The woman's voice was soft and slurred, barely audible. But she heard her own name and then another. She heard the name *Melanie*.

Melanie had called her.

Callie caught her breath.

She leaned her ear close to the machine, then pushed the replay button. The message was rambling and disconnected, hard to understand. Several mumbled apologies and then a telephone number. Callie had to listen twice before she got it down. There was still one digit she couldn't make out. Either a nine or five.

She tried it first with a five, let the phone ring five or six times. She was just about to hang up, when a groggy voice answered.

"H'llo?"

"Melanie?"

"Uh-huh."

"This is Callie. Calling you back."

"Oh . . . Hi, Callie." She sounded dazed. "I called you."

Was it a statement or a question? Callie wasn't sure.

"That's right," Callie said gently. "You left me a message on my answering machine. I've been wanting to talk to you, to find out how you're feeling."

"I . . . something happened to me. I was in the hospital."

"I . . . I know," said Callie. "I'm so terribly sorry."

"I'm sorry too," said Melanie. She still seemed confused, but her voice was stronger now, as if her mind had grabbed hold of something that she really wanted to say. "I just didn't know any better. I was young, but that's not really an excuse. I was just . . . confused and I didn't understand, but, but . . . I'm sorry."

What was she talking about? "You don't have anything to be sorry for," said Callie. "You didn't do anything wrong."

"No, no, no. I *did*. But I didn't mean to, I didn't, I didn't —"

"Shhhhh," said Callie. She was slightly alarmed by Melanie's agitation.

But Melanie wasn't listening. She'd started to talk again, her words, normally so precise, both halting and profuse.

"I thought I was better than you. That I could never ever be like you. I thought it was your fault with Steven, that you should have *figured out* what . . ."

Callie felt knocked off balance, as if she'd lost her breath. But at some level hadn't she known all along how Melanie felt? She'd always been attuned to these reactions. After all, they mirrored her own.

"You're right. I should have known. You were right about that."

"But sometimes you just . . . don't. When I fell in love with Frank, I thought it was perfect. I thought he really loved me. And he was so . . . so *sure* — about everything. He always knew what to do. But the thing is, he was never really there."

Callie's heart seemed to twist. She remembered that feeling.

The Vanishing Man. It still struck her, the irony of that name. It had started with some tabloid paper, she didn't remember which, then spread like wildfire through the press: TV, radio, print. The witnesses who'd last seen his victims often recalled a man. But except for a sense that he was good-looking, they couldn't really describe him. Or rather, whatever descriptions they gave never seemed to match. Some said his hair was blond; others said it was brown. He was five foot seven, at least six feet, well over six three. They'd glimpsed him only briefly. He was there, then gone.

Then there was the other meaning, far more personal. All those nights she'd waited alone, afraid she was losing him, afraid that one day he'd slip away, leave and never come back. She'd suspected then that he was having an affair, even confronted him. But he hadn't been sleeping with other women. He'd just been killing them.

And yet, still, she'd loved him. She couldn't let him go.

The day he'd been sentenced to death, she'd wanted to tell him that. She'd sat in the gallery willing him to turn and look at her. She'd wanted him to know that he wasn't alone, that she hadn't abandoned him.

"You know ten-b-five? The securities fraud law thing?" Melanie's voice was dreamy now, as if her mind was drifting.

"No, I don't think so."

"Well, there's this . . . this . . . *thing*." Melanie seemed to be searching for words. "It's . . . it's a law, and it makes it so you have a duty to *disclose* information if it's material. That's the word: *material*." Callie could hear the satisfaction in her voice as she managed to come up with the term. "It's not enough if you just don't lie. You have to come forward and give information in order to clarify. To make sure that other things you said aren't . . . aren't misleading."

"Mmmm," said Callie.

"I think it should be like that when people say they're in love."

"Be like what?" Callie said.

"Where it's not enough if you just don't lie. That's not telling all the truth. When I found Frank with Mary Beth, he said I should have asked. He said that he'd never lied to me. As if that made a difference."

"Steven lied to me," said Callie. She couldn't help herself.

"That's what I mean!" Melanie said. She was getting excited again. "It's the same thing. *It's all the same thing!* They say something. They don't say something. It's all still the same."

Listening to Melanie, Callie thought that this couldn't be good for her.

"Honey," Callie said, surprising herself with the endearment. "I think I should let you go now. You should get some rest."

Melanie didn't seem to hear her. "They said I was too thin, but I wasn't. You don't need to eat so much. I've read a lot about it. I'm not a . . . an anorexic."

A click, and the pieces fell into place, why Melanie had looked so haggard.

A beep on the line. Call-waiting. Callie thought of Rick.

"Melanie," Callie said softly. "Can I call you back a little later?"

"Okay," said Melanie. She sounded sleepy, like she was starting to fade. The excitement of the past few minutes seemed to have exhausted her.

But before hanging up, there was still one question that Callie had to ask. "The man who attacked you. When he came to the door, did he bring you flowers?"

"He brought me roses," Melanie said. "That's what they told me."

AFTER hanging up, Callie checked caller ID. The call that had come in showed a 413 exchange. Rick's cell phone? Before listening to the voice mail message, she went to the sink for a glass of water. Looking out the window, she drank it down fast.

Knowing that the flowers were roses made everything simpler. The connection she'd suspected was there. Everything was linked. Melanie's attack was somehow tied to what had been happening to her. Now that she knew this for sure, she'd call Mike Jamison. Tell him about the roses, both hers and Melanie's. In a way it was a relief, this resolution of doubt.

As she'd guessed, the phone message was from Rick. She quickly called him back. The moment she heard him say hello, the anger flared again.

"What the hell were you doing, talking to Lambert about me?"

He didn't answer right away, but when he did, she could tell that he was angry too.

"You know what? I don't really care if you're mad. You have no business with a gun, Callie. You don't know how to use one."

Had she expected him to apologize? She really wasn't sure. But one thing she hadn't expected was an anger that matched her own. She'd never seen this side of him before. He'd always been so patient.

"I took the class," Callie said. She could feel the tension in her jaw.

"Oh. Great. So you have, what? Three, four hours' experience at a firing range? That's just great. That's perfect."

His sarcasm was the last straw; the words flooded out. "Would you just leave me alone? Just leave me alone! This has nothing to do with you."

A long silence followed.

"Okay," Rick said. And then, with an edge, "Nice knowing you."

A click, and the phone went dead.

For a time, she just sat there, the receiver still in her hand. She'd heard the finality in his voice, knew that it was over. Rick had been a part of her life. Now he was gone. Around her everything looked the same. Light flooded the kitchen. She kept expecting the pain to start, but a numbness had settled in. She wasn't angry. She wasn't upset. She didn't feel anything.

What next? she asked herself.

She knew that she should call Jamison, tell him about the roses. But she suddenly felt so terribly tired that she could barely move. Thank God, she had at least another few hours before Anna got home. Upstairs, she fell into her unmade bed, kicking off her shoes. She thought about taking off her sweater and jeans but felt too tired to make the effort. Besides, she was only going to rest a while. She wasn't going to sleep.

The next thing she knew, there was a dim ringing. It seemed to go on and on. Disoriented, she sat up in bed and reached for her alarm clock. But the noise wasn't coming from beside her bed. It was coming from downstairs. *The doorbell, that's what it was,* she thought.

Callie stumbled up.

The hallway was dark. Callie flipped on a light and hurried down the stairs. During the time she'd slept, the sun had set. She must have slept for hours.

She flicked on the outdoor light and peered through the peephole. Anna was standing on the front porch, along with Mimi and Henry Creighton. Mimi was holding a cell phone, punching in a number.

Callie turned the lock.

"Sorry," she said. "I didn't hear you. I guess I fell asleep."

She looked at Anna. "Hi, sweetie. You have fun today?"

Anna was holding a green stuffed bear and a plastic bag of cotton candy. She had a look of happy satiety, cheeks pink, hair in tangles.

"It was so cool!" Anna said.

"It really was," said Henry.

Callie turned to Mimi. "Would you like to come in?"

"Well, maybe for just a minute."

The kids shot past their mothers, heading for the den.

"I'll make some tea," said Callie, motioning Mimi toward the kitchen.

Callie felt groggy and slightly sticky in her sleep-rumpled sweater and pants. Mimi was her usual sleek self in a navy twin-set and slacks. Gold earrings. Gucci loafers. A small leather bag. Callie couldn't imagine wearing this ensemble to an amusement park. But then, she couldn't exactly imagine wearing it anywhere.

Sitting at the kitchen table, Mimi examined a fingernail. "Do you have something herbal?" she asked Callie.

"Chamomile?"

"That'll do."

Waiting for the water to boil, Callie leaned against the counter. "So, how'd you survive the day?" she asked.

"They were fine," said Mimi. Still studying her manicure, she seemed preoccupied.

"Thanks again for taking them."

"Mmmm. Not a problem."

This time when the conversation lagged, Callie let it go.

From the den down the hall she heard the sounds of a heated Nintendo battle. Into one cup, Callie dropped a chamomile bag, into another, China Black. The kettle began to whistle. Callie turned off the gas. She poured out water and carried the mugs to the kitchen table.

The silence was leaden now. Stirring her tea, Callie racked her mind for something to fill the void. Then it struck her that this was an opening, a chance to ask Mimi what she might have seen. Mimi was in and out all day and right across the street.

She worked to keep her tone light, just mentioning a minor inconvenience.

"Have you had any trouble with deliveries lately?" That was neutral enough.

"Deliveries?" Mimi looked at her as if she didn't know the word.

"Some books I ordered never arrived. I mean they arrived — that's what the company said — but I never got them. And then, a couple of days ago, I got some flowers I hadn't ordered."

Mimi gave a brittle smile. "Secret admirer?"

Callie tried to smile back. "No, I think it was just a mistake."

"Well, who cares?" said Mimi. "I hope you enjoyed them. God, I can't remember the last time that Bernie sent me flowers."

"You haven't had any problems? Or noticed anything odd? Anyone hanging around the neighborhood who doesn't seem to belong?"

Mimi shrugged and took a sip of tea. When she put down her cup it splashed, and she dabbed at the table with a napkin.

"Bernie's having an affair." Mimi's eyes were bright.

Callie almost choked on her tea. "Are . . . are you sure?" she said. "You two seem so happy."

Mimi gave a tight smile. "Seem," she said. "*Seem*. The fact is my husband doesn't care about anyone but himself. Well, if he thinks I'm going to ignore this, he's in for a surprise."

Callie wished Mimi would just stop talking. This was embarrassing. She was sure that after some time had passed, regret would settle in. All the same, she felt the faint stirrings of something like sympathy. The disclosure was so out of character. How unhappy Mimi must be. She tried to think of something to say, something comforting. But before she could even attempt a response, Mimi was standing up.

"We should get home," she said briskly. "Thanks for the cup of tea."

Suddenly, it was like the previous exchange had never taken place. Mimi was smoothing down her hair, picking up her purse.

Callie's head was spinning as she too stood up.

"I'm glad you could stop by," she said to Mimi. "And thanks again for today."

OVER a late supper, Anna chattered breathlessly about a new roller coaster. "It's called Batman — The Dark Knight, and it doesn't have a *floor*. It's sort of like you're flying, and you go upside down, like, *five times*."

The thought of Anna suspended in space gave Callie a sick feeling. Didn't the world hold enough real danger without looking for more?

"You have to go sometime, Mommy." Anna's eyes were shining.

Callie managed a weak smile. "The roller coaster? I don't think so."

Anna pushed carrots around her plate without taking a bite. She gave Callie an inquisitive look. "Where's Rick?" she said. "It's Saturday. Don't you guys have a date?"

"Rick's tied up tonight," said Callie, and was grateful when Anna let the subject drop. There'd be time enough to explain that Rick was gone for good.

After supper, loading the dishwasher, Callie remembered the message on her cell phone. In her anger at Rick, she'd forgotten it. She should check to see who'd called. She couldn't stop thinking of Rick, of the things they'd said today. He'd had no business talking to Lambert. She still felt justified. And yet, a part of her knew deep down that he hadn't meant to hurt her.

She finished cleaning the kitchen and went upstairs to work. But instead of sitting down at her desk, she collapsed again on her bed. She told herself she'd just take five minutes and then she'd get back up. But ten, then twenty, minutes passed, and still she didn't move. She thought about seeing if Anna wanted to play Monopoly. Then she thought again of the cell phone call and got up to find her purse.

"You have one new message," the artificial voice said.

Then she heard another voice. Her ex-husband calling back.

"I've talked to my wife and she — we — think that introducing Anna to our family would create too many . . . complications. You're the one who set things up this way, and it's just not fair at this point to change the rules of the game."

There was a bit more after that, cold and vaguely accusatory. She listened until it was over, then erased the message.

The thought that Kevin didn't want to see Anna was painful to contemplate. For the first time, Callie was grateful that Anna had never taken to Rick. The last thing her daughter needed now was to lose another father figure.

But there was another more immediate reason that the message unsettled her. She realized that, at some level, she'd thought of Kevin as a last resort. She'd imagined she had a place to send Anna if things got really bad. At this point, she could no longer pretend that her life wasn't in danger. What she'd learned in the two weeks since Melanie's attack left no doubt about that. Under the circumstances, should Anna be at home? Wouldn't she be safer away from Merritt, out of the line of fire? School would be out in a few weeks. At least the timing was good.

Callie got up and walked to Anna's room, knocked softly on the door.

Anna was already in bed with a Harry Potter book.

Callie sat down on the edge of the mattress.

"What?" Anna said. She looked at her mother warily, as if she suspected something.

Callie made her voice bright. "You know, school's out pretty soon, and I was thinking you might go visit Grams and Pappy. It's been almost a year since you've seen them."

Anna stared at her.

"You mean go to Indianapolis?" By her tone, Callie might as well have suggested that she travel to the desert. "For how long?"

"A week. Maybe two."

"But what would I *do*?" Anna sounded stricken. "I don't know anyone there."

"Well, maybe you'll make some new friends. I'll bet Grams knows some people with kids right around your age."

Anna shook her head. "No," she said with finality. "No. I don't want to go."

Callie sighed. "They're your grandparents. You need to see them. Besides, I know you'll have a good time once you actually get there."

"No," Anna said. "I'm not going. You can't make me go." Now she was really angry, chin jutting out. Callie was about to argue back, but managed to stop herself.

She stood up from Anna's bed.

"There's no point in talking when you're acting like this. When you calm down, we can discuss it."

"I'm not going," Anna said again.

"Yes," said Callie. "You are."

❧

"I'm not going." Once more, Anna whispered the words.

She listened as her bedroom door clicked shut and her mother's footsteps faded. Anna got up from her bed and crossed the room to her computer. Her mother didn't think she had a choice. Well, she was about to find out.

Anna turned on her computer. When the screen flashed up,

she signed on to AOL and checked her buddy list. TheMagician93 was already there. Just as she'd known he would be. She clicked on the instant message icon, then stopped to think what to write. Did she really want to do this? She'd been going back and forth. Rick hadn't been around so much, and she'd thought things were getting better. But it wasn't like it had been before, when it was just her and her mom. It was like her mom was a different person from the one she used to be.

Yes, she decided, she was ready now.

Besides, she could always come back.

Bttrfly146   I am ready to go.

Just moments after she sent the message, he was writing back.

TheMagician93   You want to go tonight?

Bttrfly146   Right. I will meet you at midnight. Just the way we planned.

❧

Laura Seton had just turned twenty when she met Steven Gage. The past few years had not been easy, and she was ready for something to go right.

Unlike her older sister, Sarah, who had glided through college and medical school, Laura was having a hard time finding her way in life. She'd started out at Indiana University, the same large public school from which Sarah had graduated. But while Sarah had thrived, Laura languished, feeling lost in the crowd. She'd started out as an English major, then switched to psychology. She was contemplating yet another change when she decided to take a year off. A high school friend, Sally Snyder, had a sister living in Cambridge, Massachusetts, the culturally vibrant and colorful home of Harvard University. Sally, who hadn't gone on to college, proposed that they move there for a year. It was the way out that Laura had been looking for. She quickly agreed to go.

Sally and Laura rented an apartment in the neighboring town of Somerville, just a subway stop on the Red Line from the jobs they found in Harvard Square. Sally took a job at a clothing store, while Laura began to waitress. She worked the three-to-ten shift at a restaurant called The Alps, serving large portions of heavy food drenched in melted cheese. Most of the people she waited on barely registered. There was one, however, who from the first made a distinct impression. It wasn't just that he was good-looking, though he happened to be. What struck her most was how polite he was. He seemed to notice things.

The first night he came in, she'd had a difficult table of three. The food wasn't right; they were waiting too long. All they did was complain. When she reached the new diner's table, she was out of breath. When she apologized for the delay, he told her not to worry. "I saw how they were acting," he said, with a flick of the head toward the table. Later that night, back at home, she'd found herself thinking of him. When he didn't come in for the rest of the week, she was disappointed. Then, suddenly, he was back, sitting at the same table. His face lit up when he saw her. "It's good to see you," he said. When she brought his check at the end of the meal, he asked her to have a drink.

Over beers at the Wursthaus a few blocks away, he introduced himself. His name was Steven Gage. He'd grown up in Nashville and gone to school at the University of Tennessee. Now he planned to attend law school. Harvard was his first choice.

A scraping sound. He put down the book, turned off the small flashlight. Peering through the slats of the tree house, he looked across the street. Except for the yellow front porch light, her house was totally dark. Had the sound come from somewhere else? Or had he imagined it? He'd come here every night this week, hoping he might see her. Perhaps the frustration of these endless hours was acting on his perceptions.

He looked at the illuminated dial on his watch: 11:53 P.M. Then he thought of another watch, pulled from a slender wrist. The image calmed him slightly. He felt his spirits lift.

Time is fair, he told himself. *In the end, time is fair.*

In that instant, he heard it again. This time, he wasn't mistaken. But it wasn't coming from her window. It was farther to the right. A head popped out of this second window and looked from side to side. Anna. It was Anna. What was she going to do?

Fascinated, he watched her, waiting for what came next. But after a moment, she ducked inside and all was still again. Was it over? Was that it? His eyes stayed glued to the house.

Then the front door was opening. A small figure emerged. Anna stepped down off the porch and ran across the street. His heart leapt into his throat. She was heading straight for him! But she stopped directly under the tree house, stood there silently. As if she were waiting for something to happen. As if she were waiting for *someone*. She was standing right beneath him. He could hardly breathe.

Another door was opening, but this time the sound came from the house below. A second child walked into the night. If it wasn't little Henry Creighton. The boy walked straight to Anna. From his perch in the tree house, he heard their whispers, though he couldn't make out the words. Then, just moments later, they were walking down the street. He hadn't noticed it before, but Anna had a backpack. *Running away!* It came to him. That's what they were doing. At that same time, another idea burst full-blown into his mind. He'd planned to kill Laura Seton, but why not kill her child?

Sunday–Monday, May 14–15

THE desk lamp pooled yellow light on the black-and-white pages of her book. Callie was taking notes. She'd put on her Sony Walkman, and strains of Vivaldi added to her sense of calm. For a time, she was free of pressing concerns, lost in the world of thought.

Her pen moved across the paper, slowly, and then faster. She was putting together an outline for her paper on unconscious transference, having finally decided to focus on the issue of eyewitness testimony. The idea had come from the two case studies that surfaced again and again: the psychologist mistakenly accused of rape and the unfortunate ticket buyer. Both victims of mistaken eyewitness identification. She'd decided to search for more recent examples, to try to catalogue them. Her paper would start off with the classic cases, then move to her own research.

The cassette clicked off. Callie was surprised when she glanced at her watch to see that it was almost 1 A.M. She pulled off her headphones. Silence. By now Anna was asleep. As she gathered up the scattered papers on her desk, she scanned what she'd written. She'd put in a solid effort tonight, and she felt good about that. Despite everything that was happening, she'd reclaimed a small part of her life.

In her bathroom, she washed her face and patted it dry, squeezed out toothpaste, and began to brush. The faint taste of old coffee was washed away by a gust of mint. Once she'd finished brushing, she flossed, then put cream on her face. As her fingers massaged the skin of her cheeks, her eyes studied the mirror. It had been a while since she'd really looked at herself, and what she saw was disturbing. There was a tension in the muscles of her face that hadn't been there before, a deep furrow between her eyes, a tightness around the mouth. These weren't the ordinary marks of age, but a sign of something wrong. The well-being she'd felt just moments ago flickered and was gone. She'd thought her anxiety was under control, but her face told her she was wrong. And it wasn't just her physical self, it was also her behavior. Her mind flashed back to earlier, to how she'd snapped at Anna.

She turned off her bathroom light and went through her room toward Anna's. She didn't want to wake her up, just to look at her. In the hallway she left the light off, so Anna's room would stay dark. Then, gently, she turned the handle and cracked open the door. The hinges gave a faint squeak, but the lump in the bed was still.

Callie stood on the threshold for a couple of seconds, waiting to see if Anna would move. But Anna appeared to be sleeping soundly. Callie crept toward the bed. There were dim piles of blankets and sheets, a few stuffed animals. Callie leaned forward, searching for Anna's head. She reached out and touched a knot of blankets. The fabric gave way beneath her hand. She touched another part of the bed. Again there was no resistance. In a single gesture, she swept back the blankets. Nothing, no one was there.

She jumped up and ran from the room, looked into the hallway bath. The door was open. The room was dark.

Anna wasn't there.

"Anna?" Callie called softly. And then more loudly. "Anna?"

Maybe she'd gone downstairs. Maybe she'd woken up hungry, wanted something to eat.

Callie bounded down the stairs, taking two steps at a time.

"Anna?" she called again, as she flipped on the light in the kitchen. The familiar room jumped out at her, but Anna wasn't down here either.

Callie raced through the house, calling Anna's name. A hole was growing in her chest, deep and black and wide. *This can't be happening*, she told herself. *There has to be some mistake.* She ran back upstairs to Anna's room and rubbed her arms across the empty bed, threw open the closet door and pushed aside rows of clothes. On hands and knees, she looked under the bed: some books, a jigsaw puzzle. Standing up, she pressed her hands to her mouth.

Think, Callie, think.

She ran downstairs to the basement and scanned the concrete room. But, thank God, there was nothing unusual, no sign of anything wrong. Shelves lined with paint cans and storage boxes. A laundry basket filled with sheets. Crossing the floor to the furnace room, Callie flung open the door. No sign of Anna there either. She headed back upstairs.

She didn't know the number for the police department and had to look it up. Her fingers felt large and clumsy, barely a part of her. Twice she punched in the wrong number and had to start again.

When she finally managed to dial correctly, the phone rang twice.

A male voice answered. "Merritt Police Department."

Something clicked inside her.

Anna was really gone.

She began to shake uncontrollably. "My daughter, she . . . she's missing."

⤞⤝

THERE was a bus to Boston at four in the morning. They were going to be on it. By the time their parents started looking for them, they'd already be gone. "But what if they call the bus station?" Anna had asked Henry. Henry had said it wasn't a problem. No one would be awake.

But first they had to get to the bus. That was the first step. So far, they'd been walking about half an hour. Anna's feet were getting sore.

"How much farther is it?" she asked Henry.

Henry shrugged. "A couple of miles."

Anna didn't say anything. It sounded pretty far.

It was strange to be out so late at night, when everything in town was quiet. Walking through the center of Merritt, they hadn't passed a single car. The stores were dark and shut tight. The sky was full of stars. The yellow cat that lived in the bookstore slept in the plate-glass window. His name was Sebastian, and looking at him, Anna felt a little sad. "Good-bye, Sebastian," she whispered. Softly, so Henry wouldn't hear.

Now they were walking down Old Kipps Road, the street with the shopping malls. They walked past Staples and Wal-Mart, toward the Stop & Shop. In her backpack, Anna had two peanut butter sandwiches, two apples, three oranges, and some Oreos. She also had two changes of clothes and fifty-seven dollars. Henry had ninety-four dollars. With all that money, they could get to the city, buy some food, go to the movies. Henry said there were places to sleep for kids who ran away. Anna thought they'd have to call your parents, but Henry said they wouldn't.

She might have asked more questions if she'd really cared that much. But the thing was, she didn't want to run away forever, just long enough to make a point. Long enough for her mom to see that she was really, really mad. For Henry, it was different. He wanted to leave for good. That was because his parents never, ever listened to him. All they cared about were his grades, about how smart he was. For her, it was more complicated because her mom used to care. Back when it was just the two of them, before she met Rick.

Just thinking about Rick Evans gave Anna a queasy feeling. But even a couple of months ago, things hadn't been so bad. She'd hated it that Rick was there, but at least her mom had been happy. Since Easter, though, things had changed, and she'd started acting crazy. Like tonight, when she'd just barged in and said that Anna had to go to Indianapolis. If it hadn't been for that, well, maybe she'd have stayed. Even though Henry had been bugging her, she hadn't made up her mind. But the idea that she could be sent away — that had been the last straw. Her mother wanted her gone? Fine. She'd take care of that herself.

A stone caught in Anna's tennis shoe, and she reached down to get it out. As she did, a car wheeled around the corner, and lights flashed in her eyes. Henry had already jumped back. "Get out of the light," he hissed.

But Anna had one foot in the air, her canvas shoe in her hand. As the car slowed down, she started to move, but something held her back. She realized that a part of her was hoping that someone had found them. Now that they were really running away, it all seemed a little scary. With every step away from home, she felt more and more doubtful. That was why she kept standing there. She *wanted* someone to find them.

The driver stopped the car just a few yards away. He was leaning across the front seat, opening the passenger door. It was spring, but he was wearing winter clothes, a ski hat and a scarf. He had a beard, a bushy one, like someone in a cartoon.

He said something then, real soft, but Anna couldn't hear him.

She stepped up a little closer, not sure what she wanted to do. Henry wasn't where she could see; he was probably hiding now. He was going to be mad that she'd messed up everything. But right now, she just didn't care. She wanted to be back home.

The driver was sliding across the seat, getting out of the car. As he moved closer, Anna stepped back. Suddenly, she was afraid. Why wasn't he talking to her? And why did he look so weird? Then, without warning, he lunged toward her, grabbing hold of her jacket. But before he got a firm grip on her, Anna tore away. She started to run — *hard, fast* — faster than ever before. Her feet pounded the pavement, and she started screaming, "Help!"

Strong arms grabbed her, picked her up, swooped her into the air. Squirming, fighting, she looked for Henry. A piece of cloth covered her face. It was wet and smelled bad. She tried to push it away. But she couldn't get her hands to move, and then she didn't care.

⁓

"WHEN did you last see your daughter?"

The detective was wearing a black T-shirt that showed his

muscled arms. On his left bicep he had a tattoo, a long, winding vine with flowers. He'd explained to Callie that he'd just been pulled off an undercover job. Still, his appearance only added to her sense of dislocation.

"It must have been around nine o'clock. Anna was in bed. But how could anyone have gotten in? Her room's on the second floor."

Anguished, Callie looked at him, twisting her hands in her lap.

"So far, we don't see any sign that someone broke into the house. Do you think your daughter might have run away?"

Callie stared at him. "I guess . . . I guess it's possible." It hadn't even occurred to her, but maybe he was right. "We had a sort of argument about visiting her grandparents this summer. She didn't want to go. I told her it wasn't her choice."

"You know, despite all the publicity, kidnappings are still quite rare."

For the first time since Anna had disappeared, Callie felt a ray of hope. Maybe Anna had left on her own. They'd find her and bring her back.

Across from her sat the detective, whose name was Jeffrey Knight. Next to him was a policewoman, the first officer to arrive. Officer Parillo — that was her name — wore a standard blue uniform. She had short, dark hair, an athletic build, and was probably in her twenties.

"So she was pretty upset?" asked Knight.

"Yes," Callie said.

"What did she say exactly?"

"Just that she didn't want to go. She said I couldn't make her."

"Has she ever run away before? Or threatened to run away?"

Callie shook her head. "No. She never has."

"What sort of relationship do you have?"

"It . . . it used to be better. This year has been difficult. I started dating someone this fall — Rick Evans, you probably know him."

"Sure. We both know Rick." A flicker of surprise in Knight's voice, a subtle change of tone.

"Rick's out of town," Callie said. "His father's been quite ill." She wasn't sure why she said this, and Knight didn't respond.

"Did you hear anything?" Knight asked her. "Any sounds from Anna's room?"

Again, Callie shook her head. "No, nothing," she said. "But I had my Walkman on. I was listening to music."

From upstairs, Callie heard the footsteps and voices of two more detectives. She wondered what they'd found so far. She wanted to be up there with them.

Her eyes drifted around the kitchen, barely focusing. The drying dishes. The clean counters. The knives in the wooden block. *The most dangerous room in the house.* That's what Rick had called it. Suddenly, she missed him desperately. She wanted him here with her.

"Who are your daughter's closest friends? Is there someone she might have talked to?"

Of course. Why hadn't she thought of that? "Henry Creighton," she said. "If Anna talked to anyone, it would be him. He lives right across the street."

"D'you have the number?" Knight asked.

"Right there. Beside the phone."

Knight pulled out a cell phone.

"You can use ours," said Callie.

"Thanks, but I'd rather not. I don't want to disturb the scene."

The scene. Knight's offhand use of the word sent a chill through Callie. For an instant, she saw her house, her *home,* through completely different eyes.

Knight had already punched in the number and was waiting for someone to answer. After what seemed like forever, he finally started to talk.

"Ma'am, I'm sorry to disturb you, but I'm calling from the Merritt Police Department. . . . What? . . . No, it's not about your husband. It's about your neighbor, Callie Thayer. Her little girl is missing. I know it's late, but we need to talk to your son."

Another pause.

"We'll be right over. . . . Yes, of course I will."

When he hung up, he looked at Callie. "That was the mother."

"Mimi."

"She said to tell you to stay calm, that everything will be okay."

Easy for her to say. "Listen," — Callie was talking fast, thoughts racing through her mind — "there are some things I have to tell you. They might be relevant. Someone has been threatening me. Well, not threatening exactly. Oh, this is complicated, but —"

The phone rang suddenly, sharply. Callie's heart leapt. "Oh, my God, maybe it's Anna. Maybe she's —"

But before she could reach the phone, Knight had picked up. For the first time, Callie noticed that he was wearing plastic gloves.

"Is it Anna?" Callie demanded, her eyes glued to the detective's face.

Knight didn't seem to hear her.

From where she sat, Callie heard frantic speech from the other end of the line.

"Who is it?" Callie asked. "Please. I have to know."

Knight raised his hand, as if to push her back.

"We'll be right over," he said, and then hung up the phone.

"What is it? What happened?" Callie asked. Her heart tore through her chest.

Standing up, Knight looked at her. "Henry's missing too."

❧

WHEN Anna woke up, everything was dark. She didn't know where she was. She'd been running away with Henry, and then something bad had happened. All she wanted now was to go home, to be back with her mother.

Where was she, anyway? She tried to sit up, but she couldn't move. Her hands and feet were tied together. Now she was really scared.

She tried to yell, to scream *loud*, but something was stuffed in her mouth.

Rolling her head from side to side, she tried to see around her.

Slowly, her eyes grew used to the dark, and shapes started coming clear. She was lying on a mattress on the floor. The floor was made of concrete. There were piles of boxes off to one side. She saw a washer and dryer. A basement. That's where she was. She was in somebody's basement.

She heard something, a squeaking sound, a door swinging open. A slice of light fell across her face. Anna squinted toward it.

Then she heard the sound of footsteps moving down the stairs. The sound seemed to go on forever, coming closer and closer. Finally, there was a different sound, as feet landed on the floor. But still they were moving closer, and then she saw two legs. She rolled her head back a little farther, looked up into a face. It was him. The man with the beard. She felt herself start to shake.

When he crouched down beside her, she saw that he held a package of panty hose. He worked with the seal for a couple of seconds, then ripped open the packet. From inside, he pulled out the stockings. They were rolled in a small black ball. Was he going to ask her to put them on? She felt a leap of hope. If he did, he'd have to untie her. She'd kick him and start to run.

But once he shook out the stretchy black legs, he just folded them together. Grabbing one side in either hand, he pulled them back and forth.

❧

It had been hours. It had been forever. The night would never end.

Callie slumped at the kitchen table. Across from her, manning a control panel, sat a state police technician. He'd set up equipment to trace and record incoming phone calls. Beside her, Officer Parillo was knitting, something in pale blue yarn.

Upstairs, Callie heard footsteps, heavy and alien. Detective Knight and two colleagues still moving through the house. She'd been wearing a bathrobe when the police arrived, but they hadn't let her leave the kitchen. The jeans and sweater she was wearing now had been brought to her by Parillo.

Again, Callie glanced at her watch. Just a few minutes had passed. The last time, it had been 3:22. Now it was 3:37.

Callie turned to Parillo. "Why's it taking so long? They're just children, just little kids. How far can they have gone?"

Parillo gave Callie a compassionate look. "They're doing all they can."

"Like what?" Callie demanded. "What exactly, I mean?"

"They're doing surveillance by helicopter. The state police are involved. There's an alert on the regional radio network and they've brought in the tracking dogs. It's great you found that recent picture of Anna. Everyone has a copy."

The state police technician with the tracing equipment had an air of intense focus. As he took a sip of coffee from a paper cup, Callie caught his eye. "Does someone usually call?" she asked. She didn't remember his name.

"I can't say anything's usual, ma'am. Each situation's different."

"At least they're together," Callie murmured. "At least there are two of them." She wasn't really talking to them. She was talking to herself.

The beeper on Parillo's belt went off. She grabbed her cell phone and punched a number. "Nancy Parillo," she said.

It was torture for Callie to watch her face, not able to hear what was being said. Every cell in Callie's body clamored for information.

When Parillo finally hung up the phone, she didn't say anything. She stood up from her chair and crouched by Callie, taking hold of her hands.

"What?" Callie said. She felt herself start to tremble.

Parillo looked straight into her eyes. "Henry Creighton just got home."

"And Anna? What about Anna?"

Parillo squeezed her hands.

"Now, Callie, I want you to remember. We don't know anything yet. We don't know if Henry is telling the truth. Do you understand what I'm saying?"

Callie nodded mutely. Fear bloomed in her heart.

"The first part is like what we thought. They ran away together. The plan was to take a bus to Boston sometime early this morning. Now, again, I want you to remember that none of this is confirmed."

"Please. Just tell me." Callie's voice was pleading.

"Okay." Parillo's grip tightened. "Henry claims that they were walking down Old Kipps Road when a car pulled up beside them. Henry says the man who was driving the car snatched Anna and drove off."

Callie stared at Parillo. Suddenly, she was dizzy. Without warning, her stomach heaved. She threw up on the floor.

Through a haze, she heard Parillo get up and go for some paper towels. Then Parillo was back beside her, mopping up the mess.

"You shouldn't be doing that," Callie murmured.

"It's fine," Parillo said.

Upstairs, a door swung shut. Callie heard men's voices.

"When does Henry say that this happened?" Callie's voice was low.

Parillo dumped the towels in the trash, then sat back down. "He's not sure exactly. He says they met at midnight and then started to walk. I'd think it would have taken them at least an hour to make it to Old Kipps Road, another half hour or so to get to the Hicks Plaza mall. That's where he says it happened. Right across from there."

Callie's head jerked up. "But that's . . . that's *hours* ago. If they met at midnight and this, this *thing* happens at, say, one-thirty, two — that's two hours ago. Where's he been since then? Why's he just getting home?"

"I'm sure they're asking him that."

"But why are they spending time with Henry? Why isn't everyone out looking for Anna and the man who kidnapped her?"

"The man who Henry *says* kidnapped her."

"You . . . you don't believe Henry?"

"We don't know whether to believe him or not. That's why we're talking to him."

"But if he's not telling the truth, then what —" Suddenly, Callie got it. "You think *Henry* could have something to do with this?"

"We don't know anything for sure yet. We're gathering information."

"But why would he —" Callie stopped. Parillo didn't know Henry. She, on the other hand, did. She'd seen him with Anna dozens of times, watched their interactions. She couldn't imagine Henry hurting Anna. At least not on purpose.

"I need to go across the street," Callie said. "I have to talk to Henry."

Parillo touched her shoulder. "That's not a good idea," she said. "Time is important here. The detectives know the questions to ask. They need to be efficient."

Callie was about to argue when something in her collapsed. At this point, she didn't trust her judgment. Maybe Parillo was right.

Everything was too much. She wondered if she'd survive this. The desperation over Anna, the guilt over her own behavior. If only she'd heard Anna out, if only she hadn't snapped. She had no doubt that their argument had sparked Anna's flight. Whatever happened next, she was responsible. Just like before, only worse this time because now it was *her* daughter.

Someone was at the front door, talking to the officer stationed there. Seconds later, he was coming toward them through the kitchen doorway. Tall. Black hair. Piercing eyes. She recognized Lieutenant Lambert.

"Hello, Ms. Thayer. We've met before."

"What . . . what are you doing here?"

"I wear several hats," he explained. "I handle gun licenses, but I'm also chief of detectives."

As he spoke, he was pulling up a chair. His eyes didn't stray from her face. "When you came to see me, you had just applied for a gun license for self-protection. Now your daughter's missing. Is there some connection here?"

Dread was moving over her like a slow-moving fog. *He's right,* she thought. *He's right. Everything fits together.* She tried to speak, but her mouth wouldn't move; she couldn't talk at all. It was like some sort of strange dream where she'd suddenly been struck mute. But she had to tell them about Diane, about the watch and the note. She had to tell them about the flowers, the roses red as blood.

"Callie?" she heard Parillo say. "Callie, are you okay?"

Again, she tried to move her lips, and this time something shifted.

"Steven Gage," she whispered.

Lambert looked at her. "Steven Gage. You mean, the serial killer?"

Callie nodded twice.

"Steven Gage is dead," said Lambert. He might have been talking to a child.

"I know he's dead," said Callie. "That's . . . that's not what I mean."

It was so hard to talk, so hard to explain, so hard to find the beginning. Thoughts blew through her mind like drifts of snow, burying the words. All that effort for so many years, and this is where it ended. Deep in her brain, she heard something. Steven Gage was laughing. Then anger — *rage* — flared up in her. The words began to flow.

"For four years I was Steven Gage's girlfriend. I went by the name of Laura Seton. Thayer's my married name. I moved to Merritt about seven years ago to try to start a new life. No one here knows about my past. I didn't tell anyone.

"Last month, on April fifth, someone left a letter at my home. April fifth, that's the date of Steven's execution. The letter just said 'Happy Anniversary, Rosamund. I haven't forgotten you.' There wasn't a signature. Rosamund — that was a sort of pet name that Steven called me sometimes. It was a few weeks later that my daughter found a watch hidden in a basket at our neighborhood Easter egg hunt. Now, I'm the one who'd hidden the basket, but I certainly hadn't put the watch there. Later, I discovered that the watch had belonged to a writer named Diane Massey."

"The woman who was murdered in Maine?"

"Yes. That's right. She'd written a book about Steven. I . . . I helped her write it. And before Diane was killed, I think that she got a letter too. And then just the other day, I got home and found a box of roses. Just lying there on my front porch. Steven used to send me roses."

She was trying so very hard to be clear, but everything was jumbled. She couldn't seem to get the story straight, to tell the events in order. Lambert was eyeing her warily, not saying much. As she watched his face, she had a sense that he might not even believe her.

"Look," she said urgently. "I know it sounds crazy, but there are people who know I'm telling you the truth. A man named Mike Jamison. He used to be with the FBI. Or call the Maine state police. I've talked to them as well. But please, you have to find Anna first. Please. You have to find her."

"Mike Jamison," Lambert said thoughtfully. "The FBI profiler?"

Wiping her eyes, Callie nodded. The tears just kept coming.

"You have a way to get in touch with him?"

"Yes. Yes, I think so."

Callie rummaged through her purse until she found her Filofax. She flipped to the J's, where, as she recalled, she'd penciled in Jamison's number. She read it off to Lambert. Parillo wrote it down.

"Call Sheenan. Tell him to follow up on that," Lambert instructed Parillo.

Parillo headed to the hallway, pulling out her cell phone.

"This note, the watch — do you have any thoughts about who might have left them?"

Callie looked at the table. "I . . . I don't know."

Lambert gave her a sharp-eyed look. "No idea at all?"

She didn't want to say it, didn't want to *think* it. The fear was overpowering. But she knew she had to tell him. She didn't have a choice. "I keep thinking of Lester Crain," she said, still staring down. "Jamison says that it couldn't be him. The Maine police agree. But he's the one I keep thinking of. I can't get him out of my mind."

She waited for Lambert to fall in line, to tell her it couldn't be Crain. Instead, he paused, thinking.

"Lester Crain. That's the guy who escaped from prison? Down in Tennessee."

Wrapping her arms around her stomach, Callie doubled over. Anna's face floated through her mind. She heard her calling, "Mommy!" She started to rock back and forth, trying to ease the pain.

Parillo came back into the room. Callie heard her say, "What happened?"

"Okay, now, Ms. Thayer. Take a deep breath. It's going to be okay." There was a gentleness in Lambert's voice that Callie hadn't heard before. But she felt like she was drowning and couldn't get up for air. She could see Lambert, see Parillo, off in some other world. She wanted to reach out, to talk to them, but a tide kept pulling her back.

She wasn't sure how long it took for the feeling to recede. She forced herself to start talking again, to say what they needed to know.

"Lester Crain and Steven were on death row together. Steven had taught himself criminal law, and he helped out the other inmates. After he helped Crain get a new trial, Crain held a press conference. He said —" Callie stopped for a moment, then the words came out in a rush. "He promised that he'd pay Steven back, find a way to thank him."

When she'd finished, her whole body sagged. She began to sob. "But why would he take Anna? *Why?* What did she do to him?"

Lambert's voice was soothing. "There's nothing that you've told me so far to convince me that he did. This is just a theory, Ms. Thayer. There's no evidence for it."

"But . . . but there's more. The women who've been targeted — me, Diane, and another woman, a lawyer in New York — all of us let Steven down. Betrayed him in a way."

"So you think Crain is . . . trying to avenge his death?"

Somehow, when Lambert said it, the idea did sound far-fetched. But it wasn't like they had other suspects. Or any other theories.

Despairing, Callie looked at Lambert. "Please, go help them find her. Don't stay here with me."

"Ms. Thayer, we're doing everything we can. And remember, we don't even know for sure that Anna was really kidnapped. The detectives are still talking to Henry, checking out his story. She could even be hiding somewhere. We still just don't know."

"You think so?" Callie's heart leapt. She had a sudden thought. "Have you searched the Creightons' house? Because maybe she's just hiding there somewhere, in the basement or the attic. Or . . . they have this tree house! The kids love to play there. Maybe she's afraid to come home now. Maybe she's hiding there."

Lambert said, "The house and periphery have been thoroughly searched, but I'll check back on the tree house."

He'd pulled his chair closer. As he leaned forward, clasping his hands, their knees almost touched.

"Okay, now, Ms. Thayer, if you could just work with me for another few minutes. Is there anyone else who might have some reason to abduct your daughter? What about Anna's father? Has custody been disputed?"

Callie shifted uncomfortably, twisting her hands again. "No, nothing like that. When Kevin and I divorced, we agreed that I'd raise Anna myself. He's remarried now, with children. I recently asked him if he'd consider seeing Anna. He thought about it and said no."

"What sort of relationship do you have with him?"

"I wouldn't say it's good. But that has nothing to do with Anna."

"Where does he live?"

"Chicago."

"His full name?"

"Kevin Thayer."

"Do you have an address and phone number?"

"Look," Callie said impatiently. "Believe me. It's not him." But then, just as she spoke, she had a glimmer of doubt. He'd been so angry the last time they'd talked, far angrier than she'd expected.

When she'd first called, he'd been out of town. *Where had he been?* she wondered.

"I understand what you're saying, but we still need to contact him."

"He's listed," Callie said. "Kevin Thayer. Just check Chicago information."

"Have you seen him recently?"

"No, not for at least six years."

"What about conversations? How often do you talk to him?"

"When I called him about Anna last month, it was the first time we'd talked in years."

"When was that?"

"I'm not sure exactly."

"Before or after Diane Massey was killed?"

"I . . . think it was around that time. Right before or after."

Lambert took a beat to think before moving on. "Okay. Now, the note and watch — both of them were left right outside your house. Have you noticed anyone — friends, neighbors — behaving oddly lately?"

Faces flashed through Callie's mind, and then one jumped out from the rest. "Nathan Lacoste," she said abruptly. "He's a student at Windham. We have a class together. He's always been strange around me, but lately he's gotten worse."

"Strange in what way?"

"Well, it's like he's sort of obsessed with me. He drops by the office. Calls me at home. I finally told him to leave me alone. He . . . he seemed upset."

"When did you have this conversation?"

Callie's skin prickled. "Maybe a week ago, in the Windham library lounge. And . . . and there's another thing too." Her heart was beating faster. "I saw Nathan at the Easter egg hunt. He was riding by on his bike. But . . . this is crazy. It couldn't be Nathan. I mean, he didn't know. No one knows about Steven and me. No one in Merritt, I mean."

"Lacoste. How do you spell that?"

She told him; he wrote it down.

When he'd finished, he looked back up at her. "What about Officer Evans?"

"Rick?" Callie stared at him.

"Did you ever tell him about your past?"

She flushed. "I told you. No one."

But the sound of Rick's name had triggered something, a deep, painful yearning. She remembered that she was angry with him, but she didn't feel it now. It didn't matter what had happened before. She wanted him here with her.

"Rick's at his parents'," she said to Lambert. "I need to talk to him. Do you have the number someplace? I . . . I don't have it with me."

Lambert and Parillo exchanged looks.

"What?" Callie said.

"Officer Evans —" Lambert stopped. "We'll see what we can do."

Callie was about to press further when Lambert's cell phone rang.

"Excuse me," he said to Callie, as he pulled the phone from a pocket.

He listened briefly, hunched in on himself. "My God. How long ago?"

Callie's heart felt like it might explode. "What?" she said. "What is it?"

Parillo took hold of her shoulders. Callie twisted away.

"Goddamn it, you've got to tell me." She wasn't keeping her voice down.

Lambert, still clutching the phone, stood up and left the room.

Moments later, he was back. "That had nothing to do with your daughter," he said. "I'm sorry to have upset you."

From the doorway, he gestured to Parillo, who followed him out to the hall. Callie heard them whisper, then, seconds later, Parillo came back alone.

"The lieutenant had to leave," she said. "He'll be back a little later."

"Tell me what happened," Callie said. "What's more important than Anna?"

"It's not more important," Parillo said. "It's just . . . he had to go." It was like a veil had fallen between them. The air had subtly changed.

She heard someone coming up the front steps, and Callie's stomach flipped.

"I'll see who it is," Parillo said and quickly left the room. Callie stood up to follow her, but Parillo was already back.

"It's Officer Carver," she said to Callie. "He wanted to check on you."

"Tod?" Callie said vaguely. "He's here?" She'd hoped against hope it was Anna.

"Shall I tell him you're not up to visitors?"

"No, it's okay. I'll see him." A chill was creeping over her. Nothing really mattered.

Still, at the sight of Tod's familiar face, something in Callie melted. She thought of Tod's daughter, Lilly, just two years younger than Anna. If anyone could know what she was going through, Tod would be the one.

Tod headed straight to where Callie sat. She stood up. They embraced.

"I'm so sorry," he said softly, rocking her. She clung to his solid warmth.

Callie had started to sob again, and Tod was patting her back. "Where's Rick?" he asked. "Why isn't he here?"

She pulled back, wiping her eyes. "He's out of town. At his parents'. Also, we . . . we had a fight. We're not really speaking."

"Forget about it," Tod said roughly. "He'd want to know about this."

"I don't have a number for him." Hopeful, Callie looked at Tod. "You guys must have his cell number at least. He must have left a way to reach him."

"We've already called him," Parillo said.

"You have?" Callie said.

Tod shot the policewoman a look. She gestured him to the hallway.

When the two of them came back, Tod seemed uncomfortable. He was fiddling with something in a pocket. He didn't look at her.

"Goddamn it!" Callie exploded. "What is going on?"

Neither Tod nor the policewoman answered. Parillo studied her hands.

Finally, Tod responded. "Callie . . . he's not there."

"Not there? Not where?" Callie asked. She didn't get what he meant.

"Rick's not at his parents'," Tod said. "We don't know where he is."

"You mean he's gone out?" Callie said. She still didn't understand.

"No. He hasn't been there. His father . . . he's not sick."

Callie stared at Tod. She couldn't take this in. "Then, where . . . where is he?"

Tod looked at Parillo. This time she responded. "We don't know. We've left a number of messages. We're waiting for him to call back."

It took another few seconds, then Callie grasped the truth. For weeks — months — Rick had lied to her. The room seemed to dance.

"Callie," she heard Tod saying. "Don't leap to conclusions."

"Conclusions?" Callie said vaguely. The word had no meaning. She had no idea why Rick would have lied, and she really didn't care. If things had been different, she'd have been angry, but she had no feelings left.

For the next hour or so, no one said very much. It was four-thirty and then it was five. Tod left around five-thirty.

"What about you?" Callie said to Parillo. "When do you go home?"

Parillo said, "I'm not leaving."

Callie met her eyes. "Thank you."

Her mind was drifting back and forth between the past and present. The distant past in Tennessee. The recent past of this night. If only she could take back what she'd said just hours before to Anna. But you didn't get second chances. That was something she knew.

Please God, she prayed. *Please. Let her be safe.*

And thought of all the other families who must have prayed similar prayers. She thought of Dahlia's brother on the TV news, demanding Steven's death. She asked herself if this was punishment for what she'd failed to do then.

She'd lapsed into a dreamlike stupor, when the telephone suddenly shrilled. The kitchen was a blur of motion as they all sprang to life. A click as the police tech, headphones on, busied himself at the console. He looked at Callie, gave a short nod. She picked up the receiver.

"Hello?" Callie could barely speak.

"Sweetheart. My God. I just heard."

Absurdly, it took a split second to recognize Rick's voice. Without saying another word, she passed the phone to Parillo. For a moment, she felt a fierce fury that he'd raised and dashed her hopes. Then even that was gone, and she felt only despair.

"She's doing okay," Parillo was saying. "Under the circumstances. . . . Listen, we have to keep the line free. . . . Sure. Okay. I'll tell her."

When she'd hung up, Parillo turned to Callie. "He wanted you to know that he's coming home. He'll be back by noon today."

Callie stared at the blank white wall. "It's too late," she said.

~⚹~

THE man kept talking and talking, but Anna didn't understand. He was talking about people she'd never heard of, terrible things they'd done. Someone named Steven Gage, who he said had killed people. A woman named Laura. He said she was Anna's mother. Anna wished he'd take the thing out of her mouth so that she could explain. Her mother's name was Caroline. They called her Callie for short.

He was still holding the panty hose, twisting them in his fingers. He'd wind them around one of his hands and then around the other. Now he was telling her he was sorry, that he knew it wasn't her fault. But because of what her mother — what

Laura — had done, he would have to kill her. He didn't want to kill her, he said, but he didn't have a choice.

Yes you do, her mind screamed. *I don't want to die. Mommy, please help me! Somebody find me here.*

It was like a terrible nightmare. She just wanted to wake up. But she could smell the damp, moldy basement, feel the cords on her wrists. If only he would let her talk! If only she could explain! She rolled her head from side to side, moved it up and down. She tried to talk through the thing in her mouth, but the sounds she made weren't words.

The man was getting up on his knees now, leaning over her.

"I'm sorry, Anna," he said again. He even sounded sad. For a second he sounded like someone she knew, but then that thought was gone.

Leaning down toward her, he looped the panty hose around her neck. When he lifted her head, she felt his hand, big and hot and strong. *This isn't happening*, she told herself. *This isn't happening.* One more loop around Anna's neck, then he hunkered back. The fabric scratched against Anna's neck. He slowly pulled it tighter.

❧

6:25 A.M. A numbness had settled over Callie as night gave way to morning. Upstairs, she heard the flow of water. Parillo was taking a shower. The state police technician, still manning the phone, was reading a magazine. The crime scene processors had packed up and left. The house was her own again. But the heavy torpor that suffused her body kept her from getting up.

"It's looking worse, isn't it?" Callie said tonelessly. "With every hour she goes missing, the chances are less that she's okay."

The technician looked up from his reading. "It's only been six hours," he said. "A little less, maybe." He managed something like a smile, but it didn't seem convincing.

Callie buried her head in her hands. She couldn't stop the images from unrolling in her mind. They multiplied with frightening speed, the possibilities. She saw Anna raped, molested, terrified, crying for help. Or maybe — *please, God, please, God, no* — maybe she was dead.

Footsteps on the stairway. The water upstairs had stopped. Parillo appeared in the kitchen doorway, her short, dark hair still damp. Crossing the room, she touched Callie's shoulder. "You sure I can't call anyone? Someone to come and be with you?"

Callie shook her head.

As Parillo sat down to resume her vigil, a car pulled up outside. Instantly, Callie was on her feet moving toward the door. But it was only Lambert and Knight. Knight was wearing a shirt and tie; he'd dispensed with the undercover garb. Listlessly, Callie followed them into the living room.

"Ms. Thayer," Lambert said, once they'd all sat down. "I know we've been through this before. But is there anyone else Anna might have told she was planning to run away?"

Seated on the couch across from him, Callie had a sinking feeling. "You believe Henry's story," she said. "You believe she was kidnapped." She realized that she'd clung to the hope that they'd find it wasn't true, that just as Lambert had first speculated, Anna was simply hiding.

"We're exploring all the possibilities. But yes, I'm afraid that, as best we can tell, Henry's telling the truth."

"What did he say about the kidnapper? How did he describe him?"

"We have a sketch artist with Henry now, working on a drawing. He described him as having a bushy beard, but that could be a disguise."

"What about the car? Did Henry get the make or license number?"

"He said it was a dark sedan, but that's about all he remembered. He wasn't sure of the color. Maybe dark blue or green."

"Did you ask Henry if *he* told anyone that they were running away?"

"He said that he didn't. He said that they'd sworn to each other not to tell anyone."

"So what does that mean?" asked Callie. "If they didn't tell anyone, does that mean it was a stranger? Someone who just happened to be there and saw the kids on the street?"

"That's one possibility," said Lambert. "Another is that someone was watching."

"Have you talked to Nathan Lacoste?"

"We interviewed him early this morning. He let us search his apartment, and we didn't find anything suspicious. He says he was home alone last night, that he got home around eleven."

"But he doesn't have an alibi?"

"No," Lambert said. Just as he spoke, his beeper went off. He glanced down. "Excuse me." He reached for his cell phone and punched in numbers, got someone on the line.

Suddenly, Lambert was leaning forward, his whole body rigid. Was it good or bad? She couldn't tell. Her eyes raked his face.

"When? . . . Are you sure? . . . Where is she now?" Lambert looked up from the phone. "They've located a young girl who claims to be your daughter. They found her up by the Stop and Shop, alone in the parking lot. She's a little confused, disoriented. But the photo you gave us seems to match."

"Oh, my God!" Callie choked. She started to laugh hysterically, then suddenly she was crying. "Oh, my God," she said again. "Where is she? Is she okay?"

"She's in a squad car now, on her way to the hospital."

Callie looked at him, alarmed. "The hospital? What's wrong?"

"Nothing's wrong. She seems fine. But we just want to be sure. A doctor will take a look at her, and then she can go home."

Lambert was on the phone again. "Right. I'm sure she will." He held out the cell phone to Callie. "They're going to patch her through now."

"Patch her — you mean, I can talk to her? She's . . . she's there now?"

Lambert was handing the receiver to her. She clutched it like a lifeline. For a moment, she heard static and then a faint voice. "Mommy?"

"Anna." She could barely speak. "Sweetheart, are you okay?"

"I . . . I think so."

Callie couldn't stop crying. *Anna was safe! Alive!*

"Mommy? There was this man, and he made me go with him. He picked me up and put me in his car. He took me to a basement."

Anna's voice was eerily calm, like she was telling a story.

Tears streamed down Callie's face. "You're safe now," she said.

"We need to get you over there," Lambert whispered to Callie.

"Anna? I'm on my way to meet you. I love you," Callie said.

When Callie hung up, she looked at Lambert. "Thank you," she said. "Thank you."

Everything had changed so quickly, she could hardly take it in. The images that had tormented her were still seared on her brain. *Anna's safe,* she told herself. *Anna's safe. They've found her.* But a part of her wouldn't believe it until they were face-to-face.

As they stood up, getting ready to go, Parillo gave Callie a quick once-over. "Maybe you want to brush your hair? Put on a little makeup?"

Callie's first reaction was impatience. Who cared how she looked? Then she realized that Parillo wasn't thinking of her. Parillo was thinking of Anna.

"I'll do it in the car," she said, as she headed to the door.

In the powdery reflection of a compact mirror, she seemed to have aged ten years. There were deep violet circles under her eyes, and her skin was a papery gray. Callie dragged a brush through her hair, then tried to put on lipstick, but the car made a sharp turn, throwing her off balance. With a finger, she wiped away a reddish smudge. *Good enough,* she thought.

Just five minutes later, they reached the hospital. Pulling around to a back entrance, they clambered out of the car. The air was blue and luminous, smelling of flowers and dew. It was hard to believe that, here outside, the world had gone on unchanged.

Callie walked to the end of the sidewalk. Her legs felt rubbery. She stared down the main drag of the parking lot, to the busy street beyond.

In the steady stream of morning traffic, a police cruiser came into view.

"There! I see them. That must be them." Callie grabbed Parillo's hand.

A light turned red. For an endless moment, the cruiser stopped. When the light turned green, it moved forward. But not fast enough.

It seemed to take an eternity for the cruiser finally to reach them. As it turned into the parking lot, Callie was running forward. The car pulled up, the back door opened, and Anna tumbled out. She looked unbearably small and thin, with wild, unfocused eyes.

"Mommy!" she cried plaintively.

And flew into Callie's arms.

⁓

HE was trying to make sense of it, to figure out what had gone wrong. He'd been so close, almost there, when something had stopped him short.

Only time is fair.

He still believed that part.

So why hadn't he gone through with it? Why hadn't he killed Anna?

Again, he went over it in his mind, putting the pieces together.

She'd been trying to talk to him, he could tell from the sounds she made. He'd struggled to ignore the muffled cries as he calmly spoke to her. He'd needed her to understand why he had to do this. Still, at that point, he'd had no doubt that he would carry through.

When he'd finished talking, he'd wrapped the stockings tightly around her throat. Then, looking down, he'd met those huge blue eyes. That was it, he realized now, the instant when everything changed. He'd wanted to see Laura in her, but he'd just seen a little girl.

A sudden flash of insight.

He couldn't kill a child.

If only he'd realized this before! So much effort wasted. It made him sick to think of Laura's relief at having her child back. He who'd hoped to cause her only pain had now brought her joy. His only comfort was in thinking about what he had planned for her.

⤜⥤

CALLIE awoke in her own bed, Anna asleep in her arms. Light glinted in from beneath drawn shades, the rays of a setting sun.

As she listened to Anna's measured breathing, Callie snuggled closer, inhaling the damp familiar smell of her daughter's golden skin. The hours they'd spent at the hospital seemed very far away, like something they'd watched on television, not something they'd lived. She'd held Anna in her lap while detectives talked to her. Anna had answered their endless questions in a tone of polite disinterest. No, the man hadn't hurt her, hadn't touched her under her clothes. A medical exam confirmed that there was no sign of sexual assault.

When Anna started talking about the black stockings, Callie could hardly listen. Slowly, she'd stroked Anna's hair, trying to reassure her.

"He kept saying that my mother's name was Laura, but I couldn't say anything. He had something inside my mouth. I couldn't talk at all. He acted like I was someone else, except that he knew my name. He . . . he said he had to kill me. 'Cause of something Laura did. Oh, yeah, and then he told me he was sorry. I almost forgot that part."

Anna burrowed deeper into Callie's lap, as if she'd like to crawl inside her.

"Did he say exactly what your mother had done?" Lambert's voice was gentle.

"*Not* my mother. Laura."

"That's right. Laura. Did he tell you what she'd done?"

"No . . . I don't think so. Just that it was really bad."

"What else did he talk about? Did he say any other names?"

"He talked about someone named Steven. He was really mad at him."

Lambert looked at Anna closely. "Was he mad at Steven or Laura?"

"I'm not sure exactly. Maybe both of them. I can't really remember. I was really scared."

Beneath her arms, Callie felt Anna's body start to shiver.

"Do you remember anything else he said?" Lambert was leaning closer. "I know it's hard to think about this, but we need you to help us catch him."

Anna shook her head. "No," she whispered. "That's all."

The shivering was growing more pronounced. Callie couldn't take it. "Isn't this enough for now? Anna needs to rest."

They were driven home in a squad car by a young, clean-cut patrolman. As they turned off Main Street onto Linden Lane, he slowed down a bit. "When we get to your street, keep your head down. Ignore the media."

"The media?" Callie said faintly.

"Yes. You'll see what I mean."

As they neared the house, Callie saw them, reporters crowding the street. They were holding notebooks and microphones, battling for position. There were concrete barriers around her house, TV trucks, and cameras. Overhead, Callie heard the swooping roar of a news show's helicopter.

One of the reporters saw them and started to run toward the car. In an instant, the others were on his heels, and the race became a stampede. Faces and cameras jammed against the car's closed windows. Flashbulbs exploded in Callie's eyes amid a barrage of questions.

"Is Anna okay?"

"How do you feel?"

"What are you going to do now?"

Shielding her face with one of her hands, she held Anna close with the other. "Keep your head down," Callie whispered. "Don't look at them."

The car had slowed to a crawl now. They couldn't make it through. "Jesus," Callie heard the patrolman mutter. "Somebody help us out here."

Then two uniformed officers were forcing a path through the crowd. "Stay back! Out of the way!" they yelled, and the swarm of reporters fell back.

It took almost ten minutes to drive that last block. Barriers blocked the driveway. Two more cops pushed them aside.

They pulled up to the garage and parked. Callie and Anna climbed out.

Under a storm of flashbulbs, they quickly approached the front door. The patrolman who'd been their driver followed close behind them.

"Everything okay?" he asked, once they were inside.

"Yes, thanks for everything."

He smiled at them and left.

After she'd closed and locked the door, Callie steered Anna upstairs. Anna was wearing hospital garments, a big shirt and drawstring pants. The clothes she'd had on when she was found had been sent to the state crime lab.

"Would you like to take a bath?" Callie asked when they reached the landing at the top of the stairs.

"Not now." Anna shook her head. "I just want to go to sleep. Can I get into your bed, Mommy?"

Callie's heart ached. "Sure," she whispered into Anna's hair. "I'll come lie down with you."

Anna put on pajamas and climbed into Callie's double bed. Outside, the clamor of voices vied with the rumble of vehicles. But Anna, curled in a silent ball, seemed oblivious. Without bothering to get undressed, Callie lay down beside her. The world had shrunk to this single room; nothing outside existed.

Callie hadn't planned to go to sleep, but at some point she must have. When she glanced at the clock on her night table, she saw it was after six.

Careful not to disturb her daughter, she slipped out of bed, tiptoed over to a window, and peered out from behind a blind. The crowd had dwindled in the past few hours but hadn't disappeared entirely. A handful of reporters was still staked out in the fast-fading sun. She dropped the blind, crossed the room, and headed downstairs to make coffee.

She was groggy and disoriented from the long late-afternoon nap. As she dumped coffee into a filter, she realized how alone she felt. She needed to speak to another person, someone from normal life, someone besides the cops and detectives with whom she'd spent the night. Before she could stop herself she thought of Rick with a sharp sense of loss.

Martha. She'd call Martha.

At the thought of her friend's warm, worn face, her heart seemed to lift.

Martha picked up right away, almost as if she'd been waiting. "Callie," she said in heartfelt tones. "I've been trying to call you. Thank God Anna's okay. And you — how are *you* doing? How have you survived?"

"I'm fine now," Callie said. "How . . . how did you know?" Even as she spoke, though, she saw it was a stupid question. All those reporters outside the house. Of course, the story was out now.

Martha was talking again, but Callie had missed the beginning. In the flood of words, she caught Posy's name, but she couldn't make sense of the rest.

"I . . . Martha, please, you have to slow down. I don't understand what you're saying."

Martha stopped. "You haven't heard."

"Heard what?" asked Callie.

A long, long silence. "Oh God, Callie, I'm sorry. Just forget I said anything. You don't need to think about this now. Tell me how Anna's doing. That's the important thing."

Blood pulsed in Callie's veins. "I want to know what happened."

At the other end of the phone line, she could hear Martha breathing.

"There's no easy way to tell you," Martha finally said. "Posy was murdered. They found her body while they searched for Anna last night."

A tremor passed through Callie, like some small internal

earthquake. She thought of the furor that had broken out in the early-morning hours, that phone call that had prompted Lambert to rush off so suddenly. That must have been when it happened. When they discovered Posy.

"Who killed her?" Callie asked. "Is anyone in custody?"

"The cops aren't saying anything. At least not to the press."

"It must be the same person. The same man who kidnapped Anna."

"Not necessarily," Martha said. "There's no way of knowing yet. It might be totally unrelated. I'll bet that's what they find."

"You've got to be kidding, Martha. We're in Merritt, not New York. In all the years I've lived here, we've never had a murder or a kidnapping. Now, in less than twenty-four hours, we suddenly have both."

"It's not twenty-four hours. Posy was killed before that."

Martha was talking so fast now, Callie knew something was wrong. Something beyond the terrible fact that Posy had been killed.

"What happened to her?" Callie asked.

Martha didn't answer.

"Martha?" Her voice was stronger now. "Tell me what happened to Posy."

"I don't know the details," Martha hedged. "The police aren't saying much."

"Tell me what you know, then."

Another long silence.

"I don't want to be the one to tell you. I'm sorry, Callie. No."

The coffee had finished brewing, and Callie took out a mug. She lifted the carafe from the machine, and poured out the steaming liquid. But she couldn't seem to control her hand. Coffee splashed the counter.

"I understand," Callie said. "But I really have to go now."

She had Lambert's card in her purse. Now she went to find it. She dialed the number. It rang twice, then he picked up the phone.

"Ms. Thayer, I'm glad you called. We're about to pay you a

visit." He sounded brisk but preoccupied. There were voices in the background.

She dispensed with preliminaries. "Tell me about Posy Kisch."

A brief pause while Lambert regrouped. "I guess you saw the news."

"No, a friend told me. She . . . we both worked with Posy. In the Windham Alumni Office."

"Yes," Lambert said. "I know. We'll have to talk about that."

Callie took a sip of coffee. It was hot but she couldn't taste it. "Do you think the person who killed Posy is the same one who kidnapped Anna?"

"We don't know yet," Lambert said. "We're still sorting things out."

Callie took a long, deep breath, trying to prepare herself. "What exactly happened? How was Posy killed?"

A pause, this one longer.

"We can talk about that later. Right now, there's something else. We need to speak with Anna again, to show her some photographs."

LAMBERT untied a Redweld file and pulled out a stack of photographs. The three of them were at the kitchen table, Anna on Callie's lap.

"Anna, I'm going to show you some pictures. I need you to help me out here. I want you to tell me if you see the man who kidnapped you last night."

Anna was still in her pajamas. Her hair was a tangled mess. She looked at Lambert through sleep-hazed eyes, not entirely awake yet.

Lambert placed a photograph in front of Anna. She rubbed her eyes and looked. The man had a thin face, a sandy crew cut, a neatly trimmed goatee.

Anna shifted in Callie's lap. "It's not him," she said.

Lambert took the picture away, then put out another. The next man had a pudgy face and sad, doleful eyes. His hair was a dark reddish blond, his beard redder than the rest.

Anna frowned. "No," she said. "It's not him either."

Lambert took back the picture.

Then, as he laid out the next image, Callie's heart lurched. He looked younger, and he had a beard, but the features were the same. The thin, pointed nose. The foxy eyes. "Oh, my God," she whispered.

Lambert's head whipped around toward Callie. He gave her a warning look.

Anna twisted to look at her. "What's wrong, Mommy?" she said.

Squeezing Anna's shoulder, Callie gave a short laugh. "Nothing, honey. I was confused. It's okay. You can go on."

"Anna. Have you seen this man before?" Lambert's voice was level.

"No, I don't think so. He's not the man who took me."

There were eight photographs altogether. At each one, Anna shook her head. When they were finished, Lambert smiled at her. "Okay. Thanks for your help. I've got to talk to your mom for a second. Would you mind leaving us alone?"

Callie kept a smile on her face until Anna left the room. Then she took the stack of photos from Lambert and flipped back to the third one. "I saw him in Maine," she said. "On the island where Diane was killed. I'd gone out to look around. He followed me to Carson's Cove — that's where Diane was ambushed. I thought he was from the island. He said he was worried about me."

Lambert's expression was grim now. "When was this exactly?"

"A couple weeks back. May first, I think. That man in the picture, who is he?"

Lambert fingered the photograph. "This is Lester Crain."

Tuesday, May 16

I ASSUME you've all read the background material." Mike Jamison scanned the faces at the conference table. All five men nodded.

Jamison glanced at Lambert, who was seated to his left. Merritt's chief detective was hosting the task force, along with state police detective Ed Farrell, and together they'd asked Jamison to make his presentation. Farrell, mid-forties, quick gray eyes, sat a bit back from the table. There were two Maine detectives, Jack Pulaski and Stu Farkess, and Wayne Schute, from Manhattan South Homicide. All of them had followed up obvious leads without any success. They'd gathered at this state police barracks outside Merritt to pool their resources.

"Okay, then," Jamison continued. "We'll briefly review the incidents, then talk about possible links. Anyone who wants to, feel free to jump in."

Even all these years later, it was a matter of habit to say that, to make clear to the state and local guys that he respected them. He'd always gone out of his way to show that he wasn't some FBI asshole. Because of that, he'd usually enjoyed good relationships in the field. Of course, on this particular occasion, he didn't really have to worry. As a retired agent here by invitation, he had no official standing. He couldn't make anyone do anything, even if he'd wanted to.

Jamison briefly ran through the facts of Diane Massey's murder. "According to the M.E.'s report, the cause of death was blunt force trauma to the head and strangulation," he concluded. "The victim's body had been stripped of clothing and jewelry. A black stocking ligature was tightly knotted around her throat, and her eyes showed petechial hemorrhages." He didn't have to explain. All of them would know that the pinpoint blood clots were presumptive proof of strangulation. "There were straight incisions along the insides of both of the victim's arms. The incisions were made postmortem."

"Those incisions on the insides of the arms — Gage did that too, didn't he?" The question came from Schute, the New York detective, who'd been rapidly taking notes. He had bushy eyebrows, a weathered face, and dark, piercing eyes.

"That's right," Jamison said. "Gage also performed the mutilations postmortem, just like the UNSUB in this case." UNSUB. Unidentified subject. The old FBI lingo. "Another striking similarity is the black stocking ligature. Gage was tried and convicted for the murder of Dahlia Schuyler. In that case, the victim was also strangled with a black stocking."

Next on the agenda was Melanie's attack. Again, Jamison ran through the facts. "In your files, you all have a copy of the artist's sketch of Ms. White's assailant. You'll note the resemblance between this sketch and the composite of Anna Thayer's abductor."

"What about videotape?" Pulaski asked. "Did the apartment building have cameras?"

Schute gave a sour smile. "Sure did, but the one that mattered was out of service that day. Anyone who thinks you get what you pay for hasn't lived in Manhattan. Six grand a month that apartment goes for, and they can't keep the cameras running."

"What about noise?" Pulaski asked. "Were any of the neighbors home?"

"You can't hear a thing through those walls," said Schute. "The tenants pay for quiet."

As Jamison moved on to Posy Kisch, he could feel the tension building. The men at the table were all fathers. Some had kids around Posy's age.

"The victim was found near the Connecticut River during the search for Anna Thayer. The absence of blood at the scene confirms that the killing took place elsewhere. There were cuff marks on her wrists and ankles. Substantial evidence of sexual assault and torture prior to death. In addition to having her throat slit, she was stabbed eighty-seven times. It appears that the victim was raped with a knife both anally and vaginally. No evidence of semen inside the victim, though traces were detected on her face. DNA analysis is under way. The tests are being expedited."

"Kisch was last seen on Saturday, May 6, at a public dance in Greenfield. She came to the dance with a classmate who's been on our suspect list. Nathan Lacoste — that's his name — is also acquainted with Ms. Thayer. Ms. Thayer was at the dance as well, along with her boyfriend — a Merritt cop — and another couple."

"Is that a little strange?" Schute asked. "That all of them were at the same dance?"

Farrell shrugged. "This isn't New York City. There's only so much going on."

"Anyway," Jamison continued, "Ms. Thayer recalls that, during a break in the dance, Lacoste asked her if she'd seen the victim."

A little more back and forth, and then they moved on to Anna Thayer. Jamison briefly outlined the facts surrounding her abduction and release.

"Why do you think he didn't kill her?" Schute asked, once Jamison was done.

"My best guess," said Jamison, "is that this UNSUB may have kids of his own. Either that or, for some other reason, he strongly identifies with them."

Sitting back in his chair, Jamison surveyed the table.

"Let me cut to the chase. I believe we're looking for two killers. The first — let's call him UNSUB 1 — killed Diane Massey. He also attacked Melanie White and kidnapped Anna Thayer. Someone else — UNSUB 2 — killed Posy Kisch."

Schute said, "I'm having a little trouble with this. How can you know it's not the same guy? Doesn't that seem more likely?"

"I'm not saying there isn't some connection. Just that I'm fairly confident that we're looking for two different killers. With Kisch we're dealing with a sexual sadist. He gets carried away. We've got his semen on Kisch's body. It's not a clean crime scene."

"UNSUB 1 is highly organized. There's no evidence of sexual sadism, no sign of sexual assault. Even the slashes on Massey's arms were all inflicted postmortem. There's no sign that the UNSUB tried to prolong her suffering."

"But the body was stripped," Schute said. "That's not sexual?"

"In this case, I suspect not. I think the clothes were taken to keep the crime scene clean, to reduce the likelihood of trace evidence. As investigators, we're all familiar with the theory of transfer and exchange — the notion that an UNSUB always leaves something of himself at the crime scene and takes something with him. Here, we still don't have anything, no fibers, no hairs, nothing."

Schute rubbed his chin. "So one guy killed Posy Kisch, someone else did the rest?"

"That's the way it looks to me," Jamison responded. "Like I said, UNSUB 2 is a sexual sadist. His crime scene resembles Lester Crain's."

"You really think that Lester Crain killed that girl?" Schute was still skeptical. "So why's he suddenly making an appearance? Where's he been all these years?"

"I'm not necessarily saying it's Crain. I'm saying the signatures match. If Crain committed a murder, it would look something like this one."

"Still, though," Lambert said, "Callie Thayer claims she saw Crain on the island where Massey was killed. The fact that she places him at the scene — you don't take anything from that? If he didn't kill Massey, what was he doing there?"

Before Jamison could answer, Pulaski jumped in. "We don't know if she really saw him. She'd had this theory that Crain was the killer way back at the beginning. Then, when she saw his picture, she jumped on the connection."

"Maybe," Lambert responded. "But she didn't identify him by

name. When she saw the photo, she recognized the face, but she didn't know who it was. She doesn't remember seeing pictures of Crain before the one I showed her daughter."

"That's what she *says*," Pulaski said. "She probably believes it. But who can say what memories may be lodged in her subconscious? She sees the picture you showed her kid, and the picture triggers something. She thinks it's this guy she saw recently, but really it's from the past. That sort of thing happens, you know. It's a problem with eyewitnesses."

Before Lambert could answer, Jamison jumped in. "Look, both scenarios are possible, but neither changes my basic point. Whether Crain was on that island or not, I don't think he killed Massey."

A few doubtful looks from around the table, but no one said anything.

"How about the victimology?" Pulaski finally asked.

"Another link," Jamison said. "Most of Crain's victims were prostitutes, they had a certain look. Tight clothes, elaborate hair, lots of heavy makeup. Now, Kisch wasn't a prostitute, but she affected a similar style."

"What about her date that night? What's the latest on him?"

Jamison turned to Lambert, who was heading that investigation.

"We've talked to Nathan Lacoste several times. At this point, we don't have evidence against him, though we haven't ruled him out. He agreed to take a polygraph, but the results were inconclusive."

Farrell, who'd been silent for a while, started to shake his head. "I'm with Wayne. I still have a hard time believing we've got two different killers. I mean, I guess it's possible, but how can you be sure? How do you know it's not one killer who's shifted his M.O.?"

Jamison said, "It's not a question of M.O. When we talk about the modus operandi, it's just the nuts and bolts, the practical steps a killer takes in order to complete the crime. The signature is something else. It's the killer's calling card, that extra something the killer does because it gets him off. The M.O. changes with circumstances. The signature stays the same. It may evolve, it may escalate, but the core doesn't change. With Crain, torture and bondage were central to his signature. You see both in Kisch's murder and neither in Diane Massey's."

"Okay, I see what you're saying," Farrell said thoughtfully. "Now, what about Steven Gage? How would you compare his signature to what we have here?"

"Also different," Jamison responded. "Gage didn't get off on causing pain. What he wanted were the bodies. He couldn't even have sex with his victims until they were dead. Killing them was incidental, a means of obtaining control. Even the incisions on his victims' arms were all inflicted postmortem."

"Like with Massey?" Farrell said.

"That part of it, yes."

"Okay," said Schute, stretching back in his chair. "Let's talk a little about Massey's killer. The guy you call UNSUB 1. What do we know about him?"

"As I said, he's highly organized. He knows his way around a crime scene. He might be trained in law enforcement or even forensic work. If he's married, he's arranged his domestic life so he isn't accountable. Maybe he travels a lot for work, isn't home that much."

"What about Thayer's boyfriend?" Schute had turned to Lambert.

Lambert said, "He has a good reputation. I don't know him well myself. Of course, we've checked out his whereabouts, especially over the weekend. He lied about where he'd be, and that obviously concerned us. But without going into all the details, there are extenuating circumstances. He was in New York during the time in question. His alibi holds up."

Pulaski was looking over a chart that Jamison had prepared. "What about the anniversary notes? Any useful leads there?"

Jamison shook his head. "Melanie White destroyed hers. We ran tests on the other two but didn't come up with much. Staples multipurpose paper, too common to be of much use. The only envelope we have is the one delivered to Ms. Thayer. It's a Staples number ten white business envelope, also quite common. The flap tested negative for saliva."

The phone rang on a corner table. Farrell jumped up to get it. He picked up, listened briefly, then said tersely, "Thanks."

When he hung up, he turned to look at them, a stunned look on his face.

"The DNA at the Kisch crime scene is a match for Lester Crain."

⌒

"CALLIE. I know you're there. Please. Pick up. If you'd just —"

Callie grabbed the phone. "Okay. I'm here. Will you stop calling now?"

A long silence from the other end. Callie could hear Rick breathing. "We need to talk," he finally said.

"Fine. We're talking. Are you happy?"

"I mean face-to-face," he said. "I need to see you, to explain."

"You lied to me," Callie said. "That's all I need to know."

There was a beep on the line, another call. She let it go into voice mail. While the calls had slowed somewhat, she was still besieged by reporters.

"I don't think that's it," Rick said. "At least not the only thing. I think you're angry because you needed me, and I wasn't there for you."

Now Callie fell silent. Through the kitchen window, she saw gray sky. Soon, it would start to rain.

"Isn't that it?" he pressed.

"Look," she said. "Will you just leave us alone? We've already got enough to deal with. Whoever kidnapped Anna is still out there. It's just . . . it's just too much."

Another beep on the line. Didn't reporters have lives? It was a big wide world out there; there must be other stories.

"I don't want to make things harder. I want to help," Rick said.

There was something in his tone, an urgency, that made Callie hesitate. Suddenly, his face rose up in her mind, the familiar planes and angles. She wanted to reach out and touch his cheek, but of course, he wasn't there.

She sat silently for several seconds, uncertain what to do. Either way, she'd hang up feeling she'd made the wrong choice.

"Okay," she said finally. "If you want, you can come over tonight, after Anna's in bed. But only for an hour. I'm completely wiped out."

"So I'll come by around nine, how's that?"

"Make it ten," said Callie.

She hung up the phone, feeling torn, ill at ease in her skin. She had half a mind to call Rick back and tell him she'd changed her mind. If she still felt this way later, that's exactly what she'd do.

Remembering the call-waiting beeps, she punched in her voice mail number. Most of the time, when she didn't answer, the reporters just hung up. Realists, they knew full well that she'd never call them back. Occasionally, though, they left messages in winning heartfelt tones, telling her that *they understood*, that they wanted her to *tell her story*.

The first message was a female reporter calling from the *Merritt Gazette*. She sounded hesitant and very young, unsure of what to say.

"Ms. Thayer, we have some information that we need to ask you about. It has to do with your . . . past. With some things that happened in Tennessee."

There was a phone number and a name, but Callie didn't write them down. She sat there numbly, staring into space, wondering how much they knew.

The next message was from the *Boston Globe*, a reporter named Charlie Hammond. This time there were no equivocations, no room left for doubt.

"I'm calling to get your response to a claim that you are Laura Seton."

❧

AFTER the task force meeting, Mike Jamison headed for the Orchard Inn, a small hotel near Windham College that Lambert had recommended. His room had a high four-poster bed and white curtains at the windows. He was happy to see that it came equipped with a small writing desk and lamp. He planned to rent a car tomorrow and drive down to New York. Schute had offered him a ride tonight, but he wanted some time alone.

Once he'd hung up his suit, he unzipped his black nylon laptop case and removed the thin computer. He set it up on the polished desk, plugged it in, and turned it on. Outside, it had started to rain, a gentle pulsing rhythm. He'd opened a window, and the curtains fluttered in a cool gust of breeze.

Waiting for the computer to boot, he thought back on the day. The DNA was convincing proof that Crain had killed the Kisch girl. The discovery had astonished him, as it had everyone in the room. Until today, if he'd had to place a bet, he'd have said that Crain was dead. A killer like Crain never just stopped, that almost went without saying, and he knew of not a single unsolved crime with Crain's signature. Steven Gage had been a master at concealing his victims' bodies. Could he have imparted those skills to Crain on Tennessee's death row?

And yet, if that was the explanation, something had gone wrong. The attempt to conceal Kisch's body had been at best perfunctory. Even without the search for Anna Thayer, she'd have been found soon enough. There was also the question of linkage, still unresolved. If there were, as he thought, two UNSUBs, how were they connected? If Lester Crain hadn't killed Diane, why had he been on Blue Peek Island?

The questions circled around in his mind. He played out scenarios. He was conscious of that familiar stirring that came on the brink of insight. By all accounts, Lester Crain had been obsessed with Gage. What if Crain had gone to the island after learning about Massey? Maybe he'd read about Diane's murder, the black stocking ligature. Intrigued by the obvious links to Gage, he'd been drawn to the crime scene. And then, once he got there, something in him had snapped. Diane's murder could have been the stressor that pushed Crain over the edge. The grip he'd had on his murderous drives had dissolved in the excitement. Then from Maine he'd traveled to Merritt, where he'd tortured and killed Posy Kisch.

He decided to type up his notes. Sometimes the act of reviewing the facts gave birth to new ideas. But first, he reminded himself, he should check his office voice mail. He'd cleared his schedule as best he could, but there was always that random phone call.

Two messages. Damn.

It was a relief when he heard the hearty voice of his poker buddy Joe Carnowski. They were planning a trip to Atlantic City; did he want to come along? A beep and then another voice.

It was Callie Thayer.

Her voice was so soft that he could hardly hear, but he could tell she was upset. She asked him to call as soon as he could. She left her number twice.

Her phone rang four times, then he got voice mail. He left his name and number. But before he could even get back to his desk, his cell phone started to ring.

"I'm sorry." Callie was whispering. "I have to screen my calls."

He was having trouble hearing her. "Could you talk a little louder?"

"Okay." The voice was a fraction stronger. "But I don't want my daughter to hear me."

A pause.

"I guess you know who I am by now."

"Yes," he said. "I do."

"I'm sorry I didn't tell you at first. I just . . . wasn't ready. But now, well, the press has found out. That's why I'm calling you. The reporters have been calling all night. I'm not sure what to do. I tried to call Lambert, but I couldn't reach him so . . . I thought of you. It's just — everything is such a mess. I need some advice."

"Don't call them back," Jamison said. "There's nothing to be gained. At this point, you don't even know if they have enough for a story. If you lay low for the time being, it might slow them down."

"Slow them down," Callie said. She sounded hopelessly bleak.

The rain was falling harder now. Through his window, Jamison could just make out a mountain's hazy outlines.

"Everyone's going to find out. Everyone will know." She sounded so miserable, so despairing. Jamison searched for words. Something to convince her that she'd get through this, that it wasn't the end of the world.

"Maybe you're making too much of this." He was careful to speak gently. "I know it will be hard at first, but it could also be a relief. It can't have been easy for you, keeping this kind of secret."

"It wasn't really so bad." Her voice was dull, as if she'd given up.

"You still may have a day or two. At least you have some warning."

"You don't think they'll print it tomorrow?"

"It depends on what they've confirmed."

"But if I don't call them back, won't that make them more suspicious?"

"And if you call back, what would you say? You can't lie about something like this. That would just make it worse."

As soon as he got off the phone with Callie, Jamison called Lambert. He tried his private line at the station, then tried him on his beeper. When he failed to get any response, he finally left a message. "Tell him to call me as soon as he can." Then, frustrated, he hung up.

It didn't make any sense that Lambert would be out of pocket. As chief of detectives at a time like this, he should be on call 24-7. Small towns were different from big cities, but, hell, they weren't *that* different. This was a major investigation in Lambert's jurisdiction.

It was almost seven o'clock now, and Jamison decided to get something to eat.

Outside, the air was moist and fragrant, almost tropical. Umbrella in hand, he walked a few blocks to the small town center. The rain was blowing at a slant, and his clothes were wet by now. He ducked into a Mexican place with a large bright red sign. At the counter, he ordered Cajun fish tacos, then sat at a table to wait.

Next to him, a harried young mother argued with her toddler. "You liked it last time," she was saying. The kid stuck out his chin.

"One-oh-nine," the cashier called.

He checked his receipt; that was him.

He ate fast, both because he was hungry and because he wanted to get back. The mom and kid reminded him of Callie and the nightmare she'd gone through. He wondered exactly where Callie lived. It couldn't be too far. If he'd been here longer, he'd have tried to meet her, but he just didn't have time. Still, he'd have liked to see the woman he'd once watched testify. The former Laura Seton. Steven Gage's lover.

It was Callie who'd first suggested Lester Crain's involvement. Yet she wouldn't know, even now, how horribly right she'd been. The decision had been made not to go public with the DNA link to Crain. The last thing they needed was for Crain to know that they had this evidence. If he hadn't already fled the jurisdiction, that would be all it took. There'd be some concern over public safety once the truth came out. But for now, the task force members agreed, secrecy was paramount.

It seemed clear that Crain was UNSUB 2.

But what about UNSUB 1?

He finished his meal, bussed his dishes, and headed toward the hotel. His thoughts moved to what Callie Thayer had said about Gage's family, the conversation reported back to him by Pulaski in Maine. He'd never met the mother or brothers, but he'd seen them many times. The mother nervous and overweight, flanked by her hulking sons. He couldn't remember the boys' names now. The mother's name was Brenda. She'd gone by her second husband's name. It started with an *H*, he thought.

Holiday. Halliburton. Hallowell . . .

None of them sounded right.

Back in his room, the message light was dark. Lambert still hadn't called.

Jamison was hanging up his jacket when the name finally came to him: *Hollworthy*. Brenda Hollworthy. That was the name she'd used. She might have moved or married again. Still, it was worth a try.

No Nashville listing for a Brenda Hollworthy, but there was a B.W. He wrote down the number, hung up, and dialed it.

"The Lord Jesus will rise again. Have you accepted him as your savior?" A woman's voice on the answering machine, a husky southern drawl. Too many cigarettes and cocktails before God came on the scene. "I can't take your call now. But leave me a message an' I'll call you back."

He couldn't remember hearing Brenda speak, wouldn't recognize her voice. He'd never have placed her as a born-again type, but of course, that had been *before*. Before her child was convicted of murder. Before he was put to death. Maybe she, like so many others, had found solace in religion.

He hung up without leaving a message. He'd try again later.

There was one more call he wanted to make before it got too late. Tomorrow he was driving down to New York to visit Melanie. She'd been released from the hospital but was still sleeping a lot. He wanted to get hold of her before she went to bed.

He picked up his cell phone and speed-dialed her number.

"Hello?" She sounded hesitant, uncertain what to expect.

"Melanie. It's Mike. How're you feeling today?"

"Pretty good." She seemed to relax, now that she knew who he was. "I mean, better, I guess. It's slow. The recovery, I mean."

"So I figure I can be in the city tomorrow by around ten or so."

"That's . . . could we make it a little later? I have some things to take care of."

"Okay. Sure. When's good for you?"

"Eleven?"

"Sure. You've got it."

"Mike, I'm sorry to cut you off, but a . . . a friend is coming up. The doorman just called to tell me."

"Okay, then. Well, I'll let you go. I'll talk to you in the morning."

He hung up with a nagging sense that something wasn't right. For all the doctors' reassurances, she didn't sound like herself. This visitor she'd mentioned, that bothered him too. Suddenly, he felt a flash of fear. *So what if it was someone she knew? Maybe she'd known the killer.* When he'd questioned her, she seemed confident that she'd never seen him before. But what if she'd been mistaken? What if she'd been confused?

He couldn't stop himself. In five minutes, he called back.

"Sorry to bother you again, but I misplaced your address," he lied.

"Not a problem," Melanie said. And recited the street number.

"You . . . are you okay?" he asked.

"Sure. I'm fine." She sounded surprised. After all, he'd just talked to her. Why shouldn't she be fine?

Feeling a little foolish, Jamison hung up. Still, Melanie stuck in his mind like a tune he couldn't forget. He'd felt oddly close to her during the time he'd spent at her hospital bedside. As if he were just where he should be, a feeling he'd almost forgotten. He'd had it so often during those years at the Bureau, working on the profile study, during the weeks he'd met with Steven Gage just before the execution. He wondered if that was part of it, his attachment to Melanie, as if she were a sort of talisman bringing back the past.

Outside, the rain was still coming down. He could hear it, but he couldn't see it. It had still been light when he left for dinner. Now the sky was dark. He'd try Brenda Hollworthy one more time, and then he'd take a shower.

"Hello?" It was same rough voice he'd heard before, but live now, not recorded.

"Is this Mrs. Hollworthy?"

"Who is this?"

"My name is Mike Jamison. We met . . . a long time ago."

"What'd you say your name was, son?"

"Mike. Mike Jamison. We met . . . in Tennessee."

"You that boy from the FBI?"

"I . . . I used to be." His heart was beating faster now; he could feel the adrenaline surge. The past flooded over him. *Steven Gage's mother.*

Before she could hang up on him, he rushed to fill the silence.

"It's been a long time," he said.

"Sure has," she said flatly. He half expected her to hang up then, but she stayed on the phone, waiting.

"I was hoping you could answer some questions for me about a woman named Diane Massey. You probably remember the book she wrote —"

Brenda Hollworthy cut in. "You know, the Lord says that we should forgive, and God knows I try. Every night I pray for the strength to forgive, but some things are just beyond us. You have any children, Mr. Jamison?"

A pause.

"Yes. I do."

"How many?"

"Two."

"Boys or girls?"

"One of each."

"I used to have three sons. Now I've got two. That's something you never get over. You should've done something, Mr. Jamison. You should've done something to save him. The Lord doesn't mean for men to kill each other. Two wrongs don't make a right."

Her voice was emptied of emotion, as if she'd rehearsed the speech. As if she'd spent countless years preparing for this call.

"I can't imagine what you went through." That much was certainly true.

"That's why you're callin', ain't it? It's that Massey woman. You think we had something to do with it, me or the boys. Well, I can't say I'm sorry to see her gone, God forgive me for that. But you're lookin' in the wrong direction if you're thinkin' of us like that. I'm a Christian woman, and they're good, good boys. Got families of their own now."

"Please, let me explain, Mrs. Hollworthy. That's not it at all."

"You think somebody else killed her?"

"Absolutely," he said. The truth, of course, was that he didn't know, but you said what you had to say. "I just wanted to ask you some questions about a few people Steven knew. I wanted to get your impressions of them. I won't take much of your time."

"So who're you talkin' about?" He could tell she was still on guard, though she sounded a fraction less hostile.

"Do you remember a woman named Melanie White?"

"'Course. She was one of Stevie's lawyers."

"Did he ever talk about her?"

"He talked about her some. He liked her. He thought she was smart."

"Did you ever get the sense he was angry with her? Upset she couldn't do more?"

"Well, sure, he got upset. I mean, he was on death row. He knew they wanted to kill him. He got upset a lot, Mr. Jamison. I'll bet you woulda too."

"But did he talk about Ms. White in particular? Was he especially angry with her?"

"No, I wouldn't say so. She did the best she could. I mean, that's what he mostly said."

"What about Laura Seton?"

A sharp intake of breath.

"That little bitch. Don't let's talk about her." For the first time, her voice had a flash of fire. He'd clearly hit a nerve.

His instincts told him to keep quiet, to wait for her to go on.

"I'm sorry, God forgive me, but that's what she is, a lyin' little bitch. If she'd loved him like she said, she wouldn't have told them the things she did. I wish it was her that was dead now. God forgive me, but I wish it was. If I just knew where to find her, I might just kill her myself."

"If somebody did that to one of my kids, I'm sure I'd feel the same way."

"I never did understand how Stevie couldn't hate her. But he always got mad when I talked bad about her. He had a soft spot, Stevie did. Deep down he was the sweetest boy. 'She's confused, Mama.' That's what he said. He never seemed to get mad."

Confused? *Hardly*, Jamison thought. He remembered Laura on

the witness stand, twisting her hands together. She'd spoken so softly he could barely hear. Terrified, not confused.

"And what about Diane Massey? Did Steven ever talk about her?"

A long sigh ending in a heavy wheeze. Brenda's lungs didn't sound good. "You know, I warned him not to talk to that gal. She was only in it for the money."

"How did he feel when the book was published? Do you know if he actually read it?"

"Yeah, he read it all right. Five or six times at least."

"Was he angry about it?"

"Angry? No, I don't reckon so. I looked at that book once. Made me want to throw up. But Stevie — he got himself a signed copy, had her send him one. I'd say, 'Stevie, don't you see what they're doin'? Don't you see they're takin' advantage?' But he'd just sort of shrug, like he didn't really care. I remember once him sayin', 'Mama, she's just doin' her job.' 'Her *job*?' I asked him. 'Well, okay, fine. But why you gotta help her?' "

Someone was knocking on Jamison's door. It had to be a mistake. He tried to ignore it, but the sound continued, louder than before.

"Excuse me, Mrs. Hollworthy," he said. And bounded toward the door.

Through the peephole, he recognized the front desk clerk with her neat helmet of curls. "I'm on the phone," he said sharply. "Can I call you when I'm off?"

She stared gamely up at the door as if trying to make eye contact. "I'm sorry to bother you, Mr. Jamison, but it's an urgent message. Lieutenant Lambert at the police station. He wants you to call right away."

<hr />

BENEATH the yellow glow of the porch light, Rick seemed nervous. A light rain was coming down, more a mist than a downpour. Dressed in jeans, holding an umbrella, Rick was shifting from foot to foot. For a split second, she softened toward him —

he looked so vulnerable. But that was habit, nothing but habit. She wasn't going to give in.

She took a deep breath and opened the door.

"Callie," he said softly.

She could tell that he'd had to stop himself from reaching out to hug her. Quickly, she turned toward the living room. Rick followed her.

Callie gestured Rick to the couch. She sat down in a chair. From across the room, they looked at each other. The distance yawned between them.

Rick was sitting on the edge of a cushion, leaning slightly forward. As if he were trying in this small way to bring her closer to him.

"I owe you an explanation," he said.

"It doesn't really matter."

A look of pain crossed his face.

"It matters to me," he said.

There were only a few yards between them, but he seemed very far away. She wondered why she didn't care, why she wasn't more curious.

There was a constant buzz in the back of her mind: *they know, they know, they know*. Soon, her past would hit the news. It was only a matter of time.

"Callie? Are you listening to me?"

"Yeah. Sure," she said.

Rick sighed and flexed his knuckles, staring at his hands. He seemed to be searching for a way to begin, perhaps waiting for her to help. But when time passed, and she didn't speak, he finally started to talk.

"When I was a kid, I had this friend. His name was Billy O'Malley. We went to school together, played sports, double-dated at the senior prom. My dad was an English professor. Billy's was a cop. You can imagine, if you're a kid, which one is cooler. The O'Malleys had this big, rambling house. Five kids, two or three dogs. I was always hanging out there. It was just the best place to be."

Sitting erect in her straight-backed chair, Callie felt like a statue. This story from Rick's childhood had nothing to do with her. Vaguely, she wondered what he was thinking, why he was telling her this. But to ask him that, she would have to speak, and that would take too much effort.

"When I was twelve," Rick went on, "I told my dad I was going to be a cop. Billy and I had it all worked out. We were going to be partners. My father tried to argue with me, told me that I could do better. But the fact that he was opposed to it just made me more determined."

Until now, he'd been staring down. Now he glanced up at Callie. Her face was smooth as marble. He looked back at his hands.

"I went to college in upstate New York. Billy and I were roommates. We'd already taken the test to join the NYPD. 'Hired at twenty, retired at forty,' that was Billy's father's mantra. College put us a little behind but only a couple years.

"After school, it was pretty much exactly like we'd planned. We got assigned as partners, worked the midnight shift. A lot of guys didn't want midnights, but we — we both liked it. There was less supervision to worry about, and you made a little more money. The only thing was, Billy had gotten married, and his wife didn't like the hours. He kept promising her that he'd do something, but it just never seemed to happen.

"From the start, I liked being a cop. No two days were the same. I liked being out on the street, trying to keep people safe. It probably sounds corny, but I really did feel that way. And then . . ."

Rick's face seemed to darken. He took a deep breath and went on.

"There are things you learn as a cop, rules that become second nature. Never hold your radio in your shooting hand. Shoot for center mass. And another one that I'd never forgotten until . . . until that night. In a domestic violence situation, you've got to move them out of the kitchen."

The most dangerous room in the house. Callie felt suddenly cold, her mouth dry as paper. She wanted to say that she'd heard enough, but Rick just kept talking.

"It was November twentieth, a Tuesday. Right before Thanksgiving. Carla was four or five months pregnant, and Billy was just thrilled. The radio call came in around two A.M. A domestic on One hundred and tenth. When we got to the apartment, it was quiet. We didn't hear a thing. This guy answers the door. White guy in khakis and a T-shirt. He seems surprised to see us. 'You must have the wrong apartment,' he says. When we ask if we can come in anyway, he says, 'Sure, no problem.'

"It's one of those New York apartments that's been cut up from a much bigger space. So when you walk in, you're standing in the kitchen. But for some reason, I'm not thinking about that. Neither of us is, I guess. Maybe because the guy seems so relaxed, we think that maybe he's telling the truth. Or maybe because, when you first walk in, you normally don't think *kitchen*. Somebody must have been cooking, though. The place smelled like fried onions.

"Billy stays with the guy — keeping an eye on him — and I walk toward the back of the room. 'Is there anyone else home?' Billy asks. The guy says no. And then, from behind a closed door, I hear this sort of moaning.

"After that . . . everything gets confused. I think I must have moved forward, toward the door and the sound. But then, at almost the same time, Billy's yelling too. Things must have happened really fast, but it felt like slow motion. I turn back around. Billy's on the ground. The guy's lunging toward me with a carving knife. Somehow, I manage to pull my gun. I shoot him in the chest and just keep going until all the bullets are gone. Next thing I remember, I'm down with Billy. Blood's pouring out of his throat. He gives this sort of pleading look, like *Don't let this happen*. Then his head fell back and that . . . that was it.

"After I called for backup, I just sat there and cried. I kept remembering things from the past, things from when we were kids. Like how Billy was the one who told me Santa Claus wasn't real.

How we got in trouble for sneaking into the movies one day when we were broke. And I remembered his wedding, being best man, how goofy we'd looked in those tuxes. I kept thinking about Carla and the kid he'd never know.

"That's where I was when backup got there, holding his head in my lap. I'd totally forgotten about the sound behind the door. She was dead, too, by the time they got there, stabbed more than fifty times. The M.E. said she'd have died anyway, but I've always sort of wondered. The next two months are a blur. The guilt just leveled me. There were some days I couldn't get out of bed. I wished that I'd died too."

Suddenly, the words stopped. Silence flooded the room. The lights of a passing car flashed across Rick's face. Rain tapped against the windowpanes. It was coming down harder now.

"But it wasn't your fault," Callie said. "Both of you were there."

"I was the one who survived," he said. "It had to be my fault."

"And now? Is that still what you think?"

He studied his hands again. She knew those hands, the long fingers, the slight roughness of the palms.

"I don't know," he said. "Even if it wasn't all my fault, I still could have stopped it. That's what Billy's father thought. I could see it in his eyes. At the funeral, he barely looked at me, didn't say a word. After the investigation, I tried going back to work. But I just couldn't do it. I couldn't handle it. At night, sometimes, I'd take out my gun and think about killing myself. Sometimes, I'd hold it against my head and almost pull the trigger. One day, this sergeant calls me over. He looks at me for a good long time. 'Rick,' he says, 'you gotta leave this job, or you'll end up eating your gun.' I acted like I didn't understand, but I knew that he was right.

"For two years after I quit, I didn't really do much. Went out to Colorado for a while, worked at a ski resort. Sometime around that first summer I realized that Carla must have had the baby. I thought about calling her, but I couldn't bring myself to do it. She hadn't wanted Billy to work midnights, and I was the reason he stayed. If it wasn't for me, he'd still be alive. I knew that's what she'd be thinking.

"After that, I moved up here. It seemed like a good idea. Keep myself busy, get back to work but someplace totally different. And that's how it was, until last fall. Then I met you and Anna. Watching Anna, I started to wonder about Carla and the baby. I made some calls, found out she'd remarried, was living in Forest Hills.

"It took a while for me to get the nerve, but I finally picked up the phone. When I said my name, she started to cry, but she was glad to hear from me. The baby wasn't a baby anymore — he was six years old. He was William Jr. — they called him Will — and he was smart as a tack. But after Carla remarried, he'd started having problems. A year ago, she'd had a baby girl and things had gotten worse. We talked for a couple of hours about, well, everything. Then, as we're about to hang up, she asks me if I'll come to see them. She has this idea that, if I meet Will, somehow it will help him.

"Of course, I say that I will. We go ahead and set a date. The thing is, I tried to tell you, but I couldn't talk about it. You and I had been dating a couple of months. I just wasn't ready. So I came up with this story about my father. He'd been sick a couple of years ago, and, well . . . you know the rest. I thought the trip would be a one-time thing, but it didn't turn out that way. Later, I wanted to tell you, but I just didn't know how. I knew you'd be pissed that I'd lied to you. I didn't know what to do."

Finally, he looked up at her, seeking some response. Her mind was filled with the sudden knowledge of how alike they were. She'd blamed herself for Dahlia Schuyler's death. He'd blamed himself for Billy's. It seemed ironic, and also sad, that they'd both had to struggle alone. Both of them had had their reasons. Still, it was sad.

Callie took a deep breath. "I have something to say as well. I guess it's a night for confessions."

Could she just go ahead and tell him? It seemed far too easy. But of course, that's exactly what it was. A few simple words.

"Like you," she began, "I moved to Merritt to get away from something. I wanted to start over, where no one knew who I was. Before I got married, when I lived in Nashville, I —" She faltered briefly. Actually saying the words to Rick was harder than she'd expected. "I was . . . involved with Steven Gage. You know, the serial killer."

While she saw Rick's eyes widen, she didn't wait for him to speak.

"When Steven was arrested in Nashville, we'd been dating for several years."

"Jesus." Rick's voice was incredulous. "That . . . that girl who testified against him. That . . . that was you?"

Callie slowly nodded.

There. It was done.

But before she realized what was happening, Rick was off the couch. In an instant he was there beside her, grabbing hold of her arms. Roughly, he pushed a sleeve up, exposing the soft, scarred flesh.

"Did he do this to you? Is that where these came from?" His voice was thick with feeling. He was angry, though not with her.

Quickly, Callie pulled down the sleeve, cradled her arms to her body.

"No," she said softly. "I did that myself."

Rick was looking hard at her. He didn't quite believe her. But the time for lies was over. It was time to tell the truth.

"As a kid, the depression wasn't too bad, but by high school, it was pretty awful. Sometimes I had the strangest feeling that I barely even existed. When I cut myself, that feeling went away. And it didn't hurt, not at first. It gave me this sense of euphoria. It took away the pain. For once, I felt in control of my life. I felt like no one could touch me."

"Gage — he did that to the women he killed. He cut their arms like that."

Nodding slowly, Callie fingered an arm through the fabric of her sleeve. The scars had faded with the passage of time, but they'd never disappear.

"The night when I first met Steven, he saw the marks on my arms. I was working as a waitress in a restaurant where the uniforms had short sleeves. I can still picture that blouse we wore, white cotton with orange piping. In a way, it was a blessing because I had to control myself. Fresh cuts, especially if they were deep, would have drawn attention. I really needed the job. I told myself I couldn't risk it.

"Then, two nights before Steven came in, I had a sort of relapse. I drank a bunch of vodka and made a new row of cuts. The next day, I called in sick, but I was scared to do it again. I bandaged up the worst of them and tried to keep my arms down. But while I was taking Steven's order, I could tell he saw the cuts. He was telling me what he wanted to eat, but his eyes were on my arms. He didn't say anything that night, but he came back a week later. This time, he asked me out for drinks.

"We went to the Wursthaus in Harvard Square and drank a lot of beer. At first, I thought maybe he was a shrink and wanted to give me advice. But he didn't talk about the cuts at first, even though he kept looking at them. Then after maybe an hour or so, he reached out and touched them. He told me they were beautiful, like some kind of art. Even though I was pretty drunk, I knew this was weird. At the same time, I immediately had this incredible sense of relief. Someone had embraced the part of me that I was most ashamed of. It wasn't really me that he was seeing, but I didn't know that then."

"What do you mean it wasn't you?"

Callie dropped her eyes. "It had to do with his mother. When Steven was three years old, she tried to kill herself. He found her naked on the bathroom floor, wrists slit, bleeding to death. You'd never have guessed, but his mother — she used to look like the victims. Slim, blonde, beautiful really. Just like the girls he killed."

"That part . . . I never heard about that."

"Sometimes, I'd wake up and see Steven staring at my arms. The scars on my arms, I mean. I think he used them to fuel his fantasies. I reminded him of his mother."

"You can't know that for sure," Rick said.

"I'm pretty sure," said Callie.

She waited for Rick to contradict her, but he didn't say anything.

"The cutting, how long did you do it?" Rick's voice was gentle.

His voice told Callie that he didn't care, didn't mind that she'd lied. With a sort of wonder, she realized that Rick still loved her. And yet, this fact didn't seem to matter. Her own heart was frozen.

"For eight or nine years," she said, answering his question. "It started when I was in high school, went on until Anna was born."

"Do you miss it?" he asked.

She gave an awkward shrug. "I miss the relief it used to bring, but I know it wouldn't work now. It's like drinking or anything else that you turn to for escape. You feel better temporarily, then it just makes things worse. I miss what I thought it could do for me, free me from my fears. But that was an illusion, anyway. So I guess I don't miss it, really."

Rick wandered over to a window and stared out into the rain. For some reason, the sight of his back made her feel infinitely lonely.

"Why didn't you tell me?" It was the question she'd waited for.

"I . . . I don't know. It's hard for me to trust people, to trust men especially. But I trusted you a lot, more than anyone in a long time. You had a secret too, you know. You should understand."

"It's different," he said. "I lied to you. There wasn't a clear way out. But you . . . all you did was withhold something. It's really not the same."

Callie thought a moment. "I guess I don't see it that way. I was talking to someone recently, this woman lawyer I know. She said that there's this securities law that requires you to give information, that just because you don't lie straight out doesn't mean you're okay. She has this idea that relationships should be held to that same standard. A duty to disclose, she called it. I sort of agree with that."

"We're people, Callie, human beings. All of us make mistakes."

"And mistakes have consequences."

Too late, she saw him wince.

"I didn't mean that the way it sounded. I didn't mean . . . you know."

Another long silence, filled with the sound of rain.

"I still don't understand," Rick said finally, "why you didn't tell me. I know you, Callie. You're an honest person. You wouldn't want to live like that. It's one of the reasons I felt so bad after I'd lied to you."

Callie's body stiffened. "You don't know me so well. Don't you see that now?"

"But I think I do," Rick said slowly. "Sometimes better than you know yourself. And I know that this isn't like you. It's just not something you'd do."

A buzzing sensation in Callie's body, a warning of danger ahead. There was so much she hadn't told him yet, but it was time for Rick to go.

"It's getting late," she said, glancing toward the door.

But Rick stayed exactly where he was, a strange new look on his face.

"Anna," he said softly. "It's Anna, isn't it?"

Callie licked her lips. "I don't know what you mean."

But Rick's eyes were wider now, as if he'd grasped a truth. "Anna is Steven Gage's daughter. You didn't want to tell her."

A cold wind was blowing through her. Her heart was an open door.

This wasn't, couldn't be, happening.

How could he have known?

❧

RAIN was coming down in heavy sheets, obscuring the road ahead. Mike Jamison was doing seventy-five on the dark, unfamiliar highway. The sullen glow of his headlights faded into the night. Windshield wipers slapped back and forth, giving flashes of clarity.

But he wasn't thinking about the weather; his thoughts were on Lester Crain. *Lester Crain was in custody.* He still couldn't believe it. Crain had been apprehended earlier that night after running a red light. When he refused to pull over, a chase had ensued, until, finally, he was cornered. He'd been driving a stolen Toyota Camry and carrying false IDs. The driver claimed his name was Peter Welch, but his fingerprints matched Crain's.

Jamison swung into the police barracks parking lot, back where he'd started the day. There was a handful of cars by the building's entrance. No TV trucks yet. The radio call must have gone out as a traffic violation. The reporters would be pissed as hell when they discovered what they'd missed.

He gave his name to a receptionist and was quickly ushered back. In the observation room, he joined the onlookers gazing through the one-way glass. He saw Lambert at the end of the line, several guys he didn't know. The rock-faced one in a dark suit he took for FBI. There was one woman in the gathering, in a pantsuit and horn-rimmed glasses. Her hair was cut in a short blonde bob. She reminded him of Melanie.

Taking his place in the silent group, he saw Lester Crain.

There was something surreal about finding Crain here, in this small-town state police barracks. For years he'd eluded capture by the nation's top law officers. And now, when they'd all but given up, here he finally was.

Crain was slightly built with a concave chest and a ferretlike face. There was nothing especially striking about him. Your basic low-life punk. His green T-shirt was crumpled and stained. He looked like he must smell.

Ed Farrell, the state police detective, was in the room with Crain. He stood against a wall, gazing down at Crain, wearing a sour expression.

"You're not helping yourself, Lester. We already know you're lying." Farrell's voice echoed through the scratchy intercom.

"Not lyin'," Crain mumbled. "You fuckin' don't know a thing." He slid farther down in the wooden chair and thrust out his lower lip.

"Stupid-ass cops," Crain muttered, to no one in particular.

Jamison felt a hand on his shoulder. "Hey." It was Lambert.

"Congratulations," Jamison said, keeping his voice low.

"Thanks," Lambert whispered back. "Pretty amazing, huh?"

"Damn right." Jamison was watching Crain. "How's it going so far?"

"He threw us a hell of a twist right before you got here. He denies having anything to do with Posy Kisch's death. But he admits to killing Diane Massey and to kidnapping Anna Thayer."

Impossible, Jamison thought. He doesn't work like that. If Crain had abducted Anna Thayer, she wouldn't be alive.

"He's lying," Jamison said flatly. "We know that he killed Kisch. The DNA, the signature — everything adds up. He didn't kill Massey, though, or kidnap the Thayer girl. For some reason, he wants us to believe that he did. The question now is why?"

Inside the interrogation room, Farrell was talking again.

"Okay," he said. "You killed Diane Massey. So tell me about that, Lester. I want to know the details. Tell me how it went down."

Crain's lips twitched up in a cold smile. "I hit her," he said. "I was pretty drunk. I don't recall with what. Probably something I found near there. I just don't recall."

"You *don't recall*," Farrell said. "So why should I believe you?"

Crain ignored the question. "And I strangled her," he said.

"You strangled her," Farrell repeated. "I don't suppose you recollect what sort of tie you used?"

"It's called a ligature," said Crain.

"Okay. Ligature."

Crain smiled to himself, as if remembering. "Black panty hose," he said.

On the other side of the one-way glass, Jamison shook his head. "That was in the press," he muttered. "Crain just picked it up."

"You know the size?" Farrell was asking.

"Nah."

"Brand name?"

"It wasn't like I planned to wear them. I didn't pay attention."

"Where'd you buy them?"

"Don't recall. I'd had 'em a pretty long time."

"Weeks? Months? Years?"

"Yeah."

"Which one?"

"Don't recall."

From the other side of the one-way glass, Jamison shook his head. "He hasn't told us anything he couldn't have read in the papers. The stuff they held back — size, brand — he can't answer those questions."

"Like he said, he might have forgotten," said Lambert.

"Not him. Not those sorts of things."

"But why would he lie?" Lambert asked. "Why confess to a murder he didn't commit?"

"He wishes he'd done it," Jamison said. "That's one explanation."

From what happened next, it almost seemed as if Crain could hear their conversation. Until this point, he'd stared at the floor with occasional glances at Farrell. Now he turned toward the mirrored glass, gazing straight at *them*.

"I cut up her arms," he said.

Jamison stared at him, the blood humming in his veins. For the first time, Crain had offered a detail that only the killer should know. They'd withheld the part about Diane's arms for precisely this reason. To have a way of distinguishing between true and false confessions.

"Cut up her arms, like, how?" asked Farrell.

"With a knife, I ripped them straight up the insides, starting by the hands."

Lambert was slowly shaking his head, a look of wonder on his face. "Jesus Christ, Callie Thayer was right. It was fucking Lester Crain."

Jamison didn't say anything. What was there to say? He'd been so confident that he was right, so certain of his theories. And now? Now, what did he think? Again, he heard Crain's voice. "I ripped them straight up the insides, starting by the hands."

Could someone have leaked the information to Crain? Highly, highly unlikely. But how else, unless he was the killer, could Crain have known this fact? For the first time since his arrival in Merritt, Jamison felt unsure. Had he let pride — arrogance — blind him to the truth?

"What did you use to cut her?" That was Farrell again.

Crain grinned. He seemed in excellent spirits, sensing the stir he'd caused. "You're something else, you know that? Seems to me I've given you enough to work with. I ain't gonna say any more."

Farrell had taken a seat at the table. He was face-to-face with Crain. "You give Diane any sort of warning? That you were gonna kill her, I mean?"

"The note," Jamison said softly. "That's where he's going now."

Crain raised his hands. "You don't understand English? I said I'm done talkin'. You don't believe I killed Massey? Fine. Let me go."

"What about Anna Thayer? How come you didn't kill her? That's not like you, Lester, not to murder and torture the girl."

Crain's eyes glistened, but he didn't answer Farrell.

"Let's talk about Kisch again. That college girl you killed."

"I told you I'm done talkin'."

Farrell stood up, stretched his arms, and yawned elaborately. "That's fine by me. I get overtime. I can stay here all night."

Crain scowled and stared at the wall.

A minute or two, then Lambert said, "Looks like that's all for now."

He turned to Jamison. "So what do you think?"

Jamison rubbed his chin. "I don't know. There's something . . . I still don't buy it, that Crain killed Massey."

"But those gashes along her arms," said Lambert. "How else could he have known?"

"How long was the body left at the scene?"

"I couldn't say for sure. But you know the usual drill. It wouldn't have been for long. Not long enough for Crain to read about the murder and get himself to the island."

"You know," Jamison said slowly. "He could just be guessing.

That's how Gage cut the arms of his victims. He could have made the leap."

Lambert looked at him doubtfully. "So you still think we've got *two* killers, both of them obsessed with Steven Gage? One of them copying his handiwork, the other claiming to?"

Again, the flicker of uncertainty. Was it possible he was wrong? Years had passed since he'd retired. Had time dulled his instincts?

As if sensing Jamison's hesitation, Lambert pressed ahead.

"We've linked Crain to the Kisch murder. We know that he's been active. I know what you said about Crain's signature, but it's been a real long time. Maybe Crain's an exception to the rule. Most rules have exceptions."

"I guess it's possible," Jamison said. It cost him some effort to say that.

Lambert clapped him on the shoulder. "That's all I wanted to hear."

Wednesday, May 17

CALLIE woke up abruptly with a sense that something was wrong. She jumped out of bed and ran to Anna's room. Her daughter was fast asleep. She knelt down beside Anna's bed, drinking in her presence. The pink cheeks, the rosebud mouth, the faint soapy smell. Then, reluctantly, she pulled away. She didn't want to wake her.

Heading back to her own room, she felt anxious again. She knew that Anna was safe in bed. *What was wrong? What was it?* It wasn't even five yet. She had to get some sleep. But just as she climbed back in bed, the answer suddenly hit her. The reporters' phone calls from yesterday. That's why she felt so anxious. Had her silence managed to stop them, or had they run with what they had?

Her Walkman was still on her desk, where she'd left it early Sunday morning. She pulled on the headphones and turned the dial until she found the news. The announcer was talking about UMass budget cuts. A good sign, she thought.

Still in her nightgown, she walked downstairs to make a pot of coffee. The radio voice became a distant buzz, a backdrop to her thoughts. Anna hadn't been to school this week. She'd be falling behind. Callie made a mental note to get homework sent home.

She was filling the coffee pot with water when she heard the words *Lester Crain*. The container dropped from her hand with a thud and rolled in the sink.

"According to state police, Crain was picked up on I-91 after running a traffic light. His capture brings to conclusion a manhunt that's lasted for close to a decade. Crain escaped from a Tennessee prison while awaiting retrial for the torture-murder of a Tennessee teenager. State police detective Ed Farrell says there is substantial evidence linking Crain to the murder of Windham sophomore Posy Kisch. The young woman's body was found early Sunday morning near the Connecticut River. Meanwhile, police are also exploring the possibility that Crain was behind the Saturday night kidnapping of ten-year-old Anna Thayer. The Merritt fifth grader was released unharmed the following day."

Leaning against the counter, Callie took deep breaths. Her thoughts were spinning wildly. *They got him*, was her first thought. But with the euphoria came something else, a devastating knowledge. The child she loved beyond everything had been in this monster's hands. The thought was obscene, unbearable. She couldn't comprehend it.

By the time she could think clearly again, the announcer had moved on, something about renovation plans for the Merritt public library. Callie found Lambert's card where she'd stuffed it in her wallet. She pulled off the headphones, closed the door, sat down, and dialed his number.

He picked up on the second ring.

"Is it true?" she demanded. "I heard the news. You captured Crain?"

"I was about to call you," he said. For the first time since they'd met, Lambert sounded tired.

"So it's over now?" Callie pressed. "I mean, he's the one?"

"We've linked him to Posy Kisch's murder. We don't know if he kidnapped Anna."

The world seemed to tilt.

"But . . . I don't understand," said Callie. "I mean, how could it *not* be him? Two attacks right here in Merritt. The whole connection to Steven."

"We've got some . . . complicating factors."

"Did you *ask* him about Anna?"

"Yes."

"What did he say?"

"I can't tell you that."

"What do you mean, you can't tell me? My God, I'm her mother."

"Ms. Thayer, this is an ongoing investigation. As soon as we can make anything public, I'll be sure to let you know."

"So what you're saying" — she picked her words carefully — "is that the kidnapper may still be out there."

"It's possible," Lambert said. "We just don't know."

"What about Diane and Melanie? What about the notes we got? I mean, how could there be two different killers, both with ties to Steven? Unless . . . unless they're working together. Is that what's going on?"

"Ms. Thayer, I'm sorry, but I can't say anything more. I promise to contact you just as soon as we know something."

"And until then?" Callie asked angrily. "Until then, what do we do?"

"We have you under twenty-four-hour surveillance. You'll be perfectly safe."

"But how long? How long will it be like this?"

"I wish I could tell you that."

It was after ten when Anna, still in her pajamas, finally straggled downstairs. She plunked herself down at the kitchen table, with a mumbled "G'morning." Callie poured Anna a glass of orange juice along with one for herself. She'd have liked one more cup of coffee, but she'd already finished the pot.

"I thought I'd make pancakes," Callie said brightly. "How does that sound to you?"

Anna rubbed her eyes. "I'm not really hungry," she said.

"You want some cereal? A scrambled egg?"

"Maybe a piece of toast."

Callie almost said, "You have to eat," but managed to stop herself. In the big picture, what did it matter if Anna ate breakfast today? She stuck two pieces of bread in the toaster and found some strawberry jam. Outside, a thick gray cover of clouds hung low in the dusky sky. The air was heavy with humidity. Another storm on the way.

When the toast popped up, Callie spread it with jam and handed the plate to Anna.

"You sure you don't want anything else?"

"Not right now," said Anna.

As she watched Anna eat, Callie wished that she could turn on the radio. Right before Anna had come downstairs, she'd scanned the stations again. There'd been more reports about Crain's capture but no new details. Nothing yet about her own past life. For that, at least, she was grateful.

Still, Jamison was right; it was only a matter of time. She wondered if it would have been better to tell the truth from the start. But even now she couldn't imagine what she would have said to Anna. It was hard enough growing up, without this kind of burden. She herself had had two loving parents, a devoted older sister. And still she'd had a profound sense of being inadequate. Knowing that your father was a serial killer — she couldn't imagine that. She herself would have viewed such knowledge as confirming her deepest fears. She'd wanted to spare Anna this, which is why she'd never told her. Anna hadn't chosen her father. She deserved a normal childhood.

Callie tried to imagine sitting down with Anna, setting out the facts. She tried to think what Anna would say, but her mind came up blank.

"Sweetie," she said. "I need to talk to you. About something real important."

Anna looked up, fear in her eyes. "Is it . . . about the man who took me?"

"No, honey, no. It's about something else."

She looked at Anna's plate. "Are you finished?"

"Uh-huh."

"Let's go to the den."

The den was usually just a place to watch TV or play board games. But the living room faced the front of the house. The den felt more protected.

The couch in the den was brown corduroy, worn and gently sagging. Callie sat down first and pulled Anna toward her. Normally, Anna would have squirmed away. She was far too old for this. Today, though, she seemed just as happy to nestle in Callie's arms.

Callie angled Anna into a cushion so she could meet her eyes. "Okay. There are some things I have to tell you now. It's okay if you're mad."

She kept looking into Anna's eyes, the small, trusting face. She'd have done just about anything to avoid what she had to say.

"You know a few weeks ago, how we were talking about your dad?"

"Uh-huh," Anna said.

"Well, the thing is," — and here Callie held her tighter — "you have another father."

Anna looked at her, confused. "You mean, I have two fathers?"

"Your daddy from back in Indiana, I met him after you were already born."

Anna stared at Callie. "So he's not my real daddy." It wasn't a question. She'd grasped the facts, but her voice was strangely blank.

"He would have been. He wanted to be. He was going to adopt you. But before that happened, we separated."

But Anna hardly seemed to be listening. She was staring at her hands, twirling a finger round and round, over and over again. "So where is he?" she whispered.

"He . . . he died," Callie said. "He died a long time ago."

"You mean before I was born?"

"No, after that."

Anna's mouth had started to tremble. "How come you never told me? Didn't he want to see me?"

"He was too sick," Callie said. "He was sick in his mind. I didn't tell him when you were born. I didn't want him to know. But Anna" — and here she gripped her daughter's shoulder — "he really would have loved you. If I'd ever told him about you, he'd have fought until they made me let him see you."

Anna's eyes had drifted down again. "What happened to him?" she said.

"He . . . he did some very bad things. He had to go to prison. After that — this was in Tennessee — they decided to put him to death."

"Who decided?" Anna asked.

"The jury. And the judge."

"In an electric chair?" Anna's eyes were huge.

"No." Callie was rocking her now. "They gave him chemicals. It was just like he had to go to sleep. Like before an operation."

She didn't believe that, not for a minute, but what could she say to Anna? The horror of it rolled back in on her, what he'd done, what they'd done to him. This was far worse than she'd imagined, the telling of this thing.

Anna looked up at Callie. "Did he kill someone?" she asked.

Callie met her daughter's eyes. "Yes," she said. "He did."

"One person or more than one?"

"More than one," said Callie.

"His name, it was Steven, wasn't it? My real daddy's name."

A moment of shock before Callie remembered the kidnapper's ramblings. That's how Anna knew the name. She must have made the connection.

"Is your real name Laura, Mommy?" Anna's voice was small.

"My whole name is Laura Caroline Thayer. People used to call me Laura."

"Oh," Anna said.

Callie waited for another question, but Anna sat quietly, as if a part of her were trying to absorb what had just been said. In her lap, she clasped a pillow, her arms wrapped tightly around it.

"I don't want to talk anymore right now."

"All right," Callie said. As she stroked Anna's hair, she wished with all her heart that everything were different.

❧

MELANIE's home was immaculate, sun streaming through the windows. Jamison could hardly believe that it was the same apartment. He sat in a large armchair, Melanie on the couch. Both of the pieces were pristine white, either new or reupholstered.

"I'm so grateful for everything you've done," Melanie was saying. In the pale face, her eyes were the same bright blue he remembered.

Her bare feet were tucked beneath her, her toenails painted pink. She was wearing gray drawstring pants and a light pink long-sleeved shirt.

Jamison shook his head. "I haven't really done much."

"But you have. You've been here through everything. I don't know how to thank you."

The warmth of the words was at odds with her voice, which was little more than polite. From her face, he had no idea what she was thinking. Since the attack, she seemed to have retreated somewhere deep inside herself. Perhaps all her energies were consumed in the complex act of healing.

He thought back to when they'd first spoken by phone, when she called him out of the blue. At the time, he believed it was something more than a simple professional call. When he suggested that they meet for dinner, he could tell that she was pleased. But then everything had changed in that single terrible night.

Now that he was here, he felt strangely awkward. He'd come as a friend, paying a visit, and yet he barely knew her. He glanced toward her bookshelf at a small arrangement of framed photographs. His eyes lit on one of a young black woman standing by the Eiffel Tower.

Melanie's eyes followed his.

"That's my best friend, Vivian. She flew back from a vacation in Greece after she heard what happened."

He noted the careful choice of words, the avoidance of specifics. He wanted to ask about her parents, if they'd come to see her yet. But, again, he didn't know her well enough to broach such a sensitive subject. He settled for something more general.

"I'm glad you weren't alone through this."

"Not at all," she said. "My fiancé, Paul, has been wonderful. He's been here every day."

He saw it then, the square-cut diamond, glittering on her left hand. It hadn't been there in the hospital, he was sure of that. Though perhaps they'd removed her jewelry as a matter of policy.

"So you're getting married." He managed a smile. "That's wonderful. I didn't know. Is this a recent development?"

"Not exactly." She fingered the diamond ring. How could he not have seen it? "We . . . we'd been having some problems, but we've managed to work things out. After what happened, I realized that it was time for me to grow up. Paul showed me that I could count on him. There's a lot to be said for that."

"Yes," Jamison said quietly. "It's an important quality."

Looking at her, damaged and frail, he had a sudden insight. She'd been fighting some sort of private battle, and now she'd given up. From something in her tone when she spoke of Paul, he didn't believe that she loved him. But love was always a high-stakes game, and Melanie was opting out. At this point, he almost said something, then thought better of it. After all, who was he to question her decision?

She gave him an opaque blue-eyed look, then smoothly changed the subject. "How's the investigation going? Are there any new developments?"

"Nothing concrete," he said.

They were just marking time.

"I still don't think that Lester Crain is the man who attacked me. I've looked at a lot of pictures and I . . . I just don't think that's him."

Jamison nodded. "I know," he said. "They — the detectives — they're considering everything you told them."

"I had a feeling that they wanted it to be Crain. I mean, it wasn't like they tried to pressure me. They just kept telling me to take my time. They wanted me to be sure."

They talked for another hour or so, about nothing in particular. So many subjects — everything important — seemed to be off-limits. The wedding was planned for September, at Paul's mother's house in Southampton. They planned a small, quiet affair, just close friends and family. She talked about going back to work, maybe in a month or two. She still had headaches and spells of dizziness, but they were getting less frequent. Her firm had been more supportive than she'd ever have imagined. The partners had agreed to defer her consideration for partnership until next year.

When he got up to leave, she insisted on walking him to the door. Even that slight effort seemed to take something out of her. Before leaving, he surprised himself by briefly pulling her close. "Take care of yourself," he murmured, then softly closed the door.

❧

I used to be a nicer person.

The words flickered through Melanie's mind as she leaned against her door. She could still feel Mike Jamison's embrace, his hands against her shoulders. The way she'd acted, he had to think that she'd barely noticed his kindness. But she was tired, so very tired. She'd done the best she could.

Her life might not be the life she'd planned, but it was the life she had. You tried to do everything right, but things still fell apart. Investments failed. Husbands left. Terrible things occurred. You had to play the hand you were dealt. That's what she was doing.

There was no point in looking back, imagining what might have been. Crossing the room, she picked up the phone and punched in Paul's number.

Thursday, May 18

CALLIE? I just saw the paper."

That was all Martha needed to say. Callie knew that the news was out.

"Which paper?" Callie asked. Not that it really mattered. News like this would travel like wildfire via the AP. If one paper had gone with the story, all of them would have it.

"It was in the *Globe*," Martha said. "I don't know about the others."

Morning sun glimmered faintly through the kitchen window. A few minutes before nine o'clock. The beginning of another day.

"What did it say?" Callie asked. She was surprised at how calm she felt. Maybe because for the past few days she'd expected the ax to fall.

"Except for the part about . . . your past, there wasn't a whole lot new. They talked about how Anna was kidnapped. There was a lot about Tennessee."

"Did they say there was some sort of connection?"

"A connection?" Martha said.

"Oh, never mind," Callie said. "I'm not sure what I mean."

She could tell that Martha was waiting for her to say something more. But all she wanted was to get off the phone and let the news sink in. And she needed to see the paper itself, to find out what it said.

"Martha," she said, "I'm sorry, but I've really got to go. I need to talk to Anna about this. I'll try to call you back, okay?"

She'd barely hung up the phone when it rang again. Assuming

it was Martha, who'd forgotten something, she quickly picked it up. But it wasn't Martha; it was a man. Mike Jamison's voice.

"You've heard the news," she said. It was a statement, not a question.

"The news? I . . . no, I slept late. Actually, I just got up."

"I just got a call from a friend. It's out now, the part about my past."

She could hear him flipping through a newspaper. "Ah," he said.

"What are you looking at?" she asked.

"The *Washington Post*," he said. "It's not much of a story, really. A single column on an inside page."

"Oh," said Callie. She was staring out the window. The back-yard was green and empty, just like on a normal day. The sun had slipped behind a cloud. It looked like it was getting colder.

"I'm sorry," Jamison said, "if this is making things harder."

She shrugged, then realizing he couldn't see her, said, "I'm okay. So much has happened in the past week, I'm still pretty numb. Maybe it will hit me later, but right now, I'm okay."

"Listen," he said, "the reason I'm calling is to be sure you're taking precautions. I still have serious doubts that Crain is the only killer."

"You don't think he kidnapped Anna, do you?" Callie's voice was low.

"I wish I could say something different," he said. "But no, I really don't."

Callie sat down heavily. "So who then? Who could it be?"

"Profiling isn't really a science, it's more like a kind of art. My impressions are usually pretty accurate, but not a hundred per-cent."

"So what are you thinking?" Callie asked. "Do you have any ideas?"

"I think it's someone familiar with your neighborhood, some-one who may have children. He knows about crime scene inves-tigation. He's meticulous, a long-range planner."

"You think . . . it's someone in law enforcement? Someone with that kind of background?"

"A few years ago, I would have said that, but you can't say these days. With all the true crime books, TV shows, the information is out there."

"You know, they investigated my ex-boyfriend. He had an alibi, though. He was out of town, in New York, the night that Anna was kidnapped."

"It's standard procedure to check boyfriends and husbands. They're so often the perpetrators. You always look at them first."

"They also looked at one of my classmates, but I think they cleared him too."

There was something tapping at Callie's mind, but she couldn't quite get at it. Some faint intuition, a shadowy thought, struggling to get through.

"We're okay," she finally said. "We've got twenty-four-hour surveillance on top of the home alarm system. Besides, with all the press, no one could get past. I haven't looked outside yet, but I can just imagine. I mean, after the news in the paper today, I don't want to think about it."

As she spoke, she heard the swoop of a helicopter, impossibly close overhead. "There," she said. "Can you hear that? The media swat patrol."

"I talked to Steven's mother," Jamison said abruptly.

"You talked to Brenda?" Callie said. She suddenly felt light-headed.

"I wanted to get a read on her."

"And . . . what did you find?"

"She said one thing that interested me. You and the other women targeted — she claims Steven never blamed you."

"Never blamed us," Callie repeated. "I'm not sure what you mean."

"Your theory about revenge. You had this idea that Crain could be carrying out some plan that Gage devised. That because Gage couldn't avenge his own death, Crain was doing it for him. But based on what Brenda said, Steven never blamed you. And not just you, the others too. That's what Brenda said. Steven thought Melanie did the best she could working on the appeal. He actually liked Diane's book, didn't care that it made him look bad. I guess he was narcissistic enough to find any book better than none."

"Really," Callie said. "I'm surprised to hear that. But, you know, even if that's what he said to Brenda, it's not necessarily true. Steven lied a lot. Who knows what he really thought? It might even have been a part of the plan. So no one would ever suspect."

"True."

"And even if Steven didn't want revenge, Crain might have wanted it for him. Maybe Crain came up with the plan. Maybe it was his idea."

"I see what you're saying, but hear me out. When I talked to Brenda, I almost got the sense that Steven was grateful to you. Grateful to the others as well, but especially to you."

"Grateful for turning on him?" Callie said.

"Grateful for what came before. You were the closest thing he ever had to real, human contact. At some level, maybe he knew that. Maybe he was grateful for it."

"So what's your point?" Callie asked sharply. She didn't want to have this conversation.

"Okay, here's a scenario. Crain has been lying low since he escaped from prison. He's continued to kill, but he's hidden the bodies. He learned the techniques from Gage. Then he hears about Massey's murder, maybe about the black stocking. The incident serves as a stressor, what we call a triggering factor. At this point, Crain's control starts to waver. He goes to Maine, just to look. He wants to see where it happened. That's when he runs into you."

"That's a pretty big coincidence."

"Okay, so maybe he's been there a while. He's not just there for the day. But anyway, once he sees you, the compulsion just grows stronger. He follows you back to Merritt. He's keeping an eye on you. He isn't sure what he's going to do, but he has to do something. By this point, he's decompensating. He's ticking like a time bomb. He follows you to the dance in Greenfield and sees Posy Kisch. She's his perfect victim. That's when he really loses it. He doesn't even hide the body."

"So you think Crain's a red herring. Except for Posy, I mean."

"Right."

"You think someone else kidnapped Anna?"

"Right," he said again.

"It's pretty hard to believe," said Callie. But then, all of this was.

When they'd finished talking, she hung up the phone and went to find Anna. Anna was curled up on the den sofa, clutching a purple stuffed cow. On the floor next to the couch was a tray with a half-eaten sandwich. Callie realized that she'd been treating Anna as if she were home sick from school.

The TV was tuned to *The Lucy Show*, but Anna wasn't really watching. Callie turned down the volume and sat beside her daughter.

"It's hard to be stuck inside like this, isn't it?" Callie asked.

Anna toyed with the cow's purple fur. She nodded silently.

"I've been thinking," Callie said. "You don't have to do this unless you want to, but Grams and Pappy would love to see you. You could just go for a couple of days. Just to get away."

"Okay," Anna whispered.

Callie looked at her, surprised. "You . . . you want to go?"

Tears filled Anna's eyes. "I don't like being here," she said. "All those people outside. And I keep thinking that the man who took me, that maybe he'll come back."

Callie pulled Anna close. "No one's going to hurt you."

The thought of being apart from her daughter was almost too painful to bear. After everything they'd just gone through, she wanted Anna with her. At the same time, she knew in her heart that this was the right decision.

Briefly, she considered going with her daughter, leaving Merritt behind. But even as the thought passed through her mind, Callie knew it didn't make sense. For one thing, she couldn't do that to her parents, burden them in this way. Wherever she went now, the press would follow; she couldn't inflict that on them.

But beyond that was the issue of safety. Keeping Anna safe. She had no doubt that she, not Anna, was the killer's ultimate target. Wherever she went, danger would follow. She had to keep Anna away.

A whirlwind of phone calls, and just two hours later, all the plans were in place. Callie's mother would fly into Boston tomorrow and take Anna home with her. The news of Anna's kidnapping hadn't reached the Midwestern papers, so this was the first time her parents had learned of their granddaughter's ordeal. To Callie's relief, they took the news with remarkable composure. Mainly, they seemed concerned about how Anna was coping.

"I'm so sorry to put you through this," Callie said earnestly.

"Don't be ridiculous," her mother said briskly. "Of course we want to help."

Her mother was small, just five foot two, but her posture made her seem taller. Callie had sometimes wished she were softer, more prone to hugs and kisses. Today, though, she couldn't think of anyone she'd rather have on her side.

After the phone calls were over, Callie sat on her bed. So much to do — she should get started — but she couldn't seem to move. She thought about getting Anna's suitcase from the closet down in the basement. But first she had to let Anna know that she'd be leaving tomorrow. Already, her mind was running through what Anna needed to pack. Her red jacket in case it was cold. Pajamas. Bedroom slippers.

Finally, she got up. She moved toward the door and then hesitated, walked back to her dresser. Pulling open the top drawer, she took out a cherry-wood case. The key was in her jewelry box. She fitted it into the lock. Raising the lid, she peered down at her .357 Magnum. Her application had been expedited, and she'd bought it yesterday. Carefully, she lifted the gun from its blue-velvet-lined box.

Friday, May 19

OF all that is written I love only that which is written in blood. Write with blood: and you will discover that blood is spirit.

He carried the words with him on a 3" x 5" index card. Now, sitting cross-legged in the tree house, he pulled out the card to read it.

Write with blood: and you will discover that blood is spirit.

He stuck the card back in his pocket and pulled out another one.

Many die too late and some die too early . . .

The words of the German philosopher filled him with conviction. Laura had lived far too long, but soon she would be dead.

Only time is fair. Time was what gave life meaning. Once she was dead, his life would start. The burden would be lifted.

He thought about Diane Massey's book and how it had gnawed at him. In the end, though, it had served as a spur. Her book had given him strength.

Saturday, May 20

"So what did you and Grams do today?"

"We made a cake," said Anna. "Chocolate cake with chocolate icing."

"Great! That's your favorite."

As she talked to her daughter on the telephone, Callie gazed at her picture, a slightly blurry snapshot of Anna building a snowman in the backyard. The kitchen table was piled with photos that she'd taken out to sort. She'd hit on this mindless yet productive task as a way to fill the hours.

"I love you, Mommy," Anna said.

Callie's eyes filled with tears. "I love you, too, sweetheart. I miss you so much."

"Are you mad at me? For running away?" Anna's voice was timid.

"No," Callie said. "I'm just glad you're safe." She had other things to say, of course, but they could wait until later.

"I'm sorry I made you worried."

"I'm sorry you were so unhappy. That I didn't listen better."

"That's okay. Mommy?"

"Yes, sweetie?"

"When can I come home?"

"Soon," Callie said. "Once things calm down a little more. When the police have finished talking to me. When they're sure they've caught the bad man."

Anna didn't say anything.

"Hey, isn't it about your bedtime?"

"I guess."

"Okay, you better skedaddle. Don't forget to brush your teeth."

"*Mah-um.*" An elaborate sigh. For a moment, Anna sounded like her old self.

"'Night, sweetheart. Sleep tight. Don't let the bedbugs bite."

Callie blew a kiss across the phone line.

Anna blew a kiss back.

The airborne kiss only underscored the hundreds of miles between them. Callie was overcome with yearning for the touch and scent of her child.

She hung up the phone feeling desolate, worse than she'd felt for days. The piles of pictures were no substitute for Anna in the flesh. Restless, she stood up and crossed the floor, opened the refrigerator. She wasn't feeling hungry, but she knew that she should eat. The looseness of her jeans told her that she'd been losing weight.

For several minutes, she stood staring into the cold bright box. Eggs. Cheese. Carrots. Peanut butter. Bread. She finally settled on a grilled cheese sandwich and pulled out the ingredients. She put a cast-iron skillet on the stove and dropped in a pat of butter.

When they're sure they've caught the bad man.

And how long would that take?

For so long, she'd been so confident that Lester Crain was the one. But ever since her talk with Jamison, she hadn't been as sure. She thought about Jamison's theory that Diane's death had triggered Crain. That instead of being Crain's handiwork, it had been his inspiration. Drawn to Maine after the fact, he'd encountered Callie on Blue Peek Island. He'd recognized her as Steven's girlfriend and followed her back to Merritt. Posy was a victim of circumstance. Wrong place, wrong time. Posy was different from the rest of them. She'd never even known Steven. That fact, too, seemed to weigh in favor of a possible second killer.

The butter had started to sizzle. Callie turned down the heat. She put a slice of bread in the skillet and laid cheese across it.

Someone familiar with the neighborhood.

Someone who may have children.

Knows crime scene investigation.

Meticulous.

A long-range planner.

She flipped over the sandwich to brown the other side. In her mind, she ticked off the elements of Jamison's profile. Again, she had a disconcerting sense of being on the verge. There was a name, a face, just beneath the surface, but she couldn't seem to reach it.

She slid the sandwich onto a plate and poured a glass of milk, then pushed back the piles of photographs to clear a place at the table.

Bite, chew, swallow.

The sandwich tasted like oily cardboard, but she forced herself to eat.

Through the window, she saw their fenced backyard, weirdly illuminated. A few days ago, a security firm had installed a powerful spotlight. Callie found herself thinking of Henry Creighton, wondering how he was doing. Now that her fear and anger had ebbed, she could think of him with compassion. Like Anna, he must have been overwhelmed by feelings he couldn't process. She thought of her last encounter with Mimi right here at this kitchen table, how stunned she'd been when Mimi announced Bernie's infidelity. Clearly, there were tensions in the Creighton household that she'd never come close to guessing. Like Anna, Henry was a sensitive child. Of course he'd been affected.

Again, Callie sensed the sudden flicker, the glimmer of a thought. But this time she managed to get hold of it. The face was Bernie Creighton's. In her mind's eye, she saw his bright smug eyes, the puffed rooster chest. She'd always explained her discomfort with Bernie by the fact that they were such different people. They had different values, moved in different worlds, nothing more than that. Now, uneasily, she wondered if there might be something deeper.

Bernie would have had a bird's-eye view of her and Anna's comings and goings. And who was in a better position to discover Henry's plans? Bernie had been at the Easter egg hunt; he could have planted the watch. He had an erratic work schedule, even kept an apartment in Boston. With a chill, Callie thought of the phone call to the Creightons after Anna's disappearance. "No, it's not about your husband," the detective had said to Mimi. So Bernie hadn't been home that night; she wondered where he'd been.

Callie shoved aside her plate and leaned her head in her hands. For a moment, the story danced in her mind, then reality pressed in. Wouldn't Anna have recognized Bernie? Not to mention Henry? What possible motive could Bernie have? How would he know her story?

But even as she pushed Bernie from her thoughts, another face popped up. She pictured another man with children. Her ex-husband, Kevin Thayer. She'd barely thought of him at all since Lambert's questioning. At first, the idea had seemed absurd. She'd dismissed it out of hand. But as she sat here at the kitchen table, the doubts seeped back. How well did she really know Kevin? Not well at all. Even back when they'd been married, there'd been a wall between them. A few weeks ago, when she'd tried to reach him, he too had been out of town. She tried to think back, to figure out what day she'd made that call.

She was probably being paranoid, but she knew what she had to do. It was a question of matching dates and times. That was how you started.

Upstairs, Callie sat down at her desk and turned on the computer. After signing on to AOL, she pulled up Google. She typed in the phrase *Diane Massey* and clicked on the search button. A list of links flashed on the screen. She scanned for obituaries. She had to read through several before finding one where the dates were clear. Diane's body had been found on April 18. She'd been dead for about a week. That put the murder sometime around April 10.

Callie grabbed a spiral notebook and flipped to a blank page. She pulled out her Filofax, turned to April, and started a chronology.

April 5 — Anniversary note (Merritt)
April 10 (??) — Diane killed (Maine)
April 16 — Easter (Merritt)
April 26 — Melanie attacked (New York)
May 14 — Anna kidnapped (Merritt)

The roses, that was another thing. He'd left them at her door. She'd found them when she'd gotten home from shopping for the dinner party. She thought back, trying to remember exactly what day that was. It had been a hectic week, she recalled. Rick had gone out of town. She'd been on her own on Wednesday night, right before the party. She must have done the shopping on Tuesday. Monday would have been too early.

Scanning the Filofax pages, she realized how overwhelmed she'd been. On April 23, she'd gone to New York, a week later, to Maine. It came to her that she'd called Kevin the same day Rick got home. That must have been on April 11. She felt a sudden shiver. Kevin had been out of town near the time Diane was killed.

But why would Kevin kill Diane? That just didn't make sense. She flipped ahead another few pages to April 26, the night that Melanie was attacked, the night before her dinner party. In blue ink, she'd scrawled *Rick to Springfield*. He'd had that in-service training thing.

At least that's what he'd told her.

That's what she'd believed.

There wasn't a precise moment when the idea came to mind. Or rather, it was like it had always been there, waiting for her to look.

Knows crime scene investigation.

Familiar with the neighborhood.

Maybe someone with children.

Maybe, but not necessarily. And everything else fit.

She didn't have to think what to do next. She'd done it all before. One by one she compared the dates to her Filofax notations. April 5, when she'd found the note. Wednesday. Pizza night. She'd walked through the door, the note in her purse. Rick had been in the kitchen. When Diane was killed he'd been out of town, claiming to be at his parents.' Out of town when Melanie was attacked. Out of town when Anna was kidnapped.

Detectives had supposedly checked him out, verified his alibi. But after all, he was one of their own, a colleague whom they trusted. How closely would they have scrutinized whatever proof he gave? She thought of the heart-wrenching story he'd told about his boyhood friend. Was it just an elaborate subterfuge? Could he have made it up? And what about Anna? Had Rick really guessed that Steven was her father? Or was it something that he'd discovered a long, long time ago?

The doubts were eerily familiar, sweeping her into the past. She was back in her Nashville apartment, thinking, *Could he? Could he? Could he?*

But that was Steven. This was Rick. They had nothing in common.

Nothing? said a voice at the back of her mind.

You. They have you.

⁓

IT was dark in the tree house and a little cold, but Rick Evans had a perfect view. Through black branches, he peered down at the snug white house below. The only light came from behind the closed blinds of her bedroom window. In front of the house, a police cruiser silently stood guard. Inside the car was Tod Carver, supposedly his friend. Now, the single pressing question was how to get rid of him.

⁓

SHE was losing it, she really was.

She decided to take a bath.

From Bernie to Kevin to Rick. Who would she think of next? The fact was that none of these suspicions had any solid foundation. A few coincidences in timing. Nothing more than that. She tossed her Filofax back in her purse and turned off the computer.

The water was rushing into the tub when she heard the doorbell ring. Her first impulse was to ignore it, pretend she wasn't home. But that was stupid; whoever it was would know that she was here. Peering out from behind the shades, she saw the police cruiser. Reassured by its stalwart presence, she headed down the stairs.

She tiptoed up to the front door and looked through the peephole. At the sight of the uniform, her mouth went dry, then she realized it wasn't Rick. Same uniform, different face. The man on her porch was Tod.

Relieved, she turned off the security alarm and unlocked the door.

Tod was standing a bit to one side, hands stuffed in his pockets.

"Hey, Callie," he said, apologetically. "Hope I'm not bothering you." He gestured to the empty cruiser. "That's me. I'm on assignment. I saw that your lights were on upstairs. Thought I'd say hello."

"You're not bothering me at all," said Callie. "I'm dying for company. Why don't you come in for a bit? I could make us some tea."

He glanced toward the car, then, shrugging, turned back to her. "I guess I can watch you as well from inside as I can from out in the car."

"Better, I'd say," Callie quipped. "I won't be out of your sight."

❧

He waited another minute or two after Tod disappeared into the house.

It had taken several nights, but the coast was totally clear now.

Carefully, Rick climbed down the flat steps nailed in the trunk of the tree. When he reached the ground, he scanned the street. Silent. No cars. No people.

It was ten yards or so from where he stood to the bushes beside her house.

With a deep breath, Rick stepped from the shadows and quickly crossed the street.

⤛

Tod was sitting at the kitchen table piled with snapshots of Anna. He picked up a stack and filed through it. "Beautiful girl," he said.

Callie had just put on water to boil. "She's everything to me."

"You've had a pretty rough time," Tod said.

"Yes," said Callie. "I have."

It was soothing having Tod here, someone who understood.

"Do you think it's over?" Callie asked.

"Over? What do you mean?"

"There's a theory that maybe there are two killers. Crain and someone else."

Tod shook his head. "I'm just a guy on patrol. I leave this stuff to the detectives."

"And what do they think? What does Lambert think?"

"I don't know that either. I mean, I could speculate, but I don't know anything."

"Okay, then speculate," Callie said. "What do you *think* he's thinking?"

"Well, he's chief of detectives in a college town with a good bit of tourist trade. He's under a lot of pressure to make folks feel safe again. At the same time, he isn't going to want to take unnecessary risks."

Callie nodded. "That's pretty much what I thought. They're playing it both ways. They let the press think that they've got the guy, but you all are still watching me."

The kettle began to whistle. Callie picked it up.

"Caf or decaf?" she asked Tod.

"Caf. Definitely."

She dropped an English Breakfast bag into one mug, chamomile into another, poured in boiling water, and carried the mugs to the table.

"Careful," she said, setting down Tod's mug. "You'll have to let it cool."

She pulled out a chair across from him and cleared a place at the table, pushing aside a stack of snapshots so she could put her mug down.

"How's Rick been doing?" she asked. She was careful to appear offhand.

"Fine, I guess," said Tod. "I haven't really seen him much in the past couple weeks."

Callie picked up her tea and blew on it. Still too hot to drink. She wondered if Tod was telling the truth or just sidestepping the question. He was Rick's friend more than hers; his loyalty was to Rick.

"Did you go to that training thing with him in Springfield just before my dinner party?"

"Training thing?"

"A class or something. I'm not exactly sure what."

Tod dropped his eyes. "You'd have to ask Rick about that."

"So it wasn't something everyone went to?"

"You know, I'd rather not get into this."

But now that she'd started, she wanted to know. She couldn't stop herself. She was putting Tod in a difficult position, but she didn't seem to care.

"Have you ever talked to his partner's widow? That woman he claimed to visit?"

"Claimed?" Tod looked taken aback. "You . . . you think he's lying?"

Callie gave a tight smile. "I don't know what to think."

For a moment or two, she hesitated, then plunged forward.

"I was going through my calendar," she said. "Diane's murder. Melanie's attack. Anna's kidnapping. All three times Rick was out of town. At least, that's what he said."

She could see the look of astonishment spreading across Tod's face. She raised a hand to stop him from interrupting her.

"Okay, I know you think it's ridiculous. Maybe you're right. But he meets the criteria of the profile. And he had the opportunity."

Tod was shaking his head, slowly, side to side.

"It wasn't Rick, Callie. I can promise you that."

"But how do you know?" she asked him. "How do you know for sure?"

"Because I know Rick. I know the kind of guy he is."

And she . . . something was happening . . . a kaleidoscope in her brain. Tod had always called to mind her old boyfriend Larry Peters. But now she suddenly wondered why, where she'd found the resemblance. Larry's hair was dark brown. Tod's was almost red. She'd never realized until tonight how bright the highlights were. His voice, too, that was different, slow, almost a drawl.

Then she wasn't thinking of Tod, she was thinking of Lester Crain. When she'd run into him on that island in Maine, she must have noticed the accent. While it hadn't registered consciously, at some level she'd known. Southern, he'd sounded like a southerner. Just like Tod did now. Tod used to live in Virginia, which must be where the accent came from. And yet . . . and yet, there was something more. Or was it her imagination?

Her mind was out of control now, flashing random thoughts. She thought next of the Easter egg hunt, how Tod had come up behind her. It was something that Steven used to do, and for an instant, she'd been frightened.

She was aware of Tod looking at her, his face marked with concern. "What's wrong, Laura?" he asked her.

Laura. He'd called her Laura.

Confused now, she stared at him, her thoughts spinning even faster. Of course, he knew now, everyone knew, but why would he use that name? Again, for no particular reason, she thought of Larry Peters. What was it about Tod exactly that reminded her of her one-time beau? She'd always assumed it was the smile, but now she wasn't sure. But if it wasn't the smile, then what? They were two quite different men.

Misattribution. Unconscious transference.

The phrases lit up her mind.

The confusion of one person with another.

A mistake of memory.

An image, a face, was rising up through the dense fog of the past. She was back on the couch in her Nashville apartment, listening to the news. She could feel the springs beneath the sagging cushions, the pressure in her belly. She could hear the hatred and rage spewing from Dahlia Schuyler's brother. "He ruined my life. He ruined my family. Death is too good for him."

Tod had reminded her of someone, but it wasn't who she'd thought.

His face was Tucker Schuyler's face.

He was Dahlia's brother.

"You know who I am," he said flatly. "I can see it in your face."

"Know?" Callie said nervously. She stumbled to her feet.

Then Tod — Tucker — pulled out a gun. His eyes were hard and cold. He raised the gun a fraction higher.

"You're not going anywhere, Laura."

Callie stood absolutely still. Inside, her mind was racing. She thought of her newly purchased pistol, upstairs in her dresser drawer. No way that she could reach it, not with Tucker blocking the door.

"If you kill me, they'll know it's you," she said. "You're supposed to be protecting me."

"Someone broke in through the back door." He seemed to be thinking out loud. "It was dark. I didn't see them. I can't see everything."

"There's a light there now. A spotlight. They'll never believe that story."

"That's possible," he said. "But it doesn't really matter. Lives aren't measured in years, Laura. I'll have done what I set out to do. *Many die too late.* You know who said that?"

"No."

"Nietzsche. He's a German philosopher."

"Really." She gave him an engaging smile. "I don't know much about him." Anything to win time now. To give her a chance to think.

But he didn't seem to hear her. He was thinking of something else. "You know, when Gage was executed, I thought that I'd feel better. But when I woke up the next morning, everything was the same. For three months, I didn't do anything, just lay in bed, thinking. And finally I figured out what the problem was. All of you who'd supported him, you still hadn't paid. You were out there getting on with your lives. You didn't give a shit about Dahlia."

"It . . . it wasn't like that." Callie's mouth was dry.

There was a shifting, a stirring, in her mind, a tectonic re-arrangement. She seemed to be looking down on the kitchen from some omniscient place. A part of her was there with Tucker, while a part of her was somewhere else. Then, as she spoke, it all came clear, what was driving him.

"It wasn't your fault," she blurted out.

At the sound of her voice, he flinched.

"Shut up!" he said, waving the gun. But his eyes were full of fear.

If only he'd been on time. If only he hadn't been late. She could see it all so clearly now, as if she were inside him. How the guilt he'd felt over Dahlia's death had grown in him like a cancer. He'd waited for the feelings to fade, but instead, they'd just grown stronger. Finally, they'd become unbearable. Something in him had snapped. In the end, he'd dealt with the self-hatred by pro-jecting it onto them.

"You didn't do anything wrong." She said the words slowly. "Steven Gage was the one who killed her. He's the one to blame. The rest of us — we did the best we could under the circum-stances. You — we — aren't responsible. We didn't kill your sister."

A strange feeling of lightness seemed to descend on her.

"We're not responsible," she said again. "We didn't kill Dahlia."

Tucker's left eye had begun to twitch. He opened and closed his mouth. A battle seemed to play itself out on the tortured face. If only she could make him see, make him *understand.* But the coldness was growing in his eyes.

"It *is* your fault," he said.

"Tuck —" What should she call him? Which name was less provocative? "It won't help to kill me. Think about your daughter."

But this time she'd miscalculated. Tucker leapt from his chair. He waved his gun in front of her face. "Shut up! Shut up!" he screamed.

Then he was grabbing hold of her arm, yanking her upright. "Enough talking," he said to her. "Move. Down to the basement."

❧

CROUCHED in the bushes, he couldn't quite see them through the kitchen window. They must be sitting at the table, beyond his range of vision. He could just make out the sound of voices, though he couldn't hear their words.

Careful not to make any noise, Rick edged to the left. He knew that he was acting crazy, but he couldn't help himself. She didn't want to see him. She'd made that quite clear. Yet a part of him still believed that she loved him, needed him. He knew that he'd hurt her. He was willing to wait. But even now, he couldn't seem to stay away from her.

He knew what was driving him: jealousy, pure and simple. He wasn't proud of the feeling. Still, there it was. It had always slightly bothered him how Tod brought to mind that ex-boyfriend of hers. And Tod, he'd begun to suspect, was more than fond of Callie. The suspicion first came to him when Tod had agreed to go dancing. What had clinched it, though, was when Tod was so keen to get the night shift at Callie's house.

And what business is that of yours?

The question hit him hard.

Suddenly, he was appalled at where he found himself. Acting like some crazed stalker unwilling to let her go. If she wanted nothing to do with him, he had to respect that choice. How had it gotten to this point? He had to leave. Now.

Then, just as he started to turn, they crossed his line of vision. He stared at the scene framed in the window. It didn't make any sense. Tod's face was contorted in anger. Callie looked terrified. Tod was pulling out his Glock, pointing the gun at Callie.

❧

EVEN if she'd wanted to stand, her legs wouldn't support her. They felt like jelly, rubbery, out of her control. Once he got her down to the basement, she knew it would be all over. She had no choice but to act now, but how could she take on Tucker? He was larger, stronger, faster. And besides, he had a gun.

The most dangerous room in the house.

Rick's words came back to her.

She thought of the knives on the kitchen counter, stowed in their wooden block. They were just five or six steps away, but she'd never get to them. On the stove was the skillet she'd used for her sandwich, but that too was out of reach. She could make a bolt for the kitchen door, but she wouldn't get the locks undone. For a moment, she was overcome by the irony of her position. Steps she'd taken to protect herself now barred her escape.

Her eyes fell on the mug of tea cooling in front of her. With the fleeting hope that it was still hot, she grabbed the mug and hurled. The mug hit Tucker square in the jaw. Tea flew every-where. Callie glimpsed his look of surprise as his head snapped backward. Already, she was on her feet, rushing for the door. But she'd only made it a few steps, when Tucker tackled her.

He grabbed a handful of hair and yanked. Callie shrieked with pain. He threw her hard against the stove, and she buckled at the waist, her cheek smashing down against a burner with a sudden shooting spasm.

"Please! Stop!" she cried.

But just as the pain in her jaw subsided, she felt her arm wrenched back. A burning sensation in her shoulder joint as the gun gouged into her ribs.

"Goddamn it." His voice was thick. "What the fuck are you doing?"

Trembling, she waited for the gun to explode. But nothing, nothing happened.

Her right arm lay limply by her side. Slowly, she snaked it for-ward, up along the counter, toward the cast-iron pan.

"What the hell —"

Tucker jerked her back, but he wasn't fast enough.

She'd managed to grab the skillet. With all her strength, she swung.

As the pan smashed against Tucker's side, Callie heard a crack. He let out a whinnying bellow of pain. The gun dropped to the floor.

For an electric moment they both stood there, Callie still holding the skillet. She began to swing it back and forth. Tucker jumped out of the way.

She edged closer to the gun, until she stood over it. But she didn't dare to try to pick it up and give Tucker a chance to attack. Instead, she raised a leg and kicked the gun. It skittered across the floor. She saw Tucker's reflexive impulse to turn and look. But he managed to resist the urge, keeping his eyes on her.

"You don't have a chance," he told her. His voice was contemptuous.

Callie took a quick step forward and swung the pan at Tucker's head. But fast as she was, he managed to duck. He threw himself at her.

Then they were both on the ground. Callie dropped the pan. As Tucker wrapped a hand around her throat, Callie bit his arm.

"You bitch!"

Tod slapped her hard across the face, then slammed her into the floor.

Callie felt something wet and warm trickling down her face. She touched a finger to her face. Blood. It was blood.

She realized that Tucker had let go of her, and she struggled to sit up. She'd managed to raise herself onto an elbow when she saw him coming toward her. With a hopeless feeling, she saw that he had the gun jammed into his belt. The weight of his body came down on her, one knee on either side. Then his hands were around her neck. Slowly, he started to squeeze.

"I don't want to do this too quickly. I want to be sure you feel it."

Arching her back, Callie struggled to dislodge his body. But his knees dug sharply into her sides. She couldn't move at all.

His hands were squeezing her neck again, and her lungs screamed for air. In her mind's eye, she saw her daughter's face.

I'm sorry, Anna, I'm sorry.

RICK crashed through the window, sending glass and wood flying. Before Tod could pull his gun, Rick was on top of him. Over and over they rolled, but Rick couldn't get control. "Jesus Christ! What the hell are you doing? Give it up, Tod!"

But the only response was labored breathing. He couldn't see Tod's face. From the corner of his eye, he glimpsed Callie, prostrate on the floor. Her eyes were closed. She wasn't moving. *What had Tod done to her?*

That one slight shift of focus, that was all it took. Tod took the opportunity to gain the upper hand. In one powerful movement, he socked Rick in the jaw. Pain ripped through the side of Rick's face, the shock rippling outward.

Disoriented, he tried to sit up, then came another blow. The floor rose up to hit his head, then everything was over.

SOUNDS and lights faded in and out. She was lying on the ground. She'd been running, running through the thick black night, but he'd caught her in the end. Her neck hurt, something was wrong, but it didn't really matter. Finally it was over. Finally she could rest.

I'm in the mood, I'm in the mood, I'm in the . . .

Somewhere, the music played. She could hear the words. And Steven, he was here too, not so far away.

The sounds of a desperate struggle somewhere very near. *Give up, give up,* she wanted to say. *It's easier that way.*

Slowly, she let her head roll, to see what was happening. The pain in her neck confused her, though. In dreams, you didn't feel pain.

Then, as adrenaline flowed through her, she realized where she was.

She wasn't asleep.

This wasn't a dream.

And everything came back.

How Tod had come to her door that night. Tod was Tucker Schuyler.

But who was he fighting with there on the floor? Rick floated into focus. Tucker was sitting on top of him, just as he had with her. His fist slammed into Rick's stomach with a soft, sickening thud.

Tucker's back was to her. She knew he couldn't see her. She pictured the pistol upstairs in her room, measured the path in her mind. Then, she was scrambling up, racing down the hall. Almost instantly, she heard Tucker jumping to his feet.

As she hit the second-floor landing, she could hear him steps behind her. She caught a terrifying glimpse of his face as she slammed her bedroom door.

Just as she twisted the brass lock, Tucker smashed into the door. Briefly, she thought of calling 911, but that would take too long. She tore through the contents of her dresser drawer and yanked out the gun case. Her fingers wouldn't work at first, and once she dropped the key. But she finally managed to get it open and pull out the revolver.

The bullets were in her nightstand drawer. She grabbed the box and ripped it open. Bullets fell to the floor. She dropped to her knees, gathered them up, and loaded the cylinder.

Crash. The door flew open, and Tucker plunged into sight. From her sheltered position behind the bed, Callie raised her gun.

Wildly, Tucker scanned the room.

Shoot for center mass.

Fighting to keep her hands steady, she fired straight ahead.

Fired and just kept firing. He crumpled to the floor. The gun he'd held dropped from his hand. Callie ran to pick it up. She stood there a moment, breathing hard, unable to move, to think. Then, shaking, she picked up the phone and dialed 911.

EPILOGUE

Merritt, Massachusetts
Wednesday, June 28

CALLIE sat at the picnic table, shucking ears of corn. A few yards away, Rick was flipping burgers on the charcoal grill. It was shortly after six o'clock, an early summer evening. They'd swapped their weekly pizza night for a weekly barbecue.

The backyard glimmered a bright moist green beneath a heavy sun. Rick had set up a badminton net under a maple tree. A soft *thwack* as Anna sent a birdie sailing across the net. Henry swung his racquet wildly. Callie had to smile. As best she could tell, neither kid had once returned a serve.

She caught Rick looking at her, smiling at her smile. She held his glance for a long moment, reveling in his presence. *Seen.* She felt truly seen. He had given her that. And finally, now, she could see him too. They could see each other.

The hamburgers sizzled on the smoking grill.

"How much longer?" asked Callie.

Rick cut into one of the burgers. "I'd say about five minutes."

Callie peeled a last few strands from a final ear of corn. She added it to the basket and headed into the kitchen.

As she rinsed the ears at the sink, her eyes stayed on Rick and Anna, unable — unwilling — to forget the path they'd traveled to get here. Tucker Schuyler, the man they'd known as Tod, was still in the hospital. For the first two weeks, it had been touch and go, but he was making progress. Callie was tremendously grateful for this, despite everything he'd done. The fact of almost having killed someone was a thing that would always haunt her. Still, horrific as it had been, there were lessons in the encounter. She'd learned so much in the past month, and every day she learned more.

That endless night in the kitchen with Tucker, she'd been speaking to herself as well. "We are not to blame," she'd said. And known that it was true. It was Steven Gage who'd killed Dahlia and all those countless others. She hadn't been the star of this tragedy, just a minor player. For more than a decade, she'd let Steven control her thoughts and actions. He'd controlled her just as much in death as he ever had in life. Because of Steven, she'd lied to her daughter, lied to her friends, to Rick, terrified of what would happen if she ever told the truth.

And yet, now that the truth was out, none of her fears had come true. When reporters found that she wouldn't talk, they'd finally given up. Slowly, her life had begun to assume the semblance of normalcy, shopping, cooking, studying, going back to work. She'd tried to apologize to Martha for Tod, but Martha had brushed it off. "Though I have to admit," she'd said dryly, "it's sort of put me off dating." And Anna — with time and a therapist's help — Anna was getting better. So far, she'd shown little interest in the details of her father's life. When Anna asked, she would tell her the truth. Until then, she'd wait.

Which wasn't to say, of course, that the past could be forgotten. The goal wasn't to erase the past but to plumb its depths for meaning. It was Tucker's refusal to accept the past that had led to his murderous rampage. Instead of moving forward with life, he'd bound himself to the past, unable to find any meaning in life except in acts of revenge. *Tod.* It was the German word for death; that's why he'd picked the name.

The scent of burning charcoal and freshly mown grass drifted in through the open window. Anna and Henry had dropped their racquets and stood by Rick at the grill.

"Can we toast marshmallows after dinner?" Callie heard Anna ask.

"I don't see why not," said Rick. "Maybe we'll make s'mores."

Watching Rick and Anna together, Callie's heart expanded.

The two people she loved most were slowly moving closer. Once Anna had learned the truth about Kevin, something had started to shift. "She thought that her father had abandoned her," explained Anna's therapist. "That was far more painful for her than finding out the truth. Now she finally understands why your ex-husband disappeared. Over time, she may be willing to let someone else be a father to her."

"Over time," Callie whispered.

The words were a sort of gift.

Henry and Anna were back at the net, batting the birdie again. Callie marveled at how untouched they could seem after everything they'd been through. Henry, too, had fled a home where truth had been suppressed. Shortly after Henry and Anna's debacle, Bernie had come clean. Not only had he been having an affair, Bernie Creighton was gay. He was moving to Boston with John Casey, his guest at Callie's dinner party. Strangely, though, that upheaval, too, seemed to have been for the best. Mimi appeared to be calmer now. She, too, could finally relax.

The corn was bobbing in the boiling water. Callie found a pair of tongs. As she pulled out the steaming ears, her mind traveled over the years. She thought of Diane and *The Vanishing Man*. She thought of Lester Crain. She thought of Mike Jamison, how right he'd been. She thought of Melanie. They'd spoken briefly on the phone last week. Callie had made the call. After getting a report on Melanie's health, she'd mentioned their last talk.

"You know how you said that we're alike?"

A long, very long, pause.

"You know, I just don't remember. I was on a lot of drugs."

"You don't remember what we talked about?"

"I don't remember the phone call."

Quickly, Melanie had steered the conversation back to neutral terrain. Her upcoming wedding to another lawyer, her plans to return to work. *Had Melanie really forgotten their talk?* Callie still wondered. But it was one of the many things in life that she'd probably never know.

"Callie! You about ready?" Rick's voice floated in through the screen. From where she stood, she could see the kids sitting at the picnic table. Tongs in hand, Callie fished around for the last floating ear of corn. She added it to the yellow pile.

"I'm on my way," she called.

Author's Note

In writing this book, I have — for the most part — tried to provide realistic portrayals of criminal and forensic procedures. I have, however, taken certain liberties. To wit, the state of Tennessee's forty-year hiatus in carrying out death sentences ended with the April 2000 execution of Robert Glen Coe for the 1979 murder of eight-year-old Cary Ann Medlin. Due to a lengthy appeals process, almost twenty years elapsed between Coe's May 1981 conviction and his execution.

Acknowledgments

I'm vastly indebted to the following people, who supported and guided me during the writing of this book.

Thanks to my editor, Judy Clain, whose wonderful editorial eye helped make this a much stronger story, and to her terrific assistant, Claire Smith. Thanks to Pamela Marshall for a superb copyediting job, to Yoori Kim, who designed the stunning cover, and to my publicist, Shannon Byrne, to whom my debt grows even as I write this.

As always, huge thanks to my agent, Nick Ellison, who, from the start, has provided unwavering encouragement, friendship, and advice, and to his hardworking cohorts, Jennifer Cayea, Abigail Koons, and Katie Merrill.

On the research front, I'm immensely grateful to the law enforcement and forensics professionals who kindly took time to answer my questions and vet sections of my manuscript. Of course, any factual errors or creative liberties are entirely my own doing.

Thanks to Vernon J. Geberth, retired lieutenant commander with the New York Police Department, and Raymond M. Pierce, founder of the Criminal Assessment and Profiling Unit of the NYPD's Detective Bureau, who've now helped me through two books.

Thanks to former Metro Nashville Assistant Public Defender C. Dawn Deaner and Assistant District Attorney General Kathy A. Morante for help with Tennessee criminal procedure.

In Massachusetts, thanks to Detective Lieutenant Kenneth Patenaude and Lieutenant Brian Rust of the Northampton Police Department, who helped me to come up with police procedures for the fictional town of Merritt, and to Kenneth Frisbie, my firearms instructor at the Smith & Wesson Academy in Springfield.

In Maine, thanks to Detective Joseph W. Zamboni of the

Maine State Police, to Dr. Margaret Greenwald, Maine chief medical examiner, and to the Knox County Sheriff's Office, including Sheriff Daniel G. Davey, Chief Deputy Todd L. Butler, and Deputy John Tooley, who helped me to devise procedures for fictional Blue Peek Island. Thanks to State Police Sergeant Vicki M. Gardner for a tour of the Skowhegan barracks.

In New York, thanks to Sergeant Richard J. Khalaf and Sergeant James F. Kobel of the NYPD's 20th Precinct and to Sergeant Benedict Pape and all the dedicated instructors at the NYPD's Citizens' Police Academy.

For inspiration, thanks go to Delaware Chief Medical Examiner Dr. Richard T. Callery.

For answers to medical questions, I'm grateful to Dr. Brian Smith of Baystate Medical Center and to my second, anonymous, consultant (you know who you are).

For assistance on a range of subjects — including manuscript critiques and research help — thanks to Gordon Cotler, Ruth Diem, Susan Garcia, Penny Geis, Theresie Gordon, Kirk Loggins, Anne Paine, Kirstin Peterson, Marissa Piesman, Polly Saltonstall, John Shiffman, Louisa Smith, and Kerstin Olson Weinstein.

This book is once again dedicated to my family, which has supported me in so many ways in writing and all else: To my mother, Janet Franz, my brother, Peter, my father and stepmother, Froncie and Bonnie Gutman, and my sisters, Karin and Megan. I couldn't have done it without you.

About the Author

Amy Gutman, author of the widely acclaimed suspense novel *Equivocal Death*, has worked as a newspaper reporter in Tennessee and Mississippi and was the founding director of the Mississippi Teacher Corps. An honors graduate of the Harvard Law School, Amy practiced law in Manhattan for several years before writing her first book. She divides her time between New York City and western Massachusetts and welcomes mail through her website, www.AmyGutman.com.